Requiem

Requiem

Sabrina Strong Book 6

Lorelei Bell

Acknowledgments

As most authors, we always need a little help from our friends.

Dora D'agostino for help with the Italian phrases and words.

Contents

Colorado Springs, Colorado

One Week Ago…

He wiped the blood from his mouth. Three men's bodies lay among the weird shapes of the stalagmites of the uneven cave floor and debris from the cave-in. One swinging light from their rig cast a ghastly series of blipping images of what was left of the three workers going from light to dark, light to dark again and again. Their yellow or white hardhats cast aside, their necks slit open—one man's head nearly severed, the flesh ragged where it was opened nearly to the neck bone.

He had drank his fill of the blood. *How generously it had flowed.* He now was more than satiated—he was bloated with their blood. It now pooled around their bodies like dark lakes and small rivers meandering over the cave's dusty, uneven floor.

Bill Gannon sat taking in the carnage around him in the cave. The savageness with which he'd attacked them now gone. The need had made him blind to what he was doing. He now sat and took in the carnage. *What have I become? Why? Why me? I was happy where I was. Dead. At least in death I was at peace and did no harm to anyone.*

The sense of bewilderment and despair fell over him as he curled in on himself, fists to his face, pressed against his eyes. He wept. The sounds of his deep weeping filled the cavern. He was certain no one would hear him. Not here.

He didn't know how long he lie curled up, tears—blood-stained—streaming down his face, dripping onto the floor of the cave. His leathery wings were wrapped around him. *I hate them. They're ugly*—an odd ululation, like that of a woman's voice, edged into his consciousness, pausing his self-loathing. Between sobs he heard it. He became quiet and listened. It was definitely someone's voice. Somewhere nearby. She spoked to him.

"William," she said in a lovely dulcet tone, too beautiful for a mere human's voice. "Be still, my sweet. Don't cry over spilled blood."

His self-pity now forgotten, he looked up. He was certain the brilliant light was not coming from anything man-made, but rather from something ethereal, and when he lifted his head he thought the dark figure standing there was not really there, but was a vision. Something in his head. Or a hallucination from... something he ate. The light around her blinded him, and he had to block it with a broad hand.

"Look upon me," she said in a husky, yet gentle tone.

"I can't look upon you," he said, trembling with the feeling of utter loss and trepidation. He was ready to parish, if that was his fate, even though he'd only been alive for a few hours as a vampire. "But if you have come to avenge what I've done, then do so and get it over with. I deserve it." His head hung low, hair falling into his face. It dripped with the blood, feeling it wet on his face and brow.

"It would be that I should avenge what you have done, but that is not why I am here, my sweet. I have watched you, and have heard your despair and remorse for what you have done." A pause. "I know your heart," The woman's voice was rich and resonated like a musical instrument all around him. "You may look upon me now without fear, my sweet. My son."

Hesitantly, Bill drew his hand away from his eyes. The light was gone and he could see the woman standing twenty feet away. She wore black robes and a sheer, black scarf over her head. But what struck him the most was the black wings, shaped like his. Like those of a giant bat.

"Who are you?" he asked. "Or should I even be so bold as to ask your name?"

"I am known by many names down through time, for I come from a time when humans revered and respected the gods and goddesses."

"I am not of the human race," he said, wiping his eyes. "Not completely. My ancestors come from those who were downcast from heaven. Called Watchers." She paused again, letting that sink in. His eyes engaged hers. "The Fallen Ones."

He opened his mouth to speak. No words formed.

Her hand came up to halt him. "I know well who, and what you are, my son, for I am the child of Nyx and Erebus. I am the personification of retribution for evil deeds and undeserved good fortune."

He scoffed lightly. *Undeserved good fortune?* "Then I am well deserving of your wrath. I have lived longer than I should, and have enjoyed riches of untold wealth while alive." He added sheepishly, "Perhaps undeserved."

"I am not so concerned with your life-style when you were alive as a human," she said. "One seed from a pomegranate is only one seed." She smiled. "One seed among a million times infinity is too many for me to separate and single out."

He pulled his knees up and curled his arms around them, and then his wickedly taloned wings draped his circumference, as he was embarrassed that he wore no clothes. Meanwhile, he searched his memory of Greek goddesses and tried to fit her into known mythology. *Myth come to life. Who is this one? One of the Furies?*

She smiled and it lit up her dark eyes. "My son, know that I have been searching for one such as you to be my… shall we say, representative on this earth realm? In the form you are now, you have many talents that I could use at my disposal."

"What do you wish me to do, goddess?"

She smiled, then made a nod of approval that he knew what she was, and deserved reverence. "First of all, what was your full given name on this earth realm?"

"My father named me William Bartholomew Gannon. I go by the name Bill, mainly."

"You are now my Avenger, Bill, for I am Nemesis, and have need for you to keep in check the evil ones who are causing havoc. One magical creature who was born not long ago will be in mortal danger soon, and she has not yet fulfilled her role which was foretold by ancient prophesy."

Bill thought a moment, he was certain he knew who she meant.

"The sibyl?"

Nemesis nodded.

He had been tracking the sibyl for over a month—as a human—and was supposed to mate with her. Now…

"What would you have me do, goddess?"

"Go find her. Help keep her safe, for there are many who are now joining forces against her. The sibyl's life is in jeopardy."

"Gladly," he said, knowing this was so very true. "Anything else?"

"Yes. The equilibrium of good and evil has been tipped. There are many who have fallen prey to hubris, or arrogance. They join forces to kill her. Not only demons and vampires, but some humans too."

"And you wish me to be your tool to make things more even?" he asked, his words measured with thought.

"It will be a continuous job," she said with a graceful smile. "Rise up, Bill Gannon." She moved her hand gracefully from the filmy black robes.

Bill rose, banishing his embarrassment of being nude, and folded his wings tightly behind himself. Her eyes took him in, and a smile dimpled her cheeks.

"Your wings are beautiful," she said. "Hold them out so that I may see."

He did so and gazed at the knobby joints throughout the leathery wings. His gaze rose to the thumb with the large, wicked claw that curved not in, but up and back. He knew now it was how he had slit the throats of the men he had exsanguinated to feed upon from the workers who had been trying to remove huge boulders from the cave-in. He was basically a killing machine.

"You don't seem to like your wings very much. Why is that?"

"When alive, my wings were made of feathers. Pure white, as white as snow. No other like me, had such."

A finger tapping her chin, she thought on this for a moment. "Should you prove to be worthy of the task I have given you, at a time when I feel you have achieved a reward, I shall give you back your wings as they once were."

Bill could barely rein in his joy at this. Tears made him blink in order to clear his eyes. "Really?"

She nodded. "Yes. Really."

He bowed at the waist, the apex of his wings almost touching the floor, then he straightened. "I am at your service, goddess. But... tell me how do I get out of here, into the world?"

She chuckled then. "Bill. You are very capable of going wherever your mind wants you to go. Merely think it."

"How long have I been..." he trailed off, his eyes dropping to take in the dead bodies around him.

"You have not been gone all that long from the living that you cannot pick up where you have left off."

For the first time Bill's lips tilted into a half-smile. Yes. She was right. He certainly could pick up where he'd left off in his human life. But his smile vanished. "I have no clothes. I can't go about like this." His hands out. "Not with these wings especially."

Nemesis' lips twisted in thought again. "No. I can't very well allow you to walk about like that. Not in today's world. My apologies. Retract your wings."

He hadn't thought of that. It took a little concentration, but after a few seconds, they vanished.

She thrust her hand toward him and a golden light arrowed toward him. He flinched, but felt nothing, except maybe warmth cascading over his body.

He looked down to find himself clothed, in nearly the very same thing he last wore. Looking back up at her he said, "Now, though, I would drink blood to live?"

Eyes glittering, she said, "No. You are not exactly a vampire. You are something more."

"What?"

Another wry smile tilted her beautiful lips. "I will allow you to figure this out by yourself, Bill." She began to fade. "Find the sibyl. Save her from her enemies." She vanished.

Chapter 1

Demons

"Stop. I'll take an ear off if you move again."

I gaped at my cousin, Lindee, who wielded the scissors over Vasyl's head.

Vasyl made a little growl of annoyance. He sat in my kitchen blinking under bright overhead bulbs with a bath towel arranged over his shoulders. Clippings of his wavy hair on the floor around him looking like black snakes that a cat had clawed, chewed and played with. I bent down to gather one or two thick, wavy trimmings from the drastic cutting Lindee had done to my husband's hair. I held three foot long pieces. Women would pay through the nose for such extensions. I wasn't going to sell them. I wanted it for a keepsake. The notion was rather silly, or possibly romantic, I know. But I couldn't see throwing it all into the trash. It was simply too beautiful.

Moments ago, Lindee had tried unsuccessfully to use the barber scissors my dad had. "His hair is like cutting through chicken wire!" Lindee had complained—and not quietly. She then pulled out the large sheers from my mother's old sewing table. They were sharp and went through his hair easily.

Poor Vasyl. He'd lost most of his hair last night in the violent storm when he'd tackled Nicolas in my bedroom in Tremayne Towers in Chicago. They'd both crashed out my bedroom window and were side-swiped by a bolt of lightning that had hit Nicolas directly, killing him. Vasyl had made a remarkable recovery in less than twenty-four hours. Tonight he asked us to cut the rest of his hair off, because half of it had been burnt in a jagged way (and smelled bad), to the shoulders. His wings had protected him from the lightning strike, while Nicolas had taken the full brunt of it, already dead well before his ashes hit the pavement below. But the side-splash of lightning had hit Vasyl's wings, sending him careening into a building across the way where he clung until Bjorn Tremayne got to him almost a half hour later.

His beautiful hair. All of it gone in a matter of a couple of clips. Now the lengths fell a little past his collar. He looked like a totally different man. His cheekbones seemed sharper, and those violet eyes not as dark as they usually were.

"Oh, wow. What happened to your ears?" Lindee asked, as she moved to trim an uneven length from the front.

"What do you mean?" Vasyl and I both said in unison. I moved in as Lindee stepped away and brushed his hair aside to look at his ears. He had worn gold crucifixes on his earlobes. I know, weird that a vampire would wear any sort of crucifix, but he had been a priest in his former human life. The lobes looked as though someone had taken a laser and burned a quarter inch gash in each one. The earrings were gone, the cuts were healed over but blackened, almost like a weird Goth-style fashion statement.

I had a quick vision of when, and how this happened. "When the lightening hit you, the gold melted in your ears, and burned you." I said automatically.

Both Lindee and Vasyl looked up at me giving me startled looks.

"Oh, God that must have hurt like a bitch," Lindee said, grasping her own earring.

"When it happened everything hurt," Vasyl said, his French accent thick.

I stepped away, unshed tears filled my eyes while the vision made a few loops in my head. It had been a gut-wrenching scene. Horrific. The lightening had fried his wings into blackened stumps. We were told those would never grow back, or if they did, he might not be able to use them.

"It will grow back," Lindee said. "Won't it?"

I jerked my eyes to her.

"Yes," Vasyl said. "In time." He pulled off the towel, droves of his thick hair slid to the floor then. *I'll need a shovel to scoop it all up.*

"Wait. I wasn't done!" Lindee said, scissors raised.

Vasyl rose to his six-two stature. "You are done." He handed her the towel. "I am taking a shower," he announced and looked down at me. He had a bad-boy's two-days growth of beard on him. Holy crap, it gave me chills to look at him now. Especially with all his long hair gone. I found myself lost in those violet eyes of his. His face didn't match the hair. How was I going to get used to this new look? It was like looking at a stranger in my house.

He broke our stare and moved away. I wasn't sure if he had been inviting me to a shower with him or not, but I'd already showered. Plus I wasn't in that sort of mood at the moment.

"Oh, man!" Rick's voice slurried from the living room. Hobart's growly laughter rippled in. "Queenie, you ain't right!"

My two other guests were watching a reality show on TV. I half-rolled my eyes, and caught Lindee's dower expression as she took up the broom. I dipped to grab the dust pan. We worked on getting Vasyl's hair all cleaned up in near silence. It filled the kitchen garbage basket.

Our quiet mood made me remember the fact that Cho was leaving.

I took off the top of my garbage can and dumped the first bunch of clippings in.

"God, it's like we've sheered a sheep or something," Lindee said and then made her trademark laugh.

"Right?"

"Oh my God, you could fill a mattress with this!" Lindee added.

I left that alone as I tied the bag, pulled it out and put on my boots to tote it out the back to the large green garbage bin. It was cold and silent outside. I looked up at the stars, my breath making a thick cloud as I watched the many twinkling lights, thinking to myself how lucky we had all been. I returned through the side door, locking it, and went up the five steps back inside where it was much warmer.

The notes from the TV show *I Dream of Jeanie* sounded from the living room.

"Hello?" Rick answered his iPhone from the living room.

Lindee and I paused in our motions and waited to hear what was being said. Rick didn't say anything for a long thirty seconds, obviously listening to what was being said to him.

"Holy crap! He did it!" Rick's shrill voice said. "Tremayne just got reinstated as magnate for the entire North American Vampire Association!" We cheered. "*And* he got the Hunting Humans Law thrown out under a technically."

Lindee and I cheered again, jumped up and down and hugged. We surged into the dining room to see the nearly armless leprechaun jumping up and down with joy a couple of times himself. I got chills of excitement once again, only for a different reason all together.

"He's back?" I asked, noting the time. It was going on eight PM. Tremayne had left for Dark World a few hours ago. I had thought it would take him much longer to get things straightened out in Dark World, where demons ruled. I was happy to not have been invited to go this time. Not exactly your ideal vacation place.

"Is he on the phone right now?" I asked Rick.

"Yeah—wait," Rick said, ear to his phone and a hand up to me. My eyes slid to Hobart. Hobart shrugged. He was the only werewolf in the house, besides me—the half-were-creature. "Okay... yeah. Okay. U-huh." I waited and then Rick said. "Yeah, she's here." He held out the phone to me. "Here, toots. Your boss wants to talk to you."

I crossed the room and took it. "He isn't my boss," I said under my breath. I put the phone to my ear.

"Hi," I said feeling and sounding breathless, and maybe a little worried. *Why did he want to talk to me?*

"Sabrina," Tremayne's baritone rumbled in my ear, making my toes tingle and my insides go warm and mushy. "The High Council has taken the bounty off your head because you were instrumental in saving my life."

"Oh, good to know your life is so important," I said, again breathless, and near tears I was so relieved and happy. "How nice of them." I was trying to be trite.

"However, you have to become pregnant from either me or Vasyl."

"Oh. Crap," I said, and the tears of joy vanished, and I frowned. *Shit, just when things looked like they'd go back to normal.*

"They aren't fucking around, either," he said in my ear. "They're serious."

I looked around at my audience. I caught Vasyl's eyes right away, looking at me from the open bathroom door, steam pouring out. I gave him a smile and a thumbs up, since he must have missed the news. Or, he'd heard with his vampire hearing who was on the phone, and was wondering what Tremayne had to say to me.

With a razor in his hand, Vasyl shot me a warning glare and shut the door only partially.

This was not fair.

"Hang on," I said. My feet moved me to my bedroom, I opened the door and was blasted by cold air. I closed it and stepped away. I needed privacy to say what I was going to say to him. I veered to the den where the fireplace snapped, keeping it warm and toasty in there. I closed the French doors.

"What if my child is in the womb of another woman?" I said low, making glances at the closed door. The TV's volume went back up. *Good.*

"What?" Tremayne said, sounding confused.

"I said what if my egg was put into another woman's womb? You know. En Vitro? Someone is the surrogate mother."

I didn't expect Tremayne to get it right away, but it took five seconds before he said, "Who was the father?"

I bit my lower lip. "This is very secret," I said in a warning voice. "You're the only other person who I've told—I mean *no one knows!*"

"I see. You mean Vasyl doesn't know?"

"Well, yes. He does know. I mean you're the only one of my closest friends. I haven't told Rick or any of the others. I'm trying to protect the mother."

"Aw," he rumbled. "You consider me a friend."

I made a sound of exasperation.

"So, who's the father?"

"Bill Gannon."

"Oh for the love of blood," he said. "Why the fuck did you do it?"

"He was dying. I mean a humongous stone fell and cut him in half in that cave-in in Colorado Springs, and it was his last request for me to donate some of my eggs and I did."

He made one of those guy grunts.

"Anyway, the Dhampir is conceived. Maybe all you guys who wanted to be the father of my child are disappointed."

Tremayne's bitter laugh made me frown at Rick's iPhone. "I'm not half as disappointed as Vasyl is, I'm sure."

"Thing is," I went on in my hushed voice, "Vasyl doesn't realize that the child is the Dhampir."

"How do you know it is then?"

"Dante told me. He used the prophesy in order to point out the details, and it all fits. The Watchers? You know who they are, right?"

"Fallen Angels and their off-spring—*ohh.*"

"Right. Bill Gannon was off-spring of Nephilim. Their kind were having breeding problems. It was his quest to find me—the sibyl—mate with me and continue his kind. In doing so, I don't think he realized the child would become the King of Vampires."

Tremayne grunted again. "So you say you've told no one about this part of the news?"

"That's right. If Vasyl figures it out, I don't know what he'll think, but he wouldn't tell anyone. You know how to keep your mouth shut, so I'm telling you."

"Yes. But, then we still have a problem."

"We do?"

"If you announce that this child is conceived—or even when it's born—but not in, or from your body, the Powers That Be might send someone to check it out. No matter what, they stipulate that you are pregnant by either me or Vasyl, or they'll put a price on your head again. You have a month to get pregnant."

"Well, crap in fudge!" My desire to remain unburdened by a child was not going as planned. I had done my best to trick Vasyl into thinking I was not on the pill any longer—but was. Then I had to stop using it, but we had not been intimate since. Looked like my little deception was not going well. *What the hell!* If I told him that the baby that Ophelia, (Bill's sister), carried was the Dhampir—which was foretold in an ancient prophesy that the sibyl (that's me) would have—he would be pissed at me. Again. I don't know how pissed, but I feared that the news would hit him so hard it would take him even longer to forgive me than what he'd learned I'd done for Bill. In fact I was sure he wasn't actually over it. He was merely acting un-pissed in a Frenchman-like way (tight-lipped, looking at me funny, like I might run off with the next vampire to come into my life).

"Sabrina?" Tremayne's voice from the iPhone yanked me back to the now.

"I'm still here," I said on a sigh.

"Look, Morkel has told me you need to come in and give him an up-date on your files."

"Up-date?"

"Yes. He needs to know what new powers you have. It needs to be on file."

"So, you mean I have to come in? To Chicago? To the Towers?" Gak, another one of my not-so favorite places.

"That's right."

I made a heavy sigh.

"I also wish to speak with Vasyl."

"On the phone?"

"No. I'd rather talk to him in person."

"So, you want me to bring him in too?"

"Yes."

Cho's voice from the living room filtered to my ears. I peeked through the gap in the sheers over the lead-glass windows of the French door. He had his suit case in hand, jacket over his arm, ready to leave. He was going to hop on a plane and go visit his parents in San Francisco for Christmas. From there they were going to China to see the sights, and maybe find some relatives. He told me he had not seen his parents in two years. I thought that was terrible, and told him he should go and take all the time off he needed. Hobart was giving him a lift to O'Hare Airport.

"I'll bring him," I said to Tremayne, my brain working things out.

"Good." He paused.

"We'll be there in an hour or so," I said.

"Oh, and one thing I need to tell you. Almost forgot," he said.

"What?" I hated when someone said that to me.

"Talk is a war is pending between the Watchers and the demons in Dark World."

"Nifty. Why are you telling me?"

"Because, demons will side with demons. The head demon, for sure."

"Who is the head demon?"

"Naamah." My stomach sank.

"Oh, my very favorite demon of them all," I said, trying to incorporate humor into the dark sound of my voice.

"You know how he feels about you."

"Let me guess," I said. "Hates my guts?"

"Oh, much more than that. He wants to kill you in the most painful manner—his words, not mine."

"Fantastic," I said, faking a happy voice. "Just to change the subject, how are things there in the Towers?" Last night Tremayne and his minions took back the towers. Ilona was dead, thanks to me. And was now a broken-up stone statue, thanks to Cho. I wondered what happened to all her pieces after Cho broke her down using his feet as though he'd wielded a sledge hammer. With a combination of Martial Arts, and a powerful potion made with vampire blood, he'd turned her into gravel for a parking lot, basically. Good riddance.

"Things are getting back to normal. But I need to appoint a new magnate," Tremayne's voice was in my ear, yanking me out of my thoughts.

"Oh. Good." There came a pause and I might have spaced out thinking too much about things, because I didn't even absorb what Tremayne had said to me just now.

"Sabrina?" Tremayne said.

"What?"

"I never got to thank you for what you did."

"Which was?"

"Your plasma. It saved me."

"Seems we're always saving each other," I said, a smile bending my lips.

"As a result I've just up-graded you to Level Two."

"Meaning?"

"Meaning you're the second most important member of my camarilla."

"Nice. A big fat raise?" I asked hopefully. The whole "you're fired" speech from the now very dead Nicolas Paduraru coming to mind. He had no authority to fire me. Not then, and certainly not now.

"We'll talk about this more, later. But you get a special benefits package, including a free penthouse."

"Whatever," I snorted. Like I needed a penthouse. I had my own house, thank you very much.

"I have a few things to do, but someone will let me know when you get here, and I'll meet with you in the usual place."

"Okay," I said. "In your office, you mean?" I wasn't a big fan of his subterranean office.

"Yes. See you in about an hour?" he said.

"Yeah. Bye." I looked on the phone's screen and found the end button and stepped back into the living room. I had to drive to Chicago. To the Towers. *Yippee!*

"Well, Toots, how's everything with the boss?" Rick asked.

"Fine and dandy," I said, my eyes darting over the many faces in my living, and dining room. Vasyl had just stepped out of the steamy bathroom, his wet hair slicked back, shaven, a new blue shirt hung open over his shoulders and a new pair of jeans. He looked like a modern vampire magnate, ready to take on his corner of the world. *Why did I think of that?*

"Well, you ready?" Hobart said to Cho as he got to his booted feet and pulled up on his pants in that universal guy-thing, the heavy three-chains connected to his wallet in the back pocket jangling.

"Yes." Cho looked at me. "Sabrina, I'll miss you."

I strode up to him. I wanted to hug him, but he bowed deeply to me in that honoring way Orientals did. Straight black hair fell over his almond-shaped eyes. That was our relationship. He bowed to me, the sibyl. I waited for him to straighten and I gave him a hug anyway. As usual I did not get any read from this guy. I didn't know why, because in the beginning he was an open book for my Knowing, but he'd shut it down, like he could control what I could Know about him. Human, he had trained in the Martial Arts, a black belt and was a tremendous ally to have on my team. I figured he could block my clairvoyant powers whenever he wanted. Like Lindee could, but she didn't have the complete control this guy had. Cho had not seen his parents in two years and I was making him take a long needed vacation.

"I'll miss you too," I said. "But two weeks will go by fast. You'll call and let me know how things are going?"

"Of course."

Lindee stuck her hand out to him and he shook it. "Hey, eat sushi for me while you're there in China."

"I actually hate sushi," he said, grimacing. "Besides, that's Japanese."

We all chuckled.

"Well, have Peking Duck or something, then," she said. "I hope your Christmas will be great. And Santa will be kind."

He laughed. "Santa is always kind."

I turned to Vasyl. "We're going to Chicago. To the Towers." I informed. "Tremayne wants to see you, and me." Vasyl frowned.

"Why?" he asked.

"Oh! Can I go?" Lindee cried, hand up, jumping up and down wearing my sweatshirt and old jeans. "Pleeeezzzz!"

I glanced her way. "Yeah. I think we need to go shopping for you." I didn't think it would be right to leave her all alone. "I'll give you a vial of holy water and a crucifix."

"Wow. Are these requirements to go there, or something?" she asked.

"Yes. Especially if you don't want a vampire to hit on you," I said.

The loud bang, and shaking of the house made us all jump.

"What the fairy fart was that?" Rick asked jumping to his feet.

"Earthquake?" Hobart asked.

The rumbling began to shake things off the walls. *Earthquake?*

"Might be," I said grabbing for the sturdy beam of the threshold between the living room and dining room. Vasyl stepped over to me. Panic went all around.

"We should get out, if it's an earthquake," Lindee said, her voice shrill.

"Here? In Illinois?" I questioned. "We might get itty-bitty ones, but not major—" I broke off my words remembering the day I went to get the mystic ring, and an earthquake shook Mrs. Bench's house.

"OH, FAIRY CRAP ON TODESTOOLS!" Rick cried, looking up from his phone. "We've got an invasion!"

"Invasion?" I asked. "What do you mean?"

"We're under demon attack!"

Chapter 2

Bill

The Boeing 787 Dreamliner taxied on the runway of the DIA—Denver International Airport. He took Business Class so that he'd have comfort and privacy. The gentle blue, gray and white interior helped calm his nerves. Although the Dreamliner had carry-on luggage, he had little with him, just one bag.

Bill looked out into the darkness, watching the lights of the city and runway rush by, and then eased out of sight as he felt the familiar lift of the jet leaving the tarmac.

Bill had only two concerns about the flight. The first of which was possible fires on board related to the jet's lithium-ion batteries.

His second concern was the passenger seated next to him, on the other side of the privacy wall, occupied by a large businesses man on his way to Chicago. He'd said he was from L.A. almost right away, as if this made him important. He complained about the airline's on-board baggage requirements, the food, the fact that they only allowed two drinks, made a running comment about the stewardesses (who were bitches from hell), and would not shut the hell up from the moment he'd sat down, plus every fifth word he dropped the f-bomb. Finding the man boorish, and obnoxious Bill used his new powers to make the man go to sleep, and in ten minutes the man went limp, his head lolling back on the headrest.

Thankful, Bill smiled to himself and watched whatever movie was on.

Unfortunately the man began to snore. He put the headphones on in order to drown that noise out. Now, at least, he could think. After the vision of Nemesis, he had followed his inner voice, which told him he must get back home. The first place he had gone to instantly, with just a thought, was the Hyatt Place in Colorado Springs where he had been staying. He had made reservations for two weeks, as he had no idea how long it would take him to locate and snatch Sabrina.

He retrieved his luggage from the motel room. Although he didn't need to make any excuse as to why he had been gone so long (he had used a credit card and was checked in for the whole week), he had told the motel clerk that he had been in the mountains during a snow storm. He went into an elaborate story where he'd tried to hike out, fell and somehow lost his wallet and cell phone. He couldn't very well tell him his wallet had burned up with him, could he? Plus, he'd given Sabrina his cell phone in order to get in touch with his father. He felt fortunate that the car he had rented was still there. He had rented it for a week, so no one had bothered it. But he no longer had the keys. There were ways around that, however, and he used his new-found powers to open the door, and drive it to the hotel parking lot, and left it there.

Fortunately his other credit cards were in another wallet with his luggage, and he'd rented a new room for the day—to shower and sleep. He needed the time to compose himself after what had happened in the cave, and figure out what he needed to do and how to do it.

When he awoke midday, and found that sun poked in through the drapes, burning a hole in his arm. Sitting up abruptly, he moved away from the blaring sun and examined his arm where the sun had touched him. Nothing had happened. He did not smolder and other than a little redness, he was fine. *Did I imagine it burning me?*

Nemesis had been right. He was not a vampire. He could walk in the sunlight, and did not require blood to live. The throbbing in his chest from his near-panic told him he indeed had a heartbeat, like a normal human had—not like a vampire, which was one beat per minute. He felt for his pulse in his arm and counted fifty beats per minute. Not quite like a human, then.

What am I?

He rolled over, rearranged the covers and pillow, and eventually went back to sleep. It was as though he had not slept in weeks. His dreams consisted of his awakening in the cave as a vampire, and slashing the throats of the men and drinking their blood. Waking up sweat-drenched, he sat in the bed trying to steady himself. The images were hard to shake. He had killed those men. Guilt-riddled, he felt he should turn himself into the authorities. But something stopped him from doing so. It was called self-preservation.

"Why me?" He clawed his fingers through his sweat-soaked hair. The lives of those three men who had been working on the cave-in swirled around in his head. He threw off the covers and headed straight for the shower, hoping to wake up completely.

After drying off and dressing, he found he was hungry.

But not for blood. For a nice porterhouse and all the trimmings. He could find a decent steak in Denver. After all, they bred cattle here.

Now, on the last leg of the flight, his mind played out the scenes in the cave once again. They were currently over Iowa, a stewardess had said so to a passenger who'd asked nearby.

Almost there. Will I find Sabrina at home? She wouldn't know I'm alive. So his thoughts went.

Once home he would still have to figure things out. He now felt relieved that he had not sold the condo in Naperville. When he had first come to Illinois to find the sibyl, and eventually came to Emma to ask for her help. She had welcomed him and insisted he stay with her. She knew right away where the sibyl was—living right across the street from her.

Bill knew everyone would think him dead and gone, since Sabrina had been present and would have told Emma. The news would have gotten back to his parents, his sister, everyone who knew him. He had feared all his accounts would have been frozen, or dissolved. But when he'd checked, his accounts seemed to be left alone. He'd had the wording of his will to read that no one could touch any of his accounts, or sell any of his property for one full year after his death—just in case. It was well known that as a Nephilim, one might return as a Vampyr and need money and dwelling.

He had returned. What now? Pretend he was the same old Bill Gannon? Or stay out of sight? He still had a lot to think about.

Chapter 3

Payback

Hobart and Cho rushed outside, trekked through the deep snow, and jumped into his warmed-up truck.

"Why can't we use the ley lines?" I asked Rick, grabbing my purse and coat in such a flurry, I nearly whacked him in the head with my purse. He ducked. "Sorry."

The sound above our heads made us all look up.In quick succession, we ducked and dove when the ceiling light fixture swung dangerously. The ceiling cracked, plaster fell in big chunks, then all of it crashed onto the dining room table. Lindee and I screamed as bits of glass shot everywhere like shrapnel. More things in the other room crashed—lamps, and pictures falling from the walls. It was like small bombs going off. I very briefly worried about the clean-up, and then checked myself. When would I ever be able to come back and do any sort of clean up?

"We can't because it's too dangerous!" Rick yelled over the crashing noises, answering my question. "I can't protect us from demons while traveling in ley lines. This is the only way! We have to get out! Grab your keys!"

I grabbed my keys off the hook on the wall just before the rack fell to the floor. I pulled a hooded sweatshirt off a peg and shoved it into Vasyl's hands. "Here. Put this on!" I turned around to watch Lindee run around in circles, she looked like a chicken with her head chopped off. She screamed obscenities when something big crashed—my mother's china cabinet. I wanted to cry as I ran into the living room and dialed down the heat. No reason to keep the heat on high if I wasn't going to be here for a while. It was automatic for me to also turn out lights.

"What are you doing?" Rick asked, jumping up and down looking like the Mad Hatter. "We've gotta leave!"

The house itself gave a huge heave, like it were a boat riding a tsunami.

Lindee fell. Vasyl helped her up.

"Let's go! Let's GO!" Rick said, door opened to his magical whim.

"What about Hobart and Cho?" I asked.

Vasyl jerked his head. The dark form coalesced next to him and formed into the long-haired Native American, better known as Dante. "I will go with them," he offered, and smiled at Rick. "Demons will not attack an Undead," he explained, his lips curled into a humorless smile. "Unless they want to die a horrible death while I feed on them."

"Okay. That works for me," I said. He vanished. I wasn't sure how he would be traveling with Hobart and Cho, since there wasn't a lot of room in Hobart's truck, but Dante could remain invisible, or sit in the corner of a mirror, so I didn't think he would take up too much room.

"I'm ready," I said on the move. "Let's go!"

We all streamed out of my house toward my olive green Jeep. Hobart's truck took off out of my drive as we jumped into the Jeep. Gasping and panting, I plugged my key into the ignition and the engine turned over. *Thank you!* I shoved it into gear and we were out of there. Rick had his eyes on his iPhone the whole time. I didn't know what he saw in it, but it had everything to do with his protection spells.

The snow had been removed from all the country roads and were actually very good to drive on. I was seriously thinking of getting a larger SUV, because I might need something bigger if I had so many house guests—if I ever got my house back.

Fortunately, my brother, Randy, wife and kids had gone to Florida for a few weeks. Disney World was one destination. I secretly wished I could be with them.

"Seriously, this is holy water?" Lindee was holding up the vial she'd dug from my purse.

"Do not take it lightly," I firmly told her. "Act as though it were acid because it burns demons and vampires severely."

"Oh, I promise." She leaned, glancing at Vasyl who rode beside me. The crucifix I'd given her dangled from her neck. Vasyl would not have bothered her, but she did feel slightly unnerved with a vampire around the house and so continued to wear it.

"I'd never use it on you," Lindee said to Vasyl.

"I was not worried," he said. "But why are we going to the Towers to see Tremayne?"

"For one thing, it's safer than here," I said, my eyes sweeping the road and all my mirrors for any possible demons following us. "Secondly, he said he wanted to speak to you about something. Plus I've been put up to Level Two, and I'm supposed to give Morkel an up-date on my new powers."

"What new powers?" Lindee said. "You have powers?"

I laughed. Rick chuckled beside her.

"Let's see. My new powers include telepathy... um." I stopped at a stop sign and turned, using the clutch and manual shift. "Oh! Remote viewing." That was both great and not so great.

"Turning someone into stone," Rick added and chuckled again, still looking into the iPhone.

"Oh, yeah," I said, smiling broadly.

"Omygod! Really?" Lindee asked from the backseat, and leaning forward. "You can do that?" Since a lot of things happened last night, and Vasyl had been found by Tremayne, barely alive, I didn't have time or need to hash over the particular details of my night with anyone.

"I turned Ilona into stone, so I guess I can," I said, trying not to sound boastful. I had no idea that I could do this, and so it had surprised me probably more than anyone, except for Ilona herself.

"Those powers Dante gave you are very dangerous," Vasyl warned.

"No shit," I said. "I'll have to watch my temper."

"Oh, yeah. I'll be sure to never to piss you off," Lindee said and laughed.

"You never make me mad," I said. "I love you. Besides, Ilona was horrible. She was going to bite our little niece, Jena."

"Oh, my God!" Lindee said. "Really?"

"Yes. They covered my hands so I couldn't use my normal powers." I looked over at Vasyl. "They tied the bags with pure silver, knowing I couldn't touch silver, and no other person who couldn't touch silver could untie them." I hadn't told anyone of the details of my trying to find and save my brother and his family from Ilona in Tremayne Towers.

"I don't understand," Lindee said.

"I couldn't use the mystic ring to control her because of the ring being covered."

"Oh. That's the magic ring. Got it," Lindee said with a nod. She was only half right.

"She had it all planned, it would seem,".Vasyl said.

"That it does," I agreed. "But, when she lifted little Jena, saying she wanted to make a child vampire out of her, something snapped in me. I had to stop her and thought of either turning her to ice or to stone. I chose stone and it just happened."

"You mean like a statue?" Lindee asked.

"Yes. Like a statue."

We all became quiet as I pulled up to the toll booth.

"Crap. I don't think I have enough change."

Rick's snap of fingers made the light turn green and the blockade go up.

"Sweet!" Lindee said, looking at him. "You'd come in real handy. The next time I want to go to Merrilville for a concert, you're coming along."

"Sweet. I love concerts," Rick said, smiling at her.

I drove through the toll, and glanced in my rear view mirror to engage Lindee's eyes. "Look for my wallet in there. We still need money to get through tolls next time. They all have toll booth operators in them." I handed her my bag. Good thing I'd grabbed it.

Lindee opened my purse and dug out my wallet.

"Did he say what he wanted with me?" Vasyl asked.

I glanced over at him, startled as though there was a stranger sitting next to me. It was going to be a while before I got used to his new look. "No. He just said he wanted to see the both of us."

We caught up to Hobart in his white truck, and came up beside him in the other lane. We waved to him. He would be turning off to go to the airport, eventually.

Red flashing lights ahead made me slow and get into the right lane behind Hobart's truck.

"Looks like an accident," I said as we went by slower than the break-neck speed that I had been going. A wrecker was there, and so were two police cars, their blue lights strobing.

"Looks like a bad fender bender," Lindee said, turning around in her seat.

"Remember when I saved you from the car accident?" Vasyl asked.

"Oh, yeah. I was shot in the back," I said, smiling with the memory. It was the first time Vasyl had touched or spoke to me.

"You mean you were shot another time?" Lindee said, sounding shocked.

"Yes. We wcrc being followed and someone was shooting at me."

"They were werewolves," Vasyl put in. "I took you to my place to heal you."

I chuckled, remembering how he had taken me to his barn and had taken the slug out of my back, and then had me drink his blood to heal—all while I was out, or under his vampire thrall.

"That was our first intimate moment," I said, smiling.

"The first time I'd given you my blood." Our eyes met. His eyes had a preternatural glow in them. It would have freaked me out a month ago. But I was pretty used to vampires now.

"You were so handsome standing there, telling me I would have died, and there I was without a shirt on."

"You held on to that horse blanket as though it were going to hide you from my eyes when I had already seen you."

"Aw, how romantic," Lindee said, making me jerk.

Rick made a wolf whistle.

I'd forgotten about them in the Jeep, I was so wrapped up in my memories.

"You guys have a special bond," Lindee said.

"We do," I said softly. He reached for my hand. Our fingers twined, he lifted my hand, and his lips brushed the back of it.

"Romance isn't dead after all," Lindee said.

"I had been searching for her for a thousand years," he said over his shoulder. Then looking directly at me he said, "Never had I thought I would have to come to America to find you."

"You were *looking* for her?" Lindee said, sounding amazed.

"She is the sibyl. The first one in two thousand years," he explained.

"I still don't understand this sibyl thing," Lindee said, shaking her head.

"The supernatural community has been waiting for her all this time. She is important because she will give birth to the Dhampir."

Lindee was quiet for a moment. I could almost hear the wheels grinding, since I now was telepathic. "Is that why you two need to make a baby?"

"Yes." Vasyl answered first. "And we will. Soon."

Gulp.

I could not help the little zip of excitement shoot through me. Memories of how he stood in that barn and how singularly handsome he was made me hot. I don't know if my desires were ratcheted up because he was talking about us having a child together, but I couldn't single out any one reason my thoughts suddenly blossomed into desire. We had not been together intimately since the night before because of his injuries. He was now recuperated. I could see from his expression that he thought the same.

"Okay, you two. Sabrina, eyes on the road."

Lindee's warning made me turn my eyes back on the road. Ahead, Hobart's white truck turned onto an off-ramp. I noted the green sign for O'Hare. I tooted my horn at Hobart, and he honked back at me.

"There goes Cho," I said, waving. Lindee waived too. As if they could see us.

In another mile I had to pull up to a toll plaza.

"Got the money for me?" I asked Lindee.

"Oh!" Lindee made one of her laughs, as she was caught off guard. "How much?"

"Two bucks. I can get change." I pulled up behind a van and stopped and waited, then inched forward.

"Here." She handed me two ones.

I took the moment and put the dollars between my legs while I worked the clutch as I inched forward and then took it out of gear to wait while holding my foot on the break.

"Highway robbery," I complained low to the others before I powered down the window.

"This reminds me of the tolls we would have to pay when I was alive," Vasyl said.

"They had tolls back then?" Lindee asked.

"More than you think," he said. "They took anything, including money, food, clothes."

"That *is* highway robbery," I said.

"Basically," he said. "Robbers could make a great deal selling what they stole."

"You want me to put a whammy on them, Sabrina?" Rick asked.

"No." We crawled, stopped, and crawled some more until I got to the window.

Finally it was our turn. I powered down my window and was about to hand the teller my money when I saw two demon eyes glare out at me and she and a gun was in her hand pointed at my face.

"Holy shit!" I thrust my right hand at the gun and I yelled "Jam!" Directing my next words to Rick, I said, "Open the gates, Rick! Now!" He snapped his fingers. At the same time the gun clicked but didn't go *bang!* The gates shot up and I put the Jeep in gear and sped away.

"Come back here!" the demon screeched behind us.

I pressed the window button to power it up again, and cut off the cold air rushing in.

"Ohmygod, what was that shit about?" Lindee asked, her voice high pitched as she turned around in her seat to look back.

"That was a demon," I said.

"They're following you," Rick said.

"I thought you said you could keep them away," I said.

"Ah, that one sort of slipped through my defenses," he said, looking at his iPhone again.

"Make sure no more do," I said, realizing he was monitoring things from the phone, like he always did. How he could detect demons on it, I had no idea. I mean, what would be that app?

Thirty minutes later we drove into the city, and soon the entrance of Tremayne Tower's underground garage came into view. I turned off the street and through the first gates. Only then did I realize I didn't have my identification card on me. It was the only way we could get inside.

"I'm sorry," I said to the man in the gate house. "But would you please call Mr. Tremayne and tell him Sabrina Strong and Vasyl are here?"

"Okay, ma'am." The dark haired man ducked inside his window and shut it. I turned to stare at the red and white-striped gate in front of the Jeep.

"They sure have a lot of security here," Lindee said.

"Yeah, they won't let anyone inside the garage on this side of the building unless we have our ID's." I sighed. Elbow to the window ledge, I leaned on my fist. "I can't believe I don't have it on me." I straightened as realization hit me. "Oh, shit. I won't be able to get on the elevator without it and go to his office."

"Won't he have someone meet us?" Vasyl asked.

I twisted my lips in thought. The guard opened his window.

"There you go, Ms. Strong." He handed me a parking ticket as the gate rose. I'd never come in here where they gave out parking passes before. "Have a good evening." He made a three-fingered salute to me.

"Oh, thank you." I took the ticket and drove forward, into the lit parking garage. It was the same as always. But something different had been added. Parking attendants, wearing bright yellow vests, held flashlights while directing cars. I pulled up behind a car that had stopped. There were three cars in front of him.

"Wow. This place is busy," I said. "Must be something going on."

"Maybe there's a party," Lindee said.

"Yeah, a vampire party," Rick chimed in.

We were finally next in line. The young man leaned to my window.

"Are you here for Tremayne's party?" he asked.

It was the first I'd heard of any party. Clueless I said, "I'm here to see him."

"Do you have a parking pass?"

I handed him the parking ticket. He nodded and pointed. "We've got your parking slot over there, Ms. Strong. In the D parking area."

I followed the signs, turned down a different way than the cars in front of me had. I'd never liked the parking garage. I'd been shot at down here too. Ever since then I really hated coming in here.

"This place is super!" Lindee said, eyes wide open looking around.

"It's been a while for me," the new voice startled us. I looked in my rear view mirror and saw Dante seated between Rick and Lindee.

"Shit! You scared the crap out of me!" Rick swore.

"Me too!" Lindee nearly screamed.

"My apologies," he said.

"Hobart and Cho got to the airport okay?" I asked.

"They did. Hobart said he would head back to his place."

"You know what's going on?" I asked as I drove along, following more parking attendants who pointed me through when I held up my parking pass. My Jeep was the only American made vehicle in this section. Expensive vehicles, makes and models of which I wasn't familiar with, aside from the Beamers and Mercedes.

"This is Tremayne's party, and announcement of his return to the vampire world," Dante informed.

"That makes sense," I said. "After all, he'd been considered a rogue for a few weeks."

"I sense there is more to it than that," Dante said.

"What does he want of me?" Vasyl asked.

"I wouldn't know," Dante said.

"I guess we'll have to find out the usual way, 'coz I'm not getting any reads at all," I said and pulled into an empty slot next to a red Ferrari and a silver BMW.

We all piled out. I knew the way to the elevators and the others followed me. The walk from where I would have normally parked may have taken us five minutes. Today, we were much closer. Dante strode ahead, and stopped at the elevator doors, ready to press the button, but he didn't need to. It opened and two people stepped out. My gasp echoed next to me with Lindee's surprised intake of air.

"Jeanie! Heath!" I knew it had to be Heath, because they were a couple. I wanted in the worse way to run up and hug them both, but I needed to err on the side of safety.

"Going down?" Jeanie said, looking super sexy wearing a shimmery blue cocktail dress. Heath was in a very nice suit. He never usually wore a full suit. But tonight he had a tux on.

Part-ay-y-y.

"Look at you guys! You look fabulous in that dress, Jeanie!"

"Thanks," she said. Her short very blond hair was teased and the long tendrils were died to match her dress.

I turned to Lindee. "I don't know if you remember my cousin, Lindee? Lindee this is Jeanie. And this is Heath. Remember what I told you?" I prompted because I didn't want to blurt out that Jeanie was now a vampire.

"Oh, sure. I remember her during summer vacations. I went to your house once when I visited Sabrina," Lindee said. Jeanie and I were practically inseparable during the summers.

"Hi, Lindee," Jeanie said, smiling her brilliant smile. "I'm sorry that I don't remember you. Seems some things from my former life are a blank."

"Oh, that's okay. A lot of my own life is a blank," Lindee said and laughed.

"And this is Heath," I said, gesturing. I had told Lindee to not look directly into their eyes or extend her hand. You didn't shake hands with a vampire, unless you wanted to become dinner.

"How'd you do," Heath said making a little nod.

"Oh my God! I love your accent!" Lindee said. We all chuckled. Heath was originally from Liverpool, England, turned in the mid-sixties. He and his brother were both Beatles fans before they were turned.

"I hear there's a party?" I said, watching several people going to another elevator and crowding on.

"That there is. But we're to take you to Mr. Tremayne's office directly," Heath said, pointing to another set of elevator doors.

"Well, I guess we'll go with you," I said, pulling my purse strap over my shoulder.

"Blimey, Dante, it's good to see you, again," Heath said as we stepped on. "Heard there's been some drastic changes to you. An Undead, now, eh?"

"I get around much easier now," Dante said with a wicked smile.

"No doubt," Heath said.

We all entered the elevator with the vampires. The doors snicked closed. My stomach rolled. I didn't like going down to Tremayne's office. Too many bad memories there, too.

Heath pressed for Level A—Level Hell, as I liked to call it—and the elevator slid downward. It was a very short ride. Filing out, we strode through the familiar curving hallway.

"Oh, wow," Lindee said moving to the glass that made up one wall, and looked down into the next two levels. "This place is cool! Is that a billiards room way down there?"

"Yes," I said, looking down to the bottom level. The two levels were arranged below like huge steps.

"You think we might have time to go shoot some pool?" she asked.

"Mostly donors play and lounge down there, waiting for their vampires to call them," Heath told her.

"Besides, you're all going to be too busy tonight to play pool," Jeanie said, her voice sultry.

"Hey, Sabrina?" I turned to Rick behind me. My brows up.

"Alright if I leave? I had something lined up tonight."

"Sure," I said. "Thanks for helping us back there."

"Oh, no problem. See ya around, toots," Rick said. He snapped his fingers and was gone.

"Aw, too bad," Lindee said. "He's fun to have around." No doubt about that.

Dante strode ahead of us and opened the double oak doors of the outer office. As always no one sat at the desk. The only time I had seen anyone stationed here was when Nicolas assumed charge of things after Tremayne was ousted as a rogue.

The sudden vision severed me from my world. I saw a flash of someone with large black vampire wings.

"Are you alright?" Vasyl had my elbow.

"Uh, yeah," I said, blinking.

"A vision?" Dante asked.

Everyone had stopped to stare at me.

"Must have been," I said.

"What was it?" Dante asked.

"I don't know, exactly. Looked like a vampire with wings. Black wings." I looked up at Vasyl. His wings had been very dark, but they had some brown to them. Not black. This one had black wings and a very nasty looking claw at the apex of the wing, much like Vasyl's but the man wasn't Vasyl.

I shook my head. "I'm sure I'll have another one later on." I always had multiple visions of the same thing. I might even have a more detailed vision that would make me out of it for several minutes.

"We'll discuss this later," Dante said, looking grim.

"You saw it?" I asked.

"Of course I did." Dante could read my mind, and also could peek in at my visions, now that we were connected on this new higher level.

Vasyl shot him a harsh look. He said something in French.

Dante said, "The vision was of a master."

"*Sacrebleu!* What did he look like?"

"I didn't get a look at his face," I said.

"Are you alright? Can you go on?" Heath asked while standing at the sliding white doors to the inner sanctum looking at me with those serious, yet almost puppy-dog sad eyes.

I nodded. I usually feel dizzy after a vision, but this one was so brief it was inconsequential and I didn't feel dizzy at all. "I'm okay. May as well get this over with." I sighed. Anyone present didn't know why I hated meetings with Tremayne like this didn't know my history with him. There was safety in numbers, right? Especially with both Dante and Vasyl in my company. *Maybe the news will be good.*

Large red double T's of Tremayne's logo on the white doors slid apart as the doors opened. This, in my opinion, held the strangest place in all of Tremayne Towers. I'd been in this inner sanctum on a number of occasions—none of which I can truthfully say were pleasant. On one occasion I was rescuing Dante, who had become a mouse in order to spy on Ilona and Nicolas, back when he was a human shapeshifter.

Red tract lighting colored our pathway. There wasn't a right angle anywhere, and the only flat surface was where we walked. The place freaked me out, even now. But at least I wasn't alone this time. I knew the roundness and redness was meant to mimic a blood vessel. Cute vampire humor.

Vasyl looped his arm around mine and we strode behind Jeanie and Heath.

"Wow. This place is weird," Lindee gasped, overwhelmed by the strange red lighting and the ridiculous tunnel. "I feel like a hamster," she said. "Is there a huge cat at the end of this?" Her signature giggle echoed strangely. Heath and Jeanie chuckled. Jeanie looked back at us. She winked at me.

"No, but there are vampires just up ahead," Heath said, pointing. "Oh, wait. We *are* vampires." His joke was either on purpose or he hadn't even thought about it. He often didn't think of himself as a vampire.

"Lots of them," Jeanie added.

"Thanks for the warning," I said. I would have felt more uncomfortable, but I had my vampire husband at my side. What could go wrong?

We might have walked about twenty-five feet through the twists and turns before we emerged into the main section that opened up to a round room lit in yet more crimson. We came to a halt before a sunken seating area. Five steps down into a cozy seating pit in-the-round with white cushions taken up by vampires. All eyes glanced up at us. Some curious, others looked anxious, and possibly hungry.

A large curved white desk took up the back area, with a huge flat screen overhead. Below this, more vampires filled the rest of the room—some of them I may have seen on occasion working here. A few I had met, but I had to keep my eyes lowered, or not quite meet gazes. I checked Lindee. She was staring into the eyes of a male vampire. I grabbed her arm and shook her. When that didn't work, I had to step in front of her. She blinked.

"Whoa," she said, shaking off the thrall.

"I told you *not* to look into their eyes," I said, warning in my voice.

"I know. I'm sorry. I didn't meant to, but…" She took in the room. "This is weirder than anything I've ever seen on a bad trip."

"Yeah. Just be alert and don't look into their eyes." I adjusted her crucifix so it showed prominently on her chest. "There. Now be careful." She nodded and I turned back to the room.

My gaze halted on someone I recognized. Stefan Capella. Blue-black hair was styled in a business cut. He had a suave, yet dangerous look to him in the black suit he wore, which accentuated his wide shoulders and narrow waist. White silk tie contrasting with the black silk shirt and the overall combination made him look like a mobster boss. It suited him, I thought. If I had not been wearing my mystic ring when we'd met that first time, those dark blue eyes of his would have made me dance to his vampire tune. Stefan was what I like to refer to as a high-echelon vampire. I'd only met him once, but something about him—mostly his erudite eyes and pheromones—said he was a top feeder. Other than the fact that he was ruler over all of New York state, I still felt there was something more about him that I'd missed in our cozy meeting on the Leer Jet a week or more ago heading to Kansas. Those dark eyes of his caught mine. I dipped my gaze, appropriately, to show I wasn't interested. There was more significance to eye contact in a room full of vampires than one would guess.

Worried about Lindee, I leaned to Dante and whispered, "Watch over Lindee, please." He nodded. He would stay beside her, in case we became separated. All the coaching in the world would not matter, even if Lindee remembered any of it or took it to heart that this was for her well-being. I truly doubted she'd be able to both avoid looking into the eyes of a vampire, or remembering not to. I worried she would make another wrong move with one of the vampires here. We were surrounded, after all, by creatures who craved us—both our blood and sex. The pheromones alone, which filled the room, was hard to resist even for me. The vampire scents mingled like cloying incense, but oddly enough the combination threw me, and I clung onto Vasyl like a drowning person. I couldn't imagine what this all might be doing to Lindee right now. Stupid, I know, even with my nifty mystic ring exposed, but fifty-some-odd vampires all in one place proved too overwhelming for my one magical power over the total vampire thrall.

I wondered why all these vampires were gathered here—aside from the party-like atmosphere. I had thought this was a meeting between myself, Vasyl and Tremayne at the beginning of our harried trip here. When had it turned into a party? Everyone was dressed in very nice suits, and some men wore tuxes, and women had glittery cocktail dresses on. I felt so under dressed it wasn't funny. I watched them holding wine glasses filled with the red stuff. I almost expected to see a blood fountain somewhere in the back, but forced my eyes to stay on the nap of the carpet at my feet. *100% Wool, exported from England.*

Vasyl shifted beside me, and I had to look up again.

Tremayne's tall stature towered above everyone in a tight group across the room, and moved to greet us. He wore a white suit over a crimson shirt with a black silk tie. I wasn't used to seeing him so dressed up. Even his shoes were white. Well, he had returned from being ousted, and near death, so I guess it was due him.

Heath's voice brought the crowd's attention on us. "The sibyl, and her vampire husband, Vasyl, and entourage, my lord." He made a bow to Tremayne—which I had only seen him do once before.

Everyone stopped talking. The music—which I had now noticed was playing softly in the background—was silenced.

The first time I had been in this room his whole entourage of vampires had gone on one knee and made a bow, but I figured that Jeanie and Heath had already been here, since they had come up to fetch us. But suddenly, Vasyl went down on one knee and bowed his head deeply. I was struck dumb. I made a half-assed bow, only because I wasn't a damned vampire.

"I, Vasyl, humbly accept your hospitality, my lord," Vasyl's words filled the quiet room.

The tension in the room grated on my nerves. It's usually hard for me to get any sort of read from vampires, but body language was easy. There were stiff shoulders, and hard stares of anticipation. I stiffened, too, and my stomach did the usual flipping when I became nervous. I took a step back, because I'd been in front of him, and Tremayne's harsh look my way seemed to demand it. Of course, it all made perfect sense once I thought on it. Vasyl was considered a rogue and was actually interloping on Tremayne's turf (explaining why there was all this tension), even though he had been invited. It was only fitting he made some sort of bow to his authority. One monarch bowed to the other before a gathering. It was a decisive moment for both masters. I had about three seconds to ponder dreadfully that this might have been a trap for Vasyl—he was basically out-numbered here.

I, and the room as a whole, waited in silence to see what Tremayne's purpose for asking Vasyl here was. Master vampires did not invite one another to their dwellings or their areas—at least this is what I'd been told—unless there was a war going on, or something else, which I couldn't even fathom in vampiredom. In fact, if one ventured inside the other's realm there would have to be an all-out battle between them. But Vasyl and Tremayne have had some lines drawn about me, and they'd avoided confrontations. It was something like Batman vs. Superman. You knew their strengths and weaknesses. One common weakness was me.

Yep. I was as nervous as a cat in a room full of pit bulls on the whole drive into the city, and now I thought I would faint with anticipation and dread if something wouldn't happen soon to alleviate it.

"Rise, Vasyl," Tremayne said, his aqua eyes on my husband. I watched Tremayne's poker face. Even as his eyes glanced at me, he showed no emotion. Damn him.

Vasyl rose and shook the odd lengths of his hair out of his face.

Tremayne strode forward, stepping around that lower seating section, everyone's eyes on him as he walked across to where we stood. Vampires did not shake hands with one another, as a rule. This bowing and greeting thing was all a big formality. So when Tremayne walked up to Vasyl and grasped him by the arm in a sort of Viking grip, and Vasyl did the same while they held eye contact for at least one vampire heartbeat (about a minute), a shudder went through me. The crowd, as a whole relaxed, I saw movement of heads, murmurs rose, a few people chuckled. This was one of those odd paramount moments, like two opposing generals coming together for a peace treaty. A few more vampires shifted their stances. Then a grunt of approval rang out. Female vampires smiled and stared at Vasyl. A few licked their lips as though they thought of something delicious was about to be served.

"You understand that I am now the reigning master in all of North America?" Tremayne said.

"I do," Vasyl said, making a slight bow to him.

"And because of that I may choose whoever I wish to rule with me as the second master, since my brother died two months ago?"

"*Oui*," Vasyl said, holding his stare.

Tremayne turned to the crowd. He placed his hand on Vasyl's shoulder. "I know that not many of you were around more than three hundred years ago." The crowd chuckled. "But Vasyl once ruled the Vampire Association of France." This seemed to be an important historical note, because the crowd noises rose with interest.

"Three hundred and forty-nine years I ruled," Vasyl said, smiling and obviously proud of this.

This was news to me. Vasyl didn't speak to me about his past vampire life, unless it had something to do with me—his hunting for, or finding me.

Tremayne chuckled, looking at him. "You kept the Germans out during the war."

"Which war?" Vasyl said, smirking. The crowd chuckled.

Tremayne's voice cut across the chuckles. He looked out across the crowd and said in a loud voice, "Let it be known before all these witnesses of my realm that I hereby offer the command of the Eastern half of the North American Vampire Association to Vasyl."

Everyone became still again. I held my breath. I had no idea Tremayne would offer this to Vasyl. I was nearly certain he didn't want anything to do with such things.

Vasyl bowed his head and said, "I accept."

My jaw dropped. *Really?*

Cheers rang out, people clapped. I wasn't among them. I stood there in shock for about five or so seconds before I did put my hands together and clapped, but only half-heartedly. I quickly understood that this meant Vasyl would not be at my side all the time. Things would change drastically in a heartbeat. He would be busy doing whatever it is a master did. Lord over his underlings, keep them all under control. I would imagine he'd be in charge over all services, agencies and businesses which were housed here in the towers. Plus, run the two hotels here. There wasn't a chance to ask him why he was going to do this.

"Congratulations!" Heath said to him as I came out of my shock. Other vampires strode up congratulating him. A line of people came up and congratulated and bowed to Vasyl. I was squeezed out and stood next to Lindee and Dante.

"Everyone!" Tremayne's rich baritone carried over the loud voices that filled the room, his hand held high. Everyone quieted. "Now we will perform a blood ritual ceremony," Tremayne said, "Those of you who are staying on, will take part. Those of you who are remaining with me will witness." Then looking squarely at me, he said a little lower in tone, "I suggest that the two humans not attend."

That was more than fine with me. I sure as hell did not want to witness another blood ritual where—I supposed—Vasyl bit those vampires who would bow down to him from here on.

Vasyl turned to me. The violet of his eyes overtaken by the black of his pupils. The tips of his fangs slid over his ruby lips. Shit. He was already excited about this ritual if he was vamping out.

"I plan on taking my cousin shopping," I said, quickly darting a glance at both Tremayne and Vasyl.

Tremayne moved forward and quickly was at my side. "There will be a cocktail party afterwards. At my penthouse," Tremayne said, then added, "It would be a very good idea that the two of you go shop for appropriate dresses for the party." Then, as if dismissing us, he turned to Vasyl. "Gods in heaven, where did you get that awful haircut?"

Lindee made a sound of protest. "I did the best I could with what I had!" I looped my hand though her arm—the one that had bent, placing one hand to her hip—and tugged her away.

"I'll send for my hair dresser. And those clothes won't do. We'll get you a suit—uh—and shoes…" Tremayne's voice trailed off as he towed Vasyl into the crowd, away from me.

"Come on. You really don't want to see this." Dante and I trundled Lindee away. We quickly moved out of the main area, back through the crazy twisting tunnel, Dante shadowing us, now since there was only enough room for two to walk side-by-side.

"What is it they're going to do?" Lindee asked, she jogged to keep up with me.

"It's a blood ritual between vampires," I said. "Vasyl will bite whatever vampires wish to be under him. It's really gross."

"Eww. I'd rather shop, anyway," she said and then laughed.

"Sabrina! Wait!" At the sound of Vasyl's voice I turned to look down the red-lit tunnel. He jogged around a bend, and trotted up to us. He took me by the hand and stepped away with me.

I looked into his eyes. They'd gone soft, and the fangs had retracted.

"Sabrina," he said taking my hands into his and kissing them. "You must understand I must do this thing."

"Okay," I said. "I'm not sure why—"

"I will explain everything to you later." He kissed me quickly. "I must go." He turned away. Side-stepping, his hair bouncing around his face—it really was a terrible haircut—he held up a hand and then an index finger. "Later. We will speak later."

I watched him disappear around the bend. My heart became heavy. Was I about to lose him to the vampires of Tremayne's realm?

Chapter 4

Demon's Pleasure

"Pay up, Stefan."

Stefan's gaze was pulled from the sight of watching the two women strolling down the tunnel toward the exit. Mainly he was watching Sabrina. He narrowed his eyes at Russ Styles, his second in command.

"I'll have to get it for you." He sniffed indignantly, adding, "I don't happen to carry around a bank roll tonight."

"One hundred bucks?" Styles snorted, black eyes glittering, the white of his teeth contrasted against his cocoa-colored skin.

"I have no cash on me," Stefan re-worded his original answer. "I'll get it to you. Later."

Styles didn't move. He stared at the two human women walking out of the room. "I'd like to get my fangs into that one on the right."

Stefan turned to sneer at him, he almost hissed with irritation. He'd meant Sabrina Strong. "She belongs to Vasyl, now."

"What's the matter with you? You want her too. I can tell," Styles huffed.

Stefan tugged at his collar and straightened his tie automatically. "She's taken."

"Do tell. That French rogue has his fangs and dick in her every night and I can see that bothers you to distraction."

Stefan threw him a heated look. Styles laughed openly.

"I speak the truth! I see what she does to you. Too bad the rogue will also have a title which you should have been next in line for." Styles spun away after his dig. A good thing he did, too, or there would have been a large disruption to his father's blood ritual for the newly instated.

Sabrina was Vasyl's. Stefan wondered how long it would take for him to seduce her into bed with him once things had settled and Vasyl became too… occupied.

* * *

She crushed her cigarette out in the ceramic dish and blew smoke out of the side of her mouth. The moon would be full again, and she couldn't wait until it waned again to do a ritual to try and speak to the demon again.

Would he come anyway, even though the moon was waxing? She had drawn her magic circle with her Athamé—a black-hilted knife—before beginning her ritual. She had consecrated it moments ago.

Kiel St. Thomas looked over her implements—her wand, candles arranged at all four corners, other various pieces of her craft placed in spots within the circle and the five-pointed star. The thurible burned incense of the highest quality she could find. She stepped to her work station and picked up her small white hilted knife. She quickly drew it across the palm of her hand. A red line welled up, and blood began oozing from the cut. She turned her hand carefully so that the blood would drip on the black stone. The stone itself was given to her in their first meeting by the demon. He had given her the odd looking stone telling her that whenever she needed to speak with him, she only needed a few drops of her own blood applied to it. As a matter of formality, she also let a few drops drip into the silver chalice.

She raised the cup with both hands and spoke. "I, Kiel Magdalen Saint Thomas, call to you, oh dark lord, Naamah, to come to me. As always, I am your tool in all things of darkness."

The wind picked up slightly. Small ice pellets stung her face and arms as the wind picked up even more and blew out all the candles, and nearly blew the small fire out. She would have done her ritual calling up the demon inside for her own comfort, but Naamah was not a small demon, and her small apartment would not hold all of him, with his giant bat wings, and twin tails that might have been fifteen feet long.

The tingling in her feet told her that a portal had opened. The tingling shot up her legs, torso and arms and finally her head where her auburn hair whipped around her face like a ragged flag.

"Kiel Magdalen Saint Thomas, why do you bother me? I am busy," the voice echoed and carried all around her in the wooded glen where she worked. It was only a mile drive to this remote copse of trees in a field. The land belonged to a friend of the family, and she was always welcomed to spend time at the cabin.

Kiel bent at the waist and bowed, not looking up at him until she addressed him properly. "My lord, the giver of powers. I honor you, in all ways. I will honor you further. I will do anything you wish of me."

"Daughter, it pleases me to see you again. But I am very busy. What is it you want of me?" the demon's voice, which seemed to be everywhere, echoed on the night air.

Her heart skipped a beat as she watched the huge shape of the monstrous demon form before her. He stood at least ten feet tall, with huge black wings like a bat and claws at the apex that looked more like talons. Head bald, his eyes glowed red as he gazed upon her. The large double snake tales undulated beneath him. He was the most amazing and scariest thing she had ever encountered. He had seduced her in their first of three meetings. Doing it with a demon hurt like hell—it was not a lie that they had cold and huge penises. In fact, his member was huge, and pointed like a dog's. After she had pleasured him—and he her—he granted her many powers. She was the only witch in her coven (maybe in the whole mid-west), who could withstand his attentions. The other women were terrified of him. In fact one of their earlier members had gone mad after seeing him. She now was in a mental institute for the insane.

"M-my powers, the ones you granted me years ago, have been stolen," she said, speaking clearly but quickly. She didn't want to anger him.

"How did you lose your powers?" he asked.

"A shapeshifter—or I think he was—who clings to the woman named Sabrina Strong? I—my coven and I—took her powers from her. Or, were in process of doing so, and we nearly succeeded, but he intervened and stole mine as well as the rest of the coven's powers. One of them is in the hospital in a coma, she is so badly hurt by his draining of her."

The demon, Naamah, held up his hand. "I understand and know who you mean. In fact we have a common goal. The shapeshifter you speak of is no longer a living human. He is an Undead. That is why you and your coven have suffered so."

She bowed her head. "It is as you say, then, my lord."

"I need something from you, first."

Kiel swallowed hard. She feared his attentions. She didn't think she could take him one more time without bleeding to death. The last time, she had gone to the hospital—he'd torn her badly. It had been weeks before she could sit or walk again.

"I will try and fulfill it, my lord." Her voice came shakily, while eying his snake tales writhing around him. He liked to use them to penetrate a woman too, and were no less a threat by any means. One of the members of her coven, Grace Powers, had blacked out during one such session where he took three of them at once, it was the same session in which Darleen Philmore had gone mad.

"I will give you back the powers I originally gave to you, and a few more. I want you to go to where Sabrina Strong is now residing."

Kiel looked sharply up at him. Holding back her elation that he was not asking for sexual attentions, she said, "Where?"

"She is at Tremayne Towers even as we speak," he said. "I need you to be my contact through which my demons can move."

"I don't understand," she said.

"Tremayne Towers is heavily guarded by a magical shield that won't allow demons to move through. Even to enter the towers has become more difficult. A few of my demons have actually burned upon impact."

Kiel said nothing.

"What I need is for you to get inside. Since you are human, this will not be difficult. Go to the vampire side—the north entrance. There, you will remain."

"But, there are elves there. I've heard," she said.

"You will wear an elf dart to protect you from both their magic and their being able to detect you, a black witch."

"Where will I get such a thing?"

He thrust his hand toward the area between them. A piece of dark stone appeared. It was shaped like a long arrow head, made of flint. He thrust his hand forward again. Something lit up, a piece of parchment appeared. The edges burnt as the paper floated to the ground, and gradually burnt out, leaving the center of the paper un-marred.

"You will need these ingredients in order to summon any and all my demons. One is a special oil you must wear in order to protect yourself from attack yourself."

Kiel stepped forward and picked up the singed parchment and looked over the ingredients quickly. Her heart fluttered at the sight of some of the ingredients, like opium, and annamthol. She didn't dare say she would have trouble getting these things out loud, thinking it was dangerous. Opium, especially. Gathering her resolve, she pushed those thoughts out of her mind quickly.

"You have two nights in order to obtain these things and get inside the hotel where Sabrina is staying," the demon said.

"So I'm to get a room there and begin working on the spell?" she asked.

"Yes. Do not forget to rub yourself, head to foot, with the oil, some of the demons I send will be deadly, and do not discriminate. They will not harm you while you wear this ointment."

"You wish to kill her?" Kiel asked.

He laughed. "I wish to toy with her, and then I want her brought to me."

"How?"

He smiled crookedly and reached down toward his genitals. "That will be your job as well. We will talk no further, daughter. Come to me." His large penis grew hard and stiff in his hands. She balked.

Oh, shit.

"I know that I have hurt you in the past," his voice went low and sensual. "This time, let's do things a little differently," he said. One of his tails slid around her and pulled her close, another one drew between her legs. It took five seconds for the demon's tail to spear up her robe and rip it from her. His laughter made her heart beat harder, and a throbbing began in her clitoris as he stroked her there. The point of one tail slid into her and tantalized a groan from her. "My daughter, it has been a while…"

Chapter 5

Rogue

"Is this place for real?" Lindee gasped when we entered the elevator.

"Tremayne Towers is huge," I told Lindee as the elevator took us up to the main floor. "It has shops, restaurants and spas. You never have to leave, if you don't want to." I turned to smile at Dante, but he had vanished, now that the threat of vampires was gone.

"Cool. As long as we can do some shopping. I don't care." It was no secret Lindee had a penchant for shopping. I really do think she missed our modern world a lot more than she cared to admit.

"So, what does this really mean?" Lindee asked. "I mean whatever the hell they're going to do tonight with Vasyl?"

"Well, he's now second only to Tremayne in the whole United States where vampires are concerned." We stepped out of the elevator and I looked up into the five-floor atrium. A glass elevator took a person to the fifth floor, where the first four levels of the hotel were. To access the rest of the tower's ninety-seven floors you had to get on another set of elevators, or use the main ones that opened up here. I had never ridden the glass one before.

"So, he's like a vice president?"

Her words made my mouth quirk. "That's a good way of putting it." We strode along the busy mall. There were a lot of holiday shoppers around. It surprised me that many were human, but then again humans did work for the vampires. Plus, anyone could enter off the street. The only thing regular people didn't have access to were elevators that went to the "vampire" floors which required a pass card. Such as the one I had forgotten at home. *Sheesh.*

Once we entered the mall, I spotted Dante standing in the crowded hallway looking into a storefront window. He half turned to us. He looked alert, maybe slightly agitated when he turned to us. His eyes scanned the crowd around us. Ever vigilant.

"Vasyl accepted," I said to Dante, stepping up to him.

"I know." He turned away and we walked slowly along passing store fronts. Lindee paused more than once to ogle a pair of shoes or a dress.

"I don't understand why he accepted," I said, more than aggravated. I hated the thought of waiting for him to explain it "later".

"He will have to tell you himself why," Dante said. "But I do know that because Tremayne retrieved him from the storm and brought him back to your house, he is indebted to him. Vampires do not like to owe each other, and they usually pay the debt when the opportunity is presented to them. This is especially true of masters. Especially one that deals with life-preservation."

"I never thought of that." I looked down at the shoes in the display window we had stopped next to, not really seeing them, but half-noted that Lindee was drooling. I realized the call from Tremayne this afternoon was the only warning I'd had. But it wasn't much of one. How could I have known he was thinking of asking Vasyl to take on this job as a second-ranking magnate? My life was about to change, and it wasn't just that I would be moved into a higher tax bracket, but my husband was about to become one of the most powerful vampires in America. How did I fit into all of this? Me, the sibyl. Wasn't I actually their enemy? I'd killed a few vampires not more than a couple of days ago. I forced myself from lingering on that thought as it would only bring on a headache.

Next to me Lindee made a huge intake of air. "Oh! I love those shoes! I've got to go in there!" She shot away from my side like someone had launched her from a trampoline. I had the only credit cards—thank God I'd remembered to grab my purse when we were under attack—so I would pay for anything she wanted to buy—and me too, of course. I figured now that my husband had a high-end job we could definitely afford it.

Smiling, I watched her be swallowed up by the racks of clothing and followed, but I was not really into a shopping mode. My worries spun inside my head. I was given my own penthouse. What did Vasyl get? *The whole frigging towers? No. The whole eastern half of the United States. Power.*

Dante strolled along beside me in silence. It was something that I loved about Dante. We didn't have to always talk. Of course now we could merely read each other's minds.

I thought I was supposed to speak to Morkel when I got here, my thoughts came.

I think that has been postponed, Dante's voice was in my head. *The party.*

"Yes. The party," I said out loud and looked up at him.

"You need to find a dress for it," he reminded gently, gray eyes glinting as he looked me up and down.

"Oh. Yeah." This wasn't the type of store we would find a cocktail dress in. Distractedly I ran my hand across a shiny shirt on a clothes rack. The sequins against the midnight blue and the cowl neckline made it look dramatic and elegant. I looked at the size and then the price. Eighty bucks. My brows shot up.

Buy it, Dante said in my head.

Why not? I pulled it off the rack.

"I don't know why I like this shirt. It's soft, yet shiny."

"Women tend to get fascinated with shiny things," Dante said low in my ear. He knew it would tickle and I swatted him on the arm, throwing him a chastising frown. He chuckled, and threw up his hands to block me. He was in a good mood for a change, rather than the somber, sometimes too serious guy he had become. I had missed him as a human and the way he could joke and make me laugh. My heart lightened then.

"I just don't know why Bjorn didn't tell me there was a party when we spoke on the phone. He just told me to meet with him. I thought it was going to be about something else. Not…"

Dante's hand gently went to my shoulder stopping my rant. His nearness made my stomach flutter, remembering our wild exchange of power while having sex only a few nights ago.

What is wrong with me?

"Nothing," He said. "You're naturally anxious. This is a new step in your life."

I turned and looked at him. I noticed women around us stealing glances at him. He was a hot looking man with the long black hair and dark skin. Little did they know he was an Undead. I wondered if other vampires would know. Maybe they would, but these were human women shopping around us.

I don't know how I'm going to do this.

What?

Cary on as though I don't have desires for you.

Dante shrugged. *We will have time together again. I promise.* His pheromones drew me closer. The scent of smoky earth and pine making those moments of our coupling blossom in my head and sudden desire raced through me. I leaned against him because my knees had weakened. His arms enclosed around me and his scent enveloped me like the warm hug he gave. I wanted to leave this place and be with him again in his hogan, where we had made love on a different level than humans did. Some place away from here, away from vampires—away from my life.

But how? You'd have to sneak me off again.

Then I will, my Lady. He smiled, dark eyes holding my gaze. I wanted to go with him right then, the temptation was so strong, his touch at my lower back so intimate.

"Hey, cousin! Look what I picked out for the party tonight."

I looked up to see Lindee in a tight-fitting red cocktail dress with three-quarter sleeves, coming mid-thigh length. It was shimmery. She struck a pose and then did a little twirl. I was surprised to see her in a simple cocktail dress.

"Cool. Right?"

"You found that here?" I was shocked.

"Yeah. They have better stuff in the next room," she said. "You'd better get something for the party too. You can't go like that!" She swatted the air toward me.

I looked down at myself. "Wish I could just not go," I said low. Dante chuckled over my head and I felt his breath stir the hairs, making my skin tingle. I wasn't into shopping right now, but I couldn't go in my jeans. I was nearly ready to bolt, vanish from here and take Dante to my own apartment on the human side.

"I'm reading your mind," he said. "You disappear it might be considered an affront to the vampires, and insult to your husband."

I stepped back to look up at Dante. "I need to shop."

He backpedaled a few paces. "I will be nearby," Dante said. He bowed, then turned and walked between two racks of clothing and was gone.

I already missed him.

* * *

An hour later I gave the clerk my Visa, I didn't even want to know what the amount for the two dresses and accessories were. I'd found a dress for the night's activities. We both needed shoes and nylons and we picked out some make-up, since we didn't have any. We also needed some place to change, so naturally I called Jeanie.

Five minutes later Jeanie's voice pulled my gaze up to find her angling toward us. "Hey, girlfriend!"

Over the phone I had told her where we were, and she'd said she could be there in a few minutes. "Nothing like spending time at Nordstrom's."

I hadn't even noticed the store name.

"The party's just started," she said, picking up a couple of our bags. "We'll go up to my place."

"We'll be late," I said.

"Stylishly late," she said on a purr.

"Oh! Is that a Betsey Johnson bracelet?" Lindee said, looking at Jeanie's bauble around her wrist.

She shook it a little. "Yeah," Jeanie said. "You like?"

"Oh, I love her stuff."

"Me too. I couldn't afford it before, but now I'm always looking for something of hers to buy."

"Before?" Lindee gave a confused look.

"Before her change," I supplied.

She still looked clueless.

"Before she became a vampire," I said.

"Oh! I'm sorry! I'm such a ditz sometimes." Lindee giggled. "I forgot. I just thought you had perfect porcelain skin!" She laughed. Jeanie laughed and I joined in. I don't know why I laughed. This was the first time I would be with her without Heath to, well, make sure she didn't get thirsty for our blood. I should have been a little nervous being alone with her, but then I did have my mystic ring and her thrall was so inconsequential I didn't think she could really thrall either of us. She hadn't been a vampire for very long. In fact she wasn't allowed to see me at all that first month. Right now, she seemed like the old Jeanie, all her same low growling inflections, her expressions and even how she said things.

Jeanie helped us haul the bags to the closest elevators. We rode up to the fifteenth floor and walked down the hallway.

"By the way," Jeanie said over Lindee's excitement of going to a cocktail party—with mostly vampires. "Heath and I didn't change our loyalty."

I looked a question at her. "How's that?"

"I just wanted you to know, Heath and I are going to move. To L.A."

"Oh." My brows knitted, then I caught her meaning. "Right. I understand."

"Heath has always been with Tremayne for twenty years," she explained. "And, since I'm his shadow, I have to go with."

"Of course. I'll miss you. Lots." I had missed her as a human. I barely knew her as a vampire. I tried to tell myself maybe this was best. We couldn't have a real friendship like before. God, I wanted to hug her and cry, but I didn't dare.

"You will have to come for a visit," she purred and the brows danced.

"Def," I said.

One minute later, we stepped into her suite. Hers was different from mine, mainly because this was the vampire side of the towers. The living room was large, and there wasn't much of a kitchen. There was no stove. Only a counter, sink and shelves were lined with books and décor. I didn't see a large refrigerator when I swept the room with my eyes. And then I saw a mini black refrigerator, like college students used. Large enough to keep a supply of blood cold for when she had need. I wondered if she had a human blood donor or two. *None of my businesses. Sheesh!*

"I need to change too," Jeanie announced. "You guys can use the bathroom."

"To save time I'll start changing out here. You can use the bathroom first," Lindee said.

"Okay." I located my bags and found my things and chugged into the bathroom. I actually couldn't wait to see the dress on me with the high heels and the snake-skin knuckle-clasp clutch bag I'd found. It was expensive, but not as expensive as a Valentino—*probably a knock-off.* I stepped into my black pumps with the steel heels, remembering that Lindee said I could use the heels to kill vampires with. I explained that a wooden stake killed vampires (and my silver dagger poisoned them), not steel. You'd think, though that anything jabbed through the heart would kill anything, including a vampire.

My musings were interrupted when I saw Dante in the mirror beside me. I turned to him, glad I'd gotten the privacy of the bathroom. We embraced. Strong hands gliding over my curves, he drew me up against himself.

"I like this," he said. I could tell he did by the way it excited him. Our lips met in a passionate kiss that I was certain would get me out of my expensive black floor-length dress in a lot less time it took to get into.

A knock stopped our movements. "Hey, in there. You ready? We gotta go!" Jeanie's voice crashed in on my thoughts of having a quickie with Dante there on the tile of her bathroom.

"Okay," I practically choked on a half-snort.

Dante let me go. "I will be near," he said and vanished. I longed to go wherever he'd gone, right now. Not just to be with him, but to avoid tonight. Something about tonight bothered me. Something was going to happen and it would not be good.

I checked my hair and make-up quickly, grabbed my clutch and put my fingers through the loops and looked at the large rings on it that stuck out. *Gak.* If I had to slug someone, I'd do some damage for sure.

I turned and very carefully strode out of the bath—because the steel heels wanted to slip on the ceramic floor. I wondered what they'd do to carpet.

The two women were oddly quiet. Jeanie was behind Lindee, her face leaning over her bared neck, in the classic feeding position for vampires. My heart kicked with fear, and I brought up my right hand to use my mystic ring to push Jeanie aside. I was about to move her when Jeanie backed away and Lindee turned to a mirror.

"Oh, this is great! Thanks for letting me borrow," Lindee gushed, hand to the necklace Jeanie had just fastened onto her neck.

My body sagged as I realized I'd nearly made a mistake. *Fudge!*

"Oh, look at you!" Lindee said, her mouth had gone slack looking at me standing there like a dork, trying to rearrange my horrified look. My mouth hitched into a smile.

"You definitely did that dress a favor by buying it and giving it a good home," Jeanie said. That was how she looked at buying clothes and accessories. It was giving these "things" a good home, instead of being left in a store to be pawed over by others.

Jeanie grabbed her own knuckle-clasp clutch. It looked more dangerous than mine, with fangs sticking out of the top.

"Oh my God, is that a Valentine clutch?" Lindee was obviously the leading fashion expert.

"Oh, yeah." Jeanie held it up. "For my birthday from Heath. He's sweet on me."

"I should say so! That's real snake skin!" Lindee said, running her fingers over it.

"Where is Heath, by the way?" I wondered.

"Waiting for us in the penthouse. Ready?"

"I'm ready," I said. *Not.*

"Great. Let's go to the par*tay*," Jeanie said and twitched to the door.

We stepped out into the hall and something felt wrong right away. Anger leaped into me as my empathic sensitivities hummed, jarring me to alertness. I shut out whatever Lindee and Jeanie were talking about to locate where it was coming from. I scanned the hallway. I wasn't sure where Heath's suite was—or where *he* was for that matter.

Everything happened as sudden as a lightning strike. A blond man emerged from two doors down and pointed a gun at us. "Get down!" I screamed at Lindee and Jeanie and pulled them with me. We went down like three geese on an icy pond. The air stirred not two feet away, and Dante's form materialized in front of us. The loud *pop pop pop* of the gun's discharge made Lindee scream—Dante barely jerked as he took the slugs from the gun as it was fired. Getting myself into a squat, I reached around Dante's legs and thrust power toward the shooter just in time as the next series of shots came. But instead of slugs, purple butterflies appeared out of the barrel. The shooter gasped with surprise, his eyes following the harmless butterflies, disbelief on his face. I wasn't done. I fluttered my fingers again, using my mind to make something happen. The black gun he held became a large black bird. At that same exact moment Dante disappeared. The man looked down at the bird flapping its wings. Realizing he held it by the scaly black feet, he let it go and the bird flew down the hallway making its loud calls. Finding no way out, he flew back toward us.

"What the fuck?" Jeanie jumped to her feet and helped me up on my unsteady four inch stilettos.

Dante appeared right in front of the man who I now thought I recognized, but was questioning it. The man turned and ran. Through Dante's running legs I saw the man make a dash toward the stairway. I thought about his legs being tied up and shot power at him. He went down with a loud thump as Dante tackled him.

"Hey, help!" someone from behind said.

Jeanie and I turned and found Lindee on her butt, legs straight out. We both grabbed her by the hands and hauled her up on her feet. She wore red ankle booties. They were sweet looking with the dress.

"Who the hell was that? Why was he shooting at us?" Lindee asked. "God, do things never change in this town?"

"It was Leif," Jeanie said and I met her dark glance.

"That was Lief?" I said and then looked down the hallway. "He looked different."

"Haircut," she said.

The raven flew toward me. It was my fault for changing the gun into a bird. I wasn't really sure how I had done it. I put my hand up and the bird came to me, landing on my gloved hand. "Poor thing." I wondered if I should change it back into a gun. *Nah. Enough guns on the street as it is.*

"Wow. Did you do that?" Jeanie asked, both women gazing at the large black bird perched on my hand.

"Example of those powers you were mentioning, earlier?" Lindee asked.

"Yeah. I didn't want the gun to hurt us and so…" I shrugged looking up at the bird.

"You can transform things?" Lindee said. "So you're, like magical?"

I shrugged again. "I can only do it if I feel threatened." At least so far that's how it worked.

"I heard you changed Ilona into stone," Jeanie said, her blue eyes glittering at me.

"Yes. After which she was—uh—dismembered," I said.

Jeanie snorted, then laughed, her mouth opening wide with a guffaw.

"Who's Ilona?" Lindee asked.

"The scariest bitch—scarier than my mother, and that's saying something," Jeanie said.

Dante emerged from the stairs hauling our would-be assassin with one hand on his neck and seemed to be able to control him. Leif actually looked slightly dazed.

"Leif?" Jeanie said, surprise in her voice. "What the hell! You trying to kill someone?"

"Yeah. Her," Leif said, using his chin to point at me, since his hands were tied behind his back.

We all stepped a little closer, but not too close. His caramel-colored hair used to be past his shoulders. It was much shorter, now. He glared at me.

"Why?" I asked.

"You killed Darla, you bitch!" He spat, his face twisted in hate. Darla had been his female companion who I now was sure had died from the silver poisoning of my dagger. I'd caught them draining a bunch of humans in a bar/pool hall, along with a few of their underlings who attacked humans there. Actually, Darla had bitten a man's tongue off just as Dante, myself and Quist, jumped in to stop things before they went too far. Last I'd heard, the man's tongue had been saved and sewn back, but what a terrible thing to happen to anyone.

"Darla died of silver poisoning two days ago," Jeanie supplied in my ear. I nodded. I wasn't very upset that my Dagger of Delphi had claimed her.

"I'm sorry for your loss. But *I* didn't kill her. The Dagger of Delphi did it. And furthermore she bit a man's tongue off!" I shot back. "You two are really disgusting."

"If it pleases you, my Lady, I will take him up to our new magnate ahead of you?" Dante said.

"That would please me a *lot*," I said, and made a motion for him to go right ahead, thinking he was going to use the elevator. *Duh.* Dante disappeared with Leif in his grip.

I was a little surprised that Vasyl had not appeared at some point during that scuffle when my life had been in danger. *Must be busy.*

Chapter 6

Party

We stepped out of the elevator into a short hall. Two doors on opposite sides opened to the penthouses. One had been Tremayne's dead life-time mate Letitia's. The one across the hall was Tremayne's.

Two men—sentinels—standing in the hallway turned to regard us, their conversation abruptly interrupted by our arrival. Music blasted from the open doors of both penthouses.

"Nicole, Carpe noctem," the blond guy said to Jeanie, a broad smile that had some fang to it. Nicole was Jeanie's new vampire name, and I had to remind myself of that constantly. She'd taken the new name, Nicole, when she'd ascended. I simply could not call her Nicole. Besides, that was my middle name, so it was weird in more ways than one.

The dark-skinned guy—he looked Jamaican with the beaded hair—merely nodded to Jeanie.

"How's it going?" Jeanie said, her hips swaying suggestively as she walked up to both men and patted their cheeks. *Ok-aay.*

"Fine." After gleaming at her, the blond's glittering blue eyes took me and Lindee in. "We heard there was a little trouble down below?"

"A little," I said before Jeanie could say anything. "But *my* sentinel took care of him." That's what Dante was, basically. Aside from other things.

"We heard that Heath's brother attacked you?" the dark one asked, sounding incredulous.

The raven on my shoulder made a noise and repositioned himself. I had to get rid of him soon, he wanted outside with the sky above him where he belonged and I planned on letting him go soon.

"You've added an extra guest I see?" he said, smiling, looking at the bird. They both chuckled.

"He'll be leaving as soon as I can get to a balcony," I said.

"They're waiting for you," he said and gestured to what I knew to be Tremayne's penthouse. He allowed us to enter giving us a little bow as we passed.

We entered a crowded room, the noise level bombarded my senses. Vampires with either the black bottled version of their drink, or a wine glass with the same, stood in knots chatting, laughing, joking. Jeanie came to a halt in front of Heath. They embraced and lightly kissed one another. It was almost chaste. Heath's eyes fell on me. I averted mine, not because of any sense of threat from him, but embarrassed for the trouble his brother was in—plus I had to show correct decorum.

"Look down," I hissed at Lindee, whose eyes were pinging off of each and every male vampire in the room. "Don't look at them!" I grabbed her arm and jerked to get her attention off of them.

"Why? They're all so damned good looking."

"And their fangs might find their way into your neck, arm, breast, a thigh."

"Really? Oooo. That sounds so—decadent."

I released a sigh. It was an up-hill battle with her.

Following the vampire who had let us in, we entered a much larger room—one I had never seen before when I'd been up here the one time. The vampires had crowded around a central area further in. I noticed a tasteful grouping of black leather sofas. One large cocktail ottoman was pushed out of the way against the wall, several vampires—possibly a few humans—were seated there conversing, but everyone else was standing around this one area. I couldn't see through the broad shoulders and heads in front of me, which might have been nine or ten bodies deep. I knew, though, that Vasyl and Tremayne were there. I felt them, plus I could hear Tremayne's singularly rich baritone saying something. I knew he was seated somewhere in the middle of this crowd.

The man who had led me and Lindee into this room snaked his way through the crowd—basically parting them—and bent down into a low bow. The crowd noise went low, then silence, save for the background music.

Tremayne stood, his head rising above everyone. His aquamarine eyes sought and captured mine.

"The sibyl has arrived," he announced.

Everyone turned and looked at me. They parted to allow us to pass through to the front of the crowd. Vasyl stood waiting for me. The raven on my arm made a croaking raven sound and flew off my shoulder as we embraced. I didn't look to see where it went. I would find it later.

"We heard Lief attacked you. Are you alright?" he asked, and bent to look at me. The violet rings of his eyes were barely showing. I could see he was pissed. It was a good thing Leif had not tried to murder me in front of Vasyl. He would have killed him without a thought.

"I'm fine," I said. I looked around. The two masters had been sitting on the leather couch at either end. Two women were arranged in the center of the couch where both he and Tremayne had been seated. Humans. In other words, donors. Their positions on the couch told me they were definitely with both men. *That explains how "busy" he was.*

"Everyone," Tremayne's voice hushed the crowd noises, which had started up again. "I wish to present Vasyl's wife, Sabrina and her—eh—lady in waiting."

The crowd clapped lightly.

"I'm your lady in waiting?" Lindee said in my ear. "Wow, I've been promoted."

"Keep your eyes lowered. Don't let any of them touch you." I spoke my warning quickly to her, because Vasyl swiftly, but gently ushered me to his side on the couch, pretty much crowding out both women who had to then get up. The redhead who had been seated next to Vasyl slid me the bitch look. Ignoring her, I sat down as gracefully as I could, but more or less flopped down when my ankle cricked slightly. *How do women move in these dresses and heals?* Vasyl sat beside me and I directed Lindee to sit beside me. No room for extras. I shot a look at the redhead whose feathers were ruffled. She stepped over to another vampire and began snogging with him immediately.

"What happened? Dante told us Lief attacked you," Tremayne asked me, as he sat head and shoulders above Lindee (her eyes were sliding to the far left in her sneaky way of ogling him).

"He had a gun," I said. There came a few gasps from the crowd—I didn't know I had an audience, really. I blinked at the few on-lookers. A few had their phones out taking snaps of me and Vasyl. I was suddenly quite the celebrity. I was certain these pictures would be on Twitter and other social media.

"He will be punished," Vasyl growled. Something was different about him, now that I looked at him properly. The suit he wore was definitely super expensive—*Armani*—and he had shoes on—*shoes!*—and no socks. They looked comfortable, slip-ons, but nice soft leather—*Italian-made*. He looked entirely different. And then I realized what was so different about him. He'd had his hair trimmed more severely than Lindee had cut it. Now it was much shorter—to his collar—but the front was kept long and styled back off his face. Somehow the look didn't fit him, but I told myself I would have to get used to it. I hadn't entirely gotten used to the shorter length of before anyway. But it definitely was an improvement.

A man in a waiter's tux swept in front of myself and Lindee offering us what looked like champagne. We both took a flute each. Lindee slugged hers down and put the empty glass back on the tray. She took a second one.

"Hey," I said to her. "Slow down. You're under age, actually."

"Party," she explained, giggled, throwing her head toward Tremayne, who laughed and held up his glass of blood toward hers. They clinked glasses and sipped on their respective drinks. This would be a long night, I could tell.

She didn't drink this one down as quickly, and I was relieved. I didn't blame her for needing a drink, really. For that matter, I needed to belt back mine like Lindee had, to steady my nerves and took a few healthy sips. Hell, I'd been shot at—again! I'd almost sounded complacent about it, like it was part of my life and I should just get used to it, like maybe a secret agent might.

"Bring the offender in," Tremayne said to someone in the crowd.

Panic rose in me. I did not want to see Leif. My heart rattled around in my chest trying to find a way out. The crowd parted again and a knot of four people stepped through. The first being Dante. He bowed to me with a fist to his heart and then stepped off to the side. Behind him was the demon, Darius Crimmins. I had not seen Crimmins since I had begun at Tremayne Towers. He looked the same, like a disgruntled detective in a badly wrinkled gray suit. He was a Ba'al demon and was able to appear very human. He was head investigator for V.I.U. (Vampire Investigation Unit). The thin woman with him was also a demon—I'm not sure how I knew this, but I did. She had a stern, heavy jaw, in fact her lower jaw stuck out almost like a piranha, and her lips were parted. The sharp whites of her lower teeth made me shudder. Her beady eyes peered out of odd lengths of dark hair. Her shoulders leaned, one slightly lower than the other. Apparently, her human disguise wasn't very good, but then, the demons tended to have trouble with a straight posture. Even Crimmins walked with a decided limp.

The information coming to me from these two caught me by surprise. Sure, I knew that Crimmins was a demon. But I'd never seen the woman before, and yet I knew she was also a demon. How? My skin itched a little, but that could have been the dry air. I itched my nose too. Then, I saw it when they moved a little closer. It was like a shadow, only it surrounded both like a dark halo around their bodies, and I was more aware of it when not looking directly at them.

Their auras? I asked telepathically.

It is, my Lady. You see it? Dante asked in my head.

I do. Well, hell. When did that happen?

After we imprinted, after I gave the power to you. Now you are able to see who is a demon by their auras.

That will come in handy. Thanks. Okay, that was kind of lame, but I always say thanks when someone gives me a gift, and this was definitely a gift.

Behind the two demons Leif was escorted in by two vampires, his hands were in cuffs and chains. And they were not regular cuffs made of steel, since a vampire could break free of them easily. They were either made of silver or had silver nitrate inside, so that if he broke them, the silver nitrate would burn him terribly.

Neither Crimmins nor the female demon bowed or showed any sort of respect to either of the magnates seated on the sofas. Or to me, for that matter, but I didn't expect that anyway since I was very much their enemy. The female demon gave me side glances as though she wasn't real sure I wouldn't sick my dagger on her. Little did she know I didn't have it on me. If I did it would have a hard time figuring out who to go after first.

"Crimmins," Tremayne stood, eyeing the demon. "What does the V.I.U. suggest on this situation?"

Crimmins slid me a quick look. His partner gave me the stinky eye and I somehow felt insulted. I now wished I had brought Dagger of Delphi just for that slight.

"Forgive me for the delay, Magnate Tremayne, but I had to get in touch with H.Q. on this matter," Crimmins said, and made a glance around the room. "If Leif had attacked a human, then, yes. We would have to take him in and give him a trial. However, since the person he attacked was not a mere human, but the sibyl, then—" He made a nod to the female demon. "He goes free."

The female demon moved swiftly, and unlocked Leif's cuffs. I noticed she wore thick gloves to shield her from the silver. She smiled at Leif and placed the shackles into a black bag she wore like a satchel.

I gasped in disbelief.

Vasyl shot to his feet. "She is my WIFE!" He then shouted in French, and added a few English swear words to the mix. Head and hands moving with such violence, and his forward momentum toward Crimmins made Tremayne move in a preternatural quick way. He leaped in front of Vasyl to restrain him.

"Calm down, Vasyl. Calm the fuck down!" Tremayne said, his own voice calm but strong.

Lindee cowered beside me. I put my arm around her. "It's okay," I said. But really I had not seen Vasyl so violent since that day he attacked the South American master who'd tried to muscle in on his turf and take me as his prize.

Finally Vasyl's body relaxed slightly, but he still growled and stared directly at Leif.

Tremayne gave Vasyl one warning glance and turned to Leif. "Leif Sufferden, since you have not shown any allegiance to me, nor to the other master present, I, Bjorn Tremayne, banish you for the rest of your existence from any of our properties, human donors, and any other fucking thing that I can't think of at the moment because I'm so fucking PISSED!" His large sausage finger pointed at Leif. His eyes were nearly blacked out by the pupils. Then added, "You touch her, or try to attack her again, I'll come after you myself. Got it?"

Leif's expression was utterly cocky and not what I expected at all.

"Escort him out!" Tremayne's eyes caught the duo vampire males who remained standing beside him. The command put them in motion, and they took Leif by the arms to turn him out of the room. "And I mean out on the street! Take his cards that allow him entry into the towers and cut them in half!" Tremayne shouted.

"I wish to add," Vasyl said, showing lots of fang, eyes just as black as Tremayne's were, "that should I ever see you—anywhere—I will kill you."

The two male vampires escorted Leif out of the room, and not a moment too soon.

"Hey," Lindee's voice in my ear made me turn to her. "He wasn't just shooting at you. He was shooting at me and also at Jeanie. Doesn't that count for something?"

"Now you say that?" I said. I looked up only to find Crimmins and the other demon threading their way out of the room. Too late to say something now.

Vasyl flopped onto the couch next to me and the air within the leather couch expanded like a balloon until it hissed out.

"Hey," I said, leaning forward. "I think they forgot who else was there with me." I nodded toward Lindee and continued. "My cousin is human. And not only that, Jeanie was there. She's a vampire!"

Tremayne's hard look spoke volumes. His gaze went out into the crowd. I followed his gaze, feeling as though someone was looking at me. I met Jeanie's gaze and then Heath's. Guilt made me turn away. Leif could have been killed for attempting to kill me, had things gone differently. On one hand, I understood the emotions that brought him to make an attempt on my life. It wasn't very brilliant of him to try and kill me for Darla's demise, but I could see his reasons. That was me being pathetically analyzing. The emotional me said that if he tried this again he was dead meat, whether I had the dagger on me or not. I'd turned Ilona to stone—that alone should keep him from trying to mess with me, one would think. But I wouldn't hold back next time.

Another gaze that lingered on me caught me by surprise. Stefan Capella. He stood next to Tremayne, very close to him, in fact. I hadn't noticed him until now, because he stood so quiet, almost like part of the furnishings. I could tell by his relaxed pose that he was not a sentinel, or one of Tremayne's minions. Sentinels looked edgy, eager to please and ready to spring into action. Stefan was far too comfortable to be an underling, and it had me wondering. In fact it gave me anxiety *what* he was to Tremayne.

Chapter 7

Silver Eyes

The music came back on—I hadn't even noticed when it had been shut off—and the crowd broke from in front of us, drifting back into their clicks, and conversations began anew.

"Where's the bathroom?" Lindee asked low, leaning close to me.

I knew where it was, supplied by my Knowing.

"C'mon," I said placing my tall heels beneath me and feeling the restrictions of the tight dress, which slinked around my legs as I rose. I clamored best I could to my feet. Vasyl rose and so did Tremayne who helped both, Lindee and myself, to our feet. Vampires moved with such grace it made me envious. I turned to Vasyl's gaze. "We're going to the lady's room," I informed and grabbed Lindee's hand and moved her away from the main arena. I felt dozens of eyes following us. Or rather, *tracked* us. Vampires couldn't help themselves, I suppose. Two human women walking among them probably whetted their appetites. I worried more for Lindee than myself. She had not felt threatened by these vampires. Yet.

Tremayne's penthouse was huge as we wound our way through knots of people, through a couple of the rooms, and hallways until finally we came through a threshold which I knew would lead to a large bathroom. My nerves hummed when we came to the partially opened door of a lavish bathroom complete with gold fixtures, black and white tile, which was marble. Lindee peeked in beside me.

"Wow. This place is so cool!" she said.

"Okay, you go first. I'll stand guard," I said, scanning the hallway.

She looked at me. "I'm not ten. You don't have to hold my hand."

"Yes I do. You have no idea how quickly a vampire can thrall you."

She made a sputtering noise. "I'm not thrallable."

"Huh?"

"Vampires can't thrall me," she said.

"Right," I said. There was no way she was immune.

I sat in thought. She had been on a planet where vampires ruled, and lived in the palace of the most notorious vampire of all, along with various other vampires who lived there. As far as I knew she had not been bitten by any of the vampires there. Of course I'd had Jett promise me she would not be. But if that was true I might not have to baby sit her.

"Well, just keep the crucifix showing," I told her.

"Right." She ducked into the bathroom. I stood in the short hall to wait for her. No one was paying any attention, so I sat in a red leather wingback chair and relaxed back and closed my eyes. The tension of the past hour had robbed me of energy. I was wishing I was miles away from here, in my own house—alone. I wished that I hadn't come at all. I knew Leif was not through with me. To believe he'd actually obey Tremayne and leave the area would give me a false sense of security. I already planned that Lindee and I would stay on the human side of the towers tonight. We'd go to my suite and we'd share that king sized bed of mine. I still had clothes I'd brought with me over a month ago stashed there. One of us would get a T-shirt for a nighty. Since she was my guest I'd give her the choice. As my brain working out these little details, I remembered I had to check and see if my door and window were fixed first.

My thoughts were interrupted when my Were hearing caught the sound of feet softly padding toward me. I opened my eyes to find an older gentleman stepping toward me.

"You're Sabrina, aren't you?"

His salt and pepper beard and hair with the distinguishing gray at the temples put him on the other side of fifty. My Knowing supplied a few things about him quickly. Like he had been living with the vampires for decades. One in particular, which wasn't exactly surprising, but something I hadn't considered, or had come across until now.

"Hi. Yes, I am," I said with a smile, trying to figure out how to proceed. "We haven't met."

"Oh, my dear, I have wanted to meet you for quite some time, now!" He bent to me and held out his hand. I didn't have my right hand glove on, so slipped it back on and reached up to take his hand in a shake. Because he was human, I didn't want to go into a synaptic over-load and black out right here.

He shook my hand and I noticed his eyes watered slightly. Pulling my hand from him, I stood, feeling his emotions practically bursting from him. I had to put up some defenses against his emotions, since I'm an empath.

"And you are?" I said, brows raised, waiting. My Knowing was working on his name just as he told me. *Mmmm... Feee...*

"Oh!" He pressed a hand to his chest, smiling wide. "I'm sorry. My name is Malcolm McFeely. You don't know me, but I certainly know who you are, my dear."

"Oh?" That shouldn't have surprised me, since I had been announced to the room at large.

"You're the one who solved the mystery of who killed our precious Letitia."

"Oh-ah, yes."

"I was one of her donors," he said, and now I knew why he was so choked up, and why all the images of Letitia, Tremayne's dead wife, were coming at me like a freight train. "Well, I'm retired, now. But her death was such a tragedy. It touched so many of us." His eyes teared up again. Scissoring two fingers, he made a swipe across his longish bangs, which he trained to feather across his brow.

"I'm sorry," I said, feeling his emotions again. He was thinking about Letitia in a way someone did if they had loved her dearly. "I'm sorry for your loss," I added.

"Thank you, my dear!" He grabbed my hand and kissed the back of it. Good thing I still had the glove on.

Lindee popped out of the bathroom and made a startled sound. "I didn't know anyone was out here," she said pressing a hand to her chest and chuckled.

"Oh, hello!" Malcolm said brightly.

"My cousin, Lindee." I motioned. "This is Malcolm McFeely."

"Oh hi," Lindee said, wavering slightly, and I caught her by the arm.

"How do you do." Malcolm clasped her hand and made little bows to both of us. "Well, if you'll excuse me." He stepped to the bathroom, went in and shut the door.

I sighed. I had to go too. Oh well.

"I'm famished," Lindee said. "You think they have something for us to eat?"

"I'll check. I think they have the party over-flow in Letitia's penthouse," I said, as Knowing poured into me. There were more humans on that side, and the thought to maybe steer clear of Malcolm wasn't such a bad idea if he was going to paw me again. Or cry some more. His emotions might overwhelm me if I spoke to him much longer than the few minutes I had. Besides, I had to pee. There were other bathrooms up here—somewhere.

"Let's go and see if we can't scrounge up some grub," I said.

"Okay, cowgirl," Lindee said through a chuckle.

"You okay?" I asked her, when she stepped and then leaned into me.

"Yeah, yeah. Great, in fact. I guess after not having alcohol, I'm not used to it."

I threaded my arm through hers to steady her. "C'mon," I said, my stomach growling.

We slithered through the knot of vampires near the entry, crossed the hall and went into Letitia's penthouse. The two vampires on guard allowed us entry once again with bows. Stepping in, I noticed that the colors, and even the furnishings had been changed from when Letitia had lived here. I presumed Tremayne had needed to close this part of his life and had it redecorated.

As I had figured, the humans outnumbered the vampires eight to one here. This was much better. My nerves settled down, whereas before my skin crawled with the vampires eyeing us in Tremayne's penthouse.

"Oh! Food!" Lindee spotted the food table a second before I did. We crossed the room, edged around more knots of people. We found plates and worked to load them down with various finger foods. Lindee dove on something that looked like buffalo wings, and I cautioned her to taste before she took a bite.

"Oh! Hot!" She put the piece down on her plate and fanned her mouth.

"Here." I put my plate down and grabbed a crystal glass of what looked like punch. I handed it to her. She drank half of it down. Her eyes darting over the crowd.

"Damn," she said, eyes roving the room. "There's some good looking hunks here.

"Donors, I'm sure." I bit into an egg roll.

"Oh! Is that Wilburn Moon Boetteger and Freda Hall?"

"Where?"

"Over there." Holding her drink, she pointed with her pinky.

I looked at where she was pointing. One man was wearing a black rumpled-looking leather coat and a long blue scarf stylishly draped around his neck, and sunglasses. His dark hair was messy, and he had a couple days growth of beard. He was cute in a hunky human way, but the bad-boy look was his style.

"It does look like the actor," I said. "You never know who might show up at one of these parties."

"Crap! That's Helen Depu and James Gormley. God, I love their latest joint CD, *Loving You Forever.*"

"I wouldn't know," I said. I'd never heard of them or their songs.

"They won a Grammy! I've got to go and meet them."

I grabbed her arm to hold her back.

"Possibly that might be something I can help you out with?" the male voice was accompanied by strong pheromones, and the scent of licorice and leather bathed us. I knew who it was without turning to see Stefan Capella. Wearing a black suit over a black silk shirt and a purple-and white striped tie (he'd changed his tie, go figure). Dashing at six foot even, his dark eyes glittered like sapphires. He stared at me. I turned to Lindee in order to avoid his eyes.

"My cousin, Lindee wants to meet them," I said, moving my hand to indicate her.

Stefan made a little bow. "Then come." He put his arm out to her.

Lindee giggled and put her plate and drink down. Not trusting the vampire, I trailed along, feeling Stefan's pheromones hit me like a cement truck. *I wonder how old a vampire he is.*

Five hundred and seventy-two years and three months... give or take, Dante's voice came in my head. I looked around for him. Nope. He was either invisible, or hiding.

"Hello," Stefan said to the group of singers and actors, who turned a casual eye to him, at first, but then their interests perked. I was pretty sure it was the vampire pheromones. "I would like you all to meet some friends of mine." He turned to us, but I was a bit preoccupied.

Are you here in the flesh? I asked Dante through our telepathic communication.

Would my presence make you feel more comfortable?

As long as I know you're here somewhere and can flash in when I need you.

I am always close by, my Lady.

Over Freda Hall's shoulder, perched in a large potted tree, I spotted the raven preening its wings. *I forgot about the bird. It should be let out.*

No need to worry about him, Dante said. I wasn't sure why he'd said that. I was concerned about the bird. I'd brought it into the world.

After Stefan introduced us, I stood there for a few minutes smiling like I was sucking up gold dust from them. Once no one was watching, I slipped away from the group. Besides, those people would forget me in five minutes, just like they would Lindee, who would probably stand there for the entire night giggling at everything said. But then she could talk to anyone. I just wasn't that bold. I was half way across the room when I heard Lindee's trademark laugh—*ha HAH-hahaha!*

I made a quick dash into the bathroom, did my thing, washed up and came back out. Yep. No one had noticed I'd been gone three minutes.

Taking up a bit of food from my plate, I stepped up to the tree and held out the bit of egg roll to the bird. The raven blinked at me, cocked its head a few times and then spotted the bit of food. It opened its wings and sailed down to my proffered hand. It didn't seem interested in the food.

I heard a few gasps as I walked with the raven on my hand across the room. I paid them no mind. I neared the glass doors to the balcony. My hands were full. I looked around for a place to put down my plate, and the door slid open for me without my touching it.

I smiled. *Thank you, Dante.*

My pleasure, my Lady, he said.

I stepped through the doorway, into the cold night, and held my hand with the bird up.

"Go on. Fly away," I said, moving my hand up to give him the idea. The bird didn't budge.

"What seems to be the problem?"

I turned to find Stefan giving me a curious look. He was leaning against the frame of the glass door in a casual pose with arms crossed and one ankle cocked over the other. His blue-black hair lifted and swirled around his head, a few strands flitting into his eyes, giving him an even more enticing look.

"Uh, yeah, this bird? I thought he would be more comfortable out here."

Stefan crossed to the balcony railing in an easy gate. Grasping the steel railing, he bent over to look down. The sky scrapers competing with Tremayne Towers stood below and around us. "Maybe he's afraid of heights."

"He's a bird. He loves to fly," I said.

He straighten and looked across to me. "Maybe he'd rather stay with you."

At that moment, the raven flew off my hand and headed inside. He landed in the same tree where I'd found him.

"Jeeze," I gasped. "Apparently, he does like it inside better."

We both chuckled.

"Maybe he was cold," Stefan said, shifting out of his slouch and stood his full height. His shoulders were wide, and his physique reminded me hauntingly of Nicolas. But only his stature, and nothing else, thankfully.

"I know I am," I said, winding my arms about myself trying to rub warmth over my bare arms.

"Then by all means let's get you back inside where it's warm." Stefan herded me back inside and closed off the cold, winter air. I pulled up near the fireplace, turning myself around so that Stefan was not behind me—one of those self-preservation moves I'd long ago learned to do around vampires.

A man in a waiter's uniform strolled up to Stefan, as though anticipating some need. Stefan spoke low and quickly to him, I didn't hear it all, because I moved away, angling for the food table, and consequently away from Stefan. The waiter nodded, his eyes slid to me, and I knew he'd asked the man to get me something. It was more than a few words Stefan said to him, because the man nodded a few times, then bowed.

Finding a few more finger-foods, I picked up my crystal plate and a punch cup, and migrated to a stylishly modern couch. Like a dog that wanted to follow me around, Stefan folded himself beside me and smiled.

"I asked the waiter to bring you something hot to drink. Coffee?"

"With sugar and cream?" I said, placing my punch cup down on a beautiful glass table. My hand was freezing.

"I'm sure they won't forget a thing. Bjorn has excellent wait staff from Earthly Pleasures working here tonight."

"Sounds good." I hadn't been to Earthly Pleasures, the restaurant that served both humans and vampires, since Toby Hunt tried to kill us all there one night. I had no fond memories of that place. Not a lot of places in Tremayne Towers held good memories for me. I was thinking tonight was continuing that trend.

Stefan leaned forward, hands clasped between his knees. A gold watch slid down his wrist. *Expensive. Rolex?* He was keeping himself in check, and at least arms-length away. But then he knew my powers of persuasion out gunned his, as he'd had a demonstration not long ago.

"I've heard that you had some trouble at your house. Earlier?" Stefan said.

"Oh yeah. Demons," I said. God, that was old news to me.

"They attacked you?"

"They attacked the house. Rick has a really strong ward up, so they couldn't get to us. Then, since he was with us, he put one up around my Jeep as I drove us here."

"I'm not familiar with this Rick. Is he a wizard of some sort?"

"Oh, no. He's a leprechaun."

Stefan blinked, and made a little backward jerk with his head out of surprise. "You have a leprechaun who's friends with you that he would do this for you?"

"Yeah. Rick's my friend." I didn't know it was such an odd thing to be friends with a leprechaun, but I supposed it was.

Stefan chuckled and shook his head slightly. "That's one friend to keep on your good side."

"Don't I know it," I said, rolling my eyes.

"That businesses with Leif," he changed the subject quickly, "I've got men watching him."

"You do? I'm sure Tremayne's got his people on it too."

"I *am* Tremayne's people," he said with a wry smirk.

"Oh. I mean, of course," I blundered as usual. It was hard for me to talk intelligently to handsome men. Especially when they were vampires who smelled as incredible as he did. He chuckled, and that loosened things up a bit. I smiled. "Sorry. I should have known."

"That's alright. Vasyl is now in charge of the towers. He's my boss now. I'll be staying on here."

"Oh?" I said. "So, you're in charge of security here?"

"Yes. Whatever Vasyl needs me to do. I've got it covered with all my men," he said. "Bjorn has to go to L.A. and take care of the western half of things. That's why I'm here. I'm second in charge under Vasyl."

"I see." A change of guard. I suppose I shouldn't have been surprised. Thinking about it now, I remembered Jeanie said she and Heath were going to go with Tremayne to L.A. Vasyl would need his own people here, and possibly a few others. There would be new people to take up the spots that had been vacated. I was guessing Stefan was somewhat like Nicolas was to Tremayne. A second in command. I knew then he was quite powerful and probably could have seen a number of centuries.

The waiter Stefan spoke to earlier, swung up with a large silver tray, and silver coffee urn and beautiful china cups and saucers and little fancy cookies and all the things one could want to go along with, and set it down before me. Then he poured my coffee for me. The rich aroma hit me.

"Cream?" he asked, lifting up the silver cream server.

"Uh, yeah. Lots," I said, watching as he poured a little. He stopped. "More." He poured a little more. "That's great," I said.

He took up the silver tongs and grabbed a sugar cube. "Sugar, or no calorie?" He paused.

I almost chuckled. I was getting such royal treatment. "I'll take the packet. One's fine."

He ripped the packet open and sprinkled it into the cup and stirred. I didn't have to lift a finger. I felt like the Queen of England.

"Is there anything else you require, Madam?" the waiter asked.

"No. I'm great, now. Thanks."

He bowed and left. At the same time, Stephan stood. Relief drew over me as I watched him move away, his smart phone to his ear. He didn't go far, and stood behind the couch where I sat.

I carefully slid my gloved finger into the cup's finger loop, leaned and sipped. It was very good coffee. I sipped more. "Mmmm." I looked back at Stefan who was speaking into his cell phone. After a moment he leaned down next to me, over the couch and said, "I've just put more men down in the garage."

"Oh?" I said. "Why?"

"Leif took his car, and left." He slipped his phone into a pocket of his jacket.

"Good." I watched people in the room. Something about one person caught my eye, but every time I tried to look directly at him, he was swallowed up by a several people again.

"Anything else I can do for you?" Stefan asked.

"Actually, I was wondering," I said almost hesitantly. "My suite on the human side? Is the door and window still broken?"

"Broken?" he asked. Of course, he wouldn't know anything about what had happened in my suite. Or would he?

"Nicolas attacked me during that—um—you know war? A couple of nights ago."

"The siege?" he supplied.

"Yes. I was wondering if any of that is fixed?"

"Won't you be staying here, tonight?" Indicating this apartment. The smart phone still out, he looked at the screen and pressed something.

"I was thinking of Lindee, and I wanted to make sure she's safe and secure. I don't want her staying on the vampire side." It wasn't a complete lie. I was pretty sure that this party would not be over until sunrise. Vampires were such big party freaks, and I was going to want to sleep at some point. Here would not be quiet and secure enough.

"I'll check. What's the room number?" He lifted his phone to his ear again. I told him my room number. I ate a cookie and sipped my coffee while he spoke to someone on the human side of the hotel. I looked out into the room again finding my cousin. Lindee was having a conversation with Malcolm and another man across the room. Just as I'd thought, the actors and whoever else had been standing by the piano were now in another corner.

I know Malcolm is a human, but is the other one a human or a vampire?

Human. Dante was watching things too. *Stefan is assigned to you, my Lady. Tremayne assigned him right after they let Leif go. Stefan is very good. You can trust him as far as taking charge of security. But, after that...* his voice trailed off.

Good to know. And got the last part of it too.

Stefan's voice interrupted. "Yes. The door and window have been replaced. Your security will not be breached. I'll have a watch team on that as well," Stefan said, then pressed some number on his phone yet again.

Lindee drifted over and Malcolm trailed along in her wake. They were laughing as they sidled up.

"Oh-ho-ho, your cousin has just told me the most amusing story," Malcolm said, beaming.

Lindee strode to my side of the couch and settled her tush on the arm. She had a drink in her hand. "I had no idea how the two of you hop off to other worlds and have adventures. Really? Dracula?"

Lindee nodded, laughing her characteristic laugh.

"Want some coffee?" I offered.

"No," she said, lifting her drink up. "I'm having a blast! I've got autographs" —she waved some napkins with the inked autographs— "and I've met people I'd never dreamed I would." Her eyes darted at the silver setting and went wide. "Wow! That set must cost a fortune. That's got to be real silver!"

"That was Letitia's silver set," Malcolm said, gazing at it. "We often had tea or coffee—well, I did, anyway—on her balcony during the warmer months." He sighed. "How I miss her so." The man looked so sad, suddenly.

"She had a wonderful display of glass dogs, I understand?" I said.

"Oh, yes! The limited edition earthenware pieces by Woods and Sons Ltd! My God!" he gushed. "She left those to me!" He blinked and then produced a hanky.

"Oh, how wonderful," I said, happy for him.

"Unfortunately, they were stolen." He now began sobbing.

"Stolen?" I said. "Really?"

"Yes." He sniffled, blew his nose and went on. "When the will was read, and believe me, I had no idea she had left me anything, and so was *surprised* when I was named in her will." He swallowed, shook his head and went on, "Well, I won't go on and on about it. It isn't their monetary value so much as the fact that Letitia was so sweet to have left these to me. It's the mere thought that counts. Right?"

"Yes," I said. "Of course. That's really a shame."

"I've an investigator working on it, of course." He rolled his eyes. "These things always take time. I have no idea if the man even has a clue as to what happened to them."

"Who was last in here when those items were still here?"

"I had dates of the movers, you know?" He patted down his pockets and came out with a small leather notebook and thumbed through the pages. "Yes. It was three days after her death so, somehow someone still had access to her penthouse and came in and somehow absconded with them."

"That's terrible," I said, trying to sooth him. If I had some way of finding these things I'd be happy to get them returned, but my brain was too filled with too many things at the moment.

"Excuse me. I see someone I used to know." He walked away dabbing at his eyes.

"Wow." Lindee watched him. "Who was Letitia?"

"Letitia was Bjorn's life-time mate—uh, wife—who was murdered back in October," I said. "Malcolm there was her donor, retired, but sounds as though they had a real binding relationship."

"Yeah. He's bawling right now," she noted.

"He was imprinted with her," I said, sadly. "It must be hard. She didn't take blood from him anymore but I believe he really loved her." How I knew this was because Malcolm was an easy read.

My gaze went into the crowd again, and stopped. The hair style looked familiar. *Who is that?*

Where, my Lady? Dante asked.

Near the baby grand.

"Excuse me," Stefan's voice interrupted. "I need to go and check on something. In the meantime, I've called someone to stick by you." He looked up and then he straightened.

The man striding toward us was someone I didn't think I'd see alive again. But I realized that he lived only because the bullets that had entered his body were not silver. The werewolf with eerie silver eyes cast me a warm smile. We had some history, as brief as it was.

"Dan, I'd like you to meet—" Stefan began.

"I've met Ms. Strong," Dan said in a low rumbly Were voice, and nodded at me. "Hi, Sabrina."

"Hi, Dan," I said.

"Very well." Stefan looked down at me. I smiled showing I was fine with this arrangement. He gave a little bow. "I will leave you in capable hands." He swished away. My eyes lingered on the vampire's movements until he melted into the crowd.

The clearing of throat thing made me look back up at Dan.

"How's things?" Dan asked me.

"Okay, for the time being," I said, and realized that my cousin was staring at him.

"You can't be a vampire," Lindee said to him.

"I'm not," Dan said.

"Oh, sorry, Lindee. Dan, Lindee. Lindee, Dan." I moved my hand back and forth between them. Their hands came together and he held her gaze for a count of six full seconds.

Lindee went to take a drink and found her glass was empty. "Oops! I need a refill." She jumped up. "Now, don't go anywhere, I'll be right back." She was gone, and somehow I knew she would be a while.

"You disappeared last night. I was a little worried about you," I said to Dan as he stood next to me. He didn't have a drink in his hand. I knew he was on the job.

Dan chuckled. "I had no idea I caused you such concern."

I put my thumb and first finger close together. "Just a bit." He laughed again. "I'm just glad everything turned out alright. I mean, with Tremayne getting his realm back, and all."

"Yeah. Me too."

"And you," he added.

"Me? It's one thing after another with me. Stick around. You'll see."

"I plan to." He stood at military rest close by.

My Lady. Nathanial is here, Dante said in a warning tone.

I glanced across the room trying to locate him. It took ten seconds to spot him. The short man with brown hair and long bangs met my gaze. The sight of him kick-started my heart.

"Oh my God!" I said in a loud enough voice that Dan could hear me over the loud music.

"What is it?" He could tell by my expression, and posture that something was wrong.

"What is Nicolas' scion doing here? Was he invited?" I asked.

"Nicolas' scion?" The Were looked in the direction I was looking.

"Yes. He's got brown hair, sort of shaggy over his eyes. He's not very tall, and he's standing right next to the baby grand."

"I'll go check. This party is by invitation only." He was up and striding forward. I did not like the idea of another one of Nicolas' scions in the same room with me. I didn't think it likely that he had turned into a vampire, but on the other hand, why would he be here to celebrate Vasyl's rise to power, unless there was some ulterior motive? Was it me, or was I just paranoid?

Chapter 8

Bill

Bill drove up Sonata Road and knew right away something was amiss. His skin actually tingled all over. He looked in the mirror at his reflection. Yep, his hair was floaty, as though he had rubbed it with a balloon to create static. His grandmother's house was a brown brick two-story. Sabrina's house was larger, set across the gravel road from Emma's. No lights were on. He was certain Sabrina was gone. Especially since there was so much energy from demonic forces here it was as thick as cheese.

He pulled his Lexus to about twenty-five feet of Sabrina's house. He would not be able to approach the house closer than the beginning of her drive because of the ward, this he knew from experience. The unsettling feeling would become unnerving the closer he got. There was no traffic to worry about, and so, he put his car into park and sat for a few minutes longer. He became aware of some other being here, besides himself. Even though he could not see anything, he could feel a presence. Putting the car into drive, he crept closer, the wheels of his car crunching where the snow had been cleared. Within ten feet of Emma's drive, directly in front of her house, he detected an essence, or aura. *Demonic. Definitely.* It seemed stronger around Emma's house than over Sabrina's.

Emma had a very secure ward on her house—normally. But not tonight. He detected no barrier preventing him from going closer to her house and pulled into the drive. Something was clearly wrong. And the demonic signature was not a good sign. That and no signs that anyone had driven into her drive for a while, since the snow hadn't been removed, or shoveled from her walk. Who was taking care of Emma in his absence, for lack of a better word?

Lowering his window, the smell of brimstone caught him by surprise. Alarmed, he threw open his door and ran through the deep snow, up to Emma's front porch.

Sensitive hearing caught the sounds of struggles inside as he stopped at the bottom of the steps, which were drifted with snow two feet high.

"No! I banish you! Go! *Ohhhh!*" came Emma's voice from inside.

Her screams put Bill into motion. Heart hammering, he raced up the steps and burst through the door. Brimstone cloyed the air, it nearly choked him.

"Where is the girl?" a new and decidedly demonic voice said from further in the house. "I'll let you live, if you tell me!"

Bill rushed through Emma's small kitchen and entered the living room and stopped. A large and rather ugly demon stood holding Emma with his powers, high above its head.

"Let her go, demon!" Bill's voice boomed, taking the demon by surprise. It turned its red eyes on him, but still held Emma with his force. Had he been merely human, the demon would have known of his presence.

"Who are you to interfere?" it asked. It did not assume a human persona, but more demonic with a thick tail, a short snout, short, unimpressive wings, and it's skin was mottled red and black, changing colors ever so slightly, yet the mottling was always at least two colors.

"I'm her grandson," he said. "But more to the point, it's what I might do to you, if you don't release her and gently put her down. Now."

The demon gleamed toothily, like he wasn't about to do anything of the sort. Bill didn't trust that look, and rushed quickly beneath Emma, as the creature dropped her. He caught her thin body in his arms easily. Turning, he settled her down on the couch and faced the demon.

"You'll regret interfering with me," it said.

"You have it all wrong," Bill said. "I think it's the other way around."

The demon's brows dipped and it flung its hand toward Bill and a red flash burst from its fingers. Bill's hands went up absorbing the demon's powers. He felt power slide through him like thousands of volts of electricity, and yet he remained unmarred by it. He now knew how powerful this demon was, yet he could not bother the demon any more than a mosquito might a human. Gathering the power up, he thrust it back at the demon. Surprise registered on the demon's face, and it simply disappeared before the black power hit him. Unfortunately, it hit the TV, a puff of smoke spewed and then it exploded like a bomb.

Bill swiftly threw his arms up, instinctively his great leathery wings came out, using them like a shield in front of Emma. Glass and debris flew everywhere. But his wings, which had taken a number of hits, seemed uninjured.

Seconds later, when the explosion had left a black crater in the floor and a burnt area about three feet in diameter in her wall, Bill paused to test the air. The demon's stench and signature was gone. He turned and bent to Emma on the couch.

"Emma? Emma?" he called to her, touching her cheek. Then he slid his fingers under her jaw at her jugular. The heartbeats were weak. The demon's attack had sapped her strength. Emma Bench was a strong witch, but she was elderly. A demonic attack like that would be the death of any regular human. For her, he wasn't sure.

"Emma? Please." His hands brushed over her powdery white hair. Her skull felt so small in his large hands.

She opened her eyes, finally.

"Bill?" she said, her voice crackly. "Oh, Bill. You're alive?" She suddenly looked confused.

"I am here, Emma." He took in her paleness, and knowing she had certain medical issues, he didn't hesitate, but moved for the phone. He dialed 911.

"I thought you had died in a cave-in," Emma said from the couch, looking a little more than concerned now.

"I did," he said, patting her hand as the woman on the line asked what his emergency was. "I came back." He paused, holding his hand over the speaker part of her phone. "Don't worry. I'm human." *Maybe a little more than human.*

He knew he would have to leave her before the EMTs got here, to avoid a lot of awkward questions. As soon as he knew they were on their way, he said goodbye to Emma, telling her he would find out where she'd been taken and visit her. He left her door unlocked, trudged back to his car and drove away, hoping she would be taken care of.

* * *

The music tempo had changed dramatically. Instead of the loud, incessant drumming and guitar riffs charging the air around me, now the music was slow. Two musicians played the sax and piano, changing the mood of the party. Someone had brought the lights down low, and had found the mood lights—slow pulsing red, purple, green and yellow. People were dancing close. Men with men, women with men, and a few women with women. Vampires were in the mix as well.

Earlier, Nathanial Wade was escorted from the party by two Weres and a couple of vampires. He went willingly enough. From across the room I watched his head bob, the hair falling into his eyes while speaking with Dan. He indicated someone there at the party—a vampire who came to his side and spoke to the bouncers rather emphatically—as though he had brought him as his "date". Maybe Nathanial *had* been the guy's date, or blood donor, or whatever. But Nathanial was taken out of the penthouse, and my heart rate and blood pressure had returned to normal a few minutes afterwards.

Malcolm strolled across the floor, his steps faltered slightly. *Tipsy.* He sashayed up to me, took one step too far, and backed up. He bowed a little too long, his bangs falling into his eyes as he giggled. "Madam Strong, would you care to dance with me?" He hick upped and chuckled again.

"No. Thanks. I'm saving all my dances for my husband," I said to him. Honestly, if I had another man ask for a dance I was going to hide in a closet. I didn't want to dance—not with anyone and especially if they were drunk. Lindee was having enough fun for the both of us. I glanced at Dan. He stood with arms crossed watching the room, being all Mr. Guard. The couple I hadn't thought about all evening eased through the room. Heath holding Jeanie's hand, my senses were slightly charged. I thought about her leaving to a distant place. I had to finally let go of her. Maybe it was for the better. But I was feeling emotional about it, all the same.

The sound of a hoarse croaking, making a discord with the soft, sexy music, turned my attention back to that tree. The large black bird flew across the room and landed on the arm of the sofa where I sat. I stared at it. It stared at me with shiny black eyes. I offered it a cracker. It wasn't interested.

"Sabrina, there you are," Heath's voice pulled my gaze up.

"Oh. Hi," I said and smiled.

"You're sitting alone?" Jeanie said, and at once slid around the glass table and sat beside me.

"No," I said my gaze going to the bird. I stroked its chest and it actually let me. "I've got my friend right here."

Jeanie made a snort. "That isn't a bird," she said. "It has no heartbeat."

That threw me. *No heartbeat?* Well, of course not, since it wasn't a real bird.

Heath eased down beside Jeanie, both of them looking at me. I didn't know what to say, or how to say it. I wasn't sure if I should say anything at all. Fortunately Heath spoke first.

"Look, I can't apologize for my brother. What he did was wrong," Heath said, sounding angry. "He's been a bit of a dodger, a royal pain in the ass for a while. And it wasn't only just after Darla died, either. He was like this was before. But tonight, I have no idea what got into him. I would have killed him meself, if I'd been there!" He spoke loudly, with spirit, his hands working, his long hair moving with his head as it bobbed.

"Oh, hey, I know that from what he did to me before tonight," I said. Heath knew his brother had attacked me in my home about a month ago, and I'd turned into the were-creature and slashed his chest. "He's upset because he lost someone he loved. And probably feels a need to kill me because it was my dagger which did it."

"But, see?" Heath went on, hands out. "We didn't go with the hunting of humans along with everyone else, luv. We went with Tremayne to where he was hiding, after he was banished. But something happened with him." Gaze down, he shook his head slowly. "I don't know how, but he joined up with Nicolas and Ilona."

"But now they're gone," I said.

"Right," Heath said and shook his head again, the lengths of his butterscotch hair moving. "I don't know him anymore. I swear, I'd do anything to make it up to you."

"Nah," I said, batting the air. "You can't be your brother's keeper. I think that's the saying, anyway." I rumpled my brow with thought on screwing up the saying.

Jeanie made another scoffing sound. "I think he should come to his senses, think about what you're able to do, and that you killed not only Ilona, but Nicolas."

"Just so you know? I didn't kill Nicolas. But it's true I turned Ilona into stone. Maybe it amounts to the same thing. But Nicolas attacked me. I used my mystic ring to push him away. Vasyl was the one who actually tackled him and they both went through the window into that storm and the lightning struck and killed him. So, technically, I didn't kill Nicolas."

They both nodded solemnly.

"I guess we got Sabrina's version of the truth, luv," Heath said.

"What's up with that raven?" Jeanie asked, she was looking at it.

I looked over and saw that it was acting odd. No, it wasn't acting odd, it was *looking* odd. It had bloated up, the shape began to change and its size became larger as the seconds passed. I really didn't know what was going on, and leaned away from it thinking it was about to explode like one of those trick balloons. I thought that maybe my changing it had done something to it, or maybe at the clock chime of midnight was turning it back into a gun. But no gun appeared next to me. It became a man dressed all in black, with long black hair.

"Dante?" I said, surprised.

"Bloody hell, Dante," Heath cried getting to his feet, hand over his heart. "You must have scared a couple decades out of me!" He then laughed.

I stared at Dante. "How did you become the raven?"

He shrugged. "That raven, the one you changed from a gun? I let it loose earlier," he explained. "I decided it was a good way to stay physically with you, yet not be noticed, so I became the raven. It's why I didn't fly away on the balcony." I laughed at that.

"A shift-changing Undead." Heath shook his head. "That would come in right handy, I'd say."

"Yes," I agreed. Dante lifted my hand and brushed the back of it with his lips.

"Aw, you two are still doing it," Jeanie said. As with all vampires, each ascend with some special talent. Jeanie's was telepathy. She could read humans, vampires, and apparently Undeads.

My eyes slid to her baby blues. I knew I blushed.

"Don't spread it around," I said out of the side of my mouth.

"Not a chance," she purred, brows wiggling. I trusted her.

"I should check your house," Dante said. "See if those demons are still attempting to get inside." He stood and bowed to me. "If you would allow me to leave quickly and learn what is happening?"

"Oh, sure," I said. "I'll be fine."

"I won't be long." He bowed again and vanished.

We sat listening to the music.

"Ask me to dance," Jeanie said. I looked at her a little shocked. Then I relaxed. She'd said this to Heath.

"Of course," Heath said obediently, smile on his face as his eyes were only for her. They were in love. I was so happy to see this. I was happy that I'd brought them together.

She stood and they glided away from the couch into the small crowd of dancing couples. I admired how good they looked as a couple. I wondered why I hadn't seen Vasyl. *Probably still in his bull session with Tremayne.* But it had been a few hours since I'd seen him. I would have thought he would be worried about me. Thinking about him, I got up. The Were's eyes flashed at me. I pointed where I was going. He nodded. I pointed to Lindee. Dan nodded and gave me the OK sign.

I barely gave a thought over Dante's worry over whatever could be going on at my house. The ward was strong. Only Rick could bring it down, or me, if I was stupid enough, which I wasn't.

It took me a while to thread my way around the dancers, through knots of chatting people, in through the next penthouse and then beyond to the main room where the heap-big vampire moguls were.

The lights here were low and there was dancing going on here too, but I looked again and realized they weren't exactly dancing. I stepped past two people really clinging to one another and heard one of them moan. I looked again and saw that one definitely had his fangs into the other one.

Ok-a-a-y.

I strode forward more quickly, picking my way between a few more couples who were in vampiric embraces. Seriously, the moaning got to me. *Sheesh, get a room!*

When I got to the main room where I thought Vasyl was, I didn't see him or Tremayne.

Then, there was that niggle in the back of my brain and I followed its lead. Mostly I retreated from the sounds of the main room. But there was moaning down this way too. I knew there were bedrooms down the nearly dark hallway I strode through.

A wedge of light seeped out from one room. This is where my niggling feeling of where Vasyl was originated from. Self-doubts cloyed my inner being, but my need to find Vasyl led me here, and it was not a good thing to hear moaning—mostly from a woman—in the room.

The door stood ajar. I stopped. Did I *really* want to see what was going on in there?

No.

But I knew if I didn't look, I'd come back and be rooted to the spot until I had the guts to open up the door all the way. Vasyl was in there with someone. I could either distant view it, or look at it with my own two peepers. *Well, fudge!*

So, I pushed the door open just a bit. The lights were dim, only one small lamp was on. That was enough to see the naked man on top and the woman's legs wrapped around him. It was enough to make me gasp out loud and want to run.

I don't know if it was our blood binding thing, but he knew I was there. He looked over one bare shoulder. I still wasn't used to seeing short hair on him, but those huge eyes caught mine. Hand to my mouth, I could say nothing.

"Sabrina," he said, and tried to wriggle free of the woman wrapped around him.

I could stand it no longer. Tears in my eyes, I turned and ran back down the hall, dodging vampires with their blood hosts and back through the hallway. I fled into the next penthouse and grabbed Lindee who was in the arms of a large fellow—I didn't see who, I was so blind with anger.

"Sabrina, what—?"

"We're so out of here!" I said, and my brain must have fed me the picture of a place where I felt much more relaxed and in the company of friends—I needed friends who were not vampires—we blinked out of there and into a small bar. The music changed to Irish folk tunes.

Lindee screamed in my ear, she'd been so startled by our sudden exit. Another sound of someone's surprised grunt came at the same time.

"Well, I'll be fairy crap on a log! I didn't expect to see you here, Toots!" Rick's voice trilled.

Chapter 9

Tom's Hideaway

Rick sat on his favorite stool in the darkened bar. Tom moved instinctively for something under the bar, and pulled out a tankard.

"What the fuck?" The male voice standing next to me was absolutely not something I expected. I turned around to look over Lindee's shoulder and found Dan, the Silver-eyed Were, standing next to her. He looked surprised to be transported through the ley lines to another place entirely. Yeah, I hadn't planned on bringing him along, but he was here and there wasn't anything I could do about that, now. That's right. Lindee and Dan were dancing when I came up and grabbed her, and since he was clinging to her and she him, they both were caught up in my ley line. I had transported all three of us into the small bar otherwise known as Tom's Hideaway.

Tom drew a draft into a tankard and placed it in front of Dan. Full of foam, it had a rich, nutty smell to it. Then Tom turned around and chose a couple of wine glasses and set them down, poured some wine into them and set them in front of me and Lindee. We all strode forward and hopped on bar stools.

"Lindee, Dan, I'd like you to meet Tom, our bartender. Lindee you remember Rick, but I don't think Rick has met Dan," I introduced.

"How do." Tom nodded. He never said very much to anyone.

Rick said, "What the hell are you guys doing here? I thought Tremayne was having a big shin-dig at his penthouse."

"Yes, he was," I said, taking the stem of my glass and lifting it, giving Tom a little salute. There wasn't enough booze in this place to wipe out the memory of what I had just seen. But this was a good start.

"So, what are you doing here?"

"Uh," I said, using the heal of my gloved hand to soak up the salty wet trail down my cheeks. "Got sick of it."

"I wasn't sick of it," Lindee said. "I was having a great time."

I darted a look at the both of them. "From the looks of things I think I interrupted at just the right time." Dan kept his eyes cast down into his brew. Guilty as charged.

"Why did you bring us here?" Lindee asked low.

I ran my tongue around in the side of my mouth trying to find a polite way to word it. "I saw Vasyl in the arms of another woman doing the nasty."

Lindee made a dramatic intake of air, dark eyes popping. "Ugh! That bastard! Men!"

Rick was silent for a change. I had to give the leprechaun credit for not making a snide remark.

"Oh, you not included," Lindee amended to Dan, stroking his arm affectionately. *Oh, dear.*

"Anyway, I had to go somewhere I knew he couldn't come and find me, and where I felt safe, and among friends."

"Thanks toots. We love you too," Rick said. "Those demons are still trying to figure out where you went." He laughed and showed me his iPhone. I couldn't make out what he was showing me. The square outline in white was my house, and the green around it was his ward, I assumed.

"Great," I said. "Let them go ahead."

"Vasyl might be worried about you," Dan said.

"Well, he sure wasn't worried about me when last I saw him," I shot back.

"I've heard those parties get really, *eh-hem*," Rick said. He took a sip of his beer, and didn't look at me.

"Yeah," I said. "They were all *eh-heming.* I think midnight's when things begin to get really wild where the vampires are concerned."

"So, now what?" Lindee asked.

"We finish our drinks for now." I glanced at Rick. "I'll be spending the night on the human side of the Towers. I found out that my door and window are fixed and I've got serious dudes watching things." I turned and smiled at Dan. He lifted his beer to me and winked.

Rick frowned. "Watching things?"

"Oh. Yeah. Leif tried to shoot me," I informed.

"No shit?" His voice, went a full octave higher.

"Not only that, the VIU let Leif go. Saying because I'm the sibyl they weren't going to interfere."

"What the eff? That's seriously messed up!" Rick said.

Tom shook his head.

"No joke. But Tremayne has put Stefan Capella in charge of keeping watch over me and whatever Leif does from here on out."

"Capella? Don't know him." Rick shrugged.

A waitress in a Kelly-green dress and white apron swished through the door. I realized it was no longer a curtain over the door, but swinging restaurant doors with the louver-style slats. She had a huge tray in her hands. She came around to us and began setting plates in front of all three of us. Dan's eyes went huge over the T-bone steak and all the trimmings on his plate. Chocolate cake and some sort of foamy drink were placed before Lindee and I.

"I didn't order this," Dan said.

"On the house, sir," Tom said with a nod as the waitress zoomed back through those swinging doors.

"Anyone who takes care of our Sabrina here gets the royal treatment," Rick said and chuckled.

Dan smiled. "Well, thank you!" He wasted no time in picking up a huge serrated knife and fork and dug in.

"What's this?" I looked at the hot drink in a tall mug. "It looks and smells like—"

"Eggnog!" Lindee said, putting down the tall mug. She now had a foamy mustache. I pointed and laughed at her. She giggled and wiped her mouth off with a cloth napkin. "What is this place?"

"Tom's Hideaway," Rick said before I could answer her. "It's a sort of safe-haven for those in need."

"I always thought of it as an elf hideaway," I said.

Rick shrugged. "Humans who have need can find it too. Just like you did that first night."

"Yeah," I said, remembering how I was being chased by a demon down a blind alley and there Rick stood smoking against a brick wall. Little did I know there was a magic door in that wall. "I thought I was a goner."

Rick smiled. "You were on my radar even back then, toots."

I returned the smile, and grabbed up a fork. I sampled a large portion of the cake. "They make the best food here," I said through a mouthful.

"And it's like they read my mind. It's exactly what I wanted!" Lindee said, then stuffed her mouth full of chocolate cake.

I gave Tom a knowing smile.

The green door opened—this was the afore mentioned magical door in the alleyway—and two men surged in. They swept through the small room, past several tables and plopped down on two more stools. The odd—well, magical—thing about Tom's place was there were always enough stools at the bar for whomever came in out of the cold. Even if there had been only four stools, there now were six. And the bar tended to become longer as well.

The redhead threw off his coat, and the young African American unwound his red and white striped scarf from around his face.

"Quist! Fritz!" I said, surprised.

"Hey, Sabrina," Fritz said. "Surprised to see you here!" He rubbed his hands together, then blew into them.

I wanted to ask where his gloves were, but something held me back. I think it was Quist's angry look and the fact he said nothing.

"What's up, Quist?" I asked.

He unhooked the thin silver wand at his side and looked like he wanted to slam it down on the bar before him, but resisted. He placed it gently down and brooded across the way, instead of acknowledging us.

"Were you out vampire slaying?" I asked, because the wand Quist had just put down carefully was the laser with which he would sever vampire and demon heads with aplomb.

A cell phone rang. Dan dug out his phone and began talking. "Hello."

"Demons and vampires, Sabrina," Fritz said, and shot a worried look over at Quist who took the beer Tom had just set before him and began drinking it down like a thirsty man. The same waitress sailed through the swinging doors with a similar tall mug as ours and placed it before Fritz.

"Oh, thanks, Kelsy." Fritz curled his fingers around the very warm mug and visibly shivered. "God, but it's cold out there."

"Where the hell are we?" Dan asked at the other end of the bar.

"Geneva," Tom, Rick and I answered together.

"How did we get here?" he asked.

"Ley line," I said. "I tapped a ley line and brought us here."

"Why?" he asked.

"Because I had to get the hell out of there, and this was the only place I felt safe enough to go."

He repeated this into the phone.

Tom moved in front of Quist and leaned on the bar and spoke low to him in the language that elves used. Quist's very human-looking ears turned bright red and he shouted something in their language. He got off his stool and surged for the back room, disappearing through the swinging doors.

"Wow. What's wrong with him?" Lindee asked.

"We had a bad night," Fritz said. "Two humans died. We couldn't get to them soon enough."

That put all conversation to a halt momentarily. The only voice now filling the relatively cold silence was Dan's. His eyes slid to me. "She's right here. Okay. Hold on." Hc reached out, holding his cell phone to me. "Stefan wants to speak with you."

I was surprised at who wanted to speak to me. I sighed and took the phone.

"Hello?" I said into the phone.

"Why did you leave, *La mia signora*?"

I crossed my eyes then closed them in a strength-gathering moment, then opened them. I slid off my stool and walked away from the many ears around me. "Because I caught my husband doing the nasty with another woman. That's why," I answered low.

"Oh, uh, I see," he said and there was a pause. I heard Vasyl's voice in the background. His words like bullets coming out of an Uzi. "He's here and wants to speak with you."

Oh, fudge.

"Sabrina," Vasyl's voice was in my ear. "Why did you leave?"

"What?" my voice went sharp. "Did I not catch you in bed with another woman?"

Nothing like shooting a man point blank with the truth. He was stunned.

"I called to you," he said finally.

"Called to me? What am I? Your call girl suddenly? Why didn't you come and *find* me?"

"I was holding court. I could not leave," he said.

"So you found the next available slut to take to bed."

"*Mon amour*, do not slant things. I was excited by the blood ritual."

I snorted into the phone. "If you needed to have sex why didn't you have someone come and get me. Stefan was there with me."

"I do not have a cell phone."

"You could have borrowed."

"I do not know how to use one!"

"You're using one now," I pointed out.

He gasped with frustration. "Where are you?"

"I'm somewhere safe. Somewhere you can't come into." I smiled to myself.

"Wherever you are, come back."

"No."

He cursed in French. Somehow the sound of it made me hot. I don't know why. But I was not going to go to him, no matter how hot and excited he made me feel.

"Look. I'm going to let you think about what you did. I'll talk to you to-morrow night." I hit the end button, crossed the room and handed the phone back to Dan.

"Thank you," I said to him, noting he had half his porterhouse steak gone.

"Welcome," he said and stuffed the cell phone into a pocket inside his jacket. He turned back to his meal unconcerned by my little drama.

"What's up with this raven?" Rick said and pointed over his shoulder at the raven perched on the stool next to him. There had not been a stool there before, now there was. Weird that I was getting so used to this place made by elves for magical people that another oddity didn't bother me.

"Dante?" I said, peering past Rick's shoulder. At the mention of his name the raven vanished and Dante now sat in the stool.

"Fairy crap!" Rick said, blinking at him.

"That is *so* cool how you do that," Lindee said with admiration in her voice.

"My Lady, there was no one at your house, but I detected that some-one—possibly a demon—had been there," Dante said. I met his dark-gray gaze, moving toward him. His hands clutched my upper arms. He could see I was upset, but I was trying very hard not to cry in front of everyone. I looked down and away from him.

"Rick? You see anything going on at my house?" I asked.

Rick took out his iPhone and began searching it. He frowned. "Uh, hmm. Wow. Looks like there's a yellow alert on this."

"Yellow alert? Meaning?" I prompted.

"It means someone tried the barrier, but failed to gain access."

"Good or bad?" I looked up at Dante.

"I would suggest not going home at this time," Dante said. "Or using the ley lines again."

I turned to Tom. "Tom, do you have rooms available here? Somewhere?" I knew that there was a hotel within the building, but I wasn't sure who owned them.

"I'll check and see." Tom turned and picked up a land-line phone that was black and looked ancient. He dialed a single number—it might have been zero.

"I sense there is much trouble around us," Dante said, gliding up beside me. He looked at Fritz.

"I'll say." The voice belonged to Quist who pushed through the swinging doors. We all looked at him. "Vampires are still hunting humans," he said.

"What?" I said. "Tremayne got it rescinded—or whatever-you-call-it."

"Word on the street is that the vampires who went against Tremayne during his absence, are still hunting humans for blood, and the VIU is turning their backs on this."

"What?" I said again.

"That's crap!" Rick said, face turning crimson. "Tremayne got them to turn over that ruling. He told me himself he did it."

"I know," I said. "I was there when you told us."

"I don't know what's going on as far as that," Quist said, moving for his bar stool again. He cupped his hands around the mug of beer. "But if it comes down to whoever is running this town, I'd put even money on the demons are trying to take over." He looked at me then, having to lean forward. "I'd be very careful, Sabrina, if I were you. Very careful. They've got your number."

* * *

The rooms we managed to snag were in the same building, just as my Knowing had told me. There was a hotel as well as a restaurant here. I'd never been any further inside this building other than in the tavern. Rick led us through the double swinging doors, into a dark restaurant—because it was closed—with dark green table cloths. At the other end, he magicked open a locked pair of glass doors. We crossed the quiet lobby of a hotel. The night manager was apparently asleep on the job. I didn't see him anywhere. Then a thought occurred to me.

"I wonder why I didn't see Morkel when I went to the towers today," I muttered.

"Possibly because it was his day off," Rick said, turning toward a wide stairway that was very old, the stairs were covered in thread-worn carpeting, but very clean. We climbed up creaking steps.

"His day off?"

"Yeah."

"Well, that explains that," I said.

We came to the second floor, and continued up to a third floor. I was breathing hard by the time we got to the landing. It all smelled of cleaning agents, which was a good thing.

"Holy shit," Lindee said, her booted feet clumping up behind us. "How many floors?"

"Just three," Rick said, handing us each a key with a green fob with a gold number on them. "Your rooms are down the hall." He pointed. "The ones at the end, there. We keep a couple of them empty just for emergencies."

"Thanks," I said to Rick, looking at the number on my key fob. Number 34. Dante strode ahead of us with Dan bringing up the rear. I handed Dante my key and he opened the door. He ducked his head inside to check things out. Dan did the same when he got to his.

"Lindee," I said, turning to find she had opened her door and flipped on the light. "Will you be okay?"

She yawned, opening the door across from me. "Yeah. I'm beat. I'm gonna absolutely crash."

"Me too," I said. To Dan I said, "Thank you for keeping us safe tonight."

"No problem, Ms. Strong." He smiled at me and then his eyes lifted to take in Dante. Yeah. He was wondering who, or what Dante was. Or maybe he knew? *Eff it.*

I closed the door. Dante found the lock and engaged it. His hand took mine and he led me to the bed where I dropped onto it heavily. I wanted to get out of my dress badly. Only then I realized our street clothes were still over at Jeanie's apartment. There was nothing to put on to sleep in. There was no way to brush my teeth. In fact I didn't see a bathroom in this room. *Out in the hall. Crap.* I kicked off my shoes. My heels and toes hurt from them. Why did women insist of wearing such torturous shoes?

Dante settled beside me and pulled me into his arms.

"What has happened? Why have you come here?" he asked. Of course, he didn't know why I had suddenly popped out of Tremayne Towers to here.

I wiped away tears that had finally spilled over my cheeks. "I caught Vasyl with another woman." I sucked back snot.

Dante smoothed his hand over my head, quietly taking in what I'd said. He allowed me to continue when I could.

"He said he became excited by that blood ritual, earlier. That was his excuse, anyway."

"I don't condone what he did, nor do I make any excuses for it," Dante said. "But the blood which he drank from the other vampires may have tainted his judgment."

I looked up at him, wiping my eyes some more and wishing I had a tissue or three. "You think that's all it was?"

"Depending upon the vampires he drank from, his taking their blood is like having a part of them inside him. You see?" he said.

I nodded solemnly. "A part of their soul." I knew what he meant. So, it worked with vampires feeding on vampires too.

"I would give him the benefit of the doubt before taking any drastic measures."

"Drastic?" I said and a dry chuckle escaped. "You mean like taking a stake to his heart?"

"Yes. That would be drastic." He chuckled with me. "A moment." He stood. "I'll get you something for your tears." He vanished and quickly in a matter of ten seconds, was back and produced a wad of what I realized was toilet paper.

I looked at it and laughed. "Thank you." I took the wad of soft white toilet paper and cleaned myself up. Black mascara, make-up and lipstick colored the tissue. "Well, the party is definitely over."

"Perhaps," he said and put an arm around me. We sat for a little while longer while he held me, and finally my tears dried up. I hoped he was right, that Vasyl couldn't help himself. But I did have more problems than this one thing going on with my spouse.

"Dante?"

"Yes, My Lady?"

"What do you think is going on with the demons? I mean, first they let Leif go because, well, hey, it's just me he tried to kill—like my friends don't count. And, then Quist is reporting wide-spread hunting of humans. What's going on?"

"I am not certain," hc said. We looked at one another for a brief moment. I was first to look away. There was that niggle of guilt in the back of my mind. I had done it with Dante—not exactly like Vasyl had been with another woman, but it amounted to sex, nevertheless. "I could go and see what is happening on the streets, if you wish?"

I gazed at him in the dim light of the lamp near the bed. "You don't have to, if you don't want to." I muttered. I was in a very weakened state. "I'd rather not be alone."

His arm went around my shoulders again and he pulled me close and kissed the top of my head.

"You are vulnerable, right now. I wouldn't dream of taking advantage."

I made a whimpering sound in the back of my throat. There was that need in me, but I had to be strong. Didn't I?

He shook his head slowly. "No. Not tonight." His arm slid off me. "If I were your husband I would hope that those who could comfort you would merely do that and nothing more."

"Okay. But what if someone tries to get me?"

He chuckled. "You are very safe here. I will go and roam the streets nearby to see what is happening."

I shuddered. "I had some sort of vision earlier."

"Yes? What have you seen?"

"Something is coming," I said. "I think it wants me."

"It cannot find you here. Very strong elf magic disguises all who stay inside," he said firmly. "Get some sleep, my Lady." He rose from the bed. "I will see you tomorrow after you have rested." He turned and vanished.

I sighed. Reaching back to my zipper I got it down without much trouble. It slid down into a puddle on the floor and I happily stepped out of it. Now I was down to my undies and pantyhose. I peeled the pantyhose off and slid into bed. The sheets were cool and crisp. What I wouldn't give to be able to just go home. But home was where the demons were, I reminded myself. Fudge.

Problem was, that wasn't all I was worried about. I knew, deep inside, that the demons were going to be a *big* problem. I remembered the female who strode into the room with Crimmins behind Leif, the way she had looked at me still gave me pause. I might not be able to read what a demon was thinking, but their body language was a no-brainer. They were defying the ruling for some reason. Those who were in charge of VIU, like Crimmins, were not going to enforce it. The reason was just a small chunk of that particular iceberg, I realized. Earlier, when Quist informed us of what was going on, and the way he had looked straight at me, I knew I was being put to the challenge. I was the sibyl. I was *supposed* to fight demons and vampires. I was as much their enemy as they were mine. I'd had it pretty easy so far. It was like I'd been wearing a Wonder Woman costume, but it was just pretend. Like Halloween. I needed to get tough. *Damn, why couldn't my life just get easier?*

What a joke that was.

My hearing before becoming Were-girl was very good. It was now excellent and I could hear a pin drop in the next room. So, when a door opened and shut across the hall from me I lay still listening to the high-heeled footsteps of Lindee going down the hall. There was a knock on a door further down. The door must have opened.

"Oh, hi," Lindee's voice echoed in the hallway. It may have been hushed, but I heard it all the same.

The low rumble of Dan's voice came back in greeting.

"I wonder if you could help me?" she said.

"Sure. What do you need?"

I heard nothing in reply. After about ten seconds I heard the distinct sound of a zipper.

Well, fudge.

* * *

"What am I to do?" Vasyl anguished, raking fingers through his short hair while pacing like a lion in his new penthouse. The guests had been asked to leave abruptly. He was not about to have a party going on while he was in such a state.

Stefan cast his dark-blue gaze on his new Lord, Vasyl. "My Lord," he said. "You need to make amends."

"I know this! How? I have never had to make apologies to a human woman before. To any woman, for that matter! *Sacrebleu!*"

"Flowers. Lots of flowers. Chocolates, too," Stefan said, also pacing the length of the room along the other side, near the fireplace. His own desires for Sabrina were subdued to a point. There was no mistaking, he desired the sibyl. Her blood smelled delicious! "Anything she might like. She is young, barely a woman. She might like stuffed animals, like teddy bears. And for the woman in her, a little delicate thing to wear—you know—in bed."

Vasyl winced at him. "You are sure this would appease her?"

"If it is done right."

Vasyl strode across the room wringing his hands, thinking about this. When he had summoned Stefan, he'd found Vasyl cursing and screaming in a French dialect he was most certain was not used any longer. He had somehow gotten the Frenchman under control. He'd never seen a vampire cry before, and blood was very hard to get out of material. It had stunned him nearly to shame to see this rogue with such angst over a human woman. But he had to do—say—something. After all, he'd given him his oath of allegiance, although had not undergone the blood rite. Because of his father, it was deemed he was under the same rule, thus, he did not need to change his allegiance. He merely gave an oath to protect and serve Vasyl.

"How? Where does one find such things?" Vasyl asked, hands out with exasperation.

"Truly, my Lord? You've never heard of a florist?"

He shook his head. "I have told you. I have never cared for any woman until this one. She is the only woman I have ever touched that makes me want to both go insane at the thought of never touching her again, and angry because I am vampire and cannot be with her during the daytime and enjoy what she enjoys."

"Truly?"

"*Oui!*" he growled, his eyes looked both dark and menacing at once, Stefan felt some trepidation for a brief ten seconds. Vasyl was, after all, a powerful master, as old—perhaps older—than Bjorn himself. Of course, he had known him while still living in Europe. This vampire could kill swiftly and without remorse. It was difficult to understand his feelings for the human woman. But, it happened for some vampires who were smitten by humans to the point of insanity with their preoccupation with them. However, Sabrina was a special case. As sibyl she could kill vampires too. She had almost killed Tremayne for his *flagrante delicto*. He would have died too, except that she had given him her plasma, as if she had forgiven him for his transgressions. If she had not, there would have been a tyrant ruling them. Nicolas had not ruled a state since he'd left Romania in the sixteenth century. There was a vampire who was totally devoid of any real emotional needs from anyone. So, for his part, Vasyl had saved them all from that horrid possibility. And they all owed Sabrina a debt of gratitude for having rid them of Ilona—he still had not heard for certain how this was achieved, but he'd heard rumors. No telling what he would be doing now if Ilona were in charge. He scoffed to himself thinking that he would very possibly be her lap dog in the very least. He would have fled to Europe if that had happened.

So, going along with being Vasyl's second-in-command, was not such a bad deal. Especially, since he could see Sabrina, every once in a while.

"I know of several florists, my Lord. I will have one of my assistance call tomorrow when they are open. Let me work on this," Stefan suggested, looking at his cell phone.

"*Non!* This is my woman, my dilemma. You will give me the numbers and I will call them. I will be awake. I can't sleep, not while I have done such a terrible thing to her."

Stefan bowed. "Very well, my Lord. I will write down the numbers and give you a list of the things you might ask for. They could come and set it up for you, in fact."

"*Oui?* They can do this?"

"Of course, my Lord. Your riches would be the selling point." They gazed at one another for nearly a vampiric heartbeat. "I will get a cell phone for you, and show you how to work it. We'll start with a basic one until you get the hang of it."

Vasyl ran his fingers through his hair again and made a snort of disgust. "A phone is hardly one of my most important problems, *mon ami*. I had not had human blood in more than ten centuries. I've lived mostly on horse blood."

Stefan squelched his need to make a sound of disgust. "Really? Then, I shall make certain you have only Organic II. It is primarily horse blood. I will have that sent up from now on."

"*Non*. You do not *comprenre*—eh—understand. Sabrina's blood is not exactly human."

Stefan frowned. "Then what—"

"She is *magique*, and becoming more magical as time passes." He stepped toward the water buffalo head on the wall. Looking up at it, he grimaced. "Did you know she changed Ilona into stone?"

"I had heard rumors, but, I had no idea it was true."

"If she were not on our side, she would hunt us," Vasyl said, pressing a hand to his chest, and looked over his shoulder at him. "We cannot afford to have her against us, *comprendre*?"

"I do." Stefan nodded. He had not known how powerful this creature, the sibyl, was. The truth seeped into his conscience in a way that made his mouth go dry and he felt a slight tightening at his groin. Which was weird, but he knew he'd felt a need to possess Sabrina since his first meeting with her, and whenever he thought of her, his physical reaction had been the same. This new information jacked up his desires even more so. He sighed, and then quickly veiled his mental lapse of attention with a small cough. He understood Vasyl's weakness for her. Dangerous and beautiful. That's how he liked his ladies, but usually they were vampires. Magical creatures did not come along very often.

A sibyl? Never.

He knew the story behind Vasyl and Sabrina, but he had no idea how deep it ran. For a vampire to search for the sibyl for centuries and not kill her made no sense.

He would have to learn more about this woman. Much more.

"You will not send me any human females again," Vasyl said.

"I never did, my Lord."

"*Excisez moi.* It is true." Vasyl's hand dropped to his side and he looked back at Stefan, giving him an apologetic—as much as was possible from a French-man—frown. "You have done well. I have not had a second in command in centuries. I have nearly always been rogue. I had forgotten the rituals involved." He strode to the door and looked out the peek hole. "At any rate, under no circumstances allow that woman or any other to come up here to see me. *Comprendre?*"

"*Concordo, mio signore.*" As his second, any woman Vasyl rejected was his. That was an unspoken rule, and expected. The redhead he'd been given as a gift from Bjorn. She was hot. He'd happily oblige his lord's wishes on this as well. Possibly, this wasn't such a bad arrangement after all. Especially when he was to help protect Sabrina—which meant he would be close to her.

Chapter 10

Dawn

The sun was high when I awoke. Stretching, I yawned and realized I was in a strange place, not where I'd expected to be. It took about eight seconds to remember my terrible night and how I'd wound up in a small room in an old hotel somewhere in the suburbs. The walls were painted light gold and the ceiling white. The window, thankfully was covered with a shade. It was a clean room. Crisp, plain white sheets, the comforter warm, pale yellow with a delicate pattern of stems, flowers and leaves, and a crocheted throw over it as well. The small bed boasted a brass headboard and footings. Because I had nothing to wear to bed, I was nude, save my underwear and my gloves. The sheets somehow felt luxurious against my skin, and while it felt slightly naughty, it also felt freeing. I liked to sleep in at least an undershirt. I wasn't one to sleep nude. Even when with a man, I simply needed something on—aside from my gloves, that is. I know. I'm weird in that way.

Wanting to slip back to sleep I closed my eyes, not caring a lick what time it was, I wanted to pretend I had no important engagements or problems to deal with. No rogue vampires, demons or whatnot invading my world. I vowed that nothing other than hunger and the need to pee would make me stir from this bed.

The notes to *Girls Just Want To Have Fun* sounded. No. Not in my head.

"Oh, crap," I muttered knowing that was my phone's tone going off in my clutch purse. By sound I located my purse on a chair near the bed. I had to roll over and practically fall half-way out of the bed to reach it. I hauled the clutch purse back with me, scratching myself on one of those rings on top and swore under my breath. I pulled up the covers, opened my purse, and pulled out the cell phone, which was about to go into voicemail.

I looked at the readout first. I was certain it couldn't be any vampire. *Good. Lindee.*

"Hi," I said.

"Morning. Where the hell are we again? I forgot."

"I can only say we're on the third floor of where we wound up last night," I said.

There was a pause. "I'm hungry, and the only clothes I've got are the ones we came here in."

"Same here."

"Where's the bathroom?"

"Down the hall," I said. We were on the same page.

Another pause. "I'll meet you in the hallway."

"Right."

I dressed, not really wanting to put on an evening gown to go scrounging around looking for food and a toilet—not in that order. I mean, I felt so over-dressed while yanking a sequined dress up to sit on the toilet. Gak-and-a-half!

We both opened our doors at the same time and stared at one another across the hall.

"God. Do I look as bad as I feel?" I asked.

"You look rumpled. Got a mirror?"

"You don't want a mirror, honey," I said.

"That bad?" She opened her purse and tried unsuccessfully to locate a mirror. She gave up with a sigh of frustration. "Crap. Where's my—"

The sound of a flushing toilet caught our attention and we looked toward the door at the end of the hall.

Dan emerged from the water closet—which is really what it was—and stopped dead in this tracks taking us both in.

"Oh. Hell," he said, rolling his eyes.

"Speak for yourself," Lindee said, then let out a chuckle. "Dibs!" She ran—well, she scurried—on her high-heeled booties to duck into the john.

I was not going to put on my high-heeled contraptions of torture, other-wise known as shoes, unless it was required. In fact I hadn't even put on my hose—gag me. I'd rolled them up into a ball and squished them into my purse.

Okay, yeah the idea of my foot odor mingling with a comb and my cell phone wasn't exactly a nice thought, but what choice did I have?

Uncomfortable as hell, leaning against the hallway wall, I glanced at Dan.

"Sleep well?" he asked.

"Not as well as you," I said and crossed my arms. He tried to veil his guilty look but I wouldn't allow it. "Not only am I a damned good psychic, but I've got werewolf hearing," I said in a warning tone.

He cleared his throat into his fist. "Sorry. Did we keep you up?" He looked toward my door. "I thought Dante was with you."

"He left almost right after we got up here," I said. Now thinking things over, I mentally thanked Dante for doing the right thing last night and *not* spending the night with me.

"Oh," Dan said, his silver gaze meeting mine.

"She's only eighteen," I said. "If you hurt her—" The toilet flushed down the hall and a minute later Lindee emerged from the small bathroom. My warning lingered like an omen in the little hall.

"Your turn," Lindee said, heels click-clacking across the linoleum.

I took my turn for the bathroom, wishing again for a toothbrush and a hair brush. I finger-combed my hair and splashed cold water on my face. At least there were real towels in the bathroom. Once I finished up, and joined my partners, we all slinked down the three floors to the hotel lobby.

"I really had no idea this was here," I said as we moved across the dark green carpet that felt really good on my bare feet. But we stopped at the glass doorway that was the entrance to the restaurant. Crowds of people filled the restaurant. I paused to put on my shoes, leaned precariously as I did and almost fell. Dan caught me by an elbow, and Lindee grabbed me on the other side.

"Thanks, guys," I said, becoming level once again. Was I insane buying these shoes? My toes and heals hurt to put them on again. In fact, I had a bad blister on one heal.

Once I was presentable, we stepped through the doors and the smell of bacon, pancakes, syrup and hash browns hit me. The tables were set up in white linen, china and crystal. Mine wasn't the only tongue hanging out.

"What is this?"

"Sunday brunch," Dan said and pointed at the sign that would have bit me if it was a snake.

"Wow."

"Should we partake?" Dan asked.

"I think we should," Lindee said.

"Me three," I agreed.

The hostess smiled as she strode up to us. "Three?"

"Yes."

"Booth or table?" *A trough if you have one.*

"Table is fine," I said when the other two went mute suddenly.

We were seated amongst many elderly couples in suites and nice dresses, so I didn't feel too overly dressed at all, but Lindee and I got the old-men stares. The waitress told us to simply go up to the buffet tables, grab a plate, and she'd bring coffee to our table.

"Uh, there might be a problem," I said, as we moved to the line for the buffet. "I didn't bring my purse with my credit card."

Dan held up his hand. "No worry. I'm to take care of you two, and if paying for a breakfast is part of it, I can get reimbursement."

"Nice," Lindee said. "What do you make an hour?"

"When I'm on assignment, a hundred bucks, plus expenses."

"Damn!" Lindee said and laughed.

We all loaded down our plates with everything we wanted. My eyes were larger than my stomach, as usual, but I was hungry since we didn't actually have much of a dinner. And from the looks of my companion's plates, they were too.

We were on our seconds when Dan said, "My boss has asked me to make updated reports of where we are and what we're doing. Even though he's not awake right now."

"We'll be going back to the towers after this," I told him. "So, you can add that to your report."

He nodded as he made his call.

"How are we going to get back to the towers?" Lindee asked. "Taxi?"

"Yish, no," I said. "Same way I got us here."

My phone rang. I opened my purse below the table, trying to hide my smelly stockings as I unearthed my phone. A stocking became hooked and I managed to un-snag it, but not before a woman in the next table over saw it and smiled up at me. I shoved it back down into the depths of the clutch.

"Hello?" I said into the phone, working to push my smile down into a frown. Wasn't possible. This was too ridiculous.

"Ah, Sabrina, good," the familiar voice came.

"Oh, hi, Andrew," I said, smiling across at Lindee.

"I'm sorry that we had a little scheduling misunderstanding, yesterday," he said. "I'll be able to see you today, if that's alright? Will you be available later on at the towers?"

"Yes," I said. "I'll be at my suite on the human side."

"Oh," he said sounding slightly confused. "You aren't staying in the penthouse?"

"No," I said and not wanting to get into my personal problems, I went on quickly. "I much prefer my own suite during my stay at the towers."

"I heard what happened yesterday, uh, with Leif."

"Yes. I'd rather not have a repeat of that," I said grimly. "That's why I'm staying on the human side." Well, one of the reasons.

"I'm certain there won't be a repeat, but I can't say that I blame you one bit. Shall we say two o'clock?"

"What time is it now?"

"Twelve twenty-one," he said.

"I believe I can make that." I then bit my lower lip. "Eh, maybe we'd better make it two thirty. We're out, right now, having breakfast—er, brunch, I guess."

"Oh, certainly. Two-thirty is fine. See you then."

My thought was that Lindee and I would need to take showers and somehow retrieve our clothes from Jeanie's place, since I presumed they'd already left on a jet to L.A. I thought that would be a good job to put my Were guardian on.

We finished our respective meals, Dan paid the bill, and kept the receipt.

"Look, we need to be in a place where other humans can't see us disappear," I spoke low standing near the front of the restaurant. "We need to go back into Tom's Tavern." I pointed. "That way. The way we came through here last night."

Lindee and Dan both followed me through the restaurant, and headed down a hallway where a restroom sign hung. The swinging door to Tom's Tavern was at the very end of the hallway where there was a blank wall with brown shutters. The men and women's rest rooms were to either side.

"This way," I said. I strode forward several steps and pushed through the swinging doors.

"Hey, girlfriend!" Rick greeted me from his spot at the bar. *Sheesh.* The guy lived here. "What's up? How'd you like your rooms?"

"We liked them fine. I'm taking us all back to the towers."

"Who's us all?" he asked.

"Us. Them—" I pointed behind me.

"There's no one with you," he said.

I looked back. Lindee and Dan were not with me. "Well, they were right behind me!" I gazed at the swinging doors. I could see their feet and the top of the Were's head.

"They're humans," Rick said. "That's a magical doorway. They can't see it. All they see is a wall."

"Really?"

"Yep. Just tell them to walk through the wall. They'll be fine."

"Okay." I walked back to the doorway, pushed through and looked out at them. "Why are you guys standing out here?"

"Um, because that's a wall," Lindee said, pointing. "That's totally weird how you're like sticking halfway through the wall. How are you doing that?"

"Like this." I grabbed her hand and pulled. She screeched, but stumbled through. She looked around herself.

"Whoa, shit!" Then she laughed uncontrollably.

I went back for my Were guard. "Come on," I said, leaning out the door again to Dan. "It's just like Platform nine and three-quarters."

He squished his face up at me. "What?"

I grabbed his hand. "Come on, Silver-eyes." I pulled, and his feet stumbled forward, and he was on the other side of the doors.

"There," I said, turned and strode into the main area of the tavern. "Hi, Tom!" I waved.

"Sabrina," Tom said, nodding, wiping out a glass.

"I still can't figure out how we didn't see the doors," Lindee was saying, studying the louver doors.

"What was it you called me?" the Were asked.

My face warmed. "Oh. Uh, that's my nick-name for you. Silver-eyes." I hiked my shoulders up with a smile.

"I haven't been working for you for even a whole day and you've got a nick-name for me already?"

"I gave it to you back when I first met you." His eyes swam in thought. " At the bunker, when I went into that room to meet with Nicolas?"

"Oh. Yeah." He shook his head and chuckled. "Forgot. I guess we have history."

"I guess so."

I looked at Rick. "I need to get to the human side of the towers. I'm not sure if I can pinpoint our landing so well."

"You need a boost?" Rick asked.

"Yeah. I need to get a swipe card. I forgot mine at home, so I really should stop at the desk of South Tower." I felt stupid for having forgotten it. The thought had been nagging me since last night. I might need to get in and out of my suite too. I was certain they would give me a new card for my suite. If I had any trouble, I'd sick someone on them.

"I can get you wherever you need to go," Rick said.

"Okay. I guess we should try and land like at the doors so that we don't scare anyone."

"You've got it. Everyone hold hands," he said.

I grabbed Lindee's hand and Dan held Lindee's other hand.

"Here we go," I said.

Snap.

The usual odd sensations rocked me whenever Rick popped me through the ley line. When he did it I felt like my body shrank and then returned to normal with the feeling like I'd been shoved through a keyhole. My ears popped, too. Rick put us exactly where I wanted. In fact he was nice enough to place us in the foyer of the doorway so that we wouldn't freeze, since we weren't exactly dressed for the weather.

"That was too weird," Dan said.

"I thought it was cool," Lindee said. "Like the best way to travel."

We strode through the doorway. Fortunately, it was quiet and not that many people coming in on a Sunday to the towers to stay in the hotel. But some of us had suites.

We stepped up to the desk and a clerk came out.

"Good morning. How can I help you?" a young blond man asked.

"Hi, I'm Sabrina Strong and I've sort of misplaced my swipe card to get into my suite." I was twisting the ends of my gloves hopefully.

He turned to his monitor and tapped something out on the keyboard. "Okay. Ms. Strong. Room eighteen-oh-six?"

"Yeah," I said, still pulling on my gloves.

"Oh. We have some packages for you, they arrived early this morning." He turned and lifted five shopping bags that looked really familiar.

Lindee and I gasped with recognition.

"Our clothes and things!" I gasped. "Thank you! Do you know who brought them?"

"No. I don't. But probably one of the couriers from North Tower."

I nodded. He made a swipe on some instrument below my level of sight and tucked a card into a paper sleeve with *Tremayne Towers~South Tower* printed gold on black and handed it to me. "There you go, ma'am. You have a nice day. And, if there's anything we can help you with at all, just let us know. The kitchen is open until seven PM tonight."

I nodded, thanked him and Lindee took one bag, I handed Dan a large bag from Macy's and I took a couple of bags with our street clothes in them. I couldn't wait to get this damn dress off and get cleaned up and comfortable.

A few minutes later, when we entered my suite, Dan said, "This is where I leave you lovely ladies."

"Oh, well, alright," I said.

"I need to go grab a shower too," he said and backed down the hall.

"You have a room here too?"

"Yeah. Twentieth floor," he said and held up his hand. "Bye."

"Bye," Lindee and I said.

"Thanks for keeping us safe," I added.

"My pleasure." He turned and moved for the elevator.

I was actually glad to not have the Were around anymore. I'd caught eye exchanges between Lindee and the Were more than once during breakfast. I knew I would have to keep an eye on them. But I knew that the full moon was upon us. She would not be seeing him for a few nights at least.

Chapter 11

Visitors

Morkcl always dressed in a nice suit—that is, if he was not in his Sanguine Team uniform of olive slacks and shirt with the patch on the sleeve with the swirly red emblem on the sleeve. Today was no exception. He wore a dark suit that made his sandy hair look lighter, and his tan somewhat radiant.

"Sabrina, how nice to see you again," he greeted.

"You too," I drawled, "and in some place other than Tom's Tavern. Right?" He chuckled. I turned toward the kitchenette where Lindee stood, "This is my cousin, Lindee."

"How do you do?" he said with a little nod. "I see a certain family resemblance."

"Thanks," I said.

"You hungry or anything? We've got stuff for sandwiches," she offered, holding a butter knife in her hand, a dollop of mayo clung to it.

"Oh, no thank you," he said. "I just ate." He turned to me and held up his briefcase. "If you are ready, I think we can get started on my updating your files."

"Sure. Where would you be most comfortable?"

"The couch would be just fine. I've got the laptop here, and I can work from the coffee table," he said and settled on the couch. "This won't take very long." He unzipped his soft case.

"Sounds good."

"Don't let me interfere with whatever you are doing. Go ahead and eat your sandwiches. I'll ask you questions and you can answer them." He pulled out his laptop from the briefcase and began setting it up. I stepped into the kitchen and snagged one of the sandwiches Lindee was making. Earlier, I had called for makings for sandwiches from the hotel's kitchen. We'd had such a filling breakfast—well, it was breakfast to us—that all I wanted was something simple and something we could make here.

"Now, Sabrina, I've got your file up. Tell me what are these new abilities you have?" Morkel was slouched in front of his computer, hands at the ready.

"Um, I'm now fully telepathic," I began. "And I can use ley lines to travel. I'm not real good at it, but I have places I can go when I need to. Like my house or…" I looked at Lindee. "Like last night, I took Lindee and Silver-eyes to Tom's Tavern."

"Silver-eyes?" Morkel smirked as his fingers tapped on the keyboard.

"Uh, he's a Were. His actual name is Dan Huston, but I call him that 'coz of his silver-blue eyes."

"Okay," Morkel half-laughed and continued typing.

"Also I can do distant viewing."

"My lord." He looked up at me looking astonished. "Distant viewing? Really?" He sounded amazed as he looked up at me over the counter. "Tell me how it works."

"Oh, sure. I brought my plate and glass of cola over to the counter and sat to face him. Lindee joined me. "Okay, I concentrate on someone—well, it's usually someone nearby in the same area, like in a house? Anyway, I can actually see them doing whatever they are doing at that exact moment, even though I'm not with them physically," I explained. "It's like I'm there, but I'm not really."

"Extraordinary!" he said and busily typed it in.

"But if I do this, I get a really bad headache."

"It sounds like a migraine to me," Lindee put in, sliding her gaze to me.

"That has been known to happen," he said. "I would advise you not to do it very often."

"Don't worry. I won't," I said.

"Oh! Tell him what you did to Ilona, and that gun—that was just amazing!" Lindee laughed.

"I heard that you changed Ilona into stone?" Morkel said, hand fluttering next to his head. "I'm so disappointed I didn't see that!" He frowned lightly. "I really wanted to, but by the time I'd heard, they'd removed her—um—remains."

"Yeah. I did. I was extremely frightened, but also angry because she was going to bite my little niece."

"I see." Morkel nodded. "What was this about a gun?"

"Um, you remember that Leif shot at me yesterday?" I said.

"Yes. That was terrible. What did you do?" His blue eyes darted up at me.

"I don't know how, but I turned the bullets into butterflies and then the gun turned into a raven. Strange. I was only thinking of making it harmless. Nothing specific." I tucked strands of dark hair back behind my ears. If I hadn't been there myself, I wouldn't be able to believe it myself.

"That's a form of psychokinesis, it's called transmogrifying," he said and tapped something out on his keyboard. "Witches of the highest abilities can do this."

Right. That's how I got those abilities, but I didn't want to tell him how I came by these new magical abilities if that could be avoided. But from the way he was acting, he wasn't at all surprised that I had them.

"And it seems like I can see demons, or their auras, or something around them? Anyway, I know a demon, even if they appear as human," I said.

"That may be a new power I've never heard of," he said, sitting up and looking at me. "I'll put it down as simply recognizing a demon." He typed this into the computer. "I've never run across this before. Not in humans."

I took a bite out of my sandwich, chewed and washed it down with the pop.

"Now, of course, you realize you are no longer an employ of Tremayne's?" Morkel said sitting a little straighter.

"I figured that, what with my husband suddenly being the head honcho that my employ with him would end," I said. I was happy about this because it meant I would not need to work for Tremayne again. Plus I already saw the perks with this new status too. The guys in the hotel kitchen were all over themselves trying to please me. Asking me if there wasn't anything else they could bring up to me. Even the clerk at the desk seemed more than ready to do whatever it took for me to be happy. I asked for a couple of toothbrushes and toothpaste (the small travel size) for starters, and ice. I got those post haste.

"Yes. And as a magical creature, your file is in safekeeping with me," he said, tapping the top of his laptop. "I even have Rick in here," he added as he closed it.

I nodded. I wasn't used to being called a magical creature. It happened over night, really. Three months ago, I was plain old Sabrina Strong, unemployed psychic. Now, I was *magical.*

"I noticed you've proper guards on your door," he said.

"Really?" I said.

"Well, yes. Although I think the werewolves will be gone before dusk, as the full moon will be out tonight."

I choked, suddenly remembering something.

Lindee's head swung my way. "You okay? Can you breathe?"

I nodded. "Yes." But I still choked.

"Is something the matter?" Morkel asked.

"Definitely." I swallowed some pop, and I was able to get down whatever it was that had caught in my throat. I looked at Lindee. "I have to go to my place and get that potion Mrs. Bench made for me so I don't turn."

"You have a potion for this?" Morkel asked. I was surprising him a lot this afternoon.

"I do. I don't care what anyone says. I do NOT want to change into my creature. I don't like being out of control. Plus, I might wind up in a werewolf's bed. I sure as hell don't need that after what happened last night."

"What happened last night?" he wondered.

Oh fudge. I shook my head. "Let's just put it this way, my husband wouldn't like it if after the chewing out I gave him last night for his transgressions, that I wind up with another man—a werewolf, no less—tonight."

"Hmm, yes. Well, that might make things very uncomfortable," he agreed.

"I wish I could pop over to my house and get a few things." I fed Lindee a wince.

"Why wouldn't you be able to?" Morkel asked. "You have the skills."

"Demons," I said.

"They attacked the house," Lindee added. "It was like an earthquake! Shook the house. It was horrible!"

"Oh? I hadn't heard this," Morkel said. "When did this occur?"

"Yesterday. In the morning," I said. "I don't dare go back there. They're looking for me."

"I could possibly go for you, that is if you wish?" he offered.

"Really?" I said. "My werewolf potion and a few other things we don't have here would be great."

"Make up a list," he said. "Since you are telepathic, we can communicate while I'm there and you can tell me exactly where everything is."

"Wow. I didn't know you'd be able to communicate with me like that," I said.

"I can, as long as I open myself up, of course." He smiled. I could not normally read any other magical creature's mind—especially an elf. "Go ahead and make me a list and I'll go instead."

Morkel's lap top already put away, he stood and stepped into the kitchenette while we began our list. While we worked on it, he made himself a sandwich. I thought he'd said he had just eaten. I had to hide my snicker while watching him work on building it—he liked the sliced cucumbers quite a bit, and chose the tuna salad on whole wheat.

"Okay. I think we've got a pretty good list here." I handed it to him. There were probably fifteen things on it. "My potion is in my jewelry box," I said. "Which is in my bedroom, uh, on the first floor. The oak pocket door is where my bedroom is."

"Pocket doors? Really? How charming. I love those," he said, looking up at me.

"They're okay," I said handing him the list. "The potion is sort of brownish in color."

He nodded, biting off a bit of sandwich taking my list. He read it. "Oh," his mouth was full. This was funny as I'd never seen him eat before. He looked somewhat boyish, just the opposite of the stylishly dressed, obsessively neat, somewhat serious man I've only always seen.

He pointed to my list with a pinky. I noticed a silver ring on his finger. It was ornate of Irish, or Celtic design. "What drawer would these be in?"

"My gloves would be in the left top drawer. Socks and underwear in the right." Was it warm in here or what? I couldn't meet his gaze. Jeeze. I was sending a guy I barely knew to riffle through my underwear and sock drawer.

"If this is too much—"

"No. No. I'm fine," he said. "What about the dagger? Where would that be?"

"Bottom drawer, under some older jeans. My sheath is with it on a belt. Bring that too."

He put the sandwich into his mouth and took another bite and looked at me.

I heard in my head. *Okay, Sabrina. I'm off. You need to guide me to your house. I don't know where it is.*

"Oh—" I started, but he put a finger to his lips. I squinted with my thought: *Go west about sixty miles, Sonata Road. In the country, almost directly eight miles south of the DuKane tollway exit. You have GPS?*

Morkel smiled between chomps of the sandwich. *Excellent directions, Sabrina. I won't need GPS, but if I do, I'll use it. What sort of house is it?*

White farm house, three stories with a white barn and a loop for a drive.

Anything else?

Oh, and demons crawling all over it. Another house across the street. Mrs. Bench's is a brick house. Oh, God. I hope she's alright.

I'll check up on her.

Morkel smiled, waved the hand that didn't have a sandwich in it, and vanished.

"Crap," Lindee said and took her pop and sandwich to the living area. "I can't get used to all this magic stuff going on." She plopped down on the couch and had the remote in her hand. The TV blinked on.

"What's on TV?" At this hour usually nothing was on, unless it was cable, of course.

"Ugh!"

"What?"

"It's your vampire. He's on TV," she said.

"Huh?" I walked in with my plate of food and looked at the TV. Sure enough, there was Tremayne in living color.

"Sabrina?" That baritone I so recognized came out of the TV.

"Crap!" I said. I'd seen him do this once or twice before on a TV. On this set, only once before.

"Hello to you, too," he said with a sarcastic sniff.

"What is Bjorn doing on TV?" Lindee asked.

"He's not *on* TV. He's talking *thought* the TV." I'd forgotten about these two-way communication TVs they had here. Ingenious, but annoying.

"Huh?" Lindee said.

"Hi, Bjorn. You in L.A.?" I asked him.

"Yes. I'm in L.A., and the smog is just fine, thanks." Tremayne's sarcastic tone came through loud and clear.

"Good. What do you need?" I asked.

"Can't a fellow say hi once in a while without you going all snitty?" he asked.

"Snitty?" I said and looked down at Lindee. "Was I snitty?"

"I don't know," she said. "I'd be snitty too. Hey, can he see us?"

"Perfectly. Shall I tell you what you're wearing?" Tremayne asked, his brows went higher on his brow.

"No. Don't bother."

Sabrina I'm here. I'm in your house, I heard in my head. I looked away from the TV and put up a finger to Tremayne.

Good. Are you in the bedroom?

I am.

"What's going on?" Tremayne wanted to know.

"Oh, she sent Morkel out to her house and they're having a conversation that we can't hear," Lindee said.

"Why is he at her house?" Tremayne asked.

"Because we needed some things and we couldn't go because of all the demons there."

Oh, you have a marvelously old house, Morkel said in my head while Lindee conversed with Tremayne.

Marvelously drafty and cold. Did I turn the heat down? I asked. *It's over on the wall near the—*

Found it. You have it at sixty-five degrees.

Good. Carry on. I turned to Tremayne's image in the TV. His arms were crossed looking put off.

"Sorry. I've got Morkel in my house getting some things."

"Things? Like what?" Tremayne asked.

"Like my anti-werewolf potion, underwear and socks."

"Oh and nightgowns!" Lindee spouted.

"And my dagger."

"Why didn't you just send Dante?"

"I haven't seen him today. He sometimes has to feed and I don't want to know who he's feeding from," I said.

He grunted, then laughed. I stuck my tongue at him.

"What do you want?" I asked.

"I wanted to see how things were with you today." He was being snoopy.

"So, why this special tele-communications thing?" I asked. "You usually call me on the cell phone to do that. Not get on your spy TV to invade my space," I said, settling on the couch arm next to Lindee.

He pulled in a breath and let it out exhaustively, like I was taxing his patients. Good.

"I wanted to know how you were, after yesterday. I wasn't very happy with VIU for letting Leif go. Frankly, I don't know what's gotten into him. I have no control over him whatsoever. My best guess is that he put himself under Ilona's command," he said.

"Or Nicolas'?" I put in, arching my brow. I don't care how he wanted to believe Nicolas was 100% his man, I knew different. I knew he was only going along with what Tremayne asked of him, but he was really looking forward to taking control of the Eastern half of the North American Vampire Association once Tremayne died from silver poisoning. I think he didn't believe the plasma I donated would bring him from the brink of death. Actually, I, myself, didn't think it would work. But apparently my plasma had enough magical effect on him to not only keep him from dying but also bring him back to his healthy seven-foot, blond vampire-Viking brawn.

"Possibly," he agreed in a low tone as if he was unhappy to admit that possibility existed.

"And now he's a rogue," I said. "Leif, that is. If he isn't following you, and now both Nicolas and Ilona are dead, he's a *dangerous* rogue."

"Yes. Exactly." His eyes held a steady, hard gaze I didn't often see. I got that times were getting dangerous here in Gotham City.

"I don't know if anyone has reported this to you," I began. "Probably not, because I'm the only one who heard it."

"Tell me."

"Quist said last night that two humans died because he couldn't get to the vampires who were hunting them. And that the VIU turned their backs on this."

"Well, that's all fucked up," he said with a gasp of irritation.

"No shit." I was becoming such a potty mouth.

"By the way tonight is the full moon—I don't know if you were aware of that?"

"Yes. I was reminded," I said.

Sabrina, where would I find a bag to put all these things in? Morkel's voice vibrated in my head.

I held up a finger to Tremayne again. *In the kitchen. Under the sink, there should be some shopping bags. Thank you.*

Wonderful.

I turned to Tremayne. "Okay. He's almost done."

"The Weres usually leave the city for the duration of the three nights of the full moon. Which means you will not have them to guard you," he said.

"I've got plenty of help. Don't forget, I do have Dante."

"Yes. You do. But you also have one human close to you—Lindee, who might come under attack as well."

Lindee and I exchanged glances. "Morkel is bringing me the Dagger of Delphi."

Tremayne visibly shivered. Not good memories for him.

"I need to remind you what I told you about—eh—the other thing? That thing you and Vasyl need to do?"

I searched my memory.

"Has everything to do with the prophecy."

I made a heavy sigh. "Yes. I do remember."

"You doing something about it?" he asked.

I frowned. "That's a bit personal, don't you think?"

"I only asked because I saw that your husband was into Elaina, last night. She was the offering I gave him, and he accepted—meaning he accepted the position as my second in all of the U.S., mainland." He sounded affronted.

"Oh. That was all your fault, was it? I didn't get *that* memo," I said crossing my arms. So that was her name. Elaina Home Wrecker.

"My fault?" he said, looking indignant. Then his expression changed to one of confusion. "I'm sorry. What are we talking about?"

The raven that appeared out of thin air on top of the large screen TV didn't startle me as much as Dante, the man, would have. It made a loud crowing while flicking its wings.

"About your giving a human to Vasyl." I paused a couple of beats. "Yeah. I found them together in a bedroom."

"Ohhh." His arms came undone. Shrugging he said, "It's normal. An offering is used in the handing over a territory to another master."

"Yeah. Vasyl certainly took advantage of that offering, alright," I said, my face burning with anger all over again.

He let a sigh slip from his lips. "Sorry. Hell. I didn't know it would be an issue."

"It was. I left right after I found him with his *offering*."

"Humans." He snorted, then squinted out at me. "He's made up to you, hasn't he?"

"No. But, I left and when he called I didn't want to talk to him."

"He'll be up pretty soon," he said. "I'm sure he'll be making a visit after sunset. It's real important you do what needs to be done. I sure as hell don't want to have to come out there and fight the fucking demons again."

"You fought demons?" I asked.

"In the political arena, yes. Fighting them physically is not my favorite thing to do, either, especially since I've just gotten my realm back, kapisch?"

I tried not to sound weary about his reminder, but it came out that way. "Right. Okay."

"Good. Let Vasyl make up to you and then…" his gaze darted off to the side, and then he cleared his throat, eye brows flagging up suggestively. "Let him do what I couldn't." *Yeesh.*

Lindee's eyes were on me but I couldn't meet them. And Dante, of course, heard everything even in raven persona.

"I will," I said with a gush of annoyance and kneaded my forehead. An annoying headache had begun. Needing to change the subject, something flashed in my head that I wanted to ask him.

"Now, if there's nothing else?" he said.

"Wait," I said, before he flipped the switch, or whatever it was he did to interrupt our TV.

"What?" He sighed, looking put out.

"I heard that Letitia's ceramic dog collection was stolen." I don't know why, but something about it bothered me. I wanted to make sure I'd gotten the story right.

He made a huge sigh of irritation. "Not just those damned dogs, but the whole fucking curio case they were in. Oh, and by the way, they were made of porcelain, not ceramic."

"There's a difference?"

"Apparently. Yes. How did you hear about it?" he asked.

"Malcolm told me. Last night at the party?"

"You met the old boy?" He chuckled. "Pathetic, isn't he?"

I frowned. "He was in love with her."

"Whatever." Tremayne waved a broad hand to dismiss that. "Why do you ask?"

"I'm just wondering how someone would have gotten to her things. I mean, weren't there guards? Or at least someone to watch over things?"

"Only the maid, butler and cook."

"Cook?" I chuckled lightly. "I had no idea Letitia would need a cook."

"For her humans, when she had parties and such."

"Oh. Right. But still—"

"Why are you so concerned about it?"

"Well, aren't you? Something was stolen."

He made that dismissive gesture again. "The insurance guys are looking into it."

I threw him a squint. "They won't solve who stole a whole curio."

"I gather you saw it? I mean through your powers?"

"I remember it. It had a lot of glass and looked quite heavy. If someone moved it they had to know what they were doing. It looked breakable. And it couldn't have gotten past too many people without someone seeing something. Even covered up."

"It was being moved when it was stolen," he explained.

"Wow. Really?"

"Were the ceramic dogs—"

"—Porcelain—"

"Right. The dogs, were they still inside it?"

"No. They were packed up. But I'm not sure how. I never looked into it myself. I really didn't care about them one way or another."

"But the piece is quite valuable, I mean the curio?"

"Yes. Worth at least twenty-five grand at auction. At least that's what I was told."

I hummed at that.

"Is that all?"

"Yeah. I guess," I said, now my mind was working on that stolen piece of property which meant more to Malcolm than to Tremayne. But it didn't really surprise me. If it were a car, maybe he'd be a little more concerned about it. I'd had the feeling the porcelain dog collection was somewhat of an irritation to him. He never cared for them, or the curio. It was Letitia's silly little interest, not his.

"Okay." He brought up a finger. "Take care of that other thing. Don't be worrying over this other stuff."

My upper lip went into a snarl. "When I'm ready, and not before."

Tremayne's eyes rolled. "You'd better be prepared for an onslaught of demons, then."

"Bring 'em on," I said.

"Then don't come crying to me."

"Don't worry. I won't," I said.

"Bye." His face blipped out and the picture of a woman with an agonizing look on her face came on in his place during a commercial crying, "I've fallen and I can't get up!"

"Crap, Brie, why didn't you tell me he could come on the TV like that! I thought I was going crazy."

"Sorry." I winced apologetically at her.

She stood and took her plate into the kitchen.

The raven swooped down to the chair next to me. Dante's form took over the raven. He stood and bowed to me.

In the next second, Morkel appeared across the way. "I think I've got everything here," he said. "And you were right about the demons. They weren't very happy with me. But I left no way for them to track me back here."

"Good," I said.

"Oh, my God," Lindee cried from the kitchen, and the three of us looked back at her.

"What?" I said, but sudden realization hit me. We had been the only ones here a moment ago. Now there were two men with us.

"Look. I know you have this strange life, Sabrina, but I just don't think I can handle another person popping in or talking at us through the TV, or whatever." She launched herself out of the room, swished down the hall and the door to my bedroom slammed.

"Or, that I might change into a were-person?" I said in a low voice, after she'd disappeared into the bedroom. "That would top things off just right, I'll bet." Dante smiled.

"Speaking of which, the sun is setting. Do you have your potion?" Dante asked.

"Right here," Morkel held up a paper bag. I stepped over and look inside. All three vials were there.

"Great." I took the bag from him.

"Hello, Dante," Morkel said. "Did you just come in?"

"Yes." Dante gave a quelling look at both Morkel and me.

"Morkel went and got my anti-werewolf potion at the house," I explained, but he didn't seem upset with me having used Morkel for the job.

"Sunset is at four-thirty-one. Moon rise is a little afterwards," Dante said.

I looked over on the stove clock. It was nearly four-thirty now. "Should I take it now?" I wondered. "Or should I wait?"

"Wait one or two minutes and then take it."

"I'm already feeling a little itchy like the change wants to take place," I said, itching the back of my hand.

"Then, maybe you should take it now. That clock might be off a few minutes," he suggested and looked at his cell phone. "Yes, it's off by two minutes."

I nodded and pulled the cork off of one of the vials. I put my lips to it and up-ended it. I swallowed the contents quickly, as it was not pleasant-tasting.

"Well, that should do the trick."

The suite's phone rang, jarring me a little. I stepped over and answered. "Hello?"

"Ms. Strong? This is Keven at the desk. A Mr. Capella is here to see you. We don't allow vampires on this side of the hotel, but he tells me you would be okay with it, however I had to call and check."

"Tall, black hair, blue eyes?" *Dangerously sexy?* I questioned. Couldn't be too careful.

"Yes. I had him show me his ID as well."

"Then he's fine to come up," I said.

"Thank you, Ms. Strong. You have a good evening."

"Yes. Thank you." *I'll certainly try.*

"Well," Morkel said. "I think my work here is done." He picked up his brief-case.

"Thank you again, Andrew," I said.

"Not at all, my pleasure, Sabrina." Straightening his tie, he stepped out of my suite.

Chapter 12

Van Helsing, I Presume

Bill looked in the mirror. He hadn't shaved in a few days, and his beard, being thick and dark, made him look somewhat roguish. He held his razor in the stream of hot running water and prepared to shave it all off as usual. But as he put the edge of the razor to his cheek, he stopped and reconsidered.

If he shaved it all off, people would recognize him. Did he want people who knew he was dead to see him and know he had come back as a Vampyr?

Hell no.

Hand on chin, he moved his face around, examining the two-days growth of beard. He used to have a full beard, at one point of his very long life, or another, depending upon what country and century it was. It gave him an intellectual, distinguished look, when trimmed. It also made him look older, changing his looks to some degree. It covered the chin and cheek dimples. It would help to hide his identity. He often changed his looks every twenty or thirty years, because as the off-spring of Nephilim, he would not age like people who knew him would have. He would also move far away, usually to another country. But you couldn't count on it, these days, with the way people jetted around the world so easily.

The beard would stay.

He shaved only a small portion of his cheeks, and his neck—he didn't like the feel of the beard on his neck. Besides, it looked so Neanderthal.

After finishing in the bathroom, he moved to his closet—the large one behind his master suite bedroom, off the bath. Here he had many drawers and several closets from which to choose an array of suits, slacks, sweaters and shoes. He opened closets, to consider what sort of persona he wanted to have. Again the need for anonymity pushed his search exhaustively through all five closets. Then, he found the duster he he'd had for ages. Dark gray, it had the cape over the shoulders. *Perfect!* Above this was a shelf where he kept hats. He didn't often wear a hat, but he needed something with a wide brim. His brilliant-green eyes would give his identity away almost instantly if someone who knew him from before spotted him. He found the black fedora—*again, perfect!*

Quickly he chose dark charcoal pants and heavy shoes to walk through the slush of a Chicago winter. He didn't need to stay warm, but he chose a black sweater. He would be able to roam dark alleys and not be noticed. Looking in the mirror he pulled on the over-coat and fedora. With fingers he adjusted the brim over his eyes. Now he looked like Hugh Jackman as Van Helsing. He shrugged. *Eh. I'm better looking though.*

Moving swiftly, with intent, he grabbed up his wallet and exited the closet. With quick steps he swept through the bedroom, darted down the stairs. Grabbing the keys from a hook, he strode through the door to the garage. He lived in a quiet suburb. The white Lexus was parked in his garage, just where he'd left it weeks ago. He wondered if he should take it or use those powers Nemesis had given him. He realized the car wouldn't be necessary. No more than a thought, the next second he was standing at the Elburn Train Station.

There was no one around, and he went quickly to buy his ticket. He thought about where he wanted to go in Chicago, but wasn't certain he should simply pop into the city, where he needed without alerting certain magical creatures like elves who would feel his presence if he used his powers to simply pop into Tremayne Towers.

No. A train was better. He'd have time to think about what he would do, once he got there.

Chapter 13

Forgiven

The knock on the door came approximately five or six minutes after I'd gotten the call from the front desk. I'd asked Dante to stay—in his invisible form, of course—and watch over Lindee, who now had her feet up on the coffee table, munching on microwave popcorn and watching an old movie. I wanted more than ever to just hang out and watch the movie with her. But I knew that wasn't to be.

I opened the door to Stefan's smile and shimmery dark-blue eyes. He wore his usual dark suit with a black shirt and this time it was a pearl-white tie. His vampire scent of leather and licorice hit me just right, and made me want to suck him all in through my nose like a drug. He had formidable pheromones, plus that bad-boy smirk on his face should have been illegal.

Stefan took me in, pretty much the same way I had him. I wore my skinny jeans and the new dark-blue shirt that felt like velvet with a shimmery design across the front. I detected a bit of a crest-fallen look on his face. It was almost like I was going out with him and he'd expected me to dress up. Sorry. I did that last night.

"Well, are you ready?" he asked, and my eyes had gone to his mouth, watching it move. Looking forward to hearing his voice, as well as watch his lips. I couldn't help myself. *What am I doing? Stop. Just stop!*

Looping my bag over my shoulder, I said, keeping my head down, my eyes averted. "I guess." To Lindee I said, "Don't wait up for me, Lin."

"Don't worry," Lindee said. "I'm watching a movie and then going to bed. I'm beat."

"Okay, then. 'Night."

"'Night."

I stepped out of the door with Stefan. I had nothing to say to Stefan, and he was silent too as we got on the elevator and we rode down to the lobby. We stepped out and a familiar face filled my view. Malcolm McFeely.

"Oh, well hello, Ms. Sabrina," Malcolm said, smiling when he saw me, taking me in first, and then his eyes lifted to take in my vampire escort. His smile faded. "Oh. Are you going out for the evening?" He sounded slightly disappointed.

"No. Staying in. I'm just going across to the other side," I said.

"Ah!" he said, stepping on the elevator as we exited it. "Well, have a very good night, my dear," he said with a little wave.

"You too, Malcolm," I said.

We strode to the other end of the lobby and Stefan pulled out his card to swipe in order to go through to the vampire side. "Who was that?" he asked, still looking back at the bank of elevators, as though he could still see Malcolm.

"Malcolm McFeely," I said. "I met him last night at the party. He's a retired donor to Letitia."

"Ah, I see." He turned back to the door, dismissing the whole thing. The door slid open and we stepped into the lobby of the vampire side of the hotel. From there, we stepped onto another elevator with several other vampires. Stefan slid a card into a slot and pressed the button for *Penthouse* and stepped back next to me, his eyes keeping watch over the other vampires in the lift with us. The male vampires looked back at me. They all had a date on the arm. In other words, donors. One woman had long blonde hair, but when she looked back at me, I found she had skin as dark as coffee, and she wore bright red lipstick and false eyelashes. I thought she looked like she was going to model for a cover of a magazine. I had to block all the humans—especially the women. One was nervous; she'd never been with a vampire before and her thoughts were racing. Being telepathic as well as psychic made it a hell of a lot harder to block them, and their thoughts. I had to fill my head with *lalalalalal…TMI, TMI, TMI…*

Stefan cleared his throat, and moved a hand to his white tie, making a smoothing motion. A pinky ring shimmered brilliantly. I wasn't sure if this was some sort of vampire warning gesture, but the two male vampires turned back around and didn't look at me again. One of them put a hand positively on the left butt-cheek of the woman he was with. Maybe they'd caught Stefan's stronger pheromones, and knew not to mix it up with him. It was like I was with a mob boss. Maybe, in a way, I was.

When the group hopped off we were alone, and we had about sixty-two more floors to ride. At least I could now relax. Well, not completely, but I got no reads from Stefan.

"Sabrina," Stefan said. I looked over at him, standing against the wall, having taken a couple of steps away from me, giving me breathing room. "I understand that what you saw last night made you angry, but believe me, that was part of—"

I held my hand up. "Already got it. Okay? I had a talk with Tremayne, and I'm going up to speak with my husband and allow him to make amends."

"Oh. Well, good," he said, visibly relaxing. *Sheesh.* It was like it was all on his head for me to forgive Vasyl. It wasn't. I knew what I had to do, and had prepared myself for tonight—the best I could, anyway. I tried to accept the one thing I had to do to keep demons from wanting to go after me. Rogue vampires was another thing. That's why I'd retrieved my dagger (but left it with Lindee). *Am I really ready for this?* My question came while I twisted the fingers of my one glove.

"I just want you to know that he feels very badly for his actions. That's the truth," Stefan said. "It took a long time to get him calmed down, last night and assure him he could rectify this with you."

"I know. He was tempted, yada, yada. Whatever." I leaned against the wall of the elevator, cocked one ankle over the other. I wore my comfortable sneakers tonight. No high-heeled anything for me for at least a week. My toes ached so badly I could barely walk, plus I had a nasty blister on one heel, which I'd gotten a band aide from the front desk for.

He stared at me for almost a minute but said nothing more. The ride was silent again.

Once we got to the penthouse, I allowed Stefan to step off before me. He stopped outside the elevator, holding the doors, waiting for me to step off before moving down the short hallway.

I expected him to knock on the door of what used to be Tremayne's penthouse but he didn't. He rapped on Letitia's penthouse door. I mentally checked myself. I had to quit thinking of this as Letitia and Tremayne's penthouses. They were now *our* penthouses. That was difficult to accept.

Stefan used another key card and opened the door, but he didn't step in. He made a little hand motion for me to step in, while he remained outside.

"He is expecting you. Have a good evening, Sabrina," Stefan said in a slow, drawn out manner, eyes drawing down and up my form. My brows rose, letting him know I wasn't impressed by him. He made a little bow, holding the door for me.

I stepped inside, then looked back at him. Stefan let the door shut, sealing me inside. Whatever would happen, would happen. I had to check myself mentally, wondering why this felt as though I were going to be sentenced to jail time. Or that something really weird was about to play out. I huffed at myself and a smile formed. "I'm being silly," I said low to myself.

Lights were low and music played softly from somewhere within. I recognized it from the movie "The Proposal" with Sandra Bullock. The aroma of flowers filled my nose.

I realized the lights weren't low, they were off. The amber glow was given off by a gazillion little candles all over the place and created a warm, sensual atmospherc. I stood trying to understand what was spread over the various tables—and wherever there was a flat space. Then, it all became clear as my werewolf vision took over. Vases of flowers—mostly roses—and huge teddy bears sitting in chairs or along a sofa, all of them holding huge heart-shaped boxes of chocolates. Where Vasyl could have gotten Valentine hearts of chocolates in December, I don't know. Vases of roses of every color imaginable cluttered every available space where they could sit. The white Baby Grand was an explosion of roses, carnations and daises, while smaller teddy bears held more boxes of chocolates. Someone had arranged all of this—my Knowing supplied—from a local florist. They had done a magnificent job.

I stepped further in, wondering where Vasyl was, when my foot crunched on something. I looked down. It was a piece of parchment. I picked it up. It had writing all over it. It said only two words over and over and over again: *I'M SORRY.* I turned it over. The same thing was written on that side too.

I looked along the path and found another piece of parchment. I picked it up and on it was written in very large writing: *PLEASE FORGIVE ME?*

Taking two more steps more I found another piece of paper. I didn't need to pick it up, because I could read what it said where it lay: *IF YOU FORGIVE ME FOLLOW ARROWS.* A few more feet away, was another sheet of paper with a large arrow drawn on it with black marker. Then there was another arrow a few feet after that one. My heart drumming with excitement, I followed the arrows to a hallway. There were two more arrows up the hall. One pointed to a white double door with brass handles. This had once been Letitia's bedroom. I continued to the door and put my gloved hand on one of the beaver-tail handles.

Opening the door I found that the white carpet was littered with red rose petals, more candles glowed in sconces on the wall. The décor and furnishings were all new and very different from when Letitia had lived here. But then, I shouldn't have been surprised.

My eyes drifted toward the bed. Round, and on a pedestal, you had to step up to it. Draped in white chenille and surrounding it was thin red gauze hung from a central spot in the ceiling. Following the draping downward, I spotted Vasyl bare chested wearing only white draw-sting pants.

Our eyes met. His were the lightest of lavender I had ever seen on him, and the pupils, although dilated, were not over-large. His whole expression was held in his eyes, and they took on his emotions. Sad, mostly, but slightly expectant while waiting to see what I would say, or do.

"Sabrina. I beg your forgiveness," he said. "I was overwhelmed, last night." Hand over his face, he shook his head. Swallowing, he looked up at me, tears in his eyes, and gulped out, "I do not ask forgiveness very often, and I do not know how to do it. I hope I have done it all correctly—"

"Yes," I said, my voice soft. "Beautiful. Wonderful. Really. I'm not one of those women who holds a grudge." Eyes doleful, he waited. "If you can forgive me for those things I did—you know, before?—then I can forgive you."

"I will understand if you wish to not be with me tonight. It is—how you say—okay?"

I smirked a little. He had no idea what his display of his affections and desire to make up to me for last night did to me. I knew that he would do everything in his power to not do that again.

I stepped forward, and kept walking toward him until I was in his arms and looking up into his amethyst eyes.

"If I cannot have you, I would rather not go on in this life," his voice broke.

I pressed my fingers to his lips, shushing him. "You're pretty much stuck with me, since we're married and all."

He smiled and pulled me close. The feel of his arms around me made me tingle with desire. I availed my lips to him and we kissed. It lasted a while, but when our lips parted, I said, "I think if we have make-up sex after every fight, we might set a world record, or something."

He chuckled, leaned his head on top of mine, his arms wound around me tighter and he held me so close I thought I would simply melt into him, and that's exactly what I wanted to do. We would go slow tonight. It was going to be a long, long night.

* * *

Stefan's cell phone chirped. He checked it quickly and saw who it was from. He answered it.

"*Carpe Noctem,*" Stefan greeted.

"Is she with him?" The baritone asked.

"Yes, sire. She has been with him a few moments."

"Good. Make sure she stays with him throughout the night."

"I will, sire."

"And under no circumstances she leaves that penthouse. Got it?"

"Yes, sire. I am about to be relieved and have my second in command to take over."

"Very well. I know that the werewolves are out of commission for time being," Tremayne said. "You understand that in order for me to remain in charge, and the demons to take the threat of death completely off me and her, she has to become pregnant." A pause and then he added. "At this point, I don't really care who does it."

Stefan paused thinking that was an odd statement, but then after what Bjorn had gone through trying to fulfill the prophesy, it really wasn't all that odd. "I understand," he said.

"Actually, I'm telling you now that if she is not pregnant it in, say a month, then I'm giving you an order to do it yourself."

"Me, sire?" Stefan was flabbergasted, pressing a hand to his chest. He tried to not sound excited.

Tremayne's voice went low. "Stefan, I speak to you now as my son, not my minion. I sired you, yes, but you are my son first and always. You have the ability to sire children from a human female."

Stefan's brow arched and his lips quirked. How well he knew this. But tracking the child to adulthood and turning them was another thing entirely. Even that had been banned in the past two hundred and fifty—or so—years. And this was their little secret. Very few people knew that Stefan was Tremayne's son from a human woman back oh so many centuries ago. In fact, he wasn't certain if any one who presently lived in America knew this.

"I tried to do it—hell—I *did* do it, but she nearly killed me. Plus she was on the pill, which fucked the whole thing up. I had a talk with her. Actually, on two occasions, now. She understands this is necessary and I hope that she isn't going to try and avoid going through with this. Anyway, she knows how important it is."

"I understand, father."

"At any rate, you have my permission to do whatever necessary to make sure she does get pregnant."

"Yes, father," Stefan said, licking his lips, thinking about the possibility of actually having Sabrina, should Vasyl somehow fuck up.

The elevator doors slid open and Styles stepped off. He had summoned him a few moments ago. Styles nodded to him, Stefan held up a finger to hold him off for one more moment.

"I will give you a full report tomorrow evening," Stefan said into the phone.

"Very good," Tremayne said.

"How are things there?" Stefan ventured to ask.

His father sighed heavily. "Computers are down. Some little fuck of an asshole—a scion of Ilona's—actually began destroying computers and went so far as to put a virus into certain files. I've got a fucking mess to deal with here."

"I don't envy you," Stefan said. Insults aimed at the culprit over the phone made Stephan smirk.

"Anyway, I'm knee-deep in crap. I've got meetings scheduled for the next 48 hours. Lawyers, mostly. I haven't even seen the estate yet." His brother's estate, Stefan knew, was left to him after his brother's death—the only thing that was not left to Ilona. "Plus I have to prove that Ilona is dead, or at least incapacitated. So, I'm having someone fly the pieces of Ilona out tonight."

"I thought you disposed of them," Stefan said.

"I'd thought about it, and then realized I had to prove she was turned to stone."

Stefan made a non-committal grunt. "Well. I'll let you go. *Carpe noctem.*"

"*Carpe noctem.*"

Stefan closed his cell phone and looked up at Styles. "You will guard this door. No one goes in. And absolutely no one comes out. Especially the sibyl. If she is able to get past you, for whatever reason, you call me. I will take over from there."

"Understood, sire," Styles bowed.

Stefan strode to the elevator and got on. He opened his cell phone and hit the number for Donor Pool.

"Donor Pool," a rushed voice answered after two rings.

"Yes. This is Stefan Capella. I would like to request a specific female to come to room 9607."

"What's the name?"

"Elaina—I don't know her last name. But she's a redhead. She was sent up to Vasyl last night?"

"Just a moment." They would have record of who was sent up to Vasyl. "Sir, I think she's busy right now with another customer."

His temper flared and he spoke in a voice that was barely contained to a low growl. "I don't care if she's busy. She must leave whoever she's with and come to my room. Understand?"

"Sir, I realize your need, but can't we send another?"

"Look. You get this straight. I am Stefan Capella, the fucking second in command here in Tremayne Towers. I'm requesting a female to be sent to me, *now*, or I'll go and find her and I don't care how many doors I have to knock down. And then I'll come and tear your head off with my bare hands!"

"Sir, calm down, I-I can call her, okay? I have her cell. I'll tell her to be at your room in ten minutes." The man's voice was edgy, but he cowed down to him, as was expected.

"Make if *five*," he said and slapped his cell phone closed.

The elevator doors opened to the ninety-sixth floor and he strode three steps to the door of his room. With a swipe card he gained entry. His strides took him through the luxurious confines, which he mostly ignored, down a hallway and into his bedroom. There he removed all his clothes and chose a dark blue crushed velvet robe from his wardrobe, and slipped it on. His excitement had been brought on by all the talk of mating with Sabrina. How he wished a hundred times a hundred Vasyl wouldn't be able to perform his duty.

Unfortunately, he could by the looks of things.

Approximately five minutes later, the quiet knock on the door brought his attention around. His mouth turned up with both satisfaction and anticipation. Stepping back up the hall, he stood facing the door. He could smell her on the other side, slightly excited, but also had been engaged in sex with another. With only a thought, the lock disengaged, and the door swung opened.

The redhead slumped through the doorway wearing a white dress that left little to the imagination, thick hair hear disheveled, she looked tired. The dark circles under her eyes indicating she'd donated possibly a little too much, or a few too many nights in a row.

"I've already given blood tonight," she said. "I really don't think I can give any more. Sorry." She turned to leave. Stefan closed the door with his vampiric abilities. She looked back at him, with a weary look.

"Look, asshole—"

"That's alright," he said and dropped the robe from his shoulders, letting it pool at his feet. "I don't need a… donation of blood, tonight."

Her eyes glanced down at him and she smiled appreciatively at what she saw.

"I've got another problem I was hoping you could help me with," he said.

"Oh, I think I can help you with that," she said on a purr. "You're Steven, right?"

"Stefan," he corrected, upper lip slipping high. Her eyes fell on his lips. *That's right. Look at me… look at my face… my lips…*

"Stefan. I'll remember that." She nodded, her eyes almost going vacant, but definitely on his lips.

"I promise you, you will remember my name. You'll be screaming it before the night is through."

Chapter 14

Second in Command

"You are bleeding."

Vasyl's words shocked me, and especially where his eyes had gone, and, more disconcerting, his fangs were completely out.

Laying on the bed completely naked, I smelled it. Then I felt the heaviness of my lower abdomen and the twinge in my lower back. My menses had started.

"Oh, God," I said with realization hitting me. "Oh, crap." *Tonight of all nights!* My back and lower abdomen pangs had been the heralding signals all day and even a slight headache last night, and I had chosen to ignore them.

In the next second, a huge black jaguar materialized across my lower limbs, made a horrifying snarl and batted the air in front of Vasyl's face, just missing his nose by mere inches. Vasyl backed away, and didn't stop until he was completely off the bed. With the intensity of the cat's viscous hissing, growling and swatting those huge cat claws of his, I couldn't blame him.

"Dante!" I gasped, getting up on my elbows. Dante was effectively keeping me from moving much. He was a heavy cat.

Vasyl backed away, eyes on the cat, muttering words much too fast for me to understand—or maybe it was French he spoke. Whatever had him spooked—my blood, or Dante's jaguar (or both)—he backed away and then turned and shot out of my room so fast he was a blur. Crying words in French, it reminded me a lot of the first time when Tremayne had me in his bed, nicked me with his fangs and fled. That was before it was known I was the sibyl.

Propped up on my elbows, I looked at Dante in jaguar pelt. His green eyes turned to me and then he promptly lay down on me right across my abdomen and lower legs.

"You're too heavy. Get off," I said to him, pushing at him.

The jaguar lifted himself off of me, leaped and formed into a man in mid-air. He landed on his two feet, his back to me. Long black hair trailing down his nude body. In the next few seconds clothes covered him, and he turned around to face me.

"My Lady, pardon my intrusion, but you are in danger. You must get into the bathroom at once! Lock the door. I will guard you."

I moved, now my aches were much worse than moments before. I rolled over, and as soon as I stood, the pain clutched me so badly I doubled up, putting my hand to my belly. I didn't dare look back at the sheets—the wetness trailing down my thighs told the story. I scrambled into the bathroom, slammed the door shut, barely getting it locked, and sat on the toilet, pulling a wad of toilet paper into my hand to clean myself as best I could. Once I did what I could, I put my elbows on my knees, and tears slipped from my eyes.

"Shit," I cried. I said a few more things, not worth repeating here.

"My Lady, whatever you need, tell me," Dante's voice came through the door. "I'll gladly get anything you need."

I realized I had nothing here to address my menses.

"Go to my house. My bathroom. Bottom drawer. Bring it all. Also the pills—you know the ones—in the cupboard, over the sink? They help the pain." The pain, which was becoming even more excruciating as the moments passed. I worried about this. I had not had a very heavy period since going on the birth control pills. But I'd missed a couple of pills here or there. Now my ugly monthly visitor was going to get its revenge. My menses was usually very heavy to the point I needed both a pad and a Tampex. I hadn't missed any of it and vowed I'd get back on the pill as soon as this was done. Screw whatever the vampires and demons wanted. I didn't want to get pregnant. Not now. Maybe not ever.

"I will get these things for you, after I speak to Stefan," he said. "I will return as soon as I can."

"Okay," I said wanting those things as soon as possible. The pain was mounting and it would take the pills a while to work on the cramping. I eyed the bathtub. I had not been in this penthouse bathroom before. It was large. A large shower resided in a separate room, basically. The large bathtub sat on a two-step-up pedestal and was also huge. I thought it may be more of a jacuzzi than a bath tub. My Knowing told me it had jets in it and I wanted very badly to get the water going, but not in my condition without something to absorb the blood. If I moved across the floor it would look like someone had been bludgeoned in here. I didn't want to think about my having left a trail from the bed into here—*Gak!*

Elbows on my thighs again, I let my mind go blank and my Distant Vision revealed Dante and what was happening out in the hallway.

Dante stepped out into the hall, surprising the vampire there.

"Call Stefan to get his ass up here, now."

The vampire nodded. "I saw Vasyl come through. What happened?"

"Call Stefan. Tell him that Sabrina is in the bathroom. I will speak to him once I return."

The vampire nodded, held up his phone and poked at it a few times. He looked up and Dante disappeared.

* * *

The chirping of his phone interrupted him mid-stroke. Elana was moaning with another release after he'd licked one of her vampire hickeys.

This had better be important. He looked at the read out. Styles.

"Shit. I'm sorry. I'd better take this." He leaned up on his knees, pulling out of her.

Elaina made an exasperated sigh. Throwing a leg over to join the other, she rolled over and turned her naked back on him. He had noticed she didn't have very much meat on her, and now he was looking at her ribcage and backbones. *Christ does she eat?*

Stefan grabbed his phone and sat up to answer.

"What is it, Styles?"

"Sire? I'm sorry to bother you, but a situation has arisen," Styles said.

"What is it?"

"You told me to call if Vasyl or the woman came out. Well, Vasyl shot out of there like he'd gone mad."

"What? I'll be right up." He closed his cell phone and grabbed his pants. "I've gotta go. Sorry."

"Figures," she said and groped for her clothes on the floor.

While Elaina dressed, he pulled on his trousers, and then his shirt and buttoned it quickly. It didn't take her long. She didn't wear much to begin with.

She stomped out of the room without a word. *Fuck, she's mad. Oh, fucking well. She's too skinny for my tastes.*

He followed her back through his apartment, stuffing his shirt into his pants. He paused at the mirror and did his best to finger-comb out his tousled hair.

"See you," he said.

She threw her bag over her shoulder and gave him a harsh look over the other and said, "Don't count on it."

No big loss. He stepped out into the hall. Pulling his door shut, he heard it lock automatically. He watched Elaina twitch down the hall to the regular elevators. Then, he located his special key card in his pocket, turned to the elevators with the vampire glyphs above the doors, and passed it through the electronic reader. The doors hissed opened for him. It was a quick ride to the next, and top floor. He was hyper alert, felt the thumping in his chest deepen. *If something's happen to the sibyl my name is shit.*

"What is it, Styles?" he said as soon as the doors opened to the penthouse, and surged forward.

"I don't know, sire. Vasyl crashed out of there and went back into his place so fast, even I couldn't see him. Then some Indian dude told me to get you up here. I was about to, actually," he added sheepishly.

"Is she alright?" he asked.

"I don't know. I only saw Vasyl and the Indian. He said she's in the bathroom." Styles shrugged.

"Who said she was in the bathroom?"

"The Indian."

Stefan didn't know who he meant by *Indian.* He opened the door to Sabrina's penthouse with his passkey card. Stepping in he called out.

"Hello? Sabrina?"

The heavy odor of candle wax hit him. He took in the room, all aglow in candlelight. Large teddy bears, and heart-shaped boxes, and vases of flowers met his eyes. *Oh, yes, they did a wonderful job here,* his thoughts came remembering he'd had someone call a local flouriest for the touches of romance. To him, he felt they'd over done it with the teddy bears, and scowled at one holding a heart-shaped box of chocolates. A subtle scent beneath the candle's light caught him completely by surprise, quite opposite of the innocent look of the room. The heavy blood scent stopped him cold in his tracks. He had to fight his natural urges—both his desire to drink the woman's blood, and mate with her. He could do nothing about the hard-on at the moment, but he fought his blood desires before moving through the apartment. Styles said she was in the bathroom. *What's happened to her? If Vasyl lost it...*

But the blood's scent was different. Richer.

As he moved through the apartment he blew out the candles, the wicks sent up small plumes of choking smoke. The glass felt hot. He didn't want to have a fire on top of everything else. He wasn't sure if Vasyl had lit all these himself, or if he'd had help.

The heavy scent of blood brought him back to why he was here. It confused him at first, and then he knew what it was, and why it was so heavy—rich—and slightly *different.*

This was woman's menses blood.

"Sabrina?" He called out again when he entered the hallway that led to the master bedroom. "It's me. Stefan. Are you okay? Do you need—help?" This was really different. Him asking a human woman if she needed help.

No one answered. But he detected a warm, human heartbeat, so she wasn't dead. That one thing lifted his hopes—Vasyl had gotten out in time before the gushing blood had overwhelmed him to the point of no return. That took super will in any vampire to get away from a menstruating woman. Back in the day, a vampire hunted the menstruating woman if he were in bad need of a blood feast.

Stefan swallowed and paused before moving through the opened doorway of the bedroom. The scent was heavy in there. He took two steps and stopped. His eyes took in the large bed. She wasn't in it. *Bathroom.* He scanned the bed and rest of the room. Blood soaked the sheets and droplets trailed the floor to the door of the bathroom.

He turned away quickly and retraced his steps, and stepped out into the hallway where Styles waited. "We have a Hazmat situation in there," he said.

Styles grimaced and his fangs ejected from his upper jaw. "Shit! I smell it on you!"

"Just call the Sanguine Team up here now!"

Styles twirled away from him, flipped open a small metal box on the wall, and hit a red button. Right away a red light began to flash both over the button and now overhead. *That's how they do it here, like a fire alarm? My father's ingenious!*

"I'm going to stay until the team arrives. You get the hell out of here. Now." Stefan stood before the door, blocking him.

Styles didn't argue. Nodding he dashed to one of the regular elevators, jumped on and left.

Stefan faced the penthouse door across from him. He realized it was ajar and stepped in.

"Vasyl?" he called, but didn't need to. He heard someone crying. *What the fuck?*

The noises of alternate crying and blubbering continued until he tracked down the master vampire. He was huddled in his bedroom on the floor, arms wrapped around his legs. He had on a pair of white apartment pants and that was all. Head down between his knees he wept and didn't appear to know Stefan was there.

"Vasyl? What happened?"

Large, bloody tear-stained eyes looked up at him.

"I cannot be with her any longer." Vasyl wiped his eyes with the heal of his hand. "I must leave."

"Because of the blood? Get hold of yourself, Vasyl." He tried to think of what to do for him. "You need blood? I'll get you something. Just stay put." Holding a hand out to him, he ran out of the room, and into the kitchen, threw open the refrigerator, and grabbed a bottle of Real Red. But remembering Vasyl had asked for horse blood earlier, he replaced the Real Red, and grabbed the Organic II. He opened it and popped it into the microwave for twenty-five seconds—his own preference—and marched back into the bed room and handed it to Vasyl.

"Here. Have a few slugs of this." He held out the bottle.

Vasyl grabbed it and, with tears still running down his cheeks, he drank, but then stopped and spit it out.

"What is that? Horse blood?" he said. "It tastes terrible!"

"I'm sorry, my Lord. Would you prefer the Real Red?" God, he felt like a damned waiter all of a sudden.

"No! Never mind." Brows bunched, he stood. "I must go."

"What? Go? Where to?"

"Wherever. I cannot be near her." His violet-blue eyes blazed red. He'd seen that look in other vampire masters before. The blood desire so intense, they were always near madness when it came on.

"But, you're supposed to be the magnate of the eastern half! You can't leave!" Stefan argued.

"I must. Don't you understand?" Vasyl growled. "I would kill her. Her blood is irresistible to me now. I want it more than anything." He shook his head. "Tell Tremayne I abdicate my throne to whoever is next in line."

Stefan raised a hand. "Wait." But Vasyl vanished like a puff of smoke. He was gone.

Stefan stood there in cold silence taking in his new situation. *He* was next in line for the throne of the eastern half of the United States.

"What sort of turn of fate is this?" Stefan said low to himself, a smile forming. But Tremayne's reaction to what just happened would not be easy to wade through. But he had to make the call, and let him know.

Shoulders slumped, he pulled out his phone, hit his father's number on speed dial. When it connected to his voice mail, he spoke quickly, but distinctly. "Vasyl has abdicated his dominion. Call me at once. A situation involving Sabrina's blood has occurred." He paused, blew out a breath and added, "I am now in charge, in Vasyl's absence."

Stefan strode through the penthouse. Stepping out into the hall, he closed the door. He used his swipe card to enter Sabrina's side. *What's taking those infernal elves so fucking long?*

* * *

About ten minutes later (felt more like an hour), Dante brought the things I needed, handing them to me through the door—which I had to get up and open. He also handed me a robe to put on. I got myself covered as soon as I took care of things. But I was a mess.

"Dante, could you make a bath for me?" I asked, settling on the small dressing couch next to the door. "I'm really not feeling well enough." I needed to clean myself up.

"Of course." He stepped through the door without opening it—he simply stepped through the solid door. "Relax, My Lady. I will make you a warm bath." He strode through the large tiled bath. "I've had Stefan send for the Sanguine Team. They should be here shortly. They will clean things up. Until they get here, do not step out of this room."

"What about Vasyl? He didn't do anything," I said.

"I know he didn't. He left you in time."

I looked down at my trembling hands. The sound of rushing water filled the room. I watched Dante's lithe movements as he dribbled some liquid bath scents into the water. I tried not to think about anything. I felt uncomfortable to the point of shame. I couldn't get over Vasyl's look of—what was it? Horror? *No. Horror mixed with desire.*

Mortified, putting my hands over my face, I gasped.

"You will feel better shortly. Did you take the pills?"

I nodded and brushed back my hair from my face to look at him.

There was a knock on the bathroom door.

"Sabrina?"

"Stefan," Dante said. "I'll handle it. You take your bath. Don't worry about anything." Dante strode forward and stepped through the doorway again, like a ghost.

* * *

When Dante stepped through the solid door, Stefan jerked back and stared at him.

Dante leaned against the door and crossed his arms, giving him a defiant look, mixed with a slight smirk. The vampire's desires were heightened. He remembered Dante Badheart from visits here. But he thought the man had died. What the fuck?

"Shifter, you're here?" Stefan said carefully. Realization tugged at him. The man was no longer a living man. He wasn't even a vampire. What the hell—?

"I am." Dante watched a couple of expressions cross the vampire's face, one of surprise morphed into confusion, and then a light went on.

"I thought you had died," he said, then looked embarrassed. "I-I mean no disrespect."

"Do I look dead to you?"

Stefan visibly jerked again. Blinking he said. "You're not alive, whatever you are."

"You're correct," Dante said. "You called the Sanguine Team?"

"They should be on their way. How is she? She isn't hurt, is she?"

"No. Her woman's blood is all over the bed. She didn't know she was into her menses when she came here. It happened abruptly."

Stefan licked his lips and ran fingers through his hair. "Can I speak with her?"

"No." Dante stood statue-like. No one was going to get in without his allowing it. "She is taking a bath right now. I've made her as comfortable as I could." He paused and looked up. Awareness filled him. The notes of the beginning of a song sounded.

"You'd better answer that. Your father's calling you."

Stefan's phone chirped again and he pulled it out of his pocket. He looked down at the screen and stepped away from the bathroom door. At the same time three female elves surged into the bedroom looking all business, glaring at him. Two male elves surged in behind them.

In his ear, Stefan heard, "What the fuck is going on there?"

The two male elves made a wall in front of the bedroom door, arms crossed, jaws clenched.

Behind him, Dante said, "Let him pass. The woman is fine. Just guard the door."

"We need to speak face to face," Bjorn said in Stefan's ear.

"Right. One moment." Stefan slipped passed the elfin guards, stalked out of the penthouse, crossed the hall and into the other one. He eventually found the remote for the TV in the den. He hit the power button and suddenly his father was looking out at him from the screen, arms crossed, with a hard teal glare.

"Explain."

"Sire," Stefan said, working to figure out how to put all the details into organized words and thoughts. Hell. Tonight had been bizarre.

"As you know, Vasyl was with Sabrina. She apparently had her—um—monthly? And Vasyl became overwhelmed by the blood." He held his hand up when he saw his father's ire work on his face. "Sabrina is fine. He didn't touch her. He got out of there in time. As a matter of fact he is gone from the towers. Like I've reported. He has abdicated."

"But he hasn't even been in power for twenty-four hours! Where did he go?"

"I don't know. He vanished from the room."

His father sighed exhaustively. "Is the Sanguine Team there?"

"Yes. And, sire, Dante is there with her. I don't quite understand what is going on with your shapeshifter, but—"

"I forgot to tell you. He's become an Undead. He is with Sabrina, now. *Always*." Then his voice went into a deadly serious tone. "Beware of him."

"I will." Stefan paused to let that sink in. Now he knew who *the Indian* was, but this was a new one on him. He'd never seen or met an Undead before.

"Father? Am I now in power?" He wasn't sure if he could afford to assume anything at this point.

"You are. For the time being. You remember what I said?"

"Earlier? Yes." Stefan felt a delightful tingling at his groin. Just the mention of making sure Sabrina became pregnant sent messages throughout his body that would channel his mating instincts. As if he needed any more encouragement. A thrill went through him, not only for the chance to be with her, but now he was finally in the most powerful place under his father. He was now second to him only—head of the Vampire Association of the eastern half of the United States. He could hardly drink this all in.

"You will take it slowly with her, once she's done with her—eh—monthly."

Stefan bowed. "I am your second in command, father. I will not disappoint you."

"I hope to hell you don't."

Chapter 15

City Rats & Street Cats

Bill knew once he came into the city he'd find the scum that looked for opportunity. They liked dark places where they could wait for their victims—someone easy, someone not able to fight off the aggressor. Bill was confident something was about to happen.

Moving steadily along the subway, Bill used his better sight and smell to locate any humans in the vicinity. He had gotten on the train in Elgin, transferred a few times, and now was in the subway. Closer to downtown, and closer to Tremayne Towers, certain that's where Sabrina would be. He hadn't meant to get off so soon, but his gut feeling made the decision. He had to be *here* now, for whatever the reason.

Moving along the subway platform toward the exit, up ahead two people standing in the quiet station platform waiting, presumably, for a train, made him slow down. The two– a man and a woman, were not together. Again that niggling feeling that something was amiss, or about to happen thrilled through him.

That's when he saw something he wasn't prepared for. Unbelievably the man's fists were beating on the smaller woman. She screamed, held her arms up to protect herself, but it did no good. The woman's struggles subsided. Before Bill could reach them, the man—who was quite large and wearing the usual baggy pants and hood—threw the woman over the platform, down onto the tracks. That's when Bill's feet left the ground, he moved unseen, ghost-like, until he reached the scuffle. The man was already moving away from the platform, returning to where the woman's purse and things had fallen. Bill appeared before him. The man stopped and glared definitely at Bill.

"I don't think that belongs to you," Bill said evenly.

"What the fuck, muthafucka?" the man said, hands out. He turned back to the woman's bags and things.

"You hard of hearing? I said those aren't yours."

"Try 'n' stop me," he muttered, a sudden movement and he held a knife. The look in his eye said he had hurt, maybe even murdered people before, and would happily do it again.

"Very well. This is going to hurt you more than me," Bill said, wishing he had a better snide come back. But it would work for now because it was true.

"Well, c'mon. Bring it." The man stood and turned to face him, flicking his fingers as though aching for the chance to mix it up with him.

Bill moved Uber quick across the ten or so feet toward the large, ugly man. His fist slammed into the man's face, knocking him back several feet where he fell onto the cement and never moved again.

"Told you," he muttered. He looked questioningly to his fist. *That didn't even hurt.* Bill didn't bother to go see if the guy was alright. He didn't care. A train was whooshing through the tunnel, and the woman, who was unable to climb to safety, cried for help. Swiftly stepping over to the edge where the woman was moaning and struggling to get back onto the platform, his very white hand grasped her brown one, and he pulled her to safety with ease.

"Are you alright?" he asked.

"I-I'm gonna be okay," she said in a halting way, looking somewhat banged up and unsteady as she stood. She put a hand to her forehead, which was bleeding. Her nice light blue jacket had been darkened by the filth of the train tracks.

"Are you sure?" He helped her to her bags when she shuffled—maybe she always shuffled, he didn't know. She took one look at the man who had mugged her and then back at Bill, pointing. "You do this?"

Bill gave her a sheepish look. "I guess I did. I was a little angry."

The sound of the train horn made him turn to see the train light piercing the black tunnel. "There'll be people here soon to help," he said.

"Thank you," she said, moving for her things on the bench. "Bless you," she added, giving him a small smile.

"You're welcome," he said over his shoulder, keeping his head down as he quickly made a hasty retreat for the stairs to the street.

Knowing that there were cameras everywhere—and one had probably caught everything—Bill moved quickly and raced away, holding the brim of his hat down. He didn't stop until he climbed out of the subway onto the dark street and looked around. He wasn't completely familiar with Chicago's streets, but it looked like he was somewhere near the Loop.

He waited for a break in traffic and darted across the street. It irked him that he had emerged in the wrong place from the subway. But then, he was at the right place at the right time. He needed to get closer to Lake Shore Drive. Taxis flew passed him without even acknowledging his wave. Typical taxi drivers of Chicago—well, anywhere, actually. Paris was worse—but at lease he could speak their language.

It was mostly quiet at this hour. He turned to sniff the air to locate the lake, and the water's scent pulled him in the right direction. He looked up at a street sign. East Chicago Ave. Well, at least he was closer than before.

* * *

"I don't want to just build cars. I want to be the guy who designs them." Fritz opened the door for Teddie Johnson. Teddie came in to *Smilin' Mike's Diner* for the chili cheese burger combo special every Sunday night. The diner's name was a joke. There was no one named Mike, and the owner rarely smiled. Fritz, who worked there, always gave him a few extra fries with it, giving him a nod from the window in the kitchen, and Teddie would wink back at him. It was their little secret.

Fritz held the door as Teddie wheeled out into the cold night air. Traffic shushed through the slushy streets. Teddie pulled down his Bears winter knit cap, and wrapped the dark blue and orange scarf around his neck. His legs were wrapped in an official NFL blanket with the Bears logo boldly displayed on his lap. In the summer it would be Cubs regalia, in place of the Bears.

"Well, that's really good. I think you got some potential there." Teddie aimed his wheel chair up the icy sidewalk. "You just keep going to school, and it will happen, my friend."

Fritz walked alongside him. He was waiting for Quist to come pick him up, but he always walked Teddie to the end of the block because he enjoyed his company. He also was a tenant in his building, on the ground floor. It wasn't unusual that the two would walk and talk on their way out, going to the bus stop two blocks away. Fritz watched for Quist's gold Cadillac. He always picked him up after work and they would hang out. That is, until four months ago.

That's when they had begun doing serious things. Dangerous things that even to this day Fritz wasn't crazy about doing.

It took Quist at least ten minutes to get here from his job at Car Hop, so Fritz walked Teddie across the side street, said his goodbyes to him, and jogged back across the street.

The honk of the car turned him around and he stopped and looked back. Quist's 2007 gold Cadillac de Ville pulled up to the curb and he jumped in.

"Hey," Fritz said, pulling on his shoulder strap.

"Hey." Tunes were playing on the CD.

"U2? Really?" Fritz said, a little amazed at his choice.

Quist slid him that look that said *don't go there*. Crap. He realized the song "With or Without You", was playing. That had been Quist and Cinder's song.

"Where're we heading?" he said, hoping to cover up his stupid fumble with the first question.

"Same place as last night."

Fritz eyed him while an uncomfortable feeling washed through him. He resisted the urge to talk him out of it, which would only evolve into an argument. Last night had been the worse night they had seen in a long while. The vampires were becoming bold, and were now killing indiscriminately. They hadn't done that before. At least not before all this crazy stuff that happened after Ilona had begun putting things in their heads. She was dead, and her vampires were still acting like it was a free-for-all on humans every night.

"The turf wars between rogue vampires are putting humans at risk," Quist said while stopped at a light. A girl with strawberry-blond hair passed in front of them. She didn't glance their way, but Fritz looked at Quist and noticed how his friend followed her with his eyes, watching her cross the street. She looked a lot like Cinder Heartman. Her hair, her movements, her stride and body language was nearly like hers. But it wasn't her, of course.

Because Cinder was dead.

Had it only been six months ago Cinder had been grabbed by rogue vampires on the campus one night? It seemed much longer ago, and yet while Fritz loosened the scarf around his neck, because it was toasty warm in the car, he remembered it like yesterday. Quist had called him in the middle of the night, tearfully telling him about how Cinder had been attacked by several vampires. She'd died in his arms. That was the night when he had vowed to save humans who were attacked by rogue vampires and kill any he could. Fritz and Quist had gone to the same schools, becoming best friends almost right away in first grade, so when Quist said he was going to hunt vampires, Fritz was with him.

The song ended, the woman on the street had melted into the crowd and the light turned green. Quist turned the music off.

"Do you have the cross bow?" Quist asked, accelerating through the intersection.

"Of course." Fritz patted his duffel bag. "In here."

"Good. We'll need it. There's a nest I've located over on Hubbard Street."

"Hubbard? Isn't that close to the Towers?" Fritz asked.

"Yep," Quist said, eyes on the road. He turned north onto Dearborn. In ten minutes they were crossing the Chicago River. Fritz glanced right. Tremayne Towers loomed up like two white fangs. Looking down at the river he found its white reflection rippling like the other buildings next to it. The towers always looked surreal to him. He often thought about how people drove passed it and had no idea that vampires lived in the north tower.

Quist turned west onto Hubbard. There was no parking available on this street as they drove.

Fritz's stomach flip-flopped with the dread that built inside him. He wasn't exactly crazy about rooting out and then killing vampires. But then he was a good shot with the crossbow, and Quist was very handy with the laser. Most vampires didn't know what hit them when they attacked. But it was difficult to find them feasting on a human in the dark—until they'd gotten themselves the night goggles. They were slightly cumbersome to wear, but they worked beautifully.

"Bingo!" Quist said as he pulled into a slot vacated by someone.

Fritz looked around. He didn't recognize the buildings here.

Quist cut the engine and took out the keys. They rattled until he shoved them into a pocket.

"Ready?" Quist cut his eyes to Fritz.

"Just a sec," Fritz said and unzipped the duffel bag and pulled out his weapon. He had to load it, and did so now. "Ready."

Quist leaned his long body and reached into the back seat. "Here." He held out the night goggles.

"How many are there? Do you know?" Fritz gripped the goggles and fitted them on over his own glasses. It took a few adjustments to make them comfortable enough to wear.

"Maybe a dozen." Quist slipped his goggles on. As a rule Quist didn't like any vampires. But the rogues who hunted humans on the streets were the ones he targeted. The elves had a standing truce with those vampires who were in charge—like Bjorn Tremayne—and governed their own. But any rogue who now roamed the streets was definitely his target.

"How did you find out about them?"

"Remember those humans last night?"

"Yeah. The ones we actually did save?"

"One of them told me that there were more vampires down this street." He nodded in the direction. "He used to be a donor for the towers. He got out when that Tremayne bitch took over and my people—the elves—saved all those who worked at the towers, including the donors. It saved them from becoming their victims." Quist paused and added, "He didn't have income anymore, and went out looking for vampires who would pay him."

"That was pretty stupid of him," Fritz said.

"No joke. I told him that they were re-hiring for donors now at the towers. He's at least off the streets, now."

It was true that a number of street people hired up as donors. Not all were taken. For one thing the humans had to be clean of drugs, and although they didn't frown upon their donors having a drink or two, they didn't like drunks. Plus their hygiene played a role in whether or not they'd be hired. Vampires were very meticulous about having clean, healthy humans as their blood donors. It was why the elves were so important in this roll of finding the right donors for the job.

Quist emerged from the car with his laser wand in hands. He slid it into its holster—where he could flick a switch and charge it, which he did now. It made a high-pitched sound and when that stopped, in about five seconds, it was charged.

Fritz climbed out and felt slightly conspicuous about pulling the crossbow out of the car. At least it didn't look like a damned gun. Knees shaking, Fritz joined Quist on the sidewalk where he made a couple of passes with his eyes.

"Which way?" Fritz asked, hiking the crossbow's sling over his shoulder to carry it.

Quist pointed. "Let's start up here."

They walked. One block. Two blocks, then turned back in the direction they came. They walked up to the corner of La Salle Boulevard. The street was mostly vacant of humans. A few cars drove by, but no one seemed to notice them.

A siren sounded in the distance. It was typical to hear sirens all night long in the city, and both men ignored it and continued up the street.

* * *

Bill waved down an Uber cab, which actually stopped for him. He got in and told the man to take him to Tremayne Towers on Wabash Avenue. The cabby—a Pakistani—said he'd never heard of it.

Bill didn't know the address, but said. "Magnificent Mile."

"Oh, yes, yes! Magnificent Mile. I know, yes, yes, yes." He drove down Michigan Avenue. The sky scrapers of the Magnificent Mile stood tall, etched out a jagged line across the night sky. They all sparkled with the many lights on buildings and the trees along the sidewalks were graced with white Christmas lights. Bill had only seen the Towers once, and had wondered about them. Twin sharp spires drove into the black sky, looking like fangs. He hadn't noticed that before, because he had only seen them in the daytime. Now, he got it. Fangs, like a vampire. He had to hand it to Tremayne, he did tongue-in-cheek well.

The cab slowed and came to a stop. They sat there for a couple of minutes. Cars ahead of them honked. A siren sounded in the distance.

"What's the hold up?" Bill asked when he peered through the windshield and found traffic was backed up ahead.

"Sir, I think an accident," the cab driver said in his thick accent.

Bill sat debating what to do. He had no aversion to walking as they were within a few blocks of Tremayne Towers now.

"Thank you, my friend. I think I'll walk." He handed the man a twenty, told him to keep the change, and hopped out. He walked to the corner and found that he was on Grand Avenue, the river and Tremayne Towers only a few blocks ahead. The sound of the car horns became annoying. Why were they hitting the horn when obviously there had been an accident? Eventually, as he walked along, police began directing traffic around the accident. It looked to be a rather bad one, involving two cars.

There were plenty of people standing around gaping at it. Police and other first responders there ahead of the ambulance. One policeman had pulled out a collapsible yellow gurney from his trunk. The words "Shooting. Suspect on the run!" from an officer's radio came to his ears.

Well, that was typical on any night in Chicago. Just not that prevalent here on the Mag Mile.

Bill stepped around a small group of bystanders and gawkers, and moved down the street. Soon, the tapping of his footfalls the only sound in his ears, as the traffic had dwindled for the time being. He had that subtle but definite gut feeling again. *Now what?*

Bill stepped off the curb onto Hubbard, but quick reflexes made him step back when the car flew up Hubbard, made a U-turn, and the right rear tire went over the curb, where Bill had been just seconds before. Bad driver? Drunk Driver? Someone in such a hurry they didn't see him, or didn't care? The suspect from the shooting?

Bill stared after the brown sedan. It had a loud muffler. Something about it made Bill want to follow it. His green eyes squinted after it as it turned onto the next street down the block.

Ah. Vampires.

* * *

Fritz followed Quist to the end of the block where he turned and walked up Hubbard Street toward Wabash Avenue.

"There's nobody out here," Fritz said. The sound of a train in the distance rumbling across the tracks nearby nearly washed out his words. "Are you sure this is the street?"

"Positive." He moved out of the pool of streetlight into the shadows. The sound of a loud muffler made them turn. Headlights flashed in their eyes and they had to look away, the lights burned the eyes with the goggles on.

Quist swore.

The car's loud muffler was enough noise to wake the dead. The two men moved off the sidewalk and froze, pressing up against the side of the building.

Fritz's goggles became loose and he pulled them off. He wasn't sure what would happen if police happened along and saw them with these goggles on, and Fritz in possession of a weapon. He didn't know if crossbows were illegal to carry around or not. *Probably were.* Not to mention the laser that Quist had.

No one had ever seen such a weapon, he was sure of it. He'd often had sleepless nights just thinking about trying to explain it all. *We could go to jail.*

Fritz and Quist watched the car streak by, take the corner like a maniac and disappear. They stood still for a few minutes. Fritz shivered. It was freezing out here! His feet were cold, and wet. It seemed the cold seeped up through the souls of his feet and entered his body that way.

"Let's go this way," Quist suggested, pointing north.

Fritz followed. He had no choice. He hoped there wouldn't be any vampires out here tonight because people weren't out here. Well, except them. How dumb was that?

That's when the car that had passed them turned around and came back.

* * *

Ahead, above the Magnificent Mile, near the Michigan Avenue Bridge the illuminated fangs of Tremayne Towers called to Bill. *Sabrina is there.* Was she safe enough tonight? He wished he knew.

Sensitive hearing tracked the car. His abilities also alerted him that two humans were out tonight on this street. Not very far from his spot. The car, he was almost certain, had turned around to go after the two humans. *Rogues.*

With a shake of his head, Bill sprinted down the street. To ignore the possibility of trouble would haunt him. He couldn't know for certain that the vampires in the car were heading toward these humans, but he didn't want to learn that he might have done something to prevent a catastrophe, and didn't, later on. Better to error on the side of caution, he always said.

* * *

Fritz's heartbeats quickened when he saw the car careen toward them and make a sharp turn onto the sidewalk. The car bounced up wildly onto the sidewalk and headed straight for them.

Quist shouted something, but Fritz couldn't hear him with the sound of the engine in his ears. He dove away from the car's grill. Both men dodged in opposite directions. The car crashed into the wall where they had been standing two seconds ago. The sound of the crash deafening for an instant. The smell of gas and motor oil, and something hot filled the air around them.

Fritz fell across a mound of cold, hard snow. The crossbow fell out of his hands, and slid uselessly down the snow mound. His spine bent backward into a bow, and he pushed with a grunt to sit up, trying to get his footing, only to see five vampires jump out of the car. But instead of scattering—like they had in the past—two headed his way. It was all he could do to roll over and grab the crossbow, pull it out of the snow and aim. He squeezed the trigger. One bolt shot into a vampire's chest—into the heart, and he fell back. The other vampire was on him. Large hands grabbed Fritz and hauled him up. It was amazing what adrenaline did, and the natural instinct of fright or flight. But he couldn't fight a vampire.

Someone screamed. It sounded like him.

* * *

Twenty paces away, Quist took deadly aim with his laser, beheading two before the third one sprinted, easily jumped over the car and landed near where Fritz was.

"Fritz! The holy water!" Quist's words echoed far away.

A fist hit Fritz, jarring him, and his glasses flew off with the impact. His nose was broken, he was sure of it. A vampire growled something unintelligible, and opened his mouth. Fangs sunk into his flesh at the neck. Fritz screamed again. With freezing fingers, he fumbled in his coat pocket for the vial of holy water. He managed to pull it out and didn't drop it. His thumb nail pushed against the lid—the feel the vampire's bite gave him nearly made him retch. Finally the lid came loose and he jerked the vial at the face of the vampire whose fangs were in him.

The vampire let loose, screamed and fell back.

* * *

Quist jumped over the body of one vampire, and surged around the rear of the car. A flame started near the engine compartment. *It's gonna blow! I've gotta get Fritz and me outta here!*

Two Vampires had Fritz between them. Fritz was screaming something. It sounded like, "I gotta live. My grandmother will kill you if you kill me!"

"You fuckers! Let him go!" Quist yelled, hitting the button on his belt, and heard that high pitched squeal telling him that the laser was ready to go again.

One vampire shot away from Fritz—moved so quickly Quist didn't even see him. With one blow, he disarmed him. The laser wand flew out of his hands and he was hauled up against the car's trunk. Vampire fangs out, he hissed, an eager look in his dark eyes.

"Yes! Bite me, fucker!" *And die!*

The muffled sound of something beneath the car went *whoosh.* He thought if he didn't get himself and Fritz away from this car, they'd all go up like a bomb.

* * *

Bill heard the crash, and then screams coming from up the street. He couldn't run any faster, and so used his powers to get to the spot within a few seconds. He saw two men being accosted by four vampires—a few bodies on the ground he hoped were vampires. The car was on fire. The smell of gas was heavy. If they didn't get away from it soon it may explode.

All of the vampires were feeding. Bill reached the closest vampire feeding on a human and clutched the vampire's neck and flung him across the street like a rag doll.

The man who he had saved stood, shaking in the wake of the attack and looked up at Bill. He pointed behind them. "The car's gonna blow!" the young man shouted.

Bill turned, noticing the vampire who had just bitten the redhead was convulsing on the ground, throwing up dark blood.

"What's wrong with him?" Bill asked, pointing at the vampire.

"I'm part elf. My blood is deadly to vampires." He chuckled darkly.

Dismissing this, Bill turned swiftly to the young African American man further away from the car. His cries were what had brought him here more swiftly, but now he made no sounds.

Bill surged up behind the feeding vampires and took the two by the back of the necks, yanked them away from the man now crumpled on the ground. He brought the vampire heads together as if to clap two cymbals. The skulls came together more like chicken eggs smashed together. The sudden soft wetness meeting his hands made Bill drop them to the ground. He didn't look down at them, but moved away.

A third vampire looked up at Bill, his eyes taking in what he had done to his comrades. He turned, jumped, and scaled up the building like a spider.

Bill stepped over, dipped down and easily picked up the African American man, and cradled him in his arms. They were safe for now.

"This way!" The redhead ran ahead, and Bill kept up easily with him. Before they had gained more than twenty feet, the car exploded. Bill herded the other man into the alley. Debris fell as they ducked for cover. The hood fell on the cement with a clatter about ten feet away.

The red-head eyed Bill warily. "Where'd you come from, anyway?"

"No time. Your friend is badly hurt. You need to get him to a hospital," Bill said.

"My car is this way!" The red-head ran out of the alley and Bill followed him for two blocks. Finally coming to a gold, late model Cadillac, the younger man opened his car. Bill placed the other man's body into the backseat.

"Fritz! Hang in there buddy," the red-head called out.

"Thank you," he said, pulling open his door. "Who are you? How did you do that?"

"You're welcome." Bill backed away, pulled the brim of his hat over his eyes and ran down the way he had come. He ducked up another alley, and stopped. Barely winded from all his activity, he thought of where he wanted to be and closed his eyes. Aware he had moved in time and space, he opened his eyes. Above him two sharp spires cut into the night sky. He stood looking at the large lettering in red proclaiming: TREMAYNE TOWERS thirty feet above his head.

While he stood gaping at the building, wondering how he would get in, and where he should start, the gold Cadillac with the red-headed man driving it made a turn into the gated area for the private garage. Bill wasn't sure what to make of it. After a minute of debate, he decided that perhaps the garage would be the best place to begin his search.

Chapter 16

Well, Hell

The tea that the women from the Sanguine Team had made me drink was already taking affect. I felt groggy, relaxed, and my various other pains were now only minimal. I'd tasted chamomile in the concoction, but my Knowing provided me with the rest of the recipe that made me sleepy—*scullcap, Lady's Slipper, Hops, and catnip.*

The black jaguar—Dante—lay on the bed next to me. There was plenty of room on the round bed, so that was fine. I was glad that Dante chose to remain the jaguar as my personal guard. It might have looked awkward that I had a man in my bedroom other than my husband. He stayed near me as his animal to protect me from any vampire who might find my menses blood appealing—which included Stefan.

That was evident while he stood peering in at me from the doorway. Two male elves guarding the entrance from him, doing whatever elves did to keep a vampire from attacking a human. I did notice odd-looking guns at their sides, with a large barrel. They were not the kind that held bullets. My Knowing told me these held liquid-filled balls, slightly smaller than a ping-pong ball, that held holy water. Similar to paint balls with soft skin which broke easily when they hit something.

After I was helped out of the bath and dressed in a proper nightgown, and clean robe, Stefan was allowed to speak to me at a distance, and only because he was second in command. Actually, he was more than that, now, from what I understood. While I drank the tea, he explained that Vasyl had left, finding himself too terribly attracted to my blood to stay anywhere in the Towers. When he'd said Vasyl had left the towers it completely caught me off guard at first. But after thinking about it, I realized he would have had to do this in order to protect me. *Great. Now what?*

"I think I know where he might have gone," I'd said to Stephan.

"You do?" His brows deepened a furrow between them while peering in at me between the broad shoulders of the elf guards.

"I think so," I said. Vasyl would have gone back to his barn, twenty miles away from my home, and possibly eighty miles away from Chicago. In fact, because of my blood bond with him, I *saw* him in my mind, there in the dark barn, huddled against the rafters, crying.

"He has abdicated," Stefan said softly. Our eyes met.

Another moment of silence as I took this in. "What does that mean, exactly?" I needed to know, but I could guess.

"He no longer is magnate," Stefan said and after a few seconds pause added, "I am."

"Oh." This meant Stefan was exactly what I had suspected. He was a master vampire, but not quite as old as Vasyl or Tremayne.

My gaze drifted down to the brown ring of tea and bits of leaves left over in the cup in my hands. I still didn't know what it meant for myself or Vasyl. Was Vasyl now a rogue again? Overwhelmed by this news, I could do nothing, not even cry, because I was too tired and somewhat shocked by the news. At the moment, I could barely think straight. The bottom line was, Vasyl had found my blood way too appealing when he discovered I'd gone into my menses. To try and find him myself would be too dangerous. What was I to do? Sit and wait for him to contact me? He had no cell phone—he didn't even like using the house phone. Perhaps he'd find another way to tell me what was going on.

"You will have two elf guards for the night at your door." Stefan's eyes shifted between the two elves and he indicated them with a hand. "Do you require anything else from myself or—anyone?" Stefan asked.

"No. I'll leave, of course, as soon as I am able," I said.

"No need to leave, Sabrina," Stefan said, his voice still gentle, eyes glittering like gemstones. There was something about the way he looked at me that made me feel uncomfortable. It was similar to the way Tremayne looked at me. *That's odd that he almost looks like Tremayne in the features—his nose, lips, maybe the eyes too.* "You shall stay as my guest."

"Not here. Not on the vampire side," I put in, terrified he thought I would want to.

He blinked, taken aback, but thinking quickly he said, "No. Of course not. In the morning, we—or that is someone—will take you to the human side. I will have the penthouse there prepared for you. It's already furnished, of course. There will be a butler, maid, a cook on duty, at your disposal."

"I have a suite," I said, feeling slightly argumentative. I didn't need him to take care of me. My suite was paid up through the next several months. Tremayne had paid first month's rent, and I paid for six months in advance, believing I would need it. Always believing in my precognitive powers, there was that niggling thought I would have to have a place to stay here, in the towers. It had come into use more than just this time.

"No. Your suite is too vulnerable. Too many people have access to it. To get to the penthouse you need a special swipe card." He held up the one he had. "Like this. No one else will have it, except for myself, and the elves who guard you, and the help."

"But I'd like to go home. This isn't my home," I said.

He held up his hand. "I understand. But for now, it is my job to keep you out of harm's way." He made a small chuckle. "Mr. Tremayne's orders are for me to make certain you are comfortable, and safe. And let us not forget that your house has been under siege by demons."

"Right." Whatever. I'd actually forgotten about that one little detail. I was tired. A good night's sleep was all I wanted at this point, really. Tomorrow things would make more sense. Or not.

"Good night, then, Sabrina." Stefan had made a small head nod to me and stepped away from my bedroom door, followed by the two male elves. The door closed, leaving me with the elf woman, Maureen. She took my cup and made sure I was comfortable. Then, she left me for a few moments, but came back in.

"The vampire is gone. Dermont and Cassidy are staying to guard your door, outside."

"Thank you," I said.

She pulled up the blankets and comforter, humming while she did. She straightened and looked down at me with kindly green eyes.

"You will sleep a dreamless sleep, Sabrina." She turned out the lights, closed the door and my eyelids felt heavy.

Alone at last, I rolled over on my side and met the jaguar's gaze. Dante's green eyes watched my every move.

"I take it you're going to stay right there tonight?" I asked.

The jaguar rolled over on his side and yawned, one large paw flopped on my arm.

"Okay. Just don't hog the bed." I snuggled into my pillow. Sleep came swiftly. I couldn't hold my eyes open another minute. My muscles relaxed thanks to the tea. Vasyl's leaving me because of the blood problem began to fade in importance. Maureen hadn't lied. I did not dream.

I woke with the jaguar curled up beside me. I thought it odd that it's chest didn't rise or fall, but then I realized if Dante was an Undead, and didn't need to breath, then so was the animal beside me. The bedroom had a balcony, and the drapes were drawn, and yet the light of the new day seeped in around the edges. This was where Letitia had died—not exactly here, but out there on the balcony. New carpet, new paint, new furnishings would not make that go away. I could not stay here with that to haunt me. It was a good thing the tea that Maureen had given me was strong enough to hold back my visions, because I might have had a few residual ones, merely because I was in a room where someone had been murdered. Not a good place for a touch clairvoyant to reside. I wanted to get back to my suite. My suite had no history at all, since it was new when I first entered it a few months back.

Hunger came to the pit of my stomach. There was nothing here to eat, I knew that. I'd have to find something once I got to the human side. Maybe I'd order it from their kitchen. They had excellent food.

The night's events clouded my mind as I woke more fully. I threw an arm over my eyes. What was I going to do about Vasyl? Or, did I need to do anything? I missed him. Confusion and sadness drew over me.

The jaguar purred and brought his paw possessively down on my leg. I ran my hand over his large head and his purring magnified. He moved his head to rub against my hand.

I don't love him. Not as much as I do Dante. This fact hit me like a slap in the face. When Dante left me, a few months back, my whole world had crashed in on me. Then, when his death became evident—especially after he visited me in his astral shell while I lay in a hospital bed—my heart broke to pieces. If Vasyl hadn't proposed to me way before I knew Dante was dead, I wouldn't have agreed to marry him. I was attracted to Vasyl, liked him, and even felt love toward him, but not like the deep love I felt for Dante.

If only I could go back in time and change things.

"I'm glad you're still with me, Dante," I said, squelching my need to cry. If I cried now it would only show me that I was weak. I couldn't allow my feelings for a man to manipulate me, or become victim to a dark depression I would not be able to pull myself out of easily. I needed grit to help me through this.

I drew my hands around Dante's neck to hug him. It was awkward. Paw against my hip, he pulled me down easily and began to lick me. Being licked by a jaguar is an experience, believe me. The large rasping tongue is nothing like a small domesticated cat's. I chuckled and sputtered at him, trying to hold him back, but it was impossible. He was simply too strong. If he were a human right now, the sparks would fly. Yes. I loved him, and was now unable to resist him, especially after that one night of love making with raw magical energies sizzling between us. It was obvious to me that I was unable to stay true to anyone with my insatiable sexual needs for a man to make wild love to me—whoever it was. Was it because I was the sibyl? I didn't know. Maybe.

"Enough kisses, lover boy. I'm hungry." I thought about him being hungry and stalled that idea, remembering he was Undead. If he had fed on anything it would have to be through sex or death—taking a soul. How I missed watching him eat actual food. His mouth was sexy when he ate.

I managed to unravel myself from Dante's clutches and rolled out of bed. I'd been given a nightgown last night—not one of Letitia's, thank God. None of her things were still in the apartment. I had been told it had been gutted, everything replaced. I was pretty sure this nightie was brand new because I'd gotten no read from it.

I located my clothing, folded up on a chair. Obviously someone had tidied and cleaned things up for me. The sheets had been stripped last night, of course, and fresh ones put on while I was busy taking a long, soothing bath. The elf women were soft-spoken, efficient, and looked to my comforts. Plus, they were charismatic as well as pretty. I liked them at once.

After dressing and taking care of a few personal needs, I gathered my purse and opened the door. I peeked out into the rest of the penthouse. I already knew no one was there with me. *Silent, like a tomb.* The penthouse had a lot of rooms, many I had never been in, and was not about to explore.

Dante strolled out into the living area ahead of me, still in jaguar pelt. All of the flowers still spilled from their vases, but the rest of the bears, and candles and all the candy boxes and any other thing from the night before was removed or cleared out. *Put into closets.* I thought of grabbing a box of chocolates before I left. I was too hungry for real food now to take a moment for even that.

I padded toward the front door, the jaguar at my side. He looked up at the door and made a big cat sound that might have meant things were okay out there.

I opened the door and peeked out into the hall.

A blonde guy in a black button-down shirt with the word SECURITY in bold yellow stitching on sleeves smiled at me.

"Good morning, Sabrina," he said, his smile created deep dimples in his cheeks. He was handsome in the extreme. But elf guys usually were.

"Good morning," I squinted at him. In red script, over his heart was his name. "Micheal."

"If you are ready to leave, I am to escort you."

"Yes, I—"

The door to the penthouse across the way opened. Stefan poked his head out.

"Good morning, Sabrina," he said. His hair looked a little ruffled, but his clothes were not, his shirt was unbuttoned at the top, and no coat. I might have woke him—how, I would not know.

"Morning," I said, working to paste a smile on my lips. His being there only brought back memories of last night, and I really wanted to keep those at bay for as long as I could.

The jaguar snarled, making it clear he wasn't crazy about the vampire, either. I automatically put a calming hand on his head, smoothing it over his soft fur. I couldn't help but run my fingers over his soft, fuzzy ears.

"Nice big cat, you have there," Stefan said, looking at Dante.

"Yes. He eats vampires for breakfast," I quipped.

"Where are you going?" he asked, ignoring my joke.

"To my suite on the human side, like I said last night."

Stefan stepped out into the hallway. It was day time, yet, he was awake. He had to be a very old vampire for him to be able to be awake mid-morning.

"I've made all the arrangements," he said, closing the door to his apartment. "The penthouse on the human side—The Edelweiss—is now yours." He handed me a platinum swipe card. Cool.

"Oh." It had a name? "Thank you," I said, still not sure why I got a penthouse of my own, even though my husband had quit. "But I'm going to my suite first."

"Wouldn't you like to see it? At least?"

I twisted the fingers of my glove. He was persistent. Maybe I could look at it, if only to placate him and get him off my back. My suspicious of why Stefan was doing all of this, plus his interest in me had me questioning his ulterior motives. Of course, for a vampire to be interested in me shouldn't have surprised me. But something about the way his dark blue eyes drank me in—there was something deeper going on that I wasn't privy to. He wasn't exactly trying to thrall me—and he couldn't as long as the mystic ring was uncovered (which it was)—but the whole thing made me suspicious.

"Okay. I guess I have time to look at it." I looked at Micheal. "I'll allow Micheal to escort me, though. If you don't mind?"

"Not at all," he said and ran fingers through his dark hair trying to tame it down. "I'll just be a few minutes. I'll meet you downstairs." He glanced at his cell phone. Men and their toys.

"Fine," I said, glancing at Micheal. He led me to the penthouse elevator. He had a swipe card and used it. The doors swooshed open and we stepped on.

The doors paused before closing as Micheal pressed for Lobby. We took our spots against the walls, Dante sat on his haunches next to me. Micheal's blue eyes glanced at the animal by my side.

"Funny, no one told me you had a large cat with you," Micheal said.

"Oh." I looked down and patted Dante's head. "He's actually not a real cat." *Well, that was a stupid way of saying it.*

"Really?"

I chuckled at myself. "He's a shiftchanger." This was the best way of explaining it.

"Ohhhh," he said, nodding.

I wasn't sure if telling him that Dante was actually an Undead was a good idea. Micheal's dark blonde hair grew over his collar, covering his ears. His looks rivaled any vampire I'd met. Including Stefan. *Why'd I think of him?*

* * *

After straightening his shirt, and finger-combing his hair, Stefan decided not to wait for the elevator to return. Instead, he misted out of existence and reformed in the lobby. A man was running a vacuum cleaner—*such noise!*—over the carpet. He stepped away from him and his ears picked up his cell phone chirping. *Who the hell could this be?* He pulled his phone out and looked at the readout. He frowned at it. YELLOW ALLERT flashed across the screen.

"What the fuck?" Stunned, he wondered where this alert originated from. He tried to go to his menu and the alert switched to orange, then quickly to red.

"Shit!" He scanned the lobby, all around and all the way up, into where the fifth floor ceiling met his gaze. His body went into hyper alert mode when the sound of an alarm—not unlike a fire alarm—began sounding.

The maintenance guy vacuuming stopped, flicked off the noisy machine—which was now drowned out by the louder alarm—looked around, and then ran out of the lobby.

Stefan glanced at the desk. Whoever had been sitting there, vacated as well. *Obviously both human.*

He turned to the elevators expectantly. The private one's numbers glowed on floor number eight. He realized he had neither Micheal's nor Sabrina's numbers and couldn't call either one to warn them. Instead he dialed Security. They answered at once.

"Security," the voice said in his ear.

"What's happening?"

"Security has been breached," the man said.

"From where?"

"Lobby, North Tower."

"I know that! I'm standing in the lobby!" Stefan cried, hand out. "Where is it, or *what* is it?"

"We don't know, exactly, sir. The system has detected a breach, but it's acting like something has been brought in via a ley line."

"Ley line? Really?" He was not certain how the security worked at Tremayne Towers, but if something came in through a ley line—that which had no prior authority—it had to be demonic. Anyone using ley lines within the compound had to be registered. Sabrina was a registered ley line user, as were certain elves. He'd been briefed on those who were cleared to use ley lines here. Andrew Morkel was one, but he would not have opened a ley line in order for a demon to pass through. If it was not used by someone who was cleared, the sensitive ley line detection system would be tripped—as it had been. *I need to find someone who knows what's going on!*

Turning toward the elevators again, he watched the numbers countdown to ground floor. If he had either of their cell phone numbers he would have told them to go directly down to the main office—below the main floor. They would be safe there.

He surveyed the lobby, watching for whatever was coming through the ley lines to materialize. The lobby boasted a large pond with a slab of black granite. Bold red T's shaped somewhat like fangs—his father's logo for everything he manufactured or built, such as his towers, clothing line, and bottled blood.

The balconies surrounding each of the five floors looked down on the atrium. A glass elevator took people up and down these first five floors—which were kept open for guests only, no one lived on these first five floors, and they were all rooms, not suites.

He looked along the open walkways above, turning slowly as his eyes searched. Meanwhile the alarm continued to sound off in an annoying pitch. It was enough to wake any vampire, and he wondered if the guests in these rooms wouldn't come out and look to see what was going on. Unless, of course, they were advised not to exit their rooms.

* * *

Micheal pulled his cell phone from his belt and looked at the read-out.

"We have a red alert," he said, light-blond brows furrowing his brow.

I frowned. "Red alert? What's that?"

"Breach of security," he said, putting the phone to his ear.

Dante made a loud snarl and stood on all fours, looking toward the door, ready to attack.

"It looks like it's in the lobby." Michael's eyes engaged mine as he listened to whoever was on the other end.

My senses were tingling as I became hyper alert, watching the numbers above light up as we arrived slowly to Lobby.

"Got it. Right," Micheal said and put his phone back on his belt and pulled out the strange looking gun. He checked the magazine—a see-through window showed several rounds of balls. He held it at the ready in both hands, pointing at the doors.

"What is it?" I asked.

"Possible demon attack."

My pulse had already jumped. If only I had my dagger. It killed demons, no problem. I would have to use my other command of magic if it came to it.

The jaguar let loose a primal roar that startled us.

"He's going out first," I said.

"Good, kitty," Micheal said.

The elevator came to a soft halt at our destination. There was that usual pause before the doors opened. When they did, the jaguar jumped out, roaring like he was in a jungle.

Chapter 17

Gremlins

The jaguar charged across the atrium, splashed into the small pool, and then out the other side. He stopped, looked up and made a snarling cat noise that competed with the loud alarm going off.

The sound of the alarm hurt my ears. I held my hands over my ears. Not quite like a fire alarm, it was more of a ululating piercing sound that was hard for my werewolf's hearing to take.

Micheal surged out of the elevator, moving with his gun held, ready to use it.

"Can't someone turn that fucking thing off?" Stefan shouted, hands over his ears as well.

Micheal turned to a panel, threw it open and hit something.

Silence.

"Thank you," Stefan said.

"Don't step out," Stefan warned too late. I'd already taken two steps out of the elevator.

I looked around, but saw nothing. Yet my Knowing was definitely going off the scales.

Something clattered from above. It sounded something like brittle wings, but not quite. Then I saw them. Small, winged creatures circled above, but nothing like I'd ever seen before. They had large membranous wings, huge bat-like ears with large feral eyes. There were dozens of them, flying around and around at the very top of the fifth floor ceiling. They didn't seem very large, no larger than possibly a full-grown tom cat.

"What the fuck are those?" Stefan asked.

"I don't know," Micheal said. "We need back up." He barely got the cell phone off his hook when the creatures swirled as if one-mind, and became a massive, whirling dark cloud. They dove from above, down toward us. Their shrill cries nearly as deafening as the now silent alarm.

"Back up! Lobby, North Tower! Now!" Micheal shouted into his phone.

I moved to duck away from the terrifying swarm. Micheal already made a few hits with his splat gun. The creatures screamed from these hits of holy water. I jumped into the pond and hid behind the huge stone, hoping they wouldn't see me. I couldn't find Dante, but I wasn't exactly worried about him. Across from me, the exit spilled out into the hallway which led to Earthly Pleasures. The restaurant for humans and vampires was dark. No one was around—which was good, but I sure wish I wasn't here. I half thought about dodging out through the doors of the exit, but worried these creatures would only follow me.

One of the creatures darted over Micheal's head, and a long appendage—what looked to be his tongue—arrowed out of its mouth and stretched twelve feet to hit Micheal on the shoulder. He jerked from the contact as though it stung.

"Ow! Shit!" Micheal cursed. "Be careful! I think these are gremlins!"

Micheal's warning threw me. Gremlins? Obviously they weren't the kind I'd seen in movies. They were ugly as demons usually are, slimy green, brown or black skin, and nasty muzzles filled with teeth.

One larger, brown one with black ears, wings and snout swooped over my head and I ducked swiftly away from the ten-foot tongue that thrust out at me. He kept thrusting that tongue at me—and he had deadly aim. Jeans wet, my feet soaked from the water in the pond, I ducked low. I slipped and fell, hitting my knee painfully. Now I was completely soaked. I scrambled on hands and knees around the stone, in a desperate attempt to stay out of the way of that tongue. I had no idea what the tongue did, but it definitely burned like a hot iron and cut like a razor blade. I saw Micheal bleeding in a few spots on the arm, his ear and neck.

Stefan's grunts were competing with the creature's noises when Micheal's holy water hit them. Stefan had a red ax in his hand—obviously he'd taken it from the fire equipment on the wall—and chopped one gremlin's wing off in mid-flight. It went caterwauling to the floor, screeching, and trying to hit him with his tongue. Stefan swung down on the creature's head and chopped it off. But the tongue kept shooting out, seeking him. Stefan turned the ax around and smashed its head with the blunt end. Its blood and brains splattered like a watermelon. Finally, the tongue quit trying to seek a victim.

"Watch out! Sabrina! Behind you!"

I turned only to feel the bite of what felt like a razor blade on the shoulder. It burned and I screamed out. The same brown, black-faced creature flapped above me. It landed on the stone and laughed. I became an easy target.

"Fucker!" I swore at it.

Angered beyond measure, I felt a burning inside my chest that radiated down my arm and through my fingers. I rose up on my knees, and thrust my hand toward it. A red rope of light surged from my fingertips, and the power force hit the creature. It went up in flames. I smiled with satisfaction. The smell of brimstone and burning flesh cloyed the area. As the blackened corps fell into the water hissing and steaming, I splashed out of the pond to get away from it, worried about that tongue, but I need not have worried. The tongue was burnt as well.

Dante appeared as human form before me, but he had raven-black wings. "Remain in the pool, Sabrina," he said, a cautioning hand out to me while he watched the creatures swarming above us. There might have been twenty or more of them. He leaped off the floor, beat his wings, and flew into the thick of where the creatures circled. He grabbed at the creatures, catching them by a wing, or tail, and they burst into flames, much like what I had done.

Several more gremlins swirled above me. I tried to stay out of their reach, but their long tongues caught me a couple of times—it was impossible to out maneuver those long tongues. One caught me along the ribs, one shot out and caught my arm, and at third tongue seared my thigh—ripping through the jeans material as though it were paper. I knew I was bleeding. I couldn't figure out what was on their tongues that could rip open not only flesh, but heavy blue jeans material. I ducked as one tongue zipped toward my head and saw the last two inches of their tongues were edged in rows of small razor-sharp, double-pointed teeth. No wonder! It was like trying to duck away from a hundred treble hooks on a fishing lure.

Swiping my dripping-wet hair out of my eyes, I spotted three hovering above me, and I couldn't get away. I was cornered. Angry, I thrust both hands out and hit them all with power, one after another. It was like a shooting gallery at a carnival—*Zap!Zap!Zap!* I continued hitting them with my power—grunting like a tennis pro—and they all fell in fiery clumps, burning totally to crispy black things, like a barbecue gone way wrong landing with loud splashes into the pool with a hissing, sizzling sound and vapor rose from each corpse.

Quickly, I stepped out of the pool to hunt them, as they were now trying to stay out of my reach. As long as I could aim at them, they were going to become crispy critters.

"Hah! Tables are turned, assholes!" I said in a low growl and hit a few more who dared to come close.

After ten minutes of this the air became cloyed with their burning stench, the floor littered with their burnt bodies. I didn't know how the guys were doing with theirs, I didn't have time to look—I was too busy with my own bucket of trouble. I ducked back around the stone, still hitting a few more with my powers. A number of them went into a V formation and came at me like a wall, as if they thought they'd be safe in numbers. I aimed both hands and hit them with a controlled wave. Down they all went in a fiery explosion. It was like hunting geese with a flame thrower.

I jumped back into the pool, swished through the water, kicked a few blackened corpses, and hid behind the large stone where another one was hiding, waiting for me. "Think I'm that stupid, you little jerk! Take that!" I zapped him and up he went in flames and fell into the water with a splash. *God it stinks in here!*

By this time other elves had joined us. Using their splat guns, they hit the little devils. It appeared that the holy water only burned them enough to give them pain. I noticed it didn't render a fatal blow. Some of them were still clinging to life, and sending tongues after me, or anyone else who happened by. I zapped their asses into oblivion. I went along the floor and zapped every creature which had not burnt. I felt sorry for the guy who had to clean this crap up—whatever they were—of blackened little corpses.

No more creatures were left threatening us with their tongues. Exhausted, I collapsed on the edge of the pool. Red drops fell into the water, my blood made pretty little crimson clouds in the water.

Dante flew down from above and landed beside me. He bent to me.

"My Lady, you are hurt." He straightened and called to the others. "We need to take her down to the hospital."

"It burns! All over!" I said, unable to cover all of my injuries with a hand. My arm, legs, back, front, and somewhere on my head—all bleeding.

Micheal shot over to us. "We must get you downstairs," he said. "Gremlin venom is poisonous. You could die from it!"

"Well, crap," I said, woozy from either the venom or this constant bleeding I'd been doing since last night. I fell into Dante's arms and he lifted me. Without haste, he and Micheal got me back into the elevator and soon I was down on the lower level where the elf-run hospital was located. Micheal had phoned ahead. They were waiting for me with a gurney. I was placed on the gurney, several nurses and doctors swarmed around me. They started an I.V., and then a cuff was put on my arm. I heard them cut open my jeans with a rip. Crap. New jeans. Ruined. Well, they were ruined anyway, I guess. Plus the new top. Who do I sue?

"What were they?" someone asked.

"Gremlins. The poisonous kind." Micheal was bleeding too, and he was being tending to as well.

"Sabrina," Morkel's face swam into view. Someone took my blood pressure. "You'll be well taken care of. Don't worry." He scurried alongside the gurney as they pushed me down a hall. Then, he stopped following, and faded from view.

It was all I could do to stay conscious. The room seemed to whirl, and I didn't dare hold my head up. I couldn't take all the motions and people talking around me so closed my eyes.

"One hundred over seventy!" someone yelled on my right side. "It's dropping!"

"We need to stop the bleeding!" another one said.

"Get her to ICU, stat!" a man cried.

I was being wheeled quickly down yet another hall, everyone running alongside the gurney. Hands were pulling my clothes off. I didn't care at this point. Something was wrong with me. I could feel it. I thought I'd heard someone say that the gremlins had poisonous venom, but I couldn't remember who. Or if anyone had said it.

I was wheeled into a large room with a lot of lights—*operating room*—a doctor in full scrubs and a mask and gloves drew up beside me.

"She'll be out shortly," someone said.

And I was.

* * *

Bill entered the human side of Tremayne Towers. At the hour of eight a.m., it was not very busy. He took in the somewhat dark décor of the quiet lobby, and strode toward the check-in counter where he found a smiling young man standing waiting to help him.

"Good morning, sir. A room today?" he asked.

"Yes. If you have any."

"Yes. We have some vacancies," the man said. "Would you like a room or a suite?"

"If you have a suite, I'll take that," Bill said, still looking around, noticing the sweeping stair case and all the mirrors. The mirrors made him slightly nervous, and he didn't know why. *Two-way?* He wasn't certain if he would be using the suite, but he needed an excuse for being here. If he had to be here, why not go with the best?

"Very good. How will you be paying? Visa? Master Card?"

Bill gave him his gold card. In a few minutes the man told him his room number and gave him two key cards, telling him about room service.

"I noticed that there's two towers here. How do you get to the other side? Go out and around?" Bill asked.

The young man paused for a beat and then said, "Oh, you mean for the shopping mall and restaurants?" He pointed to the cards he'd given him. "Use your pass key to access through those doors." He pointed behind the desk to a wall.

Bill looked at the wall where he pointed. Two white doors stood not fifteen feet away. They looked like elevator doors. Above in gold lettering, it said *North Tower Entry*.

"Thank you," Bill said, sliding his pass cards into a pocket.

"No luggage?" the man asked.

Bill, of course, didn't have any luggage. He said, "I've had a long flight, and they lost my luggage."

"Oh, so sorry, but that does happen," the clerk said. "I hope they find it."

"They said it was on another flight and I'm just waiting for their call. I need to eat something, is there a restaurant you can recommend?"

"Yes. Idlewild, sir. Oh—" he held up a finger. "In fact I've got a coupon for it right here." he searched below in a drawer and came up with a card with the restaurant's name on it with 15% off breakfast, lunch or dinner.

"Thanks," Bill said and strode to the sliding doors, used one of his pass keys and it swooshed open.

When he stepped through he was unprepared to find people in Hazmat suits vacuuming the floor. The unmistakable reek of brimstone heavy. A number of people were draining the pool where a huge slab of black granite stood in its center. He had to pick his way around a section, which was cordoned off with yellow caution tape, where a pile of small blacked, weirdly shaped bodies lay. *Was that wings I saw on that one?* He could just make out small leathery wings on some of them, and the heads were definitely of some demonic creature—not much larger than a small dog.

Bill stepped across the lobby, and up to an older man standing with an upright vacuum, watching the whole process off to the side with a grimace on his face.

"What happened here?" Bill asked the older man.

"Aaah. Who knows?" he said. "You never know what goes on over this side—weird shit," he muttered at the end. "As soon as I can transfer to the South Tower, that's what I'm doing." He looked up at Bill. "Someone said seagulls got caught in some sort of vent." He added in a low tone. "Right."

Bill looked around at the blackened ashes. "Seagulls did this?" He highly doubted this was the work of seagulls.

"I don't know. Don't seem at all right." He pulled off his baseball cap and itched his balding pate.

"How is it they all burnt to a crisp?" Bill wondered.

"How?" he said, gray eyes slitting, itching his unshaven jaw now. "Crap if I know. I was in here earlier, cleaning like I normally do. An alarm went off. They told me if that alarm ever went off to get the hell out. That's what I did." He shrugged. "Just come back to find they've got someone cleaning this crap up. Thank God they didn't expect me to do it!"

"Well," Bill said after a while of watching along with the old man, "you have a good one." He was certain because of the old man's confusion as to what had actually happened, he had been thralled by a vampire in order to block him from saying much to anyone who asked.

"You too," the man replied, and returned to watching the Hazmat team clean.

Sabrina is nearby. Their connection—however thin—tingled inside his head. She was near. But how would he be able to watch for her and not have anyone become suspicious? Or worse, be seen by her. Even in this disguise, she might recognize him. He hoped the growth of beard helped hide some of his features. He adjusted the brim back over his eyes and walked on. There were cleaning people everywhere in the lobby. Someone turned something loud on. He turned to see that they'd begun draining the pool below the large slab of marble which had the *TT* logo on it. And if there had been any furniture, it was all gone.

He shook his head, and moved away, out into the corridor, and searched for the restaurant.

Chapter 18

Visitation

I woke up woozy and unable to focus at first. But I wasn't in pain, which made a big difference.

"She's coming around," a man said and my eyes swung to the other side of the room. Morkel moved into my periphery. Stefan was somewhere nearby—I don't know how I knew this—and so was Dante. Micheal stood beside Dante. At least that's who I thought it was as I tried to focus them in. I closed my eyes.

"Sabrina? Can you hear me?" Morkel said.

I opened my eyes again. "Yeah. Woozy," I managed. My mouth felt dry as sandpaper.

"You should feel better soon. We were able to stop the bleeding. Gremlin's venom has anticoagulant in it, plus a poison that could have killed you if we hadn't acted quickly." He looked up at the others briefly. "You were very lucky that Stefan agreed to donate a pint of his blood to counter act the poisons. Your vitals are coming back to normal nicely."

"Wait a minute," I said. "Who donated blood?"

"Stefan, here," he said, hand gesturing toward him.

"Vampire blood? His blood?" I said, startled.

"We had no choice. There were no other vampires awake. Besides, only the oldest vampire's blood would work against the poison quickly enough." Morkel went on, "We wouldn't have been able to get Tremayne here in time." He sounded apologetic, like it made all the difference in the world which vampire's blood I'd prefer.

My eyes found Stefan's sapphire eyes. Wonderful. Now we were connected in that weird way that vampires had the upper hand over you. Thank goodness we had not swapped blood, as a scion and vampire might. The vampire would know everything about you from your blood. It was bad enough I would know a bunch of things about him.

"Excellent job killing those demons, by the way," Morkel said, sounding both proud and impressed.

"She's a one-woman demon killing machine. She must have killed over fifty of them!" Micheal also sounded impressed with me.

I had no idea I had killed that many. I had no idea there *were* that many.

"Do we know where the breach came from?" Morkel asked.

"Only that it was a ley line breach," Stefan said. I would have thought they would have talked about this hours ago. How long had I been here, anyway?

"What time is it?" I wondered aloud.

"Three-thirty."

"Afternoon?" I asked.

"Yes."

"I'm hungry. I never got breakfast."

They chuckled.

"She deserves a huge steak and all the trimmings," Micheal said, beaming.

"Actually, I would love that."

"I'll have them bring you something up," Morkel said. "I'll see if they can do a steak."

"I need my anti-werewolf potion," I said, looking straight at Dante.

"Why?" Morkel asked.

"You want me to turn?"

"It would help your injuries to heal," he said.

"I. Don't. Want. To. Turn." I slid my gaze to Dante. He bowed and vanished. He would get the anti-werewolf potion for me—wherever the hell it was.

Morkel stepped out of the room and snagged a nurse requesting her to get some food for me. I hoped their food came from the food court. It was pretty darn good, from what I remembered—although I didn't know if steak was on their menu, but anything was possible here.

Stefan stepped closer to my bed. "I'm sorry this happened to you," he said, and I couldn't help but watch the weird way his lips moved. He was like a snake hypnotizing his victim. "We can't seem to find where, or how this breach happened."

"Inside job," I said. I simply Knew this. "Call Rick."

"Leprechaun Rick?"

"I can call him," Micheal said, eyes glimmered at me.

"Thanks," I said. "He's the best on wards and ley line magic. If there was a breach, he'll find it."

"You're right about that," Morkel agreed as he reentered the room.

Micheal busily poked at his cell phone and as he waited for the number to connect, he and Morkel stepped out into the hallway. I was now alone with Stefan.

I looked straight ahead, my eyes going slightly out of focus as the vision came.

"Sabrina? Are you—"

"I'm fine." The vision actually had me more than frightened. I was a tad pissed off by it too. My work was never done, it seemed.

I glanced away and closed my eyes. I needed something else, and with only a thought, I told Dante what else I needed from my suite.

Get the Dagger of Delphi, too.

Done. Dante confirmed inside my head. I smiled.

"I'll find out who, or where this attack originated from," I said.

"How?" he asked

"I'm the sibyl." I smiled confidently back at him, even though I felt no confidence at all.

He made a deep sigh and relented. "Very well, Ms. Strong."

"And don't think for one moment because you've given me your blood that you can call me to you," I said, the anger bringing my brows together, but I felt so weak right then my hands began shaking.

Sensing my energy drop, Morkel moved back inside, pulling up beside Stephan.

Stephan glanced up at Morkel but to me said, "That isn't possible," he said. "I gave my blood to you. Not the other way around. If anything, you'll be able to track me." He paused and held up his hands. "I donated because you needed it. It was a matter of life or death."

"Yeah, thanks, then," I said sheepishly. I looked into his dark blues and then I saw it. The eyes turned a slightly different shade. Teal. Like Tremayne's. How utterly uncomfortable that made me.

A second vision played quickly, taking no more than ten or so seconds, but I saw a great deal.

Stefan stood with an older woman—old enough to be his mother—who wept. They stood in a room, lit only by candlelight. The house was more like a one-room hovel. His hair was very long and pulled back and tied with a length of red ribbon. He wore a white ruffled shirt, stuffed into short breaches and black boots. She wore a simple dress, its dirty hem touched the floor. An apron tied around her looked only slightly soiled. Their raiments were from a much distant time, the clothing was simple; that of peasants. The room was lit by candlelight.

"Mother, I have consented to allow the master to turn me into a vampyr," Stefan announced.

The woman gasped. "Stefano! No!"

"He approached me and told me he was my real father and offered me my own realm to rule."

"You cannot!" the woman cried, hands clasped, begging, then she buried her face into them and wept.

"Mother. Think about it! The duke has taken Maria—your daughter; my sister—to be his chamber maid against her will. We have no choice. I become vampyr, I will have more power than a human. I will be able to destroy The Baron Edwardo and no one will be any the wiser what became of him. I will bring Maria back. Without his iron hand, you'll be left alone, too. I will bring you into the palace. Mother, think about it!"

"No, Stefano! Your soul will be damned!"

"If that is what it takes to defeat him, it will be worth saving you and my whole family." He grasped her by the shoulders. "Don't you see? This is the only way we will survive! I don't act now he'll have our land and our heads!"

The vision ended. The two were speaking Italian, and yet I understood everything they had said.

I said to Stefan, "Bjorn Tremayne is your actual father, as well as your sire."

His gaze lit over my face, landing on my eyes, my lips and then he blinked and let his head dip, momentarily gathering himself. I had surprised him.

"It is true. How did you know? I did not give you any vision."

"Your blood," I said. "It tells me things about you in little bits—your life before, and things you did." I was able to see who Stefan was before he was turned because I'd had his blood. "Did you rescue your sister?"

Again, I'd surprised him. His mouth dropped open for a few seconds before he answered. "Yes. But it was too late. He had already raped her," he said somberly. "That was a very long time ago."

"And Bjorn was—is—your father," I said.

"Yes." He nodded. "I would have told you sooner, or later."

"Won't have to now," I said, a smile crimping my lips.

"Oh, my God!" Someone burst into the room, a whirlwind of sound and her movements interrupted Stefan's admission to me. Lindee's excited form stopped two steps inside my room after seeing I had a visitor. "Oh. Sorr-he-he-he," she chuckled, putting her hands to her mouth. "I didn't know you had someone with you."

"That's alright. I must go, anyway," Stefan said. He stepped somberly to the door. Then he stopped and looked over his shoulder at me. "I will speak with you later," and then left the room.

"And, I believe I'll be running along as well," Morkel said and also left.

When the door closed Lindee said, "Wow. That guy was hot. You always have such hot men around you!"

"Which one?"

"The swarthy one," she said.

I frowned at her. "Unlike you?" I said.

She smiled and made a nervous chuckle.

"You went out with Dan, the werewolf, this morning."

Her eyes went huge. She didn't have to ask how I knew. She hadn't blocked me because she had been so worried about me.

"That's okay," I said and took her in. She must have been crying, her eyes were red. "I think I knew you two were into one another that first night."

Lindee lowered her head but I saw the smile. I wasn't stupid. They'd spent the night together in that elf-run motel—or at least until the middle of the night, when he left her because the bed was just too small for two people to sleep together.

I looked up to a soft knock on the door.

"Come in," I called.

"Hi." Dante ducked his head in. "I've got your anti-werewolf potion." He stepped in, holding out a large shopping bag from one of those elite stores that Jeanie liked to shop in. "Plus something else you may need, my Lady." He brought the bag over to me.

I smiled. "Thanks. You read my mind."

"Of course, my Lady." He set the bag down, and from his pocket he took out a vial. "In an hour you must take this." He held it up between two fingers.

I nodded and took it from him, placing it in the bed with me. "Can you take my dagger out too?"

"Yes, my Lady." He turned to the bag and pulled out the box.

"Remove it from the box," I said. I couldn't do this, because my one hand was still hooked up to an I.V.

"So, anyway, they said you were attacked by something nasty," Lindee said while Dante opened the box.

"Gremlins. They have poisonous tongues. I could have died."

Lindee screwed up her face. "How did you get away?"

I shrugged. "Burned them up."

"With what?"

"My powers," I said, smiling.

"Wow! Cool!"

Dante held the dagger, still in its sheath, in his hands. I took it from him. "Thanks." I slid it under my sheet next to me. It would be safe there until I needed it.

In a few minutes, food was brought in and I ate while Lindee yammered on and on about Dan. She told me he'd been a bouncer for some place I'd never heard of, and security for some band I'd never heard of. I told her that my night sucked, and went into the whole story. She was shocked to hear that Vasyl had left.

"He'll be back, I'm sure," she tried to humor me. She didn't know vampires very well.

After I ate (yes, steak and all the trimmings as promised), I took my anti-werewolf potion.

Then the nurse came into the room and announced, "Visiting hours are over."

"I'll see you in the morning," Lindee said, stepping out the door. I was glad that the nurse had come in and made her leave. She sucked the energy right out of me.

The nurse turned down the lights for me and I did get a short nap in before I was awaken by a knock.

I cracked my eyes open. An awareness brought my whole body awake. My hand moved to my dagger at my side. My fingers went around the hilt. I sat up a little, expectantly. The demon I had had the short vision of earlier was here. I hadn't expected it to actually knock.

"Come in," I said. I was prepared for this little meeting.

It was the same female demon who had been with Crimmins at the party, the night before. She limped in, wearing a black leather jacket over jeans and a black turtleneck shirt. Not exceptionally stylish, but a better dresser than most demons I'd had the displeasure of meeting.

Anticipating a kill, the dagger in my hands shifted, then began to vibrate slightly. I held it down.

"Sabrina Strong?" I wondered where the guards were I had requested. Possibly this one found her way in, the same way that the gremlins had. Or, maybe her human facade was good enough to get past all the elves in here. But I reminded myself, visiting hours were over with. She must have somehow gotten past the nurses station.

"Yes?" I said. My right hand, which had the mystic ring was exposed because that's the hand where the I.V. was hooked into. With a mere flick of my hand I could throw the demon into the wall, or out the window, for that matter. But first I wanted to know why she was here. It might be vital to my survival.

She squinted at me with those beady black eyes as she spoke. "My name is Villarreal. I have come directly from Dark World, from my lord and master to give you a message." I noticed that if I shifted my eyes just slightly off the demon, a dark shadow draped it. I wasn't sure if it was an aura, or what it was.

"Who is your master?" I asked. Because she couldn't refuse a direct question from me, I decided to get to the bottom of things quickly.

The demon blinked and pulled in a breath and held it. Her cheeks puffed out, doing her level best to not answer. But she had to. "Naamah," she said on a gush of air, looking disgusted with herself. She squinted at me with a hateful look. "So, it is true! You *can* control us."

I thought it was apparent that I could, so I didn't bother to answer.

"So, what's the message?" I asked, continuing with the grilling session.

"He has told me to tell you that this morning's assault was merely a demonstration of what he can do."

"Really."

"He intends to kill you for cutting off his beautiful twin tails."

"I see." I paused. "Didn't they grow back?"

"Yes. They have. Lovely as ever." She made a toothy smile. Gag me.

"So what's the problem?"

"He wants revenge," she said, sharp chin jutting out at me. "No one does that to him and lives."

"I see." I had loosened the binds on the hilt of my dagger all the while she had been talking. The dagger tried to hop out of my grasp, but I held it down. "Thanks for the message. Can you take one to him for me?"

She looked a little surprised by my coolness under her threats.

"I suppose," she said looking defiant.

I flopped back the covers and let go of the dagger. The dagger flew across the room and hit the demon in the heart. "Go to hell!"

The demon's eyes went huge with surprise. It cried out in pain, then went silent, and dropped to the floor. At the same moment, an elf bodyguard shot in. He found the demon on the floor sputtering in its death throes for about twenty seconds and went still.

"Sorry," he said. "She got past me. I didn't see her."

"No problem. She's done sneaking around," I said. The Dagger of Delphi extracted itself from the demon and swooped back to me. I caught it and replaced it back into its sheath. I yawned. "Tell Morkel to report this to Stefan. I don't think we'll get any more attacks from the ley lines. But just in case, he should keep vigil."

"Right," he said and bent down to look at the demon. It suddenly burst into flames and he stumbled back. Blue and orange flames licked up about three feet and went out in a puff of black smoke that dissipated rather quickly. The only thing left was the ashy remains.

"Damn demons," I said. "They sure do leave a mess when they die. Don't they?"

"I'll go and get someone to clean this up." The guard left.

Someone else burst in.

"Hell, Sabrina!" Rick said, eyes huge. "I just got word about what's been happening around here. You alright?" His eyes took in the strange gray pile of ash in the form of a body on the tiled floor.

"Fairy fucking crap on toadstools! What the hell was that?" Rick asked, pointing. He didn't often use the f-word, so this meant he was hyped up and scared shitless.

"Oh, that?" My eyes went to the burnt corpse on the floor. "A demon, of some sort. She sent a message and told me who was responsible for sending those gremlins."

"Who?"

"Remember Naamah?"

"Oh, hell! Mother of heavenly God!" His whole body sagged at the news.

"Did you figure out where they breached security?"

"Yeah. I got a ward up over the whole building. I don't think they can get any-thing past it again. But if there's any demons here already—like that one" —he pointed to the blackened corpse on the floor— "then we've still got problems."

"Well, I killed that one. It claimed her lord was Naamah."

"She say why he did this?"

"Why do you think? I cut off his tails. Plus, we've heard rumors that demons were beginning a war with the Watchers, remember?"

"No. I don't think I got that email."

"Well, I think it's happening right now."

"Hey, Rick! I've been looking for you." A man with red hair stuck his head in.

"What is it now?" Rick sounded harassed as he turned.

"Oops." It was Quist looking slightly disheveled. "Hi Sabrina."

"Hi." I would have waved, but I held onto the dagger, just in case a vampire stepped in.

"Oh, Quist. Sorry. I thought—never mind," Rick said, his hands flapping at his shoulders. "What's up?"

"We were attacked by rogues last night. Fritz was attacked, and I brought him here, last night," Quist said.

"How is he?" I asked, my heart going out to them both.

He shook his head. "He lost a lot of blood. He's in a coma. They have him in ICU."

"Oh, God," I said, the pit of my stomach squeezed. "Poor Fritz. What hap-pened?"

"We were ambush by rogue vampires." He paused and scratched the back of his head as though thinking about what he was going to say. "Then, this guy in a big, long coat and hat came along, busted two vampire's heads together—I mean he actually cracked them in half! He helped me get Fritz into my car and then he left like he was on fire."

"You mean he left the scene?" Rick asked.

Quist looked down at him. "No. I mean he ran so fast I couldn't see him."

"Like a vampire?" I asked.

"I guess," Quist said.

Chapter 19

Donor

"Is this the sector where the breach was?" Stefan asked the man at a control panel in the computer room where hundreds of monitors were fed hundreds of camera shots throughout Tremayne Towers.

The young man looked up at Stefan. "The closest we could figure is that it came through here." He pointed to the ceiling of the fifth floor—exactly where the gremlins had first appeared.

Stephan nodded.

"Then, there was another breach," the young man said.

"What do you mean? Where?" Stefan's voice went loud and all the other monitor attendants looked at him.

"Looks like in the hospital," he said.

Stefan surged away and pulled his cell phone out. He pressed the number for Styles.

"Yes, sire?" Styles answered.

"There's been another breach. In the hospital!" Stefan shouted into his phone, exiting the all-glass monitor room. His eyes felt grainy from staring at computers too long. He had stifled a couple of yawns while in the monitor room where the young man—whatever-the-fuck his-name-was—explained how the monitors worked for each section. He had been the one who'd discovered the breach earlier that morning and the alarm was sounded. Was that really eighteen hours ago?

"I know. I'm there now," Styles said. "The demon has been vanquished. Repeat: the demon is dead."

"What? How?" Stefan was still moving Uber-vampire swift along level C. He stopped in front of his private elevator. Using his swipe card, the doors opened and he got on.

"Apparently the sibyl's dagger?" he said it as a question, as though he couldn't quite understand it.

"Ah. Yes." Stefan rubbed his brow. It had been a long fucking night already, and it had only just begun. He needed a snack and something to warm him up.

"Everything is fine." Style's voice was balm in his ear. "Ah, sire. Could I go take sustenance? I haven't—"

"What? Oh. Yes. Go ahead, Styles. You did a splendid job. See you later."

"Right. Have a good one," Styles said.

"Right." Stefan hit end and tried to remember which level the donor pool was on. No matter, he retracted his cell phone and pressed for Donor Pool.

"Good evening. Donor Pool," someone actually answered. Stefan looked at his watch. He had no idea what time it was and now that he looked to see it was well after midnight, he didn't wonder why he was dead on his feet.

"Yes. Uh, I don't suppose you'd have a female for a late libation, do you?"

"Um, actually we do have one," the woman said haltingly as though looking for her. "I think she's still taking a nap. Should I wake her?"

"By all means," he said, and remembered that the Donor Pool was on level B. He pressed for it on the elevator panel. "I'll be there in ten seconds to pick her up."

The elevator went up one level and stopped, the doors opened and he stepped out. He looked at the signs in front of him on the wall. The sign read DONOR POOL and the arrow pointed left. He moved in that direction. The desk was currently unoccupied, but he guessed that the woman who had answered had gone to get the donor.

He stood waiting for five minutes and two women strode up. She had limp mousy hair cut to just below her chin, and wore glasses. She pulled them off as soon as she sighted him. He had hoped it was the blond. Oh well.

"I'm sorry," the woman who worked there said. "I didn't catch your name?"

He breathed a weary sigh. "It's Stefan Cappela. I'm now magnate of the towers."

"Oh. Congratulations!" the blonde said brightly. "This is Beth." No last names. It was forbidden to know the donor's last name.

"Hi," she said looking sheepish, unable to look directly at him. He didn't need eye contact to thrall her, as would a lesser vampire.

His eyes dropped to her donor tag. He reached for it and read it. The red swirl with a black drip meant that she was a new donor. If the red swirl was gold, she was an exclusive donor. Depending upon how it went, he might add her to his harem. Then he saw a red X where it would show whether or not they would also have sex with the vampire who chose them. The red x meant no they wouldn't. Didn't matter, there were ways around this. He was very good at blanking their minds of it.

"Come along, Beth. I hope you don't mind a long elevator trip to my floor?"

"Uh, no," she said, and giggled nervously. She stepped into the elevator, and yawned. "Excuse me."

"I'm not keeping you up?" he said, smiling. He had to control his hunger. He had not felt so hungry in ages. He'd simply been too busy working, trying to figure out his new job, and also had to get caught up with the demon problem of that morning.

"Oh, no," she said. "I just didn't know any vampire would want me. But, here you are, and here I am." She shrugged. No make-up at all, she looked like the bottom of the barrel, as they say. He wasn't attracted to her. But as a feed and something to fuck, she would do.

"This is your first time? With a vampire?" he asked, sending out the pheromones.

"Yes. My friends all said that it was real easy way to make fifty dollars."

"I see." He smiled, eyes holding contact with hers. "But actually, if you only give blood, it's only thirty dollars. Unless you agree to having sex, of course."

"Oh." She bit her lower lip. "I didn't know that. I mean they gave me a form to fill out and I did that. Then they gave me this card thing-y"—she held up the card—"and I was told to wait." Her eyes went round. "Oh, gosh. I hope you didn't think—"

"No. No," he said with a wave of his hand. He glanced at the number floor they were at. They were at the twelfth floor now, still rising. This was his own private elevator and no one else could get on, so his privacy was assured. "But I think we will be able to have a little fun, Beth." He stepped over to her. "I believe it said on your card you didn't want the bite to show?"

"Yes," she said, making a little face. "I've got a boyfriend. He doesn't know that I'm doing this."

"I see. I won't bite where it will be visible." He stood in front of her and put his hands on her upper arms. He would not kiss her, but he could tell she thought that's what he intended.

"Oh, are you going to bite me now?" Her eyes zeroed in on his fangs, which had now dropped down over his lower lip.

"Uhuh," he said, still smiling. He preferred to bite from behind, but tonight was a little different. He reached for her scarf. "Why don't you take this off?"

"Oh, yeah. Sure." She made that nervous laugh again and unwound the scarf from around her neck.

"Beth, look at me," he said, tipping her head back with his fingers under her chin. His thrall would be very deep, especially after the bite. She looked into his eyes. "That's right. Good. You'll remember nothing, except that it felt wonderful and you'd like to come back again. To be my donor, exclusive." After a moment he said, "Oh, and wear this dress again."

"Ok-ay," she said, eyes glazed over.

The tingling in his groin intensified like it always did when he was about to feed. He tried to imagine she was Sabrina—which was difficult. If he could not have Sabrina in his bed for a while, this would have to do. His fangs actually ached as he slid the neck of her collar down over her shoulder to gain access to it. A late feeding would help him sleep. But his other need began to rage as an exquisite throb began along the length of his cock.

He sank his teeth into the fleshy part of her shoulder at the back. She made a sudden little shriek, then succumbed to him, melting in his arms as though she'd fainted. Holding her up with one hand he unzipped his pants, then leaned his shoulder into her to hold her upright. His other hand went under the dress, found her panties and slid them down. Under vampire law this was basically rape. But she would not remember it and he had the ability to coax her into wanting to change her sexual preference on her card. Boyfriend or no boyfriend, she was his.

Lifting her above himself and pressing her into the corner of the elevator, he gradually entered her. He leisurely lapped at her blood while thrusting into her and holding her in position with both hands. He imagined what Sabrina would be like, holding her like this and pounding into her. *Soon, I'll have her in my bed.* He kept an image of Sabrina in his mind. Her hair, her lips, her eyes, her smell. He wanted so badly to be with her—not with this one. Not with anyone else.

Once the elevator reached the 96th floor, he was finished. He zipped up, and pressed for lobby again. While the elevator went back down, he drew up her panties, straightened her dress and hair, and replaced her scarf about her neck. Other than wetness between her legs, she wouldn't know anything had happened. His bite alone would have given her an orgasm, but she'd orgasmed several times while he took her.

She was surprised when she came to, finding herself stepping out exactly where she had stepped on. She had to grab the handrail a few times, because she was a bit dizzy from the one less pint of blood—more or less. He thanked her and gave her a twenty, telling her to get herself something to eat and said goodnight to her . Once rid of her, he pressed the button for his floor. The ride up made him re-live the moments with—whatever her name was. He closed his eyes and wished he could go pound on Sabrina's door and—*no, wait. She was in the hospital, still.*

The elevator arrived on the floor of his suite, and opened up. He crossed the hall to his door, but paused to eye the door across from him. Styles was enjoying his donor—you couldn't hear all that moaning and crying out, and not know.

His day had begun that morning, with Sabrina. He'd been worried about her all morning, and waited—stayed up—in order to see her when she was out of surgery. The doctor said she'd be released tomorrow morning. After speaking with her, he'd gone and took a two hour nap, until dark fell over the city.

Now, exhausted, he wanted to get to bed early. He planned a nice dinner for Sabrina in her new penthouse for tomorrow evening. He had already hired on a staff of three for her new penthouse. Actually, they were the same who had been Letitia's servants, and were unemployed still. They were more than happy to work for a human again. Especially the cook.

Stepping into a hot shower, he wondered what Sabrina liked to eat. *She wanted a stake tonight.* But for tomorrow's dinner something more classy. More dignified. *I want it to be perfect.* The cook had a refined skill in culinary arts, he'd noted this on her file.

Ten minutes later the hot water spiking down on his skin felt good, and he thought about Sabrina, conjured her in his mind. He'd never met such a woman before who was so… deadly. That, in a blink of an eye, she could kill him. That, more than anything, excited him.

Chapter 20

Lemon Meringue

In the morning I was being discharged, and called Lindee. She sounded excited over the phone, but I knew it wasn't because I was getting out of the hospital. Then she became quiet. It was one of those dead sounds on the phone you think that maybe the other person hung up. But then she sighed.

"What?"

"Mother called," she said in a dead tone over the phone. "Mother" meaning her mother.

"Good."

"Not good! She wants me to come over. Today!"

"We were going to go there soon, anyway," I said. "We'll go in my Jeep. I've just been released from the hospital. You need to bring me some clothes."

"Clothes? Why do you need clothes?"

"Mine were ruined in that attack. Plus, they pretty much had to cut them off me."

"Oh. Right. Didn't think of that."

Rick stood to one side, waiting for my call to end. He had come to see how I was. Minutes later, my phone conversation ended—which is not easy to end if you are speaking with Lindee—and I looked up at him. His hair was combed back, and it looked wet, like he'd just stepped out of the shower.

"Hi, Rick," I said.

"Good morning, toots. How are you today?"

"Great," I said. "My dagger took care of another demon last night."

"Really? Girlfriend, you kick ass!" he shrilled and did a little fist pump—as well as he could without a whole arm.

"I'm being released. I need to get Lindee to her mother's today. Any chance you can ride shotgun?"

"Me? I'd be happy to, toots, you know that!"

A half hour later, Lindee had brought me a change of clothes and I was dressed. I thanked the nurses, doctors and all the uniformed guards for their help before I left. We all three hopped on the elevator and went up to Garage.

I was amazed—no—I was startled that no one tried to shoot, bite or spit at me, or stop me in some way from leaving the towers. I was so giddy I didn't even mind the insane traffic while driving out of the city.

Lindee and Rick filled the Jeep with their voices, so I didn't bother turning on the tunes. They compared their childhoods, and I couldn't decide which one had it worse: Lindee growing up in a strict Catholic home, or Rick growing up in an orphanage in a convent. I could see the two had more in common than I did. I had asked Rick to come with me to be my back-up, just in case I got demonized again. You just never knew when a demon might try to attack you. That message the female demon, Villarreal, had given me was not an idle threat. Naamah was a big, ugly, nasty demon and just thinking about it made me shiver in my shoes.

We had just gone through the Aurora Toll Plaza when my phone made one of those annoying sounds telling me I had a message. I dug it out and looked to find I had something from Stefan. My stomach dropped wondering what the hell he wanted. Then I remembered we never did get to the human side to inspect my "new" penthouse, because of the demon attack.

"Here," I handed Lindee my phone as I drove through traffic. "Scroll to my messages."

She pressed until she got to messages and I had her retrieve the one I wanted. Stefan's sexy voice came over the speaker (and Lindee had to go "*WooOOo*" suggestively).

"Hi, Sabrina. I hope you will get this message. I wanted to make arrangements to meet you at The Edelweiss, um, your penthouse, tonight… say around seven o'clock? Dinner will be prepared for you, so don't eat beforehand. I look forward to seeing you tonight. Alone, of course," he added, his voice going deep and somewhat suggestive. "See you then."

"Wow!" Lindee crowed. "He's into you too? And Vasyl only just left?" She fanned herself.

I rolled my eyes. "He's next in line," I said, exasperated. I wished I could just go home, that it was not dangerous to go somewhere, like to Beyond the Veil, and just leave this world behind. I'd go there and hide for the rest of my life. Rick had checked the status of my house, earlier. The ward was still "compromised". He didn't want me anywhere near it. It was like the demons had camped out, just waiting for me to be stupid enough to return.

"That's right," Rick said from the back seat sounding slightly awed. "He's Bjorn's son. You knew that didn't you?"

"Not at first. I figured it out just recently," I said. Earlier, while waiting for Lindee to bring me my clothes, I filled Rick on what had happened the night before (with as little detail as possible, because men just don't want to hear about that part of a woman's physiology). It relieved me to know he had already heard that Vasyl had left, and why—yes, news gets around as fast in the Towers as any small town. At least he was up to speed on this aspect of my life.

"And he wants to date you?" Lindee said. "Cool."

"No. Not cool and the date part is just a preliminary thing." I sucked a breath in through my nose and then blew out with frustration. "I'm to mate with him."

"Mate?" Lindee's voice went high and ended on a giggle, throwing back her head and laughing full bore. "What? So, are you a brood mare? Like on that goofy world you just rescued me from?"

"Black Veil. Yes." I snorted. "It would seem so." She knew all about that stuff since she had spent almost a month on Black Veil where human women were considered breeders.

"She doesn't know, does she?" Rick said.

"No," I said. "I don't like to talk about it."

"About what? What are you guys talking about?" Lindee said, eyes going back and forth between us as she sat sideways in the front seat. "C'mon, you guys! Don't leave me out of the loop!"

"She's supposed to give birth to the dhampire," Rick said.

"A what?"

"It's sort of a hybrid vampire/human creature. Anyway, she's supposed be mated with a master vampire. Bjorn tried—and nearly died..." he trailed off. I glanced up in my rearview mirror. The leprechaun looked slightly embarrassed. He had been part of the plan to help dupe me into thinking I was not being thralled by Tremayne, but I was and I wound up in a *ménage à trois,* which ended badly—with Tremayne having the Dagger of Delphi in his chest.

He nearly died, but I came to the rescue and gave plasma, which was experimental, but it worked.

"I was on the pill, anyway, so it wouldn't have worked. It was too bad Dante stabbed him with the dagger," I said, looking up in the mirror again. Rick stared back at me with sunglasses. "Just to set the record straight. It wasn't me. It was Dante. Just so everyone knows," I added.

Lindee had the look of horror on her face. "Dante stabbed him with that dagger of yours?"

"Yep." I nodded. Rick had become quiet in the backseat. I quickly changed subjects. "So, when we get to your mom's you need to remember that you've been in a rehab, and also learning the culinary arts while there," I said to Lindee.

"Is that the story you're going to tell her mother?" Rick asked.

"That's what we've already told her, and we have to go with it since it would be really hard to convince her mother she's been on another planet since November," I said.

We were quiet for a few minutes. Then Rick said, "Hey, I could pretend to be from this rehab place, and that way we can have a story for me."

"Okay. That might work."

"Wait. Really?" Lindee looked doubtful. "I don't know. My mother can spot a lie a mile away."

"I think that might work," I said, ignoring Lindee's doubts. "You'll need a name. Not just Rick."

"Mr. Latimer," Rick said as though he had the name ready to use.

"Mr. Latimer?" I repeated.

"Sounds respectable," Rick said.

"I don't know," Lindee said. "My mother can see through a con, believe me."

Rick chuckled. "Honey, I'll have your mother eating out of my hand before I've been there five minutes."

"Really?"

"A saw buck says I'll have her inviting me to eat in her kitchen before we leave," he said.

"Okay, you're on!" Lindee growled and laughed. I hated to remind Lindee she had no money to speak of.

"I wouldn't wager him," I warned. "He's very talented. Plus, he does have the leprechaun thing going for him."

"Wait. What's a 'sawbuck'?"

* * *

A half hour later I pulled up to Lindee's house. It was brick two-story, in DuKane. It was nice to be back on home turf—so to speak. Lindee needed some clothes, and personal items—the excuse I used to convince her she needed to go. We were basically living out of suitcases without the benefit of suitcases. Plus, she had no money, and none of my clothes fit her.

We all piled out of the Jeep. Lindee went three steps and stopped dead on the sidewalk staring up at the red brick house with white shutters. "I can't go in there," she said, eyes huge.

"Oh, come on," I said. "It's your mother for crying out loud!"

"That's just it. It's my mother. She has a tongue as sharp as a machete!" She looked at me and then her eyes dropped to Rick. She put her hand out at him. "And how am I going to explain Rick to her!"

"Hell-ooo," Rick said, both hands wagging. "I'm a guy who was born without arms. What's she going to do, put me out on the street?"

"You just insulted Rick," I said. "Not only that, he's a leprechaun. He can do crap on you if you don't behave yourself."

Lindee bit her lower lip. "I'm sorry, Rick. I'm *so* sorry!" she began to hiccup. Great. She hiccuped when she was nervous.

"Don't worry about it, kid. Just go in there and face the music," he said.

Lindee turned to him and said, "Who are you again? What's the story you're going to give my mother? Because she can smell a lie ten miles away, I swear!" The mile just became ten. Great.

"Lindee, get a hold of yourself." I grasped her by the shoulders and shook her a little to stop her from hyperventilating. I was about to slap her if she didn't cut it out. "Look, your mother misses you, she needs to see you to know you're alright," I said. "And I'll introduce Rick myself, so it will take the stress off you." I knew she was worried that her mother would mistakenly think Rick was one of her weird boyfriends. Actually, he would be more normal looking than any of the guys she had dated—and that was the god-awful truth.

"Okay. Okay," she said batting the air with her hands. I knew when she began repeating herself she was really nervous, so I wasn't going to harp on the comment she made about Rick. Besides, I knew Rick could handle his own—in his own way.

Lindee went up to the door. She tried to open it.

"It's locked." She turned to me like I had a magic spell to open a door for her.

"Knock," I said.

She knocked. Then she rang the doorbell. "It's freezing out here!" She jumped around a little to emphasize that she was cold. Hell, I was cold, too.

We actually didn't have much for jackets and we waited on the sidewalk that had been cleared of snow. Someone had made a snowman in the yard. I *Knew* it had been her brother; he and his friends had made it yesterday. Icicle lights hung from the eves of the house, and small colored lights draped over the bushes, all lit and glowing through an inch or two of snow.

The door opened to a middle-aged woman. Her dark hair curled and styled just so, had silver strands running through it. Her mother's voice went high. "Oh, my God! You made it! Come in!"

We all stepped into the warmth of my aunt and uncle's home. Lindee chuckled nervously as her mother hugged her—they were a hugging family. She knew better not to hug me, because I'd blurt something out. Like when I was small and she and my uncle hugged me. I'd pointed at my uncle and blurted, "He dropped your earring in the garbage disposal!" and that started a fight between them. But I had more control of myself these days. Really.

We entered the living room, everything was just as I remembered it. All beige furniture with plastic covers over the couch. You did not put your feet up on the coffee table or any chair. Above the fireplace, and between a family portrait (from five years ago, before Lindee had gone into her Goth look), and a slightly yellowed one of my aunt and uncle's wedding photo, hung a huge crucifix. Off to the side stood a fake Christmas tree draped in ornaments and lights, with piles of wrapped presents underneath.

"Hi, Aunt Ann," I said.

"Oh-h, my goodness!" My aunt's tears gleamed in her eyes. "Sabrina!" Her arms out-stretched, she came over and put her arms around me and I blocked her emotions, and everything I didn't want to know about her, best I could. "You found my daughter, and I haven't even had a chance to thank you at all!" She kissed me on the cheek. "I sent you a Christmas card. Did you get it?" *Crap.* I hadn't even sent any out. It was too late, now.

"Uh, yes. Very nice card. Thanks," I lied through my teeth. It had probably come in my mail and I had no way of going to get my mail. In the back of my mind I thought that maybe I should call my post office and ask them to hold all my mail until further notice.

My aunt's eyes slid to where Rick stood, hat in hands. I suddenly realized he had a suit on. He'd magicked a change of clothes while we were still outside. He looked more dignified, to tell the truth, than was warranted.

"This is Mr. Latimer," I said right away. "He's sort of escorting us today."

"Oh—uh—hello," she said, not quite sure if she should shake his hand. Obviously reconsidering that, she said, "Thank you, Mr. Latimer. You must be from the—uh—rehab? I'm so grateful to you for taking my daughter in."

"Yes, Mrs. Strong," Rick said. "You know we do a lot for the kids and young adults at the school." I felt a blush coming on as Rick began to work his charm. "We at Saint Felicia's Academy have always taken in the most difficult of cases." I had no idea where he came up with the name of some bogus academy, but he was doing great.

"Oh, really?" Aunt Anne said, looking at him a little more closely. If her eyes were lasers, he'd be cut in half.

I twisted the ends of my gloved fingers. Lindee hiccuped.

"Well, take me for example. My mother abandoned me when I was only a baby. The sisters all took me in and" —he shrugged—"I turned out great!"

"But of course you did!" she said, her cheeks flushed, smiling like a toothpaste commercial. "So, how is my daughter doing?"

Lindee tried to escape her mother's perimeter, but Aunt Anne caught her by the shoulder and wrangled her back into the spotlight.

"Oh, she's doing just fine." Rick beamed. "She's very good at her studies, and I think we're getting down to why we are still just a wee bit angry."

"Angry? Why should she be angry?" Aunt Anne asked and I saw her Italian ire flare up. "We took care of her! Put her through the best schools, and—"

"This isn't something that can be undone in just a few short weeks, you understand. Kids, like your daughter, here, need a firm hand but also understanding. So, we've gotten through the hard part of cleaning her up."

"Hmnnn," she said. Crossing her arms, she eyed Lindee critically. "You look like a hooker in that shirt, by the way."

Lindee's shirt dipped low, and was showing cleavage.

"Well, I inherited your boobs, Mom, so it's not my fault I look like a hooker."

Her mother pulled in a shocked breath—I thought she would slap her silly for that remark. "That's enough, young lady!"

"Now, now," Rick said, shaking a finger at Lindee. "What did we say about disrespecting your parents? Especially your mother."

Face turning pink, Lindee turned and made huge eyes at Rick as if to say, "Knock it off." But Rick was on a roll. He was like a steam roller, in fact.

"There's a few things we should discuss, Mrs. Strong," Rick said and moved to Lindee's mother's side, a hand toward her as if to guide her off to one side. "Alone," he added, giving me a look.

"Of course. Why don't you come into the kitchen? I've just made a lemon meringue pie. We can talk over coffee, and a piece of pie," my aunt said to Rick.

"Oh, you drive a hard bargain, Mrs. Strong," Rick said with a chuckle, and threw us the cat-ate-the-canary look. "I can't remember the last time I had homemade lemon meringue pie." He turned his head and winked at us. The two of them strode through the house toward the kitchen.

I looked at Lindee and shrugged. "Told you."

* * *

Stefan woke to the sound of rustling in his bedroom. It startled him, knowing he was very much alone. He turned in the bed, and saw a disturbing sight of a large black bird sitting staring at him from his bureau. He remembered the black bird Sabrina was so concerned about at the party, and tried to get it to fly off the balcony. It had refused, of course, because—he realized much later—it wasn't a bird at all. Why was he here in his room? How did he get here? Wait, he knew the answer, but it just wouldn't come to him at the moment.

"What do you want?" Stefan asked, voice tight. He rolled over to his back, arm flopped over his eyes. He lifted his arm and peeked at the bird.

The bird opened up its wings and inside of ten seconds the bird turned into a man, who now stood at the side of the bed. This made Stefan sit up. It was the Undead Indian, of course. He still had the wings, though. *What the fuck?* He looked rather formidable.

"I want nothing," the Undead Indian said. "I have come to warn you."

"Warn me of what?"

"To be careful where Sabrina is concerned."

"Because she's dangerous? She might kill me? I know that. She nearly killed my father with that dagger."

"That's where you are wrong." The Indian's black eyes glowed preternatural green in the semi-darkened room.

"What do you mean?" Stefan asked. The man was making little sense and he wanted him to say whatever the hell he was going to say and to go away so that he could sleep. He was accustomed to at least ten hours of sleep. He'd be lucky if he got eight.

"She did not wield the dagger."

"Who did?"

"I did." His brows lifted with the significance. "She never called it to her aide."

Stefan held a poker face. *Why is he telling me this? Maybe he's jealous. That must be it.* Stefan smiled inwardly. "I know you possess her—"

"In ways that you never can, white-eyes," the Indian said, smirk broadening, showing his very white teeth.

"No doubt," Stefan said. He couldn't imagine what sort of crazy sex he and the sibyl enjoyed. No one knew much about Undeads, only that they took the souls of those who died—some primarily took souls from people who died in accidents or had been murdered. It was how they fed. But some fed by having sex with multiple partners. In a way Stefan was a bit jealous of his closeness with the sibyl. But it didn't matter. He was going to mate with her and that was final.

"Oh, I see," Stefan said as realization hit him. "You're upset because I'm supposed to knock her up?" He held back the snicker in the back of his throat. He'd nearly forgotten that the Undead had been her lover before he died. No wonder he was constantly with her.

"I warn you, Capella, I won't use the dagger on you. I'll rip out your black heart if you should mistreat her in any way, and that includes deceiving her or tricking her, or hurting her physically, or emotionally."

"Why do you think I would do any of those things?"

"Because I know you, Capella. I know you better now than when I was human." Arms crossed, he smiled again, showing teeth. The black wings resting on his back like some deviant fallen angel. "Remember I can be anywhere anytime, remaining invisible. I know your escapades with women and I find you disgusting."

"Never mind how you feel toward me. Bottom line is, you want me to treat the sibyl with kid gloves?"

"That would be the general idea," he said. Dante glared at him for a long moment, and then very, very slowly, he faded to nothing.

"Finally!" He fell back and glanced at his clock. Three fifteen in the afternoon. Fuck. Three hours before he had to get up and begin making arrangements for Sabrina and their evening together. Stefan pulled the sheet back over himself. *At least two more hours!*

Chapter 21

Drink and be Merry

We said good bye to Lindee's mom—who practically wanted to adopt Rick before we got out of the house. She had told him that he was welcomed to come by again for lasagna dinner some night. He actually gave her his cell phone number. Knowing Rick and his enjoyment of food and ladies, he'd be on that in a New York minute.

It was still early and I sure didn't want to go back into Chicago, or back to the Towers—yet. I didn't wish to brood, fret and worry about tonight, or whatever Stefan had in store for me. Yes. He couldn't do the nasty with me—not yet, ha-ha. But there were things he could do to, or with me, or *at* me. Sheesh!

"I need a drink," I announced as I drove out of DuKane. "Rick, tell me how to get to Tom's Tavern from here."

"Sure, sweetheart." He looked down at his phone. "Just take this road all the way to Randal. That will get you there," he said. I looked up in my rear view mirror. He was back in his street clothes. Good. He was beginning to give me the creeps in the suit. He'd looked like a Jehovah Witness ready to spout Bible verses.

"Are we going to that little bar again?" Lindee asked.

"Yeah," I said, shifting into fourth, as we headed out on the highway. A sign told me Geneva was twenty-six miles ahead. I wanted to turn right and go home, actually. Thinking about my home brought tears to my eyes. "Rick," I sniffed after a few miles, "what's going on at my house? Any change?"

"Let me see. Just give me a few seconds to get that up," he said looking down at his smart phone. "Oh, how I love my apps."

Using my rearview mirror I looked back at him. Next to him sat a large black garbage bag filled with Lindee's clothes. She didn't have a suitcase, I guess, so she'd gotten a jumbo black garbage bag from her mother. I was glad that Lindee had been able to get all her things she needed from the house. I told her that since I now had a penthouse, she could have my old suite for herself. As far as I knew the penthouse was something that Stefan had given to me—not that I'd wanted, or asked for it.

"The ward is still up, but it's constantly being tested. Someone or something wants in," Rick reported.

"Naamah," I said.

"Or his minions," Rick said.

"Who's Naamah?" Lindee wanted to know.

I glanced into my rearview mirror again. "Since Rick is good at storytelling, I'm going to let him tell you about when we went to Dark World and met him, and all those nasty demons there," I said.

"Oh, I'd love to tell this story, sweetheart! Let me see. Where to start?"

"With saving Bjorn who was trapped in that church?" I suggested.

"Oh, yeah. Good idea, otherwise she won't know why we had to go to Dark World to begin with," Rick said.

"Why did you?" Lindee asked.

"Bjorn had to get there for his trial," Rick said. With that, he launched into the story.

* * *

An hour later, Rick directed me down an older section of Geneva and I found a handy parking spot near the front of a place called O'Fallon's Inn. I had no idea what the name of it was, since I'd never gone in through the front of the establishment.

"This is it?" I questioned Rick as we walked up to the glass front doors arranged on the corner of the building, and up two slightly crumbly, rounded steps. It looked eighty years old, if not a hundred.

"Yep." Rick stepped up to the door, grabbed the door handle and held it open for us.

"Thank you," I said.

"You are quite welcome," Rick said.

"This is where we stayed the other night?" Lindee asked.

"This is the place."

We stepped through a narrow foyer. There was a dark stained phone booth and a small closet for hanging coats and hats. I was surprised that the owners had not gotten rid of these reminders of the older days. Nostalgia was "in" these days.

We stepped into the hotel lobby. I recognized the green carpet and the stairs we all had climbed that night to go to the third floor. To the other side was the door to the restaurant. Without breaking stride we all headed through the door. A hostess smiled and greeted us.

"Hello," she said. "There's a private party today."

I paused, feeling almost like I'd be doing a discourtesy by advancing through the restaurant.

"Hi, toots, these ladies are with me," Rick said as he strode ahead. "Party at Tom's today? Cool."

"Oh, hi, Rick," she said brightly, and smiled up at us. "Go on through." She directed with her hand.

We all followed Rick through the quiet restaurant, which was deserted, no one was seated at the tables or booths. We entered the short hall at the end of which were the swinging doors. Lively music, and lots of voices filtered out to my ears. It did sound party-like.

"Oh, God. Not the wall again," Lindee said as we walked into the hallway, and Rick strode through those swinging doors.

"Ri-i-ick!" Came a chorus of voices, greeting the leprechaun.

"Don't you hear that?" I asked her.

"No. I don't hear a thing." Lindee looked at me. I pushed her forward. She stumbled through the doors, screeching, and stood blinking around where she'd wound up.

I stepped through right behind her and a greeting from the same group came, "Hey, Sabrina! Hey, Lindee!"

I wasn't sure who all was speaking, until I saw Micheal standing at a long table with a crowd of people seated around it. He held a large mug of dark beer in his hands. Tom smiled at us from behind the bar. There may have been a dozen faces looking at us from the bar, but dozens more on the main floor.

"Hey, Micheal!" I shouted back at him because the live music was really loud. The Tavern had become larger, with more tables—some of them ten feet long with dozens of people sitting at them. I figured there must have been fifty people here. There was a small stage in the back with four people performing some very spirited, foot-stomping Irish tunes. Bar maids in their Kelly green dresses and frilly aprons worked the floor, carrying huge trays with drink and food to the tables. I had to wonder what the occasion was. Everyone seemed really happy. It looked like a celebration.

Rick snagged his usual stool at the bar. The bar had become more than twice the length it was originally—I figured it might have grown to about twenty feet long. Lindee and I found stools a little further down the other end. Tom smiled a lot more than I had seen him smile before, and engaged in lively chatter as well. Two other bartenders worked along with him, and barmaids scurried to get their drinks filled. I settled in a seat, feeling among friends, even though I knew maybe only a handful. I spotted Andrew Morkel, seated at one of the tables, laughing and talking.

"Hello, Sabrina!" Micheal swooped in beside me and leaned his forearms onto the bar, a tankard of dark beer in his hands.

"Hi, Micheal," I said. "Looks like a great party. What's the occasion?"

"It's my birthday!" he said.

"Well, happy birthday!" I beamed.

"Happy birthday! I just love parties!" Lindee chimed in beside me.

Tom placed two drinks in front of us. I wondered what he'd chosen for us. Mine was a white wine of some sort, and Lindee had a beer with a huge head on it. Tom always knew what one wanted to drink. He waited for us to take a sip.

Mine was a wonderfully sweet Moscoto. "Oh, that's perfect, Tom!" I said.

"Oh, I like this!" Lindee said. "Tastes a little like root beer." She sipped again. "Has a little kick to it."

Tom nodded. "Old family recipe," he said to her. "Food will be out soon for you two, and there's cake for later."

"Great!" I said. Looking at Lindee's drink I thought, *I hope it isn't real booze.*

It isn't, Sabrina. A little elfin magic is all, and will make her think she's drinking, when she's not.

Startled, I stopped and looked up at Tom. He gave me a little wink.

You can hear my thoughts? I sent my telepathic message forward.

It's more that you can hear me, Sabrina. Tom winked again, nodded and moved to the next customer.

I turned back to Micheal and had to shout above the music. "I've never been here when there were so many people!" I tapped my foot on the stool's footrest to the beat. "Great band. Makes me want to dance."

"Well, by all means!" Micheal took my hand and before I knew it I was out on a cleared spot where other people were dancing. I didn't know how to dance to this music, but I sort of followed Micheal's footsteps. His feet were very quick and he went into an Irish jig. I got lost, gave up and stepped back, out of the way to watch and clap in time with the beat. Other people stopped dancing, and those who were seated turned to watch and began clapping along. Holy cow, this guy could have given Micheal Flatly a run for his money.

Lindee sidled up beside me, clapping. "Wow. He's good!" her voice in my ear. She smelled of the root beer she was drinking. I had to wonder about it—she would have normally demanded a "real" drink. I had been prepared to say to her, "You aren't of age, yet." Tom had never carded her, or anyone else in his establishment. Since he was telepathic, I wondered if he didn't "know" Lindee was not of drinking age and did a little magic to whatever he served her so that she *thought* she was actually drinking something she shouldn't be.

Two waitresses, a blond and a redhead, joined in with Micheal, and all three began tapping and stomping together in synchronized steps. The band began to play a more up-tempo tune to go along with their steps. They were so good they got whistles and yells from the crowd.

"Yeee haw!" I cried enthusiastically, clapping along.

They kept dancing, and then a couple of other women—barmaids and servers in their Kelly green skirts, their hair in traditional tight, long curls that bounced with their steps—went out and joined them, keeping Micheal in the middle of a line. Arms down at their sides, they did a turn, still side-by-side, and without touching, and then the music stopped—it now was just their shoes stomping and tapping vigorously, making the floorboards sound like they might cave in at any moment. I'd never seen this Irish dancing live before, and this was fun to watch and be a part of.

About ten minutes later, they were done, and everyone cheered and clapped. Lindee and I meandered back to our stools and drinks, and now plates of food had been placed there too. I hadn't sat for ten seconds when I heard my name being called out. I turned to see Morkel motioning to me. I grabbed my drink and went over to him where he stood at the end of one of those long tables.

"I don't mean to interrupt your good time, or your meal," he said as the band began playing again—this time something softer, and we didn't have to shout.

"Oh, no problem," I said, my glance taking in the people at the table. Some were young, and some were quite old.

"I'd like you to meet some of my relatives," he said and went on with the introductions. "This is Paudeen and Annora Tallach. And over here is Timothy and Noreen Morkel—my parents." He motioned to the older people at the table. He looked like his father the most.

"Oh, how do you do," I said and they took my hand in a little shake.

"And," he turned around to introduce four more people. "Deaglan, Cassidy, Patrick and Annora—all of them O'Fallon." Two of the older couple had pure white hair, faces full of wrinkles, and yet their eyes were bright as they smiled at me.

"O'Fallon? As in the name O'Fallon on the front?" I asked.

"Yes. They are the owners," Morkel said.

"Well, thank you, Mr. and Mrs. O'Fallon for your wonderful hospitality, food and drink!"

"You're quite welcome, my child," the woman, Annora, said, her lips drawn up in a kindly smile, and the crinkles around her eyes and mouth deepened.

"I think of this place as my home away from home, or a port in the storm—so to speak," I was speaking the truth on this.

"Any time you have need to come to our place," she said. Then Mr. O'Fagan said something in Irish. His wife giggled.

"What was that?" I asked.

"It means, more or less, that our house is your house," Morkel said.

"Well, thank you!" I nodded to them.

"Now, go ahead and enjoy your food, before it gets cold," Morkel said. I thanked him and gave a little wave to the people I'd just met—*could they all be elves?*—and returned to my place at the bar. Lindee had her elbow on the bar talking to a tall man sitting next to her. I didn't recognize him. He had black hair, and normal looking ears. I guessed him in his mid-twenties at least. From where I sat, I didn't think he was hitting on her. It sounded more like he was telling her the history of the place.

Hungry, I eyed the large individual pie. I knew it was some sort of pot pie. Seven o'clock, my dinner date, was a long ways off yet. I'd eaten only that wedge of pie at Lindee's house, and it had worn off. I picked up my fork and knife and dug in. Steam curled up out of the thing like a smoke signal. The aroma took me back to my mother who made such things. If I ever got back home I would have to go through her recipe box and hunt down this recipe. Maybe Lindee and I could work on it together.

"Great. I'll give you a call," the dark haired man said. He got up and stepped away.

Lindee turned to me. "Do you know who that was?"

"No," I began eating, because I wasn't sure that I would be able to eat anything tonight with Stefan seated across from me. A vampire was not the best dinner partner, if my past experiences told me anything.

"He's Shaun O'Fallon, manager of the restaurant. I told him I'd like to work here. He told me they were looking for kitchen help and I could start next week!"

I gaped at her. "Lindee!" I said, startled by her change of plans. "I thought you told me you didn't want to stay here. I mean in this world. That it might make you return to the life you once led."

She shrugged. "I don't know. I like these people. I could try it. See how it goes."

"What about everything back on Black Veil? What about Joha?"

"Huh? Oh, him." She made a disparaging sound with her lips, and batted the air dismissively. "I don't want to go back there. I don't like not having everything we have here, like electricity, and toilets that flush and hot water you don't have to heat over fire. You know that soot gets all over you, your clothes, and the whole house?"

"Okay, whatever you like," I said. Actually, it might be the best thing for her to get a job in the field she liked most. "Like I said, you can stay in my suite, if you want."

"Well, about that… Shaun said that they have rooms here I could rent. He said it would start out as room and board."

"You mean the small hotel rooms? No bathroom?"

"No. They have efficiencies here. I'd have my own bathroom—thank God. Besides, I don't have a way to get here."

"Oh, okay. Sounds like a plan," I said. We turned to our food, and ate without talking. I think we were both hungry.

A man settled beside Lindee, in the now vacated stool. It was Quist. I wanted to speak to Quist. His mood felt really gloomy. I didn't want to bother him, but

I wanted to know how Fritz was doing. I hadn't thought to ask anyone before I left the hospital.

"Trade places," I told Lindee. A waitress came and picked up her empty plate.

"Huh?" she asked. I made a motion to indicate I wanted to speak to Quist, sitting next to her. She mouthed the word, "Oh." Nodding, she got up and we traded seats.

I settled beside Quist. He didn't seem to notice as a pint of stout was placed before him and a plate of soda bread.

"Hi," I said. "How's Fritz?"

"He's still in a coma," Quist said without looking up at me. He stared straight ahead, one hand around his pint of beer. He looked at me. "Sorry, I didn't even ask how you were. Or why you were in the hospital yourself."

"I'd been attacked by Gremlins. Poisonous kind."

He nodded. "You're lucky to be alive, from what I've heard of those bloody things."

"They got to me in time. Good thing the hospital is in the same place."

He nodded and sipped his drink almost absently.

"So, you guys were attacked by a bunch of rogues?" I asked.

"Yeah. That's pretty much what happened," he said. "They were definitely after us."

"Wow. You're lucky to be alive," I said, fingering the stem of my glass.

"Wouldn't have been if that guy hadn't come out of nowhere to help," Quist said after another sip.

"Tell me again about him." I said. "I was a little distracted at the time you told me about it."

"Yeah, he just showed up out of nowhere—he wasn't driving, just walking. He took two of them and cracked their heads together like eggs!" It was the first emotional thing he'd said. His hands opened as he told the story. "Then he carried Fritz for me, and ran—I mean he ran—to keep up with me, put him in my car, and then he disappeared."

"Yeah, that's right. I remember you saying that," I said.

"He wasn't a vampire," Quist said, looking steadily at me. "And I know he wasn't an elf. Elves can't do that."

"What did he look like?"

"I never got a good look at him—his face. He wore a big duster, with a mantle and hat. I think he had a beard, but it was hard to see. He was big, too. Had to be six-four easy."

"Brawny?" I asked.

"No. Not really brawny, or outwardly muscular that I could see. Just well-toned."

"How did he disappear?"

"I watched him duck into an alley," Quist snapped his fingers. "Then he vanished. He wouldn't tell me who he was or anything."

"Well," I said on a little sigh, "I guess you're lucky he came along when he did and he was on your side."

Quist nodded. He finally looked at me and a small smile crimped his lips. "I heard you killed at least fifty goblins."

My face went warm. I shrugged. "It was me or them."

"So I hear it told," he said. "Poisonous? No human can survive a bite from a gremlin."

"Uh, yeah. A kindly vampire gave me some blood to counter act it," I said.

He smiled. Then, he gave me a pat on the shoulder. "First the rogue vampires, now the demons. We need an army to fight them."

I stared back into his blue eyes. "Yeah. I think we do." I looked around the room. "Anyone in here likely to sign up?"

"They don't get involved with vampire or human politics."

"Politics? Rogue vampires are killing people on the street! That's not political!"

"If it doesn't directly involve them, or their lives, they don't really care." He took a sip of his beer and stared ahead.

"What about you? You got hurt, too," I said.

"That was my choice to go after vampires."

"Why? If you don't mind my asking."

"Vampires killed my fiancé a couple months ago. I began hunting rogues then."

A memory of something interrupted my conversation. It was from a vision I'd had months ago when I was standing in a cemetery with Nicolas and the twins the first night I began working for Tremayne.

"I think we came across one of your kills. Did you use a bolt and a crossbow?" I asked.

He turned his head to me. "Yeah. At first that's all we used."

I shut my eyes. "I'm trying to remember the cemetery we were in."

"Who's 'we'?"

"That was when I first started working for Tremayne. I was trying to discover who had killed Letitia," I explained. He nodded. "So, you're not one hundred percent elf?"

"I'm only part-elf on my mother's side. I'm more or less half-elf and half-human. Anyway, the other elves here aren't likely to come to my defense—or yours—unless they're paid." He made a little grunt. "Or work for Tremayne Towers, of course."

That put a new light on things for me.

"What about when they brought all those humans over here from the towers, keeping them out of harm's way when Ilona took over and was going to have them for dinner?"

"That was different. These were co-workers. People they knew and couldn't very well leave for the vampires."

"No I suppose not. It might have embarrassed them." I now looked around the room. Tom stood in front of us, and gave us both fresh drinks.

"So, you're only part elf?" I asked Quist.

Quist looked up at Tom. "Yep. Like Tom. I'm part elf."

"Tom is only part elf too?"

I looked up at Tom again.

He looked slightly embarrassed as he said, "I'm just a rogue." Then he chuckled. "Sabrina has the real gifts. Or so I've heard."

It was my turn to feel embarrassed. "Well, I'm not anything but me, and every day I keep on finding out I can do something new and magical."

"Like incinerating gremlins?" Quist looked at me, head sagging over his drink.

I looked back at him and then up at Tom. "That was something new I didn't know I could do."

"How would that work on vampires, I shudder to wonder?" Tom was the one who asked this.

We both looked up at him.

"I would guess it would incinerate them just as well," I said, and smiled at Quist.

Chapter 22

Emma

When Bill entered the hospital where they had taken Emma, he knew what room number she was in without asking. The usual chemical smells that he associated with hospitals caught him off guard. They seemed stronger than he remembered. Not that he visited people in hospitals much.

He knocked on room 109. A frail voice said, "Come in."

When he pushed the door open, he tried to prepare himself, but there was no way to prepare to see Emma, a frail woman of 79, in a hospital bed. If she were human, instead of the descendant of Nephilim, she would not have sustained the injuries she had and lived. Her hip was broken—this he knew the moment he stepped inside her room. How he knew, he wasn't sure. Possibly he had some sort of second sight, now. But, he knew the demon in her living room had dropped her. It would take a long time for her to recover. During his drive out, he had been thinking on what he could do to assure her the best of care. He made a mental note of private nurses he could call who could take care of her, wherever she decided to go afterwards.

"Emma, how are you?" Bill said, stepping up to her bed. Smiling, she reached for his hand and he took it in both, gently holding the cold, frail, blue-veined hand that felt more like a cadavers hand. His heart lurched at the thought of her not making it, and yet that's what he was thinking. Again, he didn't know where that had come from.

"I've been better," she said. Her voice was strong, but her eyes looked tired. An I.V. hooked up to her other hand, he guessed it had pain medication in it. She looked at him for five or so seconds, seeming to try and remember who he was, and made a small chuckle. "The last I heard you were dead, cut in half in a cave-in." She spoke slowly. "You were the last person I would have expected to come in and stop that demon." She made a weak chuckle.

"I did. Die, I mean," he said truthfully. "Then I came back as a vampire—at least for a short while. I don't know how, or why."

"But, it's daytime," she said, pensive. "If you're a vampire, how would you walk in sunlight?"

He smiled and patted her hand in his. "Very observant, Emma."

She smirked, and her hand lifted as if to play-slap him—as she'd so often did—and missed by six inches. They both chuckled. "Stop that. Tell me. I want to know. I *saw* that you were killed in a vision."

"Yes. It took me a while to put things together." He pulled up a chair to sit closer to her. "I think someone who was working over the area where I had died bled. The blood fell into my ashes and—*poof*—I became a vampire."

"But, now you're not a vampire," she noted. "How can that be?"

He shrugged. "I have no explanation. I also seem to have extraordinary powers, as you saw yourself." Something inside him prevented him from revealing the vision of Nemesis to Emma. At the moment it felt wrong to speak of how she came to him and what she had said to him.

"Yes. You chased that demon off," she said. "Do you have a heartbeat?"

He turned his free arm upward and allowed her to find his pulse with cool fingers. "Oh, my," she said, eyes going wide. "A human heartbeat and you're warm. It's as though you were brought back to the living."

"It is," he said. "What about you? What were you about to do when the demons came?"

"Let's see." She paused to ponder this, looking down the length of the bed. "Ah! I was about to take a read, like I usually do in the evenings." Emma often used her crystal ball to reach one of her spirit contacts on the other side. "That's when it happened. I don't know how it got through my wards." She shook her white-mantled head.

"They are looking for the sibyl," he said. "They were there, at Sabrina's house too."

A worried look rippled her forehead as she place two fingers to her lips, glancing away momentarily as if in thought. She looked back at him.

"That isn't good. She isn't there at her house now, is she?" she asked.

"No. I've located her, however."

"Where?"

"At Tremayne Towers in the city."

"Is she safe?"

"It would seem so. There are many elves who live and work there. And I know she has one leprechaun who seems to be her friend."

"Ah, yes. I think I saw him once in one of my reads," she said nodding. "Have you made yourself known to her?"

"No."

"Why?"

"Because, she saw me die," he said. "I'm worried that she may see me as an enemy. She might even kill me."

"No. Never." Emma's hand gripped his arm. She gripped it with a strength that was surprising for everything she had been through.

He smiled and returned her grip—but gently. He needed to remind himself of the destructive strength he now had, and had to concentrate on using a gentler touch on humans he cared for. "I only came to see how you were. And to warn you to not go back home when you are released. I'll make sure you have the best of care. A private nurse—whatever you need."

"Oh, Bill," she said, almost tearing up. "You needn't do that."

"I'm going to, and you can't stop me," he said, a smile to back it up. "Where will you stay afterwards?"

"My sister can put up with me for a while, I suppose." Then her eyes went large. "Oh! Mr. Jangles! He's still at the house."

Bill chuckled. "The cat. Of course. Don't worry. I'll go to your place and take him to mine. He can terrorize my house for a while. Until you can come and get him, of course."

She chuckled, and patted his large hand.

"Oh, my heavens!" she said, fingers touching her lips again.

"What is it now?"

"I've forgotten. You're going to be a father!"

"I beg your pardon?" he said, confusion riddling his face, a grin working against the frown.

"Your sister Ophelia, she's—" she stopped and shook her head, blinking her eyes. "Oh my goodness, that sounds terrible!

His brows dipped now in confusion. "Emma, what are you trying hard not to tell me?"

Her hand went up weakly and flopped back down. "Forgive an old woman."

He made a small grunt. "You need not ask my forgiveness, and I hardly think of you as old." After all he outdated her by more than twenty years. But then he was full-blooded Nephilim, she was not.

She took a breath and started anew. "Ophelia, your sister, is surrogate mother of yours and Sabrina's child."

Bill felt a chill go down his back. The memory of what he'd asked of Sabrina before he died resurfaced. Odd how he could remember up to the very last seconds of his life. He remembered the look on Sabrina's face—her tears—as he lie dying cut in half by the rock. She had felt something for him—he was certain of this now—since she had gone ahead and donated some of her eggs toward the cause of helping their species.

He smiled, patted Emma's hand and looked down at her in the hospital bed. "Thank you for telling me, Emma. I would not have known, otherwise."

A half hour later, he left Emma, and drove out to her house on Sonata Road. Dark, the house looked sad and lonely to him. But the demons had moved away from her house. Unfortunately they had concentrated on Sabrina's house across the street. He could detect demons very easily by their phosphorous glow—whether they were allowing themselves physical bodies or not. He was very certain that Sabrina's wards were still up. Whoever had put them up for her was very strong. *The leprechaun?*

He used the extra key Emma always kept underneath the back porch steps. It hung from a nail, under the third step. No one would know to look there, and it was still there. Once inside, he could still smell the demon's residue of brimstone. He moved methodically through the house, calling "Mr. Jangles? Mr. Jangles, where are you? Kitty, kitty, kitty?" He walked through the dining room toward the steps, which went up to the second floor. He decided to grab a few things from his old room. Once he finished placing his clothing into a suitcase, he went back downstairs with it. He would need the cat's travel cage and a few other things. He found it in the usual spot on the porch. Mr. Jangles, if memory served, hated the cage, nearly as much as he disliked Bill.

Instinctively, Bill knew where the cat would be, and went to Emma's bedroom. There he spotted the black and white, long-hair feline on Emma's made bed. It jumped off the bed and darted underneath it.

"Well, it's good to see you too," he said. Mr. Jangles was Emma's familiar, and it showed devotion and idolatry only to her. Bill was not worthy of its time, apparently, as it always slinked off into another room. One would never see the two together. It had become a running joke between himself and Emma that people would think they were one and the same. Oddly enough, Mr. Jangles hadn't been with her that long—possibly a year, or less. In fact, it seemed odd to Bill that just suddenly the cat had simply been in the house, and Emma had said nothing to Bill about it, only calling it Mr. Jangles, and when it ran upon seeing Bill, she had decided it didn't like Bill very much. She thought it was cute. Bill was not amused. In fact, he found it down-right odd that an animal would not be able to come under his powers of persuasion.

He bent down onto his knees and flipped back a corner of the bedspread. The cat hissed and spat at him. The cat didn't like him any more now than it did before he had died. Possibly it sensed that Bill was different. Still there was no need to be so distasteful.

Bill had no time to waste with the cat, and so harnessed his magical abilities—the ones he'd always had with animals, but now there was added power—and lured the cat out from underneath the bed. The cat came out from hiding, meowing, as though it thought there was some treat in it for him.

"Come, come, Mr. Jangles. You can't dislike me any more now than you did a week ago, can you?" Bill picked it up—he had never touched the cat—and now petted its soft fur, and it purred. Cats were strange animals. He should easily make the animal obey him without any great difficulty, yet, he'd had to resort to more mental effort. His annoyance was pushed aside as he sensed that the cat was more than what he appeared. Not a mere cat. Power emanated from him. How was it he'd never sensed this before? He caught himself in mid-thought. *Because I've never touched it before.*

He walked back into the kitchen. The cat was out of food and water. What did it think it was going to subsist on?

As Bill opened the cage Mr. Jangles made a yowling protest and attempted to thwart him from placing him into the dreaded cage. It scratched him on the back of the hand. Bill managed to push him inside—all the while snarling and growling at him—and closed the door.

He was certain he would need stitches the way the cat had scored him. He examined the back of his hand. No scratches. No blood. No pain, in fact. He hadn't imagined what he'd felt—the cat's sharp claws had ripped into the back of his hand, he was certain of it. Yet, he was unharmed. His self-healing qualities seem to be even better than before.

He had questioned what exactly he had become, in the back of his mind since his return to the living—especially since speaking to Emma. The cat's attack and inability to leave a mark on him now brought it to the forefront. And what of last night when he'd killed those two vampires? He had smashed their heads together like two melons. *What the hell have I become?*

Chapter 23

Sabrina

Lindee and I returned to the towers. Rick stayed, since The Hideaway was his regular hangout. Tonight's meeting with Stefan in the back of my mind, I barely listened to Lindee's non-stop gibbering about working at the O'Fagan Restaurant. I reminded her that she would have to get some sort of restaurant certificate from a cooking school before she could actually cook. That didn't deflate her ego one bit. She said she'd work her way through school even if she had to waitress. I hoped she was up to that challenge. She had the out-going personality for waitressing, though, and I thought she might make a pretty good one. I was hopeful that the elf-run place would be good for her.

I parked my Jeep in the south side parking garage of the towers. I had no intentions of stepping one foot into the vampire side ever again, if I could help it. I had no need to, now. If someone wanted to see me they could frigging make an appointment and come up to my penthouse. *Penthouse. In Chicago. It even had a name. The Edelweiss... Listen to me, I'm up in the world, now.*

I opened the back door of the Jeep and lugged out the large garbage bag of Lindee's clothes and held it in my arms. "You can hang these up and use any of the drawers you want in the suite. I'll get my stuff out of there eventually," I said, stepping around a moving van next to my Jeep. It was a rental, with the price and phone number splashed all over it.

"Okay. No big," she said looping her hand through the backpack.

"We'll get these things to the suite, first. Then we'll go up and take a look at my penthouse."

"How cool!" she squealed. "My cousin has a penthouse."

"Well, you've got a frigging suite," I reminded.

She looked at me. "Really? It's mine?"

I shrugged. "Yes. I've paid rent for six months. It's mine, and I'm letting you use it."

"Nice!" She strolled away. "I won't have to move back home. Ever!"

A car door shut six vehicles down from us. A white car. It looked expensive. My attention paused on the tall man in a leather fedora who emerged from the car. He moved around to the trunk and leaned down to take out a garment bag. Tall, I guessed him at least six-four, and well-built, neither lean nor heavy. Something about the way he moved seemed familiar to me. And yet I could get no read from him. I didn't know if he was an elf or a vampire. But not likely a vampire, as it was still daytime.

"Hey," Lindee called, breaking my steady gaze at the hunk hunting around in his trunk—*what's he got in there? A dead body?* Funny how I couldn't get a read on what was in his trunk, even.

Embarrassed, I turned toward Lindee who was half-way across the garage heading for the elevator. "You got enough men to lust after—jeeze! C'mon. This thing's heavy!"

"Listen, you," I said, stepping to catch up. "I've got the heavy stuff, you twit."

* * *

Aware of Sabrina, Bill lingered near his trunk, back to her. He worried she might recognize him, even with the beard, so he stood bent over his trunk until her friend called to her and she stepped away, her footfalls tapping further and further away. After about thirty seconds, he turned and watched the two women enter the elevator. *That was close.* He could breathe again. He had no idea she would be there in the parking garage at the same moment he was—he had recognized her Jeep right away with that "Only In A Jeep" emblem on the wheel cover as he followed her through the garage in his car. Sabrina would probably not get a read from him, but that only meant she wouldn't know who he was—or *what* he was. That part was still a mystery to him.

Bill waited until the two were on the elevator before he closed his trunk. Beeping the remote, he turned with his garment bag over his shoulder, which he had traded at his house for the suitcase, when he'd dropped off Mr. Jangles. He had prepared the cat's bed and filled his food and water bowls, and arranged the cat litter box in the bathroom—for now, since he couldn't think of where else to put it.

He thought of getting on the elevator as he headed toward the stairs and then cautioned himself. Something told him to take the stairs. He stared at the door with the word STAIRS in bold letters. Shrugging, he opened it. A brisk climb up to the 20th floor would do him good. He didn't want another chance meeting—an even closer one, say, on the elevator—than this one in the garage with Sabrina. He wasn't ready to meet her face-to-face.

Emma's words, before he left her, came back to him. Her eyes had looked bright and clear when she'd said, "Bill, you were meant to be with Sabrina. I know this," she said and patted his hand. "Some things just take a while to happen. You'll see."

He smiled at the memory. But, deep inside, he really doubted her words.

Chapter 24

The Edelweiss

I remembered to get the special key-card for the penthouse that Stefan said he'd leave for me from the hotel clerk before we went on up to my suite. We must have looked like bag ladies striding across the hotel lobby with a huge black garbage bag and a backpack. But the clerk didn't say anything to us, and called me "Ms. Strong."

We carried our bags back across the lobby and I noticed that man in the hat and long coat again from down in the garage. He had a garment bag over his shoulder. Head down, the brim of the hat keeping his identity safe, he jogged up the winding steps quickly as though he had some sort of meeting and he was late. Either that, or he was trying to keep from being seen. Something about the way he moved up the steps, his strong strides, seemed familiar to me, but I was clueless. Maybe because he was so obviously trying to avoid being seen, I thought that perhaps he was someone I knew. But who it could be, since I could not get a read, I had no clue. I stared out through the elevator's doors with these thoughts and then they closed.

"Who is he?" Lindee asked.

I glanced at her and realized she'd seen the man too.

"Same guy as down in the garage. Bet he's handsome. Probably one of your past lovers, no doubt." She was joking. I think.

"I don't know. I can't get a read on him."

"You mean you don't know things about him like you do everyone else?" she asked as the elevator rose. "That's really weird."

"Yes. The only people I can't read are vampires, elves, Weres and certain magical people." I slid her a look, my brow arching. "And sometimes you." She giggled deviously.

"Maybe he's magical," Lindee concluded.

Tired of holding on to the bag I eased it onto the floor at my feet. "What do you have in here? Your entire wardrobe?"

She laughed. "Yes. Basically what I like, and what my mother doesn't like."

"Right. The low-cut blouses and skin-tight jeans?"

"Exactly." We both laughed.

About ten minutes later, we placed her things in my suite, then resumed our trip up to the penthouse. I slid my card into a slot before I could press the button for Penthouse. This was the so-called security, I gathered. What would keep someone from getting the card and using it to gain access was my worry.

In just a few minutes we arrived at the penthouse. The double white doors stood in front of us. And a little white sign engraved in gold said unnecessarily *The Edelweiss.* It was the only penthouse on this floor, unlike the double one on the vampire side. I spotted a doorbell and rang. After thirty seconds the door was opened by a straight-backed middle-aged man who wore a neat black suit over a white starched shirt and black tie.

"Miss Strong?" he looked first to me and then to Lindee, and back to me. Two women stood off to one side, waiting and looking expectant.

"Yes," I said. "I'm Sabrina, and this is my cousin, Lindee." I was getting a read from someone. Nervous. Someone, maybe all of them, were nervous. I wondered why. Maybe they had heard I was clairvoyant? Or, just that I was coming and would be their new mistress.

"Welcome home." He stepped back from the door to let us in.

Lindee snickered, and I headed her off from making a comment by glowering at her in warning. She tucked her chin in, trying to keep her smile wiped off her face, but she failed and hid it behind her hand.

A few seconds after entering, I took in the entrance hall. Neutral gray, and warm colors helped create a sleek contemporary look. Track lighting, hung from the low ceiling emphasized a narrow painting on the wall that looked like Japanese writing, and a corner display of pre-Columbian sculptures (which I knew were reproductions). Large ferns and potted trees—all real—stood around a black sculpture. The walls were covered in a gray textured fabric, the carpeted floor solid coffee-colored. A small doorway off to one side led to a sort of den, and the window beyond looked out onto Lake Michigan—which to me always looks like an ocean, only not as pretty blue-green. Straight away, the hallway that led from the main entrance, opened up into an octagonal hallway, with at least four, or five doors, and one hallway leading into another room. But the central focus in this octagonal room was a winding, open-staircase of white marble and brass handrails. It disappeared almost mysteriously into a hole in the white ceiling. A very large jade plant in a terracotta pot stood to the side, and a large statue of a Tiger made of wood stood guard, slightly beneath the open stairs. The area was no more than perhaps nine-by-nine, so the whole thing felt cozy.

"May I introduce you to the rest of your servants?" The butler gestured to the younger woman first. "Mindy is your maid, Dolores is your cook, and I am James, your house servant." He bowed.

The first woman was young, in her twenties, with large, expressive eyes, with dark hair pinned back. The woman next to her had gray hair pulled up in a bun. Her narrow eyes glinted through glasses. She was heavy set, and from my read, she was married to James. Both women wore black dresses and white aprons. More emotions pressed into me. The thought of Malcolm flitted around. Why Malcolm I couldn't figure out. Did they know Malcolm? I had to block them. My gloves protected me from most second sight, but not all. And emotionally, these people were off the charts. I had no idea why they were so nervous. Not over me, surely.

Maybe something they'd done? Somewhere in the back of my mind, the little red flag was waving frantically. *Hmmm.*

Lindee snickered and elbowed me. This was becoming too much fun for her. I didn't really think I needed three people to take care of me—but then someone had to pick up after me, and feed me, since I was a lousy cook, and clean this huge place. Maybe a butler wasn't such a bad idea either. He could answer the door for me. I was beginning to get flits of the different rooms throughout the place. There was actually a suite on the second floor, more open, but unfinished. The furnishings had not been completely put together, like the beds, and a few other things weren't quite done.

"Uh, hi, everyone," I said, nodding to the two women.

"Is there anything you would like me to make special for you tonight, Miss Strong?" Dolores asked.

"Uh, well…" I looked at Lindee. I'd been craving something all day, and I simply blurted it out. "Prime rib?"

She allowed herself a half-smile. She was thinking *My specialty.* Straightening her back, hands cupped together, she blinked rapidly, her eyes actually going back so all I saw where the whites when she said, "When would you like to be served?"

"Oh, um—" I thought back to Stefan's message. "I'm expecting a guest at seven," I said, and almost said he was a vampire, and not to worry about feeding him, but I caught myself.

"Will this be a formal, or casual affair?" She asked. She wanted to show off the crystal and silverware.

I was stumped.

"Formal," Lindee whispered to me. I looked at her. "Well, he's your date, isn't he?"

"Uh, not quite formal?" I wasn't sure, really. "It's only for one other person."

"A man? I'll make it special for you," she said, smiling more. "Thank you, miss." She made a quick little bow turned and went down the hall, and disappeared through a doorway. Off to the kitchen—I got a visual from my Knowing. It was a functional kitchen with two huge stoves and ovens, lots of counter space, and every sort of utensil and culinary do-dad you might need to entertain most of the people who lived in the towers.

The maid stepped forward. "I will take out some dresses for you to choose from," Mindy said. "May I show you to your bedroom?" She gestured ahead.

I looked at Lindee and made a face. "Dresses? I've got *dresses*? Here?"

"Several were brought up, madam" Mindy said in answer to my question which I thought had been in a stage whisper. "Come this way, if you please?"

I was so unused to being served and catered to, this was stepping way out of my comfort zone for who I was and how I'd grown up. Other little girls may have dreamed of being the Cinderella who became rich, but I didn't. I had a practical side to me that thought my adult life would be as hard, if not harder, than my childhood because of my abilities.

I was both right and wrong. Now I had to fight demons and other supernatural beings in order to survive, but at this point money was no problem.

We followed Mindy through the large foyer, through an open doorway, and down that one short hallway where she opened up a set of double doors. The expansive room was—as with the rest of the place—tastefully furnished. The bedroom was opulently draped in mint and dark brown fabrics, dark green carpet and trimmed in gold, walls scrolled with gold at the top. The canopy bed was large with matching drapes and comforter and a gazillion little pillows of every shape, size and color to compliment the room. The headboard was upholstered in matching mint fabric, and a matching ottoman at the foot of it.

"Silk sheets, you think?" Lindee wiggled her brows at me.

I paused to get a read. "No. Satin."

Mindy stood at a walk-in closet. "If you'll step in here, madam?"

Lindee and I walked through the room and into the walk-in closet which was about three quarters the size of the bedroom itself, and furnished nearly as well. Two mint upholstered armless chairs were stationed in corners, and one bench before a mirror and assortment of drawers.

"How long have you guys been here?" I asked Mindy.

"Only since yesterday. We were told you would be here yesterday," she said, doing her best to not look at me. Her eyes fluttered, she would not look directly at me. To me, this spelled guilt of something. But how could she feel guilty of anything, especially since we never met before this day?

"Right," I said. "Stefan told me he hired you three." Then, I got a read. It was of Letitia's penthouse. Oh. Not only Mindy had been there, but also the cook and butler. My flitting visions involved Malcolm seated at the table with Letitia. Next to them was the curio and Letitia's collection of porcelain dogs. Strange. They were seated in the kitchen. I worked to push this unrelated vision away.

Mindy opened one of the closets—there were a couple of them—with beautiful dresses. All in my size. Whether or not I'd like them was another matter entirely. I supposed if I were to "entertain" certain guests, I might need some of these things. But I had news for these people, I wasn't about to "live" here. I might stay for a few nights at the most. That was it. I had to get my house back from the demons. How I would do this, I didn't know at the moment.

"Oh. My. God! These dresses… these shoes! Ak!" Lindee went into a full drool, complete with ogling everything while going through all of the things on the rack. There were short dresses, there were floor-lengths, and there were your every-day sort of dresses, and pant suits for casual.

"Here's a very nice Dior," Mindy said, pulling a long formal dress out. It was peach. I wasn't crazy about it. That's when I got a vision and staggered a little. Lindee caught me.

"Oh-oh. There she goes," Lindee said, holding me up.

Stefan wearing a lavender shirt with a matching tie, dark suit (a slight deviation from what I've normally seen him in). He looks like a typical hot Italian dude.

Me wearing an electric blue sleeveless gown with a silvery band of sequins that began at the lower back curved over the left hip and down the side ending in a relaxed curl near the end. I looked stunning.

I came out of the vision. Lindee held my arm and Mindy looked a little startled.

"Did I say anything?"

"No," Lindee said.

I looked up at Mindy. "You might as well know, I'm a touch clairvoyant. I will, from time to time, go into a vision. I'll be alright as long as someone catches me, lays me down and leaves me be."

Mindy's eyes went large, then she pulled the reins in on her outward show of emotions and said, "Yes, miss," she said, avoiding my eyes again. I knew my statement had caught her off guard.

I had another image of the porcelain dogs and that curio. Why, I wasn't sure. I needed to get Mindy out of here. I stepped up to the closet, found the dress I saw myself wearing in my vision and pinched the material between my gloved fingers. "This one, I think."

"Oh!" Lindee gasped, and stepped in front of me, hogging the space. "This is a gorgeous dress!" Lindee touched it. "You could wear those earrings you wore the other night with it."

"Maybe," I said, distracted.

"There's jewelry, as well as shoes." Mindy pulled out drawers lined in red velvet holding expensive-looking jewelry. There were several drawers full of shoes—all of them the spiky heals I hated. Who knew what my shoe size was? *Tremayne. That's who. Duh.*

"Who had these things sent up here?" I asked.

"I am not exactly certain, madam. They were here on a rack when I arrived. I only put them away, just yesterday."

"I'm sure it had to have been Stefan," I said to Lindee. We stepped out of the bedroom. "What time is it?" I asked.

Lindee looked at her watch. "It's ten after five o'clock."

"Shoot. I'd better get ready." I turned to her. "You gonna be okay tonight all alone?"

Lindee made a funny sound with her lips. "Of course! I got along fine without you last night. Remember?"

"I'd like to forget that, but yes." We both chuckled.

"Besides, I'll be busy putting my clothes and shit away. I'll order a pizza."

"Sounds like a plan," I said, following her out of the closet, through my bedroom and out into the hallway. The hallway was as wide as most rooms, with furnishings, like a side cabinet and chairs with crystal lamps.

"I'll be fine." Lindee moved through the Octagonal Room and looked up at the corkscrew stairway. "I wonder where that goes."

"It's a small suite," Mindy said before I could answer. "It's for guests—"

"It has three bedrooms," I interrupted her, then, realizing my error I put a hand to my lips. "Sorry. Just sort of popped out."

"You've been here before, madam?" Mindy asked, the look of surprise on her face.

"No. I told you. I'm clairvoyant. I simply know things," I explained. I could also tell her that I knew she was from Clinton Iowa, went to the state university, taking Child Development, but after two semesters, decided she really didn't like children as much as she thought, and switched to housekeeping, and had eventually moved with her husband to Chicago, where she had more opportunities for a maid position. I got all of that with one sweep of our eyes meeting. She dipped her gaze back down. I presumed she was used to being under the beck and call of a vampire, and feared I had the same powers. It would shock her what I could and couldn't do. I was better than a vampire, as I was now. I knew everything about her past and present, and if I had another moment of holding her gaze, I'd know all her little secrets. If I touched her, I would get a vision of all she did yesterday, the day before, last week, last month, etc. Maybe something that happened when she was a child. Or, I could simply touch one of the dresses with my un-gloved hand. That was when an evil thought raced through my mind and I banished it quickly.

Deciding I didn't want to know more than I had to about my servants, at least for the time being, I turned to look down a new hallway. It was a wide enough hallway that there was furnishings in it. A sideboard—or whatever they called them—and a couple of tastefully upholstered chairs.

Seeing my curiosity, she opened her mouth to tell me all about where it headed to, but I beat her to the punch. I pointed and said, "That goes through the Entertainment room, and eventually to a sun room with lots of plants and a hot tub." I glanced at her and saw Mindy's fearful look. Hands wringing, her eyes darted to me, then went almost guiltily to the sideboard two feet away. I pressed my fingers to her arm and the vision of her placing a large black box into the bottom drawer played out in my head. *Hmm.* She's very guilty about whatever she put in that drawer. I needed to know what it was, but my attentions went back on what was happening around me.

"If that is all, miss?" Mindy asked. She wanted to escape. I let her go and turned to Lindee who chuckled with a knowing look.

"You used to do that all the time, and it upset my mother so much," she squealed and tapped my arm. "I think that's one of the reasons I love you."

"Oh, yeah? How comforting to think you would love me because I gave your mother a migraine."

Lindee laughed, and it filled the room, but the fabric walls absorbed the sound.

"By the way, there's also a pool and garden up on top, through another stairway on that second floor." I pointed, continuing with my knowledge of the place.

"Really?" Lindee gasped. "You have a pool?"

"We won't be able to enjoy it until this summer," I said.

"Sounds like I'll be visiting you a lot this summer!"

We both laughed.

A few minutes later, we said good bye, and Lindee left, excited to get her things moved into my old suite. I looked over at James who stood near the door, having appeared from the other room off the entryway. "I need to make a call to Earthly Pleasures, but I don't know the number."

"I can make that call for you, miss. What do you need from that establishment?" he asked, chin slightly up, hands in front of him like a good waiter.

Knowing my servants had once served Letitia, I didn't pause in saying, "Have them send up a four-pack of Real Red."

Without missing a beat, he said, "Yes, miss." He stepped back to a small table near the display of artwork, and picked up a land-line phone.

"That's for my guest tonight," I added, unnecessarily.

"Stefan Capella? Very well, miss," James said, waiting for the call to go through. After a moment, I heard him speak with someone. Meanwhile, I returned to my bedroom and found Mindy laying out the dress I'd asked for, plus the matching shoes, jewelry and underthings. The shoes, bra and panties were blue to match the dress. I wanted to pinch myself.

"Will you be taking a shower, or a bath madam?"

"A bath."

"I will draw it for you." She paused and added, "Bath salts or bubble? I believe there may be Himalayan salts, and there's some jasmine and also lavender bubble bath." She moved away from the bed and headed toward the large bath.

"Uh, bubble bath. Lavender." I said letting her swish ahead of me onto the large bathroom. It was similar to the one in the penthouse I'd been in the other night, only not peach in color. Mint tile with dashes forest green. The large tub was on a platform, essentially the same as the one I'd used last night. A lush fern and ivy seemed to grow out of a limestone wall on the other side. The counter and sink matched the colors exactly.

Sound of the water rushing into the tub pulled my attention to the mirror, which had a marble effect throughout. Plus I found Dante looking on from a corner. Only I could see him, which was a blessing.

Mindy busily put out a wash cloth and a huge super fluffy towel for me in the same colors as the bathroom in forest green with mint satin along the edges. I, meanwhile, went back into my room and pulled a few things out of my bag and brought them into the room.

"Would you like anything to drink or munch on while you bathe, miss?" Mindy asked as she paused in the bedroom before leaving.

"That's not a bad idea. Wine and dark chocolate, if you can find any—the chocolate, I mean."

"Oh, I'm certain that Dolores would have something you would like."

"Good." I smiled, waiting for her to leave.

Once she was out of the room I stripped and stepped up to the large bath tub. I slowly lowered myself into the warm water, which drew a sigh of absolute relaxation from me. My lower back and abdomen were still aching from my period. Every molecule in my body shuddered and I lay my head back against the little pillow, closed my eyes and wanted to sleep in there forever.

"Miss?" a voice brought me out of a light sleep.

"Yes?" I didn't open my eyes to Mindy who had returned.

"Here is your glass of wine—a Merlot—some chocolates, and some wedges of cheese that Dolores has made up for you."

I cracked my eyes open to watch her place a small plate of expensive-looking chocolates and slices of cheese, some green grapes, and a glass of wine down on the side of my tub. There was at least six inches of ledge for her to place the silver tray on.

"Thanks," I said, drawing my hand out of the water to dry on a small white towel. That's when I saw Mindy in my mind. I jerked with the vision, pulled in a breath and my eyes had become huge.

"Is everything alright, miss?" she asked, finding my reaction slightly unusual.

"Uh—" I didn't know what to say, or how to say it.

I had to work on blocking this image coming from Mindy who had touched the washcloth. I had to rearrange my look of shock.

"Is everything alright, miss?" Mindy asked.

"Don't go home the same way," I said.

"What?"

"There'll be an accident on the toll road, involving two semis and five cars. Take an alternative route."

She blinked, stunned. Then she said, "Alright."

With a shaking hand, I picked up the stemmed glass of wine, and sipped, then choked. Continuing to act as though everything was fine, I chose a piece of dark chocolate.

"Enjoy," she said, left the room, and closed the door.

Left with my thoughts, I took a sip of the wine trying to bring up the image again. It wasn't an actual image, now, but a feeling. The collection of porcelain dogs that was to go to Malcolm was worming it's way through my conscience. These people knew something about them and I needed to get to the bottom of it. Trying to console my conscience, I took up a chocolate and sank my teeth into it. I thought I'd found a small bit of heaven in that one bite. "Ohh, yum!" I said, my taste buds working on the pairing. I took another bite of chocolate and sip of wine.

"You are looking well, my Lady." The voice made me jump and I almost dropped a chocolate into the water. Dante stood at the other end of the tub chuckling. He was fully clothed this time. I shouldn't have been shocked that he decided to become visible.

"We really have to quit meeting up in bathrooms like this," I said.

He smirked. "Yes. I'd rather it be in bed."

"Men."

He shrugged. "You'll have your hands full tonight."

"Tell me something I don't know."

"Okay, then I don't really need to tell you Stefan is a pig." He crossed his arms and I watched the muscles bulge under his black T-shirt. His hair was in that loose braid again. I wanted to reach out and undo it.

"Already knew that," I said, scrunching up my nose and nodding.

"He has desires for you," he reminded.

Raising the wine glass to my lips, I looked up at him. "Jealous much?"

He gave me another shrug.

"Listen, don't go after him with my dagger. I won't take the rap for that again."

"I won't. But I'll be near." He stepped back, as though he were about to disappear.

"Wait," I said. "Something's going on here. I just had a vision—"

He held up a hand. "I saw it."

"Was it Mindy?"

He looked up in thought. "I'm not sure. But you're not involved."

"Yes, but if she's about to be killed in an accident—"

"There is no way to prevent it."

"Wow. That's really negative," I said. I'd already warned her to go a different route, and hoped she would listen to me.

"I'm sorry, but I'm keeping my eyes on you, and only you."

"Okay, but the butler, the maid and maybe the cook are all acting... odd. I can't put my finger on it. And each time I get close to learning about it, you know, through a vision? Malcolm gets into the picture."

Dante's gray eyes glimmered. "I suggest you look in the living room." He disappeared.

Eyes rolling in exasperation, I gasped. *That's all you've got?*

You only need to worry about Stefan.

Great.

* * *

Stefan lapped at the blood running down the woman's breast where he'd bitten her. She moaned while his fingers moved inside her. *What was her name? Heather?* He made two quick thrusts into the second woman beneath him.

Bridgette wriggled. "Don't stop, please, Stefan, don't stop!" Bridgette cried. She dug her nails into his buttocks. It wasn't so much that it hurt—because it didn't—he found her desperation enjoyable to the point he wanted to prolong her... needy suffering. His own climax was close, but he could prolong that indefinitely.

Stefan smiled. Someone had actually written a book on the sexuality of vampires, complete with diagrams and graphic pictures. One whole section was devoted to the vampiric three-way, or ménage à trois. He wasn't sure what position this was, but this was definitely his favorite.

"Goddamn it, don't stop!" Bridget said through gritted teeth. Her nails scored his back and he knew she'd drawn blood. *What the fuck!*

Stefan lifted his head from the breast of the other woman to regard Bridget. Black hair fell in waves around her sweaty head. She was not the donor tonight. Heather was. He had enjoyed his feast of Heather's blood, but this one, Bridget, had him thinking of Sabrina—up until she began clawing and swearing at him like a bitch.

In an Uber move, Stefan pulled his fingers out of Heather, and moved to top Bridget fully with his body. He grasped her face with both hands and kissed her on the mouth hard. He then rose up on his hands and rammed several times into her, drawing sharp cries from her. When he stopped, she smiled back at him. He lifted his lip and snarled at her.

"Not enough for you?" he questioned.

She shook her head. The women who signed "yes" to having sex with a vampire were only one or two steps away from being whores. Bridget's former life had been exactly this, so it was no surprise to him how hard or rough she liked it. Thing was, a vampire could be prone to as much violence as any of the johns she'd done, with the added threat of being drained of blood.

She brought her hands around in front of his face, fingers arched into claws, trying to scratch him. He swiftly caught her by the wrists and pinned them down over her head.

She laughed at him. "Tie me up?" she said.

Stefan had not quite released Heather from his thrall. He said to her, "Heather, gather your clothes and get out. Now."

Wordlessly, the blonde moved off the bed, picked up her various clothes and scooted out the bedroom door.

"You like to play rough, do you Bridget? Eh?"

She play-struggled, tossed her head around, biting her lower lip, then burst with a laugh. "Too bad you sent the other girl away. I could have done things with her, and you could have watched.

"I don't like watching. I like doing." He switched to one hand holding both wrists, the other went to her throat and tightened until she choked. She laughed as she did, thinking this was all fun and games.

"Now, you listen to me, bitch." He lowered his face to hers. "I can either drain you of blood, or I can snap your neck like a twig." He tightened his grip on her throat. She quit laughing. She quit breathing and began to turn red in the face. "You don't make demands of me. Got it? *Comprendre?*"

The look of superiority was gone as she nodded slowly. He loosened his grip on her throat. She pulled in a strangled breath, choked a few times, but he didn't let go of her wrists. Not just yet.

"Now, I'm going to finish with you. After I do, you will leave and never come back, bitch." He let go of her wrists, grabbed her legs and drew them up until her feet nearly went over her head and began slamming into her, each thrust made her grunt sharply. Fifteen minutes later, he came and roughly pushed her off the bed. She fell to the floor with a screech.

"Get your clothes, bitch. I don't want to so much as see your face ever again."

Moaning, Bridget scrambled around on the floor, picking up her clothing.

Stefan strode to the bathroom, slapped her ass on the way–Making her screach–and slammed the door and locked it. He started the shower, now looking forward to his date with Sabrina. She would take his mind off these two whores. Bridget, mostly.

Looking into the mirror before stepping into the shower, thinking about Sabrina. Sensitive ears picked up movements on the other side of the door. Bridget hadn't left yet, and furthermore she was near the door, which meant she was at his bureau, where his wallet was.

He threw open the door. Startled, Bridget jumped back. Something dropping from her hands. He looked to find his wallet on the floor, greenbacks littered around her feet.

"You promised us a bonus if we were good!" she said, having put on her jeans and bra and nothing else.

Stefan surged toward her faster than she could take one step. He grabbed her by the arms and shook until the money in her hands fell to the floor.

"You weren't that good!" He pushed her away. She stumbled to the floor, and went to her knees crying, black hair down in her face. "Now, get the hell out of here before I call someone to throw you out!" *Not that I need anyone to do that.*

Sniveling, she crawled partially, then rose, grabbing her shirt from the bed.

"Asshole," she said, glaring up at him.

"You want a fight?" he said, and shook his head. "No. I won't give you that satisfaction. I'm not stupid." He pointed toward the door. "Get the hell out or I will grab you by the hair and throw you out myself!"

She moved for the door, pulling on her shirt, but left it unbuttoned, it fluttered with her movements. He watched her leave his room, a moment later his front door slammed. He stepped out to make sure. *Yes.* The bitch was gone. *Finally!* He went and bolted the door.

Chapter 25

The Date

Dressed, and oh-so not ready for my date with Stefan, I strode out into the odd-shaped room—what I would refer to as the Octagon. Music played from several speakers. It was like I was in a concert hall. I knew it was only a CD, but it sounded so real it made me think there was a quartet playing somewhere in the penthouse.

I knew I was expected in the dining room to my left, but thinking about Dante's suggestion, I took a detour and stepped across the Octagon into the living room.

Aside from a panoramic of sky scrapers through the large floor-to-ceiling windows, the room consisted of large-scale sofas wrapped in pigskin—yes, my Knowing told me *pigskin*—with over-sized miss-matching pillows strewn about to give it a casual look. Armless chairs were covered in that same gray textured fabric that covered walls throughout the penthouse. Brushed stainless-steel panels masked the heating and cooling systems, and made a somewhat unusual design interruption. The fireplace, gas, of course, was surrounded by a rock wall that looked as though it had come out of a cave. I missed my own house, my own fireplace, my own bed. Especially tonight. I could sit in my own house, and think of Vasyl. I felt guilty for not missing him enough. I wondered what he was doing tonight-and where he was.

Why wasn't I missing him that much? My brain asked.

Did I miss him? Of course I did. I thought about all his quirks, and even all his demands of me. Not to mention his gorgeousness, and his love making. Tonight I was not in any shape to have sex with anyone.

Running my gloved fingers over the soft pigskin-covered couches, colored to match the deep chocolate thick rug, I remembered why I had come in here. Dante had said to go to living room. Why? I looked around to find what it was that James, Mindy, and Dolores were so nervous about. I took in the modern paintings—which were pretty awful. I mean if I threw paint on a canvas like this, could I also charge thousands for one piece, even though I had never claimed to be an artist? I doubted it. But still, I was appalled at what people would pay for junk.

The hard-surface gleam of the coffee table moved my eyes to yet another huge jade plant enjoying the breathtaking panorama. I swept my gaze over the expanse of glass, the room's breadth was extended by the reflection of a mirror. The subtle neutral palette worked well with that dark chocolate carpet that had the look, and I was certain, the feel of lamb's wool. I had to admit it was inviting, and I folded myself into one of the armless chairs, almost afraid that if I sat in one of those couches, I'd want to curl up like a cat and take a long nap.

Releasing a sight, I stood, feeling the pencil-thin heels of my shoes dig down into the thick carpet.

And then, as I turned to go, I saw it in the corner, beyond three large black urns, next to a floor lamp, partially reflected in the window. It was about four feet tall, covered in one of those gray mover's blankets. Curious, I walked over to it. My hand itched to pull the blanket off. I was already getting a read, but I couldn't believe what I saw in my head. I had to confirm it with my eyes and reached down to the corner and lifted to reveal a beautifully carved claw-foot. It was stained darker and didn't match any of the furnishings around me. The glass of the case made me gasp. My next gasp came when I heard a voice from behind say, "Miss, I hope everything is alright?"

I straightened, and turned to James. I don't know why my heart beat as though I had been caught in doing something bad or devious, when I knew full well this piece of furniture didn't belong here.

"Oh, you startled me," I said, hand to my breast bone, hoping my face wasn't as red as a beet. It felt warm enough to be.

"I believe your guest will be arriving shortly, miss," James said.

"Uh. Yeah, I was just wondering what this was doing here," I pointed to the covered piece of furniture. The one that was "stolen" from Letitia's penthouse. I wasn't about to point the finger at him, nor was I going to admit I knew what it was. I went into my dumb act. "I mean, why is it covered?"

James had stepped silently across the carpet in his shiny black shoes. He glanced down at the covered piece. "We have been working tirelessly, getting your home ready. You must understand we only had a few short days in which to make your place comfortable. Furniture arrived yesterday. The movers did what they were supposed to do—deliver everything. But we had to uncover everything. We are still putting together the rooms upstairs. Why, some of the beds haven't even been put together yet." He wasn't lying. Not exactly, and that was just the thing. He did it all so poker-faced. The curio, the one that had been missing, according to Malcolm, was here. A mistake? I wasn't quite sure. Did James know what was underneath that blanket? I couldn't just come out and ask him, could I? But I did know that this portion of the penthouse had been put together by a designer by the name of Peggy Yord. Months ago, commissioned by Tremayne himself, on the off-chance I'd become a permanent fixture here at TT.

"So, where did all this furniture come from? Letitia's place?" Again, me doing the dumb act. I needed to see how deeply he would lie.

With a hand, not quite touching me, James guided me out into the hall while he explained. "I really don't know where all of the furnishings have come from. Possibly some are from Letitia's penthouse, but not all. Especially, the living room. That's all new, and it was here, and put together when we got here."

"I see." His words rang of truth. Mostly. I could not read him further than—well, no further than I could throw him. He was very good at guarding his emotions and thoughts. Interesting. Only people who had a tight rein on their emotions and thoughts could keep me out. But I only needed to touch an object to get a read from it. I made plans to go back to the living room when I knew everyone was gone.

"James, do you or Dolores stay here in the penthouse, or do you leave at night?" I asked.

"Dolores and I have a small quarters beyond the kitchen," he said. "We are on duty all hours of the day and night. We will answer if you buzz us."

"And Mindy?" I asked.

"She has certain hours. In fact," he glanced at his watch. "She has just left for the day."

"I see." It was going on six, I knew this because I'd glanced at a mantle clock in the living room before we exited.

"This way to the dining room, miss." James led me to the double black lacquered doors of another room and opened them.

I had not been in this room before, but knew what it looked like way before I'd set foot inside. Yet, to see how it had come together in proportion to the rest of the apartment was something to experience in person. Similar to the rest of the penthouse, it boasted a floor-to-ceiling view of skyscrapers through a panel of five or six windows. An intimate, round table in the center of the room was covered in a silky material that sparkled. Two chairs with the same textured upholstery on the seats, as on the walls and ceiling, were simple in construction and brought the whole room together. The wood looked like cherry. My Knowing told me they were 19th-century Chinese chairs. Dolores had chosen over-large plates with a simple black line design running through the center, and fluted Champagne glasses, an elegant orchid for the centerpiece, and two strategically placed candles in round glass holders. The room's hypnotic sense of elegance was focused mainly on that small table. Two floor lamps on either side of the room lent to the relaxed feel, the black vertical blinds dispersing the light up or down. I realized the opposite wall was, again, all mirror, making the room look much larger. The music, I noticed, had gone to a sultry saxophone in the background.

"What time is it?" I asked, hand to my nervous stomach as James pulled out one chair for me. I did my best not to drop into it out of habit, but rather settled my butt into the chair demurely.

"Five fifty-five, madam," James said, having pulled out a gold and silver pocket watch from his vest pocket to check. I only then noticed he'd dressed up for the occasion. Not quite a tux, but something nicer than his day suit.

The doorbell—it was a single-note chime—rang. Stefan. Crap. My stomach flipped a few times. I looked for a place to hide. Behind a drape, perhaps? I found no drapes. *Crap.* Maybe behind the baby grand, nearby. Or, could I fit inside? The hood was up. Gak!

James left the room to answer the door.

"Will there be anything else, tonight, madam?" Dolores asked. I nearly jumped, because I hadn't seen her, hadn't detected her at all. In a black dress wearing a more frilly apron and a little hat. She was standing near another door across the room. Ah, right. This led to the kitchen, of course. That's where she'd popped in from.

I thought a moment. "Yes. When you are ready to serve, please take one bottle of the Real Red, open it, put it into the microwave for twenty-five seconds, and pour it into a wine glass, please?"

"Of course. As you wish, madam." She made a little head bow.

"Oh, and after you serve us, you may—uh—retire for the night." I hoped that sounded right. I wanted to make sure that they knew to skedaddle once the vampire got here and we were seated enjoying our respective meals. I didn't need humans to protect me from a vampire. I had my ring, and I had Dante, in case anything should happen.

"Very well, miss," Dolores said and went through a narrow black, swinging door, and headed back to her kitchen.

James stepped in after Dolores left the room.

"Stefan Capella," James announced, from the open door. Once Stefan stepped into the room James exited the room, and closed the door quietly.

"I see you've found the penthouse," Stefan said, looking around. As I had seen in my earlier vision, Stefan was wearing a dark suit with a lavender shirt and a simple silk tie to go with it.

"Yes." I had to clear my throat, while keeping my eyes lowered to his lips. I wanted to watch his lips move erotically again. I couldn't help myself and had to peek.

"To your liking I hope?" he asked.

"Oh, I suppose it's alright," I said.

"Why? What's wrong with it?" He looked surprised by my not being grateful, or something.

I smirked and dipped my gaze down to my table setting. "To be honest, it's too much—servants, and just—everything." I grasped my dinner dress, looking down at myself. "This isn't me."

"It *is* you, Sabrina. You look ravishing," he said, eyes taking me in. *I'll bet.*

"Dinner will be served—huh—for both of us," I explained. "There'll be the red stuff for you."

He smiled stepping toward the table. "You needn't have bothered. I've fed well tonight."

"Oh, good! I-I mean… good," I said, flustered. I moved my silverware slightly to the right, closer to the black linen napkins, which were held with a brass napkin ring. Because of my movements, one fell to the floor. Stefan was up instantly and came around to pick it up before I could bend to get it. We sort of met half way from the floor to the table. Eyes locked, I straightened and yanked my eyes away from his. Damn, was this going to be a tough evening to get through, or what?

"Thank you for your hospitality, in any case, *cara*." He stepped around the to the other place setting and folded himself into his chair, doing that hand-smoothing thing to his tie again.

As if on cue, James stepped in with the wine. He poured a deep red wine into Stefan's glass first and paused. I was somewhat puzzled until I watched Stefan take a sip and nod to James as though he approved. Stefan winked at me. James poured more wine in his glass, and then poured some in mine. He bowed and exited through the little swinging door.

Smiling, Stefan leaned toward me and said, "You've got a nice deal here. I don't know why you wouldn't enjoy it."

"I know it seems like I'm being ridiculous about it. But I do have my own house. Eventually the demons will leave it." I hope.

"Exactly why we have to go with plan A."

"You and your plans," I said on a little chuckle, remembering he'd said something of the same thing on our flight on a private jet out to Kansas.

His mouth twitched, and I have to say I was back to watching his sexy mouth—nearly as sexy as Dante's. White bottom teeth showing when his lower lip made an odd quirking movement as he spoke. It was hard to tear my eyes away from his face with the stark blue eyes, his sexy lips and white teeth. I felt like a moth attracted to a candle's flame. I wanted to move in for a closer inspection.

"Let us refer to it as 'plan A' for now, since there might be ears bending to hear us," he said low, while leaning a little bit over the table.

I let it go for the time being. "I've told my servants once we're served, that they were to go to their own rooms."

"Bright girl, *cara*." He seemed pleased with this.

At that precise moment, Dolores came through the doors with our plates of food on a tray—well, mine, anyway. She placed the wine glass of blood down in front of Stefan. I'd nearly forgotten about it and shut my eyes to the concoction and involuntarily shivered.

James came through the room, freshened my wine and stood nearby. "Madam Sabrina, if you require nothing else?" James said, placing the bottle into an ice bucket nearby.

I blinked up at him. "Uh, no. This is fine. Looks wonderful," I said. The prime rib was exactly as I'd requested; not too pink, yet not overly done, the red juices flowing out.

"Very well. Good night miss. Sir," James said, and made a little bow and Dolores followed him out the door.

"Nice," Stefan said. "They came highly recommended."

"Ah, I thought you'd hired them," I said.

"No. My—" he broke off, made the motion of straightening his tie, looking as though uncomfortable. He couldn't remember that I knew.

"Your father? Tremayne?" I smiled, picking up my glass of wine.

He picked up his glass of wine, held it up and inclined his head toward me. "Yes. My father. To your new penthouse, *carissima*."

I took a sip and put the drink down.

"Please, enjoy your meal. It looks exceptional. I wouldn't want it to spoil on my account." He sat back with his other drink, and looked around the room. "Beautiful night." He spoke while I picked up my knife and fork. Once again I was eating before a vampire lord. He was right. The meal was delicious. He threw one arm over the back of his chair, which was pulled away enough so that he could hang an ankle over a knee. We sat listening to the soft jazzy saxophone. He sipped on his Real Red, and I ate my meal—which was, by the way, more delicious than I could possibly say. I devoured it. Who says women can't eat hearty? I sure did. Meanwhile, he stood up and wandered the room to look at the paintings and sculptures, giving me some privacy to eat. Maybe he was one of those vampires who didn't like to watch humans eat.

After ten minutes, and after I'd finished my plate, he sauntered back and broke the silence. "I have researched you, *cucciola mia*." Stefan sat back down. Folding his hands on the table, he leaned forward slightly. I noticed he had strong-looking hands I hadn't actually looked at his hands before (yeah, too busy looking at his sexy mouth). His fingers were blunt and thick. My mind went to an earlier vision of those hands on me—everywhere. I slid a hand over the back of my neck, working to push that away. "I understand you were bitten by a werewolf?"

I reached for my water glass and took a sip of the ice water—the wine was making me tipsy, because it was a heavy dark red wine.

"Yes," I said after swallowing.

"That explains the slight tang in your scent," he said, smiling.

"A turn off?" *One can only hope.*

"Not at all, *carissima.*" He smiled with those quavering lips, showing more teeth this time. Jewel eyes sparkled from the candlelight. He was using Italian endearments. Some I'd heard before and some I hadn't. *He's flirting with me.* "I like a little danger in my women. It makes it *molto interessante.*"

His scent of leather and licorice was driving me up a wall. *Damn him.* I was in two minds as to whether I wanted to take a bite out of him or straddle him. Both, actually. *Why does he make me crazy like this? His scent, his sexy mouth. Hell.* I looked at my gloved hands. *No wonder!* I had left both gloves on because they had the tulle on the backs of the fingers, allowing my mystic ring to work on his pheromones. I didn't want to go into a stupid vision from touching things Dolores and James had touched. But somehow my ring wasn't working to block his thrall. Was it his blood that he donated to me working on me? How? I was told there would have to be an exchange of blood—in other words he would have had to have bitten me in order to control me this way.

"I've studied your file, supplied by Andrew Morkel, of course. You are more than sibyl, Sabrina. Being a sibyl would only make you tremendously talented psychic, it would not give you so many powers that you would prove to be invincible to any opponent."

I stared at him for ten seconds. "I'm not invincible."

"You are more than mere human, Sabrina, *amore.* You fried fifty gremlins!"

"It was either them or me. Besides, their tongues hurt!" I rubbed a spot on my arm where I still had stitches, remembering the sting. Looking down at it, now, I realized it had healed completely. My werewolf hormones doing their job.

"You also turned Ilona into stone—that in itself tells me you're quite dangerous to all vampires."

"Am I on your most dangerous list?" I asked, chuckling dryly.

He looked down at his Smart Phone. He must have had my file there.

"I understand you have something called a mystic ring?" He smiled up at me. "Oh, that's right. I had the experience of its powers on the jet a few weeks back."

"Yes. I could give you an even better example of its powers, if you wish." I smirked.

He held up his hand. "Not necessary. I hardly think after watching you turning those gremlins into crispy critters that I need any more examples of your powers, *carissima,* thank you. You could be very deadly to a number of your adversaries."

"You'd think they'd leave me alone, wouldn't you?"

"I agree. Moving on. The Dagger of Delphi." He paused and took a short breath and said, "How did you come by it? No one knew it existed."

"Vasyl, when he was human—as a priest—was charged with protecting it with his very life. He was hunted by the Nephilim, and when it was clear that they would kill him, he had no alternative but to have a vampire turn him." Leaning his chin on his hand, elbow on the table, he didn't interrupt me, so I went on. "It took him something like ten years to return to seeking the next sibyl. He had told his sire—prior to his turning him—all about his mission and where the dagger was kept. Neither one could go to retrieve it because it was on holy ground. It was later that he thought of approaching the elves to ask them to keep it safe. Since the Nephilim are also their enemies, they agreed."

"And he waited and watched until he found you after all this time?"

"He found me when I was still a child. I was to get the ring and prophesy from my mother—who was dying of cancer. She was supposed to be the one to come back in spirit form to give it to me. But, as a sort of exchange, Vasyl turned her so that she wouldn't die. I didn't get the ring and prophesy until a few months ago."

"I see," he said. "And on the subject of the prophesy, you know that a master must mate with you?"

I pulled in a breath and let it out in an exhaustive sigh. We were finally to *that* subject. "Yes." I was so tired of this. "Is this on my file as well?"

"Sabrina, the Council has decreed that you must become pregnant by a master, otherwise they will not stop hunting you down. Even with your numerous powers, you would not be able to thwart them all, plus it might become very exhaustive. There are millions of demons who would gladly risk their own lives to try and kill you—merely for the prestige factor. You must understand they are the terrorists of the nether world. And, I might add, you have not seen anything yet. The gremlins were nothing."

"So I've heard. All to bring forth a Dhampire?"

"Well, yes."

"What if I were to tell you my child is conceived and carried inside the womb of another woman?"

This stumped him slightly. "How?"

"In Vitro."

"Who is the father?"

"I'm not saying who. But he was the off-spring of Nephilim."

He gave this a few seconds of thought, then said, "No. The prophecy states it must be a master vampire, not Nephilim or their off-spring. My father attempted to complete this task, and although I don't agree with the way he tried to trick you into it, he is no longer willing to take the risk of becoming the victim of your dagger again."

"I don't blame him," I muttered.

"Vasyl was the next in line. I was to make sure you two mated. When he fled, because of your blood's potent allure to him, that put him out of the running."

"Well, shucks," I said, snapping my fingers, but it was a dull sound from my gloves. "Looks like we're all out of masters."

"Not at all." He smiled, sitting back again. Drink in his hand, he swirled it some, the red sheeted down the sides of the glass. "Even if there were no masters left in the United States, we would be able to call someone from any place on the globe to come and mate with you."

I couldn't catch a break.

"But we need not import a master, since I am next in line."

My eyes went large. I hadn't thought of this. Damn!

"You and Vasyl should have mated by now. Why aren't you pregnant?"

His question stumbled me. My mouth opened, then closed. Blowing my cheeks out, I let out a slight puff of air. "I was on the pill," I finally said.

"No longer will you be." He picked up the napkin and dabbed at his lips. "Tell me, *cara*, why did you resist having a baby, when you knew the prophecy?" His brow rumpled, as if this one thing stumped him.

"I didn't want to become pregnant. I'm only twenty-one."

He smiled. "I understand that. However, the Council is not going to wait until you feel like having a baby."

"No shit," I said, watching him loosen his tie. He slid it off his neck slowly. He folded it in thirds and placed it on the table. I was well aware of the vampire's undressing before taking his meal. But I knew I was not to be his meal tonight. This made me even more nervous because my visions are never wrong.

"I've made a promise to my father, *cara*, that one way or another you *will* become pregnant. Once you are finished with your period—well, in fact starting tonight—we will be together every night."

"Uh, tonight?" *Gulp.*

"Yes. I want you to feel relaxed with me. I am not a threat to you. I can resist your blood—probably better than either my father or Vasyl could, since I've never had it." His eyes glittering, he added. "I vow, Sabrina, I will not bite you. Ever." It was exactly what Vasyl had said to me too. But, he had bitten me. Once.

My nerves on edge, my stomach twisted. He got up and walked over to me. I looked down at my shaking hands and pulled off both my gloves.

"*Cara,*" he said in a soothing way, stepping around the table to stand behind me—the classic feeding pose for the vampire. I stiffened when his hands gently smooth the hair from my neck and he bent and kissed me on the shoulder. "You need not be so nervous." He made a sliding chuckle, it was somewhat devious.

I closed my eyes and gripped the sides of the chair, actually bracing myself for his fangs to slide into me (even though he had already vowed he would not bite me). His lips lightly touched my skin along my neck, giving me tingly sensations to the point I nearly screeched. When I no longer felt his lips on me, I opened my eyes and breathed in that leather/licorice scent.

"You act as though I'm going to torture you." He chuckled. "That is the furthest thing from my mind. I only wish to give you pleasure, *cara.*" His fingers massaged my shoulders. The muscles there were tight. His fingers, the way he massaged me, felt *so* good.

I couldn't help but moan as he hit a nerve that made me go all shivery.

"Ah, you are so tense, Sabrina. No need for such tension." One large hand slid down my arm, to cover my hand. Fingers twining with mine, he drew it up and kissed the heal of it. Gently he coaxed me out of my chair. Standing next to him, I realized I had never been so close to him before this. His exotic scent—pretty much like most vampires—had an allure all its own. His pheromones were another matter, entirely. Even though my ring gave me resistance, I could feel his power. No question in my mind—he was definitely a master.

My hands pressed against his broad chest, I couldn't look up into his eyes, and so, naturally they fell on his lips. His pheromones were hitting me. *How? My gloves are off!* His hands slid around my back, and pulled me closer. Okay, we were now hip-to-hip.

"Uh. We—we can't do anything tonight," I said, still looking down. "Because of—you know."

He chuckled. I thought he chuckled at my naïveté. But mostly just chuckling at my expense.

"You would be amazed at how much we *can* do tonight, *coccolissima*." His lips snagged my attention, and I simply couldn't stop being in his thrall. Fingers under my chin, he lifted it so finally, I looked up at him—dared to look directly into his sapphire eyes. His expression so intense, it took me a moment to realize he was probably finding the temptation of biting me as overwhelming as my own inability to resist him.

His eyes dropped to my lips. Then he moved in for the first kiss. I held my breath and closed my eyes. Gently his lips touched mine, as though they wanted to learn the contours of them first, before exploring more deeply. His hands, meanwhile, drew around my waist—at first. Then, as the kiss deepened, his hands roamed—one went up between my shoulder blades, and the other dipped to the curve of my butt. A delicious tingling started low. I had to admit I was attracted to him. Everything about him felt hauntingly familiar—his touch, even his kiss.

When our lips parted we opened our eyes and stared into one another's for several seconds.

"Well, that was pleasant on a number of levels," he said on a low growl.

My brain had apparently gone on vacation because I had no come-back. My hands were perched on his shoulders, and I still felt a definite throbbing between my legs in anticipation. I hated to disappoint myself, we couldn't do anything while I was on the rag.

Or so I thought.

His hands left my back, and I felt a chill when they did. Odd. Vampires were chilly creatures, but he was not. It was almost like he had warmed his hands in an oven. *Hot Italian?* He pulled off his jacket. I didn't see what he did with it because in the next second he lifted me into his arms and carried me across the room. I thought stupidly there would be this awkward moment where he would have to somehow open the door. Nope. Vampire magic opened them for him. Into the hallway, he strode with me in his arms.

"Where are we going?" I asked. He slid me a look as though I were silly to ask. I looked down the hallway. Yes. Of course. To the end to the gold-trimmed double white doors of my bedroom.

"Uh, I didn't invite you—uh—"

The doors opened via vampiric magic once again and he strode in.

"Hey!" I must have been coming to my senses, suddenly.

Candles strategically placed on the mantle, and a few in wall sconces, whooshed with flame. Another vampire trick.

"Put me down!"

"Gladly, *carissima*."

Stefan settled me on the bed, and his lips covered mine again. This time the kiss was demanding. I sank into the mattress with his added weight next to me, his hand traveling up my thigh, to my hip and then my waist, learning my curves, until his thumb pressed against a nipple. At his touch it stood erect like an obedient soldier. His other hand busily undid the buttons of his shirt, all the while pressing his lips to mine as if anchoring me to the bed with them. With his other hand he reached back and un-zipped me. Stefan did not waste time with sweet talk. In fact I got that he wasn't a talker, but a doer in bed. Mr. No Nonsense peeled my dress off and gazed at my half-nude body. I expected him to pounce like a lion on a piece of meat.

He didn't.

When he paused to let his eyes drift over my form, I wasn't sure what he'd do next. I had equal chance to look him over. He'd unbuttoned four buttons of his shirt. I expected a mat of black fir on his chest. Not so. The hair grew only in the valley of his chest and disappeared at the V of the open shirt. I supposed that having a Viking father may have left him with sparser body hair than I'd heard Italian men usually sported—all over. That would have been a definite turn-off for me to feel hair on a man's back. Maybe he went and got it waxed, I didn't know, and at this point didn't care.

He unbuttoned the rest of his shirt and pulled it out of his pants and shrugged it off. It was almost as though he'd read my curious mind. I had only a second to take in his viral chest and six-pack when his hands went to his belt and unbuckled it and slid it out of the loops.

I swallowed hard. I didn't go to bed with men I hardly knew. Dante was the first man I'd had sex with after knowing him only a few days. This was slightly terrifying. Not only was Stefan a sexy man, but he was a vampire, and, as the record showed, I had no reason to trust him, since he was equipped with fangs and had a definite hard-on. But I knew he would not do the nasty *that* way while I was having my period. Some men had no problem with doing it during (my ex-boyfriend, Jack had insisted), but since my menses blood had driven Vasyl away, I was pretty sure there was not going to be much he could do but have a wet dream tonight. Or so my poor innocent mind thought.

Stefan's eyes still lingered on me as the belt in his hand was all but forgotten and dropped somewhere on the bed. His eyes traveled over my body as though to memorize it. Then when he found what he had been searching for, he took my right arm and examined the inner elbow.

Oh, crap.

"Vasil's bite?" he asked.

I turned my head away. "What do you think?" I said, hoping he would not touch it.

"No other vampire has bitten you?"

"Two others," I said, after a moment's pause. "Nicolas on the wrist, same arm. Another vampire bit me here." I moved my other hand over my breast. Alucard from Beyond the Black Veil had bitten me too—the memory still fresh. There was one on my foot too, but that he could find on his own, if he wanted. He had several places to induce an orgasm from me.

He brought my wrist up to look more closely. "You were hurt badly here," he said, his fingers slid up my arm, and the sensation was one that both tickled and hit one of those erogenous zones. My eyes shot up into the back of my head, it felt so yummy. "Not just a vampire bit you here." His voice brought me back to what we were discussing.

"Huh? Oh. That's where the werewolf bit me, too," I managed through the haze.

"Before or after Nicolas?"

"Nicolas bit me afterwards. I guess he couldn't resist my blood, telling me he was going to suck out the werewolf venom, but he wound up biting me."

"He had possession of you before my father?"

I looked sharply up at him. I didn't know exactly what he meant. Maybe it was a vampire term, but basically the answer was "Yes."

"And Vasyl, you say, bit you when you were much younger?" His hand had slid up to my inner elbow, but carefully didn't touch the old bite scars. Not yet.

"I was eleven."

"Why? To mark you?"

"That's what he said, so that he could find me, just in case he lost me some-how."

Stefan sat on his haunches and took in this information, and seemed to make up his mind about something.

"The other vampire. Who was he? The one who bit you on the breast?"

"His name was Alucard. Not of this world, but another world, where I traveled to."

His gaze lifted. "Yes. I remember being told of your travel to Beyond the Black Veil. What happened to this vampire?"

"He was killed," I said.

"By your dagger?"

"No. Drakulya killed him."

His mouth opened only slightly and his eyes flashed. "Yes, yes. This too, I was told." He released my arm, and then settled beside me. Arm bent, he leaned his head on his palm to look down at me. The fingers of his free hand slid up my shoulder, and underneath my bra strap. He bent to kiss me along the collar bone. A shiver went through me.

"Cold?"

I nodded.

He got up and grabbed the extra quilt at the end of the bed and drew it up around us both, but mostly around me. He rearranged himself beside me, fingers worrying the bra strap again.

"Did Dracula touch you?"

"No. I wouldn't let him. I would have killed him, had he tried."

"I have no doubt," he said, his lower lip dipping again showing teeth. I nearly swooned at that. Shit, I was too easy.

I slid my eyes to his briefly, but wandered back to his lips. They bent into a crooked smile, a breath rushing out of his nostrils in a sort of half snicker. Then he swallowed. The smile gone. I might have been mistaken, but he looked nearly as fearful of me as I was of him.

"I feel somewhat like the male equivalent of the Black Widow spider's mate," he said quietly. "I tread carefully with you, since you could kill me in so many different ways."

"I don't have the dagger, so you don't have to worry," I said.

"Oh, but your other powers are so well cataloged. I do not doubt that this Alucard suffered at least something from your hands?"

I smiled with the memory. "Yes. He discovered the dagger." I met his gaze. "His world was stuck in the Victorian age, and so I was dressed in a ball gown, and hid it underneath all my—whatever I wore—when he overpowered me."

He made a scoffing sound. "How could he have overpowered you?"

"He put something in a drink to knock me out," I said.

"Ah." He nodded. "Then he bit you?"

"Oh, yeah." It was my turn to swallow. "He bit me on the ankle." I lifted my foot out from beneath the blanket.

"Really?" He reached as he sat up, gently took my foot in his hand and examined my ankle.

"He was going to drain me of my blood and make a huge profit."

His gaze slid back to engage mine, releasing my foot. "Really? But you said that he found your dagger?" He settled beside me again. "Didn't this kill him? Eventually?"

"No. It didn't poison him completely. You see, nearly all the vampires on that world are part human. The silver doesn't poison them with the same potency as here."

Stefan's fingers stilled at my shoulder and he removed his hand from where it was. He leaned to kiss along my collar. His hand slid across my belly and drifted south. I was pretty sure the talking part of the evening was over. His lips feathered kisses up my neck and found my lips again. The hand had drifted further down, slid beneath my panties and settled at my mound. Nimble fingers found me throbbing and began a warm massage there, sometimes teasing and sometimes stroking. Arousing me, his fingers worked on my swollen nub. I couldn't help but twitch from what he was doing to me.

His mouth and tongue pressed against my lips, I couldn't help but part mine in a moan, and he filled me there. I reached down where his hand was and for several long minutes I helped him work me toward a climax that had me teetering on that illusive glow until it burst from my toes all the way to my core. Lips leaving mine, his tongue trailed down my neck, to my right breast, where he found Alucard's bite to invoke it. His fingers still manipulating me, I gripped his shoulders until another explosive orgasm rocked me and I cried out. If I were dynamite and Stefan were a match I would have blown this whole penthouse off the top of the tower.

"Wowie—" I breathed a few minutes later.

"Yes. Wowie," he said, that crooked smile in place again.

Panting I looked up at him. "Exquisite, *carissima*." His fingers released me and took one of my hands from his shoulder and kissed the back of it. His longest bangs hung over his brow. It looked mussed up—*did I do that?* Plus there were bloody scratches all along his shoulders, chest and one arm. I checked my fingernails. Long. Sharp. Some long fir growing from the knuckles—gross!

"Oh, crap!" I said, jerking my hand away from him. "My werewolf is coming out of me."

"What? Really?" His eyes went wide when he saw the claws cutting through the ends of my gloves. *Crap, another nice pair ruined!*

"I need to get my anti-werewolf potion. Quick!"

"Where is it? Maybe I can get it for you?"

"It's in—um—I think my purse. *Grrrrr.* No!" I had to try and think. *Why is the were-creature coming out so late? It should have been out an hour or more ago!*

The moon's rise was clouded over. Supplied Dante in my head.

Crap. Fudge. Help!

Stefan slipped off the bed. He stood there waiting for me to tell him where the anti-werewolf potion was.

You had it in your suite. I will get it, Dante said in my head.

"Where is it?" Stefan asked again.

I held up my hand to Stefan as I squeezed my eyes, feeling the Were-creature's grasp on my physical as well as my mental being try to take over. My skin itched, which meant the hairs were growing. *Wonderful. Now I'll look so sexy to him.*

"It might be too late," I growled. Some shifting of bones and internal organs began to make their transformation inside my body. The ache that went along with the change was terrible. "Don't shh-tay—" I managed to garble past canines. No wonder my ring did me no good against his thrall. The were-girl coming on seemed to fuck up everything.

Dante appeared in physical form on the other side of the bed. "My Lady. Here." He moved to my side of the bed, and lifted me up, placing the vial to my lips. "Drink."

"What the fuck? Who do you think you are barging in like this?" Stefan snarled.

I managed to choke down the anti-werewolf potion. It was barely a swallow, but it was enough.

Dante looked up at Stefan, brows knitted, eyes narrowed, but he didn't move away from me. "You are the one who is intruding, vampire. You need to leave."

"Sabrina?" Stefan said, looking down at me. "What's going on?"

My eyes snapped shut while the magic warred with the werewolf inside me. It hurt too much to speak. The portion of me that was still human prayed it was in time.

"Go," Dante said in a warning tone. "No man holds her heart but me. No man can claim her soul, but me. Go. Now!" That's all I remembered him saying.

It took possibly a minute, or so before things settled within me. I looked at my hands. The nails slowly retracted and the hairs that had grown on the backs was sucked back inside my skin. My hands became the human ones, not the were-creature's. I now looked up at the two men in my bedroom. Call me a man glutton. Whatever. Both shirtless men looked hot to me. *Were-creature wants to mate.* I knew this and bit my lower lip against the little ripple of cries that wanted to escape. Both the werewolf and the woman inside me wanted to cry out of frustration.

Stefan looked confused, crushed and pissed about Dante muscling in on our private moments. He had planned a long night with me. But it had been cut short.

"You'd better go, Stefan. I'm really not myself tonight," I said. Understatement of the year.

"Very well." He snapped up his belt and shirt. "*Buona notte, carissima.*" He stalked out the bedroom door. Using his magic again, the door slammed shut this time.

I gave Dante a weak smile when he turned to me. One knee on the bed, he leaned and touched my face.

"How do you feel?" he asked, concerned.

"Better," I said sitting up further with his help. "I just need to sleep it off." I reached back to undo my bra—odd that Stefan hadn't undone it.

"I will go," Dante said, moving away.

"No," I said. He turned back to me. "Please. Stay with me tonight. As a man, this time?"

"Of course," he said, turning back to me, his face holding that small glimmer of happiness on it. I could see he'd gotten rid of his competition. Well, yeah. He sort of did. But again, I was not myself. Not totally.

"Hold me," I said tearfully.

"Of course." He brought the blanket up around me, careful to not touch me in an intimate way. I wasn't sure why, but then, again he knew I couldn't do anything tonight.

"Shit," I said, wiping tears away. I imagined mascara ran down my face like sooty tears.

"Why are you crying?" he asked, and leaned back to look down at me. He was kneeling on my bed while I sat crying like an idiot.

"I can't do this—what they want me to do." My hand went out in gesture.

After a moment Dante asked, "What is it that you don't want, or like about it? Is it having sex with Stefan? Or getting pregnant?" Great. He was my therapist as well as lover, constant companion, and consultant on all things metaphysical.

"I don't know!" I cried and tried to pull away, but he held me firm. I stared back up at him. I wiped my eyes again with the edge of the blanket. "Maybe the pregnant part. Or the having the baby part. I don't know! That's just so scary to me. I mean—jeeze, I've heard how hard it is to carry that baby around for nine whole months. Then, you know, going through labor."

"Now, you've answered that question honestly," he said, holding me close.

"You once told me that life wasn't fair," I said.

Dante smiled, ran his hands down the back of my head and looked into my face. "I remember that."

"If life isn't fair, is death fair?"

"I don't know, as I am Undead."

I gazed into his smoky eyes and took a tour of his chiseled features, the full lips, proud nose and high cheekbones. "Maybe being Undead you get to have more than the living get to."

He did a one-shoulder shrug. "Maybe." His brows wiggled. "I get to have you."

I couldn't help the smile that etched across my face. He lifted my chin with a finger. "I will be with you tonight, as you wish, my Lady. But know that when you are able to be with Stefan I will not interrupt. Unless something goes wrong, that is."

I looked down again. "I don't want to do this. I don't understand why I'm supposed to do this."

"Nor do I. But the demons will not allow you to get out of this again. Not this time."

"Fucking demons."

Chapter 26

In The Works

Pulling his wet hair back off his face, Bill gazed into the mirror of the steamy bathroom. He looked the same as always, well-muscled body, handsome face. But something had changed. Something inside, and yet he looked no different.

"Nemesis, you have helped me so far, but what am I supposed to do? The sibyl is safe, as far as I can tell."

"*You will know when the time comes, my son,*" a female voice said.

He looked around expectantly. Was she here? He didn't see her.

"What am I? Can you at least tell me that?" he asked.

"*That is something I cannot reveal as yet. For you are not completed.*"

"I'm not completed? What does that mean?" He grasped the edge of the counter and leaned forward, looking hard into the mirror, but not at himself. He expected to see the goddess somewhere in the mirror. He wiped away the fog revealing more of the bathroom, the shower curtain moved—*maybe*. Something moved. He caught her dark eyes and raven hair looking at him from over his shoulder. She was a beauty beyond compare, he wondered why he'd never noticed that before.

"You are not quite done," she said again, her voice seductive and barely above a whisper, still looking at him from behind his left shoulder. He turned around, expecting her to be there, in the bathroom with him. But no. She was only in the mirror.

She giggled, almost child-like again.

"That makes no sense. Am I a cake that has time left in the oven?" he said, feeling foolish.

"You might say that. In a way. Yes." She said, gleaming at him.

He shook his head. Wet lengths of hair fell down into his face. "I didn't want this," he said finally.

"No. You were chosen. And as a chosen one, you must complete your task."

"My task being?"

"To save the sibyl, for she will be in danger. Soon."

"You keep saying that. And yet I've seen her powers—or the direct result of it," he said.

"Her powers will not be able to take on that which wants to destroy her forever."

"Who?"

Silence. He waited for an answer, but she said nothing more to him, and when he looked again, she had vanished from the mirror. He sighed heavily and let his head sag again.

Goddesses are impossibly trying.

* * *

I heard a light tap on the door. Because of the quiet of my room, it woke me from sleep. It took a few seconds to remember where I was, and the memories from last night slammed into me. *Oh, hell.*

I felt around to see if Dante was gone. He was. I didn't know when he'd left me, but he can do a quick vanishing act. I could have sworn his arm had been around me the whole night and we had snuggled like old times.

"Miss Sabrina? Are you up? Would you like breakfast?" I recognized Mindy's voice.

"No. I'm not up. And yes. I would like breakfast." Was that a confusing response?

The door opened and Mindy surged into my room. What would she have done had I a man in bed with me, I had to wonder. Too bad Dante was shy around humans.

Mindy swept in, proceeded to open the drapes and let the sunshine pour in.

"Hey. What's the idea?" I threw the covers over my head. It was nice and dark in here, I didn't need to have my eyes burned.

"Come, now." Mindy bustled around straightening things, picking things up off the floor. My bra, the expensive dress, shoes… God, what a pig I am. "Dolores has been waiting to serve breakfast to you. It's after ten o'clock!"

I made a snarky response under the covers, hoping she couldn't understand it.

"Shall I lay out clothes for you this morning?"

"No. Go away. I can dress myself," I said.

When I heard nothing more from Mindy I peeked out from the covers. Gone. I needed my privacy. I was not going to be treated like an invalid or a child. I'd have to get that straightened out with all of these people. Last night I had considered dismissing them all, but then I realized this was a job, it was a paycheck for them, and I couldn't possibly put them out of a job just because I was cantankerous about people taking care of me. I simply had to put down some ground rules, that's all. *Yes. I'll do that.*

I found a pair of jeans and my sweatshirt that I'd worn yesterday and as I pulled them on I remembered my vision and realized Mindy was okay. That gave me a big relief. Maybe my powers of seeing the future gave her the insight of doing what I'd told her. Maybe she did go a different way home, last night, avoiding the accident.

I took a quick shower. A few minutes later, dressed in jeans a simple shirt, I swung out into the hallway, and stopped at the bureau that Mindy had been looking at and wringing her hands when we stopped near it, yesterday.

I looked up and down the hallway. I detected no one nearby. Quietly, I opened the bottom drawer. Folded gray quilts—like the one that was over that piece of furniture which I knew was Letitia's curio—met my eyes. A guilty conscience almost made me close it up right away, but my Knowing made my hand move the quilts back. A large black box, was hidden underneath, something like a jewelry box, but much larger. I couldn't very well pull it out without taking the quilt out, and what would I do if I did take it out to see what was inside? Instead, I pulled off one glove, and pressed one finger to it, hoping I would just get the very last person who had touched it, and what it contained.

I touched it. The vision flitted through me, and I was able to control it so it wouldn't put me out. It unnerved me, nevertheless, what was inside and who had put it there.

"Oh, crap." I had to call someone.

But who?

Voices made me replace the quilt and close the drawer.

My werewolf's hearing was heightened at this time, and I heard:

"You just stay away from him!"

"I *told* you I didn't *do* anything!"

It was James speaking to Mindy. It was odd that the voices had been loud, just a moment ago, but became suddenly hushed, as though they knew I was up and about. Well, they would, I guess, since Mindy forced me out of bed.

A door slammed somewhere further in the penthouse.

Shaken from my little detour, I continued to the dining area where I found my breakfast sitting waiting for me under domed lids on the table. I suppose Dolores was tired of waiting for me and simply kept everything warm this way. I used my clairvoyant abilities to get a bead on everyone, and what they were up to. I didn't like doing this, but in the interest of espionage, I had to make sure they were all busy in some other part of the penthouse.

Nope, James was coming down the hall, so I had to make it look like I was going to have breakfast, and sat down. Quickly, I pulled off the lid of a plate of home fries.

My stomach turning inside out, I lifted a dome over another large platter. My eyes took in scrambled eggs and sausage links—they were huge. A glass of orange juice from fresh squeezed resided next to a glass of milk. Poor woman went to a lot of trouble just to feed little ol' me.

I lifted a fork of food to my lips when James walked into the room.

"Good morning, miss. How are you?" he asked.

"I'm fine. How are you, James?" I wore a pair of gloves that completely covered my hands so I wasn't able to get a clear read of him. And, when I probed, I found that his mind was not the easiest to read, either. He might have been something other than human. But what, I couldn't guess. Possibly he was part elf, which would explain a lot.

"Well, miss, thank you," he said, eyeing my gloves. "Do you have anything special you would need today. Anything I might get for you?"

"Oh, uh, no. I'm going down to my suite and bring up some of my clothes."

"Mindy would be happy to help, of course, and if I can be of any service to you?"

That wasn't what I had in mind. How was I going to get that black box out of here? Or look at it? I switched gears, thinking that if they didn't know I knew about it, they might not move it or do anything drastic. My best route was to act stupid. In my case that didn't take extra acting skills.

"Well, actually, I'll have my cousin help me bring my stuff up," I said. The last thing I wanted was to have any of them around me when I made a call. I still didn't know who to call. Tremayne wasn't all that concerned over the missing porcelain dogs, or the curio. My only choice was to get in touch with Malcolm. Besides, I had to get my belongings up here. Whatever else Lindee might be doing today, she could help me pack up my belongings in the suite and haul them up here. Sounded like a fun-filled day.

"Dinner was great, last night, by the way, and breakfast is awesome," I said and slid another mouthful in. "Is Dolores here?" I asked through a full mouth. *I'm so frigging hungry!*

"No, miss. She went out shopping this morning."

"Oh, I see."

"If there's nothing else?" he asked. "Would you like to read the newspaper?" He tapped the folded newspaper on the side.

"No. I'm fine for now," I said, smiling.

After James left, I finished breakfast, thoughts about calling Malcolm about the curio filling the back of my head, plus looking into the box of those porcelain dogs I'd found. It's as though I needed to see the pieces for myself.

Excited with my thoughts, I took the elevator down to my suite's floor and knocked on the door. I thought I could hear the hair dryer going, so I waited and waited and knocked again and waited. Finally Lindee opened the door.

"I should have called, but I figured you'd be here," I said to her.

Lindee stepped back, took one look at me and said. "God, you must have had a great night."

I stopped. The words *I had great sex last night* was written on my forehead again. But I hadn't done anything. Oh, right. Stefan had done *something* to me.

"Whatever," I said, stepping past her, almost folding in on myself with guilt. "I'm going to move my stuff out—" I stopped. Every chair had piles of my clothes on them, neatly folded, of course.

"I didn't get a chance to put them into anything," Lindee said, looking sheepishly at me. "I hope you don't mind. I needed to make room for my things."

"No. That's fine. I hadn't even thought about your having to make room for your stuff." I strode into the bedroom. My suitcase was still in the closet. It would help carry about half my things. The empty black garbage bag she had used for her things was folded on top of some of my stuff. I figured I'd use it in the same fashion.

"So, how was your night with the Italian stallion?" Lindee said from behind me, making me jump.

"Oh my God," I said, hand to my sternum when I turned around. "First of all, I don't kiss and tell, and second, does anyone actually use that term anymore?"

"My mom does," Lindee said with a shrug. "And it looks like you had a good time."

"Whatever," I said, throwing my hands up before reaching for my humongous black suitcase in the closet. My face was hot when I wheeled it past her and out into the living room.

"Well, jeez, I just thought I'd say something, because you were so up-tight about it all day, yesterday, and I thought that maybe things would go bad, but I can see that things went fine. Right?"

"Yes. Now can we just change the subject? Please?" I bent over the folded clothes on the couch. I couldn't remember bringing so many clothes here. I wasn't sure why her bringing up the fact that I'd had a good time with Stefan last night annoyed me so. Maybe because I didn't want to admit I had liked it.

"Oh, wait," she said. "No wonder you're out of sorts. You're on the rag and—" She came to a halt with an intake of air, and expelled it on, "Oh my God!" and a look of wild shock on her face. "You didn't—" Both hands to her mouth.

I threw her an annoyed look again. "No. I didn't. Just help me, please? I'd like to get these things up to my new place so that I don't have to keep wearing the same jeans and shirt every day. I certainly can't walk around in those expensive dresses that someone picked out for me."

"There were a lot of them. You think Stefan bought them for you?"

"On his account? Maybe. Or on Tremayne's account. Tremayne was the only person who knows my size."

Lindee caught my look and then went in a completely opposite direction. "Wow. So, you have lots of vampire guys who know your bra size? Big deal."

I couldn't help but laugh. Lindee was so casual about men and sex it was ridiculous.

Lindee helped me pile things into the luggage bag. In an hour we had made three trips up and down the elevator with all of my clothes—the last of which we hauled in her black garbage bag, because I didn't want to take another trip down and up again.

"When did I bring all this crap from my house? I didn't know I owned this many clothes and shoes! I don't even remember having half of them!"

"You'd be amazed. I think Opera had a show on how much shit a woman owns. Fifty pairs of shoes is not uncommon."

"Oh, please! I know I don't own fifty pairs of shoes," I said, watching the elevator doors as we rose. There had only been ten pair in my suite's closet. But then again, no telling how many pairs were in my penthouse closet, supplied by my vampires.

The elevator came to a stop at a floor in between mine and the penthouse. The doors slid open and Malcolm and another man stepped on. Our surprised greetings rang out. I hadn't called him because I didn't know his number, and was glad we happened to bump into him.

"Oh! Sabrina!" His hands had taken mine into his. "This is so fabulous, you have no idea." He turned to the other man he was with. "Charles, this is the woman I was speaking to you about. This is Sabrina, Sabrina Strong."

There were how-do's and hand shaking all around.

"And this is her cousin—um—don't tell me!" His hand had gone to his temple and he squeezed his eyes in deep thought. "Ah, it's Linda!"

"Lindee," she said, making a disparaging sound. She'd always hated when people had gotten her name wrong.

"Oh, right. Lind*ee*! So sorry. Yes. And this, of course, is Charles Barone. We were going out on the town. It's such a glorious day, don't you think?"

"I've been too busy to notice," I said, indicating my suitcase. Which was empty as we were going back down to my place. "But I am very happy to see you, in fact, I would have called you, but I didn't know your number."

"Oh? You could have asked directory in the hotel. What is it my dear? You look distressed." Malcolm turned to Charles who wore a peach ascot with a black suit coat and violet shirt. The combination reminded me of sherbet. Malcolm was dressed down in jeans and a dark overcoat and a casual shirt.

"I think I know what happened to the curio, and I might also have the whereabouts of the earthenware dogs."

Malcolm became excited by my news, and he grabbed me by the wrists. I really wished he hadn't done that.

"Where? Oh, you must tell me, my dear!" He turned to Charles and said, "You see? I told you she had great powers. I had all the faith in the world she'd find them." He put his hand to his heart. "Oh, I think I'm going to faint!"

Charles put his arm around Malcolm to steady him. As a pair they sort of matched. Charles had sandy brown hair, a bit of a three-day beard going. I had been right about Malcolm's sexual orientation, but I had to look past all this and get to the jest of things.

"Look. I can't tell you right now where they are. But do you have a photo of the curio? And of the collection?"

"Oh, do I!" He pulled out his phone to show me the picture. "It's by Jon Widdicomb. The curio. She ordered it specifically for the display of the dogs. I remember her telling me all about it."

"Can you send them to me?" I asked him.

"Certainly!"

We exchanged our information, because I needed his phone number, anyway. I didn't get off on my floor, but went all the way down with him and Charles while I told him where the dogs and curio were. My thought is that somehow the curio and dogs were moved here by mistake. At least I hoped so.We said our goodbyes at the main floor.

The elevator's doors closed and Lindee slid me a look and said, "What the hell was that all about?"

"I'll tell you on the way back up, but you have to keep it a secret. You have to pinky swear it."

The elevator stopped on the eighteenth floor to let someone on. The doors opened. My brown eyes met those of green looking out of a handsome face. He was a tall man with a short beard. He swiftly turned away and ran down the hall and disappeared through a door.

The elevator's doors shut and I stood there gasping, "Oh my God!"

"Now What!" Lindee would have a brain hemorrhage before too long, I had a feeling.

"I think I know who that was."

"Why'd he run like that?"

"He's supposed to be dead."

* * *

Heart hammering in his chest, breathing harder than he really should for such a short distance, Bill stopped half-way down the stairs he had begun to descend.

Why am I running like a fool?

He leaned against the cold white wall to gather himself.

She saw me. Now what?

The woman with her. She had to have been a relative. There was definitely a family resemblance. Sabrina had no sister, so perhaps a cousin? He played back those five excruciating seconds of recognition that had passed between them. Seeing her again had spun his head like it always did. The two women were going up in the elevator. He had been waiting for the elevator that would take him *down*. Why had he stepped over to it then? *Idiot!*

He raked his fingers through his long hair. She would know he wasn't exactly a vampire, wouldn't she? Hell, he didn't know what he was. *Would she now hunt me?*

No. Get a hold. Why would she hunt me? I'm not a vampire. She'll figure that out in ten seconds, after recognition hit her.

Making his way up the stairs to the doorway that opened out to the hall, her startled expression remained in his mind's eye. A smirk slanted across his face, despite himself. He could always startle her. There were times he knew he had become an irritation to her—what he termed "stalking" her. If she hadn't gotten a ward up to prevent him from coming over to her house every day, she probably would have called the sheriff's police to give him a warning in the very least.

Too bad he couldn't follow her with a GPS dot. It wasn't like before. It was up to his wits and whatever magic he had at his disposal, now. But now she knew he was in the towers. Would she leave to escape him?

No. She'd be too conflicted, too curious as to why he was alive and here—*and ran like a bad dog who'd pooped on the rug.*

Bill reached the same bank of elevators he had stood at two minutes before. He checked where each elevator was, and whether it was going down or up. She had been going up in the third elevator, and it had stopped at the ninety-sixth floor, now. *Penthouse?* If she came back down she wouldn't likely stop at this floor to confront him, would she? *No. Not likely.* He felt safe in assuming she would not. He had done nothing to her.

He pressed the down button once more. Fifteen seconds later the elevator arrived and opened. No one was on, thankfully. He got on and pressed for Lobby. He had become a frequent visitor to the lobby on the north side in the last two days. He greeted the man at the desk by name.

"Jim, good morning," Bill said with a nod.

The tall blonde manager waved. "Morning. Going for a jog today?"

His stomach growled. "Not now. Maybe later." It was lunch time by his stomach.

* * *

"Oh. My. God!" I said again as we rose in the elevator.

"Who was that?" Lindee asked, gaping at me. "You said he was supposed to
be dead? He looked pretty alive to me."

"He was dead! I know it! I saw him killed in a cave-in. I'm sure it was Bill
Gannon. Omygod!" I shuddered. Feeling slightly dizzy, I leaned back against
the wall because my knees wanted to go out on me. I covered my face with
my hands.

"He isn't dead now." Infallible Lindee logic. She stood looking at me as though
I'd sprouted a pair of horns. "You must be wrong."

"I saw him die, don't you understand?" My breath came out in raged pants
as I tried to figure this out. He had grown a beard, but I recognized his eyes
easily. "He is—er, was—the off-spring of Nephilim, and they say if one of them
dies and comes back they become vampires." I said this out loud so as to try
and understand.

"Oh, wow. So, he's a vampire now?" Lindee said, working to understand me.

"No." I said, thinking about it. "Wait. It's day time. If he's a vampire, he can't
walk around in daylight. Plus, he's on the human side of the towers. That's
impossible! How can he be alive?"

My reasoning was emphasized by the ping of the elevator bell and the doors
slid opened to my penthouse door.

Lindee pulled the luggage on wheels out into the short hallway, and I lugged
the large bag out of the elevator.

"This doesn't make sense," I said frowning hard, dragging the large bag to
the door of the penthouse.

The door opened and James stood looking out at us, like he had every time
we had hauled my stuff inside. He grabbed the bag that I was having trouble
pulling—it had mostly shoes in it and weighed a ton, plus it had several holes
in it and the shoes were poking through them. Holding it by the twisted neck
a foot off the floor, as if it weighed nothing, he took it inside.

"Will this be all, miss?" James asked looking hopeful he wouldn't have to
open the door for us again.

Mindy stood a short way past the foyer entry and took the suitcase from Lindee, looking slightly uncomfortable. She kept looking up at James, but he didn't look back at her at all.

"Yes. Thank god," I gasped.

"I highly doubt that God has anything to do with it, miss," James said. "By the way, you have a visitor."

I stood gaping at James, my heart had begun a rapid beating again.

"Who is it?" I don't know why I envisioned Bill to have gotten up here by some magical way, but that was how jumpy that encounter had made me.

"He said his name was Hobart. He looked rather... scuzzy, and I really wasn't sure about letting him in—"

"No, that was fine. Where is he?" I asked, panic attack averted.

"This way, miss." Putting down the bag, James turned on his heal.

"Stay here. I need to go speak with Hobart," I said to Lindee, and followed James passed the corkscrew steps, down a long hall, following my majordomo until he opened up the doors of a nicely furnished room—one I had never been in before—with more of those pigskin chairs. I scrunched my nose at the dark paneled walls, stone fireplace, dark everything. It looked like a man cave. Maybe it was the den.

I stepped in and Hobart stood up from the chair he'd been sitting in. His face looked pinched with worry. He wore his usual black leather jacket and blue jeans and huge belt buckle that doubled as a weapon. His face unshaven did give him the look of a guy who might be unsavory. The handlebar mustache, however stood out from the nest of brown beard that had grown around it. Frankly, I was surprised that James had let him in.

"Sabrina? I was hoping I'd see you," Hobart said, a smile creasing the beard.

"Hobart," I said. "How are you? You look like you've been traveling."

"I have. I came to speak to you on Vasyl's behalf."

My jaw dropped. My spine tingled. "Where is he? What's going on with him?" I stepped closer, and as much as I never touch people, I wanted to grab Hobart by the coat and shake him into telling me right then.

He stepped even closer to me. The fresh scent of the outdoors and that heavy musk of werewolf overpowered everything.

"I need to speak to him!" I reached for him. He grabbed both my arms to calm me.

"Don't try to find him," he said in his most warning tone, his voice so gravelly it sounded like the bottom of a cement mixer. The big Were's words had me holding my breath for what he would say next. "He is extremely attracted to your blood, now." He straightened slightly, and released my arms. Eyes drew away from me and he blinked a few times. "As a matter of fact I'm terribly attracted to you in a Werewolf way, but—" he shook his head "—that's neither here or there."

"You've seen him? Spoke to him?"

"Yes," he said. "Vasyl wanted me to let you know that he loves you, very deeply. Those were his words." His pointing finger shook like a baton between us as he spoke. He blinked and lowered his eyes. "You know—" his head dipped, hands dropped to his sides. He looked back up at me. "You've got a hell of a lot of people who love and care about you, Alfa Girl." He stared directly into my eyes. One hand scraped across his lips, the beard making that scratchy sound against his coarse palms.

"Oh, hell," I said. Tears threatening to leak, I had to glance away. Blinking, I took a gloved finger and wiped the wetness away from my cheek. His hand came up and grasped my shoulder in a tender way. I looked back at him through my tears.

"Now, that's a fact, so face it, honey." He'd never called me 'honey' before, his voice had gone soft—as soft as Hobart's baritone voice could go. "So, I'm telling you what he told me. You stay away from him. But he's going to get as far away from you as he can. He didn't tell me where, so don't even ask."

France. Probably. I still had a thread of a link to Vasyl, and I knew he would go to his homeland.

Looking away, I swallowed the tears that wanted to come again. I truly didn't know why anyone loved me. I didn't understand what it was they loved or even liked about me. I was a misfit. I had to wear gloves *always*, and even when I did I could still go into visions that put me on the ground if someone wasn't there to catch me. While under a vision I muttered incoherently, and drooled too. I was strange to be around. My parents guarded others from me by putting me upstairs in my room, locking me in until guests were gone because I scared them, because I knew things about them—secrets—that no one should know. Some of them thought I was the devil's spawn—like Grandma Rose.

Hobart's hand was still on my shoulder, and his thumb worried a spot there. As though realizing it, he removed his hand. I knew he actually wanted to do more right then, but he resisted. He had not touched me in any way that was untoward since he'd become Vasyl's scion. I now wondered if he had released Hobart of his hold.

"I'm sorry I couldn't be here sooner, uh, see, I've been in my pelt during the full moon, trying to find Vasyl, because he called to me. I found him when I woke the second morning as a human—I won't say where—and I came here to deliver his message. It took me another day and night to get back home—as a wolf."

"Oh, God, Hobart." I shook my head. "Thank you for doing that and coming here. How did you get up here? I thought they had security in place."

He smiled. "I asked for Morkel, security called him and he got me in."

"You haven't been to my house by mistake, have you?"

"I did go there, at first. There's still some weird shit happening over there."

"Yes. I know. That's why I'm not there." I looked around myself. "I feel like Rapunzel, or something. I'm living in a dream world."

He looked around the opulent room. "Looks like you're doing alright to me. You have a butler and maid. And all this." His hands went out, eyes darting around the room.

"Well, it's my station as sibyl, I guess you could say." I frowned, remembering my manners suddenly. "You thirsty or hungry or something?"

"I don't want to put you out."

"Put *me* out?" I pressed a hand to my chest. "Huh. I've got a butler, a maid *and* a cook. I don't have to lift a finger. My only problem is I don't know how to call James, my butler. I've only been here like a night and a half a day."

He chuckled. "Yell for him."

"Actually, I need to get you up to speed," I said, walking to the double doors and opened them. I scanned the hallway. "James!"

James glided down those spiraling stairs. "Miss?"

"Could you get my guest something to eat and drink. He's been on a mission for me and I think he's hungry. Maybe we could all use some lunch. How about sandwiches with pickles, chips, and drink? Something like that." I must have been reading Hobart's mind, because he looked as though he was about to drool.

"Very well, miss. Where would you like it to be served?"

I thought that was an odd question, at first, but then thought about my evening with Stefan in the dining room. Eek.

"Might I suggest the Sun Room?" he said.

"That's right. I've got a Sun Room!" I turned back to Hobart and had to snicker.

"I say let's go for it. Sun is out today, real bright," Hobart said.

"Yeah. Sun Room would be great," I told James.

James bowed and left to order some munchies from Dolores.

"Sabrina? Where are you?" Lindee's voice carried down the hall.

"We're in here," I called, waving.

She appeared in the open doorway. "Jeeze. I didn't know this place was so huge."

Lindee strode into the room, her hair slightly disheveled.

"Hey, Big Bad!" she said with her usual giggle at the end. She arrowed straight for him and gave him a big hug. She was from a hugging family. He hugged her back, but not too much.

"Hey, there, little cuz," he said.

"Lunch is about to be served—in the Sun Room," I announced in a very bad British accent. Stepping toward the door, giddiness overwhelmed me. It's amazing what a little good news could do to a person's mood. At least I knew Vasyl was safe.

"Sun Room? Where the heck is that?" Lindee asked as we all stepped into that octagonal room.

"Follow me." I turned down the hallway. At the end, we came to a pair of French doors that stood open, and stepped down three flagstone steps. Windows on one end curved over the room at least half-way. Tropical plants filled the entire area. A nice patio set with a glass table resided underneath bamboo trees, and was already set for three—Dolores moves fast. Nearby, a waterfall spilled into a pool, and large gold fish swam around in it. At the other end of the sun room, and up three steps a whirlpool beckoned my achy body. The chlorine from it tainted the air. The greenery, sunshine, perfume of different flowers, and food brightened my mood even more. I had my Were, Hobart, back. I already decided he would stay in a suite upstairs. He was my protector, after all, when a vampire couldn't be around. I needed him to stay with me, if I were to remain here.

We all sat at the table and Dolores brought us lunch, which consisted of a huge array of cheeses, thinly sliced tomatoes, cucumber, sliced homemade whole-grain bread, and thinly sliced ham off the bone. Plus a large pitcher of iced tea, and tall glasses with ice and lemon wedges awaiting the refreshment.

I picked up a piece of white cheese and took a nibble. When the taste hit my tongue I was happily surprised. Munster.

Dolores poured the tea, asking if she could get us anything else. Our eyes were big, and I know we'd eat most of it. I let her return to her kitchen. She told me to ring the little bell, which she'd supplied, if we needed anything else.

While making a huge sandwich, I got Hobart up to speed. Lindee threw in her little comments for good measure and entertainment. After explaining what had happened the night when Vasyl left (doing my best to not go into great detail), I continued with the gremlin's attack the next day. Hobart grimaced when I told him how the tongues had razor-sharp teeth on them, showing him my scars, and that I would have died had I not been treated for the poison—given Stephan's blood.

"Then I wound up here." I motioned around myself and slathered butter on a slice of whole wheat bread.

Twenty or so minutes later, Dolores brought out a cherrypie and coffee in a silver carafe. She sliced it up and served us and left.

"You remember Bill Gannon?" I asked after making sure Dolores was gone.

"Yep," Hobart said.

"I just saw him. Here."

"Really?" He wiped his mouth off with a cloth napkin. Taking up a cup of coffee (Dolores made splendid coffee), he said, "Bill? You mean that guy that died in that cave-in?"

"That's the one. He's alive. Don't ask me how."

"I wouldn't dream of it," Hobart said. Lindee barked her laugh.

"She thought he was a vampire," Lindee said. "But it's daytime."

"So, he can't be a vampire," Hobart said and looked up above us to the glass terrace windows. "Sun's out."

"Yeah. I couldn't get a read from him either. But I never could before." I continued to stare across the room at a palm tree, then down into the goldfish pond and watched the gold and white and gold-spotted ones swimming around. The water rushing over large rocks was splendid white noise. The sound was soothing. I wondered who took care of all of this, and then the Knowing hit me. There was one guy who came in and took care of all the plants, and even fed the fish. He was Japanese. I couldn't say the name if you asked me.

"He can't be dead and he can't be a vampire, so, he must just be human," Lindee concluded.

"No. He isn't human. If he was plain old human, I'd have gotten a read—even the short few seconds he stood there." I shook my head. Stumped. "Why is he here?" That was my other question. *Looking for me?*

We all exchanged blank expressions.

"But, listen," I stepped over to the doors and closed them, to make sure I had privacy. I darted back to the table and spoke low. "I need the two of you to help me with something."

Lindee and Hobart exchanged glances.

Hobart said, "Is it dangerous?"

"Will we get in trouble?" Lindee asked hopefully, rubbing her hands together.

Chapter 27

The Curio

We all migrated back to the hall, and I directed them to the living room, and closed the doors. Dolores had come in, right after I told the two my plan, and what I needed them to do. I gave Lindee the sneaky project, since she was so bent on doing something devious, or glaringly wrong.

We waited for Dolores and Mindy to become busy clearing the dishes from the Sun Room. I, meanwhile, took the two into the living room, and had them sit and relax. I used my clairvoyant powers to Know where the cook and maid were, as well as James. Once I knew James was still working on the rooms upstairs, I said to Hobart, "Go stand at the door, and listen for anyone coming."

He was up and jogged to the door. With his werewolf hearing, he could hear a pin drop anywhere in the penthouse. He gave me a hand up, for me to hold back from doing the one thing I had been wanting to do since I'd seen it. Dolores and Mindy must have walked by the door, and Hobart gave a thumbs up.

I turned to the covered object, and pulled off the gray cloth. Standing about five feet, I had a little trouble lifting it. Lindee helped me pull it completely off the piece.

"Oh, just as I thought!" I said, looking over the glass case. I checked the picture that Malcolm had sent me. Lindee stood at my shoulder looking at the picture too.

"Yep. That's exactly like this one," she said, nodding.

"Hang on," Hobart said quietly at his station.

Lindee and I moved to block the view of the piece, in case someone walked in. After about thirty seconds, Hobart gave the thumbs-up again.

"Okay, I'm going to touch it," I said, looking directly at Lindee. "You'll have to catch me if I swoon."

"Right." She stood behind me, arms positioned to catch me. Hobart had argued he should be the one to do this, but Lindee was pretty strong. And if she needed help, he could rush over and help her carry me to the couch.

I slid my glove off, and touched the curio. The images zipped through me, but I was able to control them, and not go into a swoon. Maybe my new powers helped me get beyond my swoons.

When I didn't fall back into Lindee's arms, she asked, "You okay?"

"Yeah," I said, working to pick out all the information I got through touching the curio. I saw so much stuff, it's a wonder I survived it.

"I need to sit," I said, moving for the nearest chair.

Hobart was there and the two of them helped me plop into an overstuffed chair.

"Quick, get that thing covered," I said to them while I sat forward, putting my head in my hands, elbows resting on my knees. They worked the cover over the curio.

"There, we've got it," Lindee said.

"Did you see who brought it here?" Hobart asked.

"Just some guy in a uniform, like a mover," I said. That was the last image I got. I couldn't get any more from what happened to the curio, or why it was here. I passed my phone to Lindee.

"Can you text Malcolm for me?" I wasn't very good at texting, yet. In fact, the last time I tried it, I fried out my phone because I had to take my gloves off.

"What do you want me to say?" she asked, taking my phone from me.

"Just tell him that the curio is in this penthouse, and possibly the dogs are too."

After a few moments of her thumbs working frantically, she said, "Done. Now what?"

"It's your turn. You still want to do this?"

"Sure," she said, full of enthusiasm.

"Great. Hobart, how's it sound out there?"

"Quiet."

"Okay, I'll call for James." I got up and walked over to the door, opened it and called at the bottom of the stairs. His muffled response came, and then his footfalls followed. He came down the steps, a little out of breath.

"You know you can ring me," he said.

"I didn't know how." I asked.

"A button, near the door. Looks like a doorbell," he said.

"Cool. Well, since you're here, I was wondering if you have any of the bedrooms finished, upstairs?"

"Only one," he said.

"Could you show it to Hobart?" I moved to the doorway of the living room.

"Of course. If you would, Mr. Hobart?" James was accommodating, and took Hobart up to the suite of rooms to show it to him.

Meanwhile, Lindee and I moved to the sideboard, where I had found that box earlier.

"Ready?" I asked.

"Ready," she said.

We quietly slid open the drawer, lifted the quilt and I managed to open one of the boxes. Our eyes went wide.

"This is it," I said in a whisper. "Why are they here?" My earlier though was that the curio, and what was in it, was brought here by mistake. I wanted to give them the benefit of the doubt.

We closed the box replaced the gray quilt and closed the drawer before anyone saw us. My cell phone chirped and made us both jump. I dug it out of my pocket. I looked at the read-out. I didn't recognize the number, but the name I did. Quist.

"Hello?"

"They moved Fritz to a city hospital about thirty minutes ago," Quist said. "He's still in a coma. They had to move him."

Chapter 28

Requiem

"Where are you?" I asked Quist into the phone.

"In our hospital. On the vampire side." He sounded slightly winded.

"I'll be there as quick as I can." I ended the call and looked at Lindee. Hobart walked into the room.

"I've just got a call," I explained to Hobart. "Fritz is in a coma."

"What?" he said. "You mean that scrawny black kid?" Hobart looked startled. I realized I hadn't told Hobart about this. There was so much to cover.

"Yeah. I'll tell you about it on the way down." We strode out of the room. "He was injured the other night when they were out hunting rogues. I'm going down to the hospital where Quist is. He probably could use some friends right now."

On our way out, we passed James who stood at the entryway almost expectantly.

"Will you require anything else, miss?" he asked.

"Yes," I said. "I know you had one room ready, upstairs. Is there a possibility you could get a second one ready? Mr. Hobart and Lindee are both going to stay the night."

"No. I've got a date tonight," Lindee protested.

"With Dan?" I asked.

"Yeah."

"Okay," I said. "Just the one room for Mr. Hobart, then."

"It's ready, miss. What would you like for dinner?"

"Whatever Dolores wants to make would be fine," I said.

"My complements to the cook," Hobart said. "Thank you."

James bowed.

In ten seconds we were out the door and hopped into the elevator.

* * *

Bill had been sitting in a chair, only ten feet behind the demon for forty-five minutes. He'd come here after sitting on the human side for about thirty minutes. He worried that he'd be seen too easily and he feared Sabrina might bolt if she saw him again. But it occurred to him that most of the bad things that had happened, happened on the vampire side. Apparently demons were not welcome on the human side. Of course, the sliver embedded in balustrades, and railings of the stairs, and buttons of the elevator, and the crude cross and Star of David designs along the edges of the rug might have been part of the plan to keep vampires and demons at bay there.

Following his gut instincts, Bill had crossed to the vampire side and found the demon loitering in the lobby of the vampire side. He could detect a demon a mile away. This guy was a Ba'al Demon. Dark, longish hair, he styled it in bangs trained across his brows—whoever he had decided to mimic. He pretended to watch TV, but all the while, his eyes kept darting to the door that led to the human side.

The little snit. He's waiting for Sabrina. How many demons do they have in this place, anyway?

His gut instincts had told him to be here. He had been following these little premonitions, and they had worked out well. It was just a fluke that he and Sabrina had met by accident when the elevator opened while he stood there. *Or was it by design?*

Bill leaned to pick up another magazine to idle away the time. The show on the TV was a ridiculous game show. The hosts looked too young to have continued to run a game for fifty years. No humans could possibly keep doing the same damned thing for so long and not look ancient.

The door from the human side slid open. Sabrina advanced through with a bearded, rough-looking man in her wake. He recognized him. The werewolf who had been with her on several occasions, in and out of her house. While that irked him on a different level, what happened next had him jerking to his feet.

The demon with the mop of hair jumped up, moving toward Sabrina.

"Oh, hi Sabrina. There you are. You know, I've wanted ask you over for tea sometime?" He moved into her space.

Bill surged across the room in long strides, ready to knock the son-of-a-bitch to kingdom come.

But once again, he hadn't moved fast enough.

The werewolf's move was lightning quick. He had his arm around the man's neck in two seconds flat, and in his other hand was something shiny with three deadly claws pointed at the man's throat.

"Wait!" Bill shouted his warning. "Don't cut him! That's a Ba'al Demon."

"Bill?" Sabrina's voice filled the atrium.

"He bleeds, it might be deadly to you," Bill said, not exactly ignoring Sabrina, but he had to warn them. Ba'al demon's blood, if spilled, could burn like acid.

"Bill, what are you doing here? How can you be alive?" Sabrina nearly shouted.

The werewolf pulled the deadly belt buckle weapon away from the man's neck, but now held him with both arms. *He must be strong as hell.*

"What do you know about him?" the werewolf growled, indicating the demon.

"Just trust me. I know plenty about demons," Bill said, hand out in a cautioning way.

Sabrina's eyes narrowed and she looked over the man in the werewolf's grasp. She seemed to go through a little decision.

"Malcolm?" she said.

The man made nervous head nods at her. "Yes. Yes. It's me."

Afraid that Sabrina might be taken in by this impostor, Bill said, "Remember Grandma Rose?"

"Okay, trick question. We saw each other in the elevator, today. What was our discussion about?"

"Uh," he chuckled, choked some before saying, "Have your friend let up a little. Hard to breath."

She nodded to Hobart, and he loosened his grip, but still held on to him.

The demon straightened his jacket and tie, then he shook his bangs out of his eyes. Bill watched Sabrina observe the creature's movements carefully.

"Uh, what was the question again?" the demon asked.

"What were we discussing, today?" she repeated.

"Oh, well, that's easy. Your new penthouse?"

Squinting, Sabrina turned away, stepped over to a small glass door on the wall, opened it revealing a large red button. She hit it with the palm of her hand and a loud siren sounded, similar to a fire alarm.

The woman seated at the hotel desk jumped up and whisked through a door behind her. Other people who were in the lobby dashed away.

* * *

I turned back to Bill and Hobart who both now held the demon. I noticed the dark smudge—his aura—around the guy's body. *Funny, I didn't see that until now.* And that odor of burnt eggs—sulfur—was pungent. But what really had my attention was Bill Gannon, former Nephilim, standing looking cock sure of himself and handsomer than I remembered him looking. *What is up with him?*

"Bill? What is going on with you? You're supposed to be dead. If you're not a vampire, what the hell are you?"

Bill shrugged. "I really don't know. But I've been sent here to protect you."

I slid my eyes to Hobart and the demon. "Not very good at protecting me, are you?"

"I would have been on the demon, but your Were got to him first," he said and shrugged.

The demon struggled in Hobart's arms, and tried to break free.

"Damn it, he's strong!" Hobart grumbled.

"Sabrina, tell the demon to stop struggling," Bill said with an exhaustive sigh.

"Stop struggling, demon," I said. The demon quit wriggling and became docile.

"Good boy," I said, as though he were a black lab.

"You haven't figured out how to use your ring?" Bill asked, looking slightly annoyed at me.

"Well, it didn't come with an owner's manual," I complained bitterly. But I knew how to use it all the same. I just forget is all.

"You have the power to command demons," Bill reminded.

"I know. Pretty useful on vampires, too." I looked at the demon and it threw me a worried look.

"If you wanted to you could make him poke himself in the eye," Bill suggested.

"I couldn't do that. Unless he was going to harm me, of course."

The demon smiled and made a nervous laugh.

The elevator doors swished opened and out poured four security elves. Micheal among them.

"What's the breach?" Micheal asked, striding forward, ahead of the others.

I pointed. "Got another demon in here."

"I thought we had that breach closed up!" Micheal motioned for his men to grab the demon. Two men moved on his silent command and grabbed the demon who looked like Malcolm.

One of the other men, standing five feet away, spoke into a walkie-talkie. The painfully loud alarm was turned off. *Thank you!*

"Are you alright?" Micheal asked me, his large hand grasping my upper arm. The warmth of it surprising.

I nodded vigorously. "Yeah." My eyes slid over to Bill. Lindee, if she were here, would goggling him. She had gone on to her suite, leaving me and Hobart to go and see about Quist and Fritz. Whatever Bill was, he was no threat to anyone, unless they were allergic to drop-dead gorgeous men. Even his beard didn't detract one iota from his looks. Not only that, his eyes were more startling green than I could remember. Plus his scent had changed. I tried to decipher it. It smelled of clean, fresh outdoorsy man with a hint of hazelnut. *Weird.*

"Take him to the VIU," Micheal motioned to the others who had the demon in a pair of silver handcuffs. The demon's wails and yowling carried throughout the lobby and all five stories of the atrium. The two elves disappeared through a door with the demon.

"If every thing's okay, I need to go with them, and then file my report," Micheal said.

"I'm fine," I said to Micheal. "But I need to get to the bottom of how these demons keep on coming in."

"I understand," he said.

"Who do I speak to?"

"Right now, I think Andrew Morkel would be in charge. You want me to call him?"

"Yes. Do that. Have him meet me down in the hospital."

He nodded and took out his cell phone. He and his other security man vanished through the same door.

I tossed my hair back over a shoulder. Hobart stood beside me, waiting.

"Now what?" Bill asked.

"Well, I was going down to console a friend. His best friend is still in a coma," I said.

"I'm sorry to hear that," he said. "Anything I can do to help?"

"Nothing at the moment," I said, moving toward the bank of elevators. Hobart on my heals. I pressed the DOWN button. The doors slid open.

Bill slipped into the elevator with us. "Don't mind if I tag along?"

"It's a free country," I said, hitting the Level D button. I settled against the wall and crossed my arms to study him in a preternatural way. "So, Bill. How did you go from being dead to being alive all of a sudden like?" He had pheromones, just like a vampire, yet different. Sort of made one exceedingly happy to see him, and I was struggling to maintain an air of indifference.

"I don't know how exactly it happened. But I was, for a very short time, a vampire," he said.

My brows went up and I slid my gaze to Hobart. "But you aren't a vampire anymore. I would know," I said and waved the hand with my mystic ring at him, concentrating on pushing him across the elevator to see if it did anything. He stayed right where he was two feet away from me. Why was it I wasn't as annoyed with him as I used to be? If anything I couldn't keep my eyes from raking over his body.

"No. I'm not." He glanced down and nodded at my ring. "Your mystic ring would work on me if I were either a vampire or a demon."

"But it doesn't. Which leaves what?" I asked.

He shrugged. "I'm not sure. I'm not complete."

"You're not complete?" I repeated, looking him over. "You look complete to me." *Actually more than complete. Why am I suddenly wanting to put my hands on him?* My mouth stretch into a smile. *I'm smiling. Almost giddy he's here. This is stupid!*

He shrugged. "I can't say more. I'm sworn to silence."

Squinting, I looked slightly away from him—like I did with demons to check out their aura—I saw a brightness all about him. *Aura's almost frigging white.* Bill oozed cheerfulness, and it was contagious. Even Hobart was smiling.

"But you said something about keeping me safe or saving me?" I said. "That's what you said. You think I'm in danger?"

"Sabrina, you are always in danger," he said, smiling. His teeth seemed so white and perfect, and the dimples in his cheeks deepened. *Save me.*

Hobart's rumble told me Bill had hit a man button. I slitted my eyes to him.

"It's true, Alfa Girl. You tend to attract trouble," Hobart said in his own defense.

I rolled my shoulders and then tilted my head side to side, hearing the vertebra crack some. I tried to pretend I was working out the kinks and not pissed by what he'd said, *and* not look at Bill's handsome face. *Did I actually attract trouble?* After thinking about it, I couldn't deny it. *How many times had I been attacked this week? Twice? Three times? I've lost track.*

"So, you're here as my safety net?" I asked him.

"That's a good way of putting it. Yes."

The elevator came to the end of our ride, making my knees buckle—I hated that feeling. The door opened and put an end to this strange, yet enjoyable ride.

Both men allowed me to step out ahead of them into the disinfectant-smelling, ultra clean front office of the elf-run hospital. It hadn't been that long ago when I'd been a patent here. We stepped up to the main desk—a horseshoe-shaped, white work place that housed computers, and nurses with pointed ears wearing either sky blue or teal green scrubs. I saw no doctors at all. (In many cases, they were on call, if there were no emergencies.)

I stepped up to the head nurse, a redhead with large blue eyes and freckles splattered across her nose. I was about to ask her a question—not really knowing how to form it—when a voice stopped me.

"Sabrina? Over here."

I looked to see Quist standing near the white upholstered chairs along the wall, holding his phone. I stepped over to him.

"Quist. What's going on?" I asked.

"I thought I'd better stay here to tell you," he said, blue eyes taking in the two men who stood with me.

"Oh, you remember Hobart, and this is Bill Gannon," I said, motioning to them as I introduced them.

"Yeah. Hi. They've removed Fritz to a hospital downtown. I'm waiting to hear which one. They moved him because they didn't want his family to come here, and they had to inform them because he was in a coma. Sort of not cool with a human's family knowing about the vampire's dealings, or the fact elves run this hospital. They left about forty-five minutes ago."

"You mean, they couldn't or didn't want to explain what happened, and so—"

"They're going to go with a car accident," Quist said, running his hand over his mouth, fingers scraping the light blonde stubble there on his upper lip. His eyes darted away from me and became out of focus. "It was my fault. I shouldn't have pushed him. He really wasn't that into it. You know? My wanting revenge. I shouldn't have brought him into it."

"Revenge?" I said. "What happened?" I realized I didn't know that much about Quist or Fritz, for that matter.

"A bunch of rogues killed my girlfriend a few months ago," he said, his voice became gravely, and he cleared it. Turning away he made a harsh cough, hands went to his head as he slumped. "I wanted to kill those responsible for her death. But now…" his voice trailed off, a hand went up and fell to slap his thigh with anger.

I put my gloved hand on his shoulder. "Take it easy," I said. "You couldn't have known that they were going to attack you."

He pulled in a shaky breath, and let it out. His shoulders sank further with his sadness and he dropped into a chair. He wiped the back of his hand over his eyes before he went on. "I went back to the spot, where we were that night," he went on. "Found my laser wand. It was bent. It's useless now." He looked up at me. "See, they were waiting for us. Like I told you."

I licked my lips. "Are they part of Leif's gang?"

"I'm pretty sure they are. I know I've seen at least one or two of them before—hey," he said looking up at Bill as if just noticing him. He pointed at him, looking somewhat shocked. "You! You were the one who came that night."

Bill nodded at him. "All in a night's work. I'm sorry I didn't get there in time to save your friend. They drove right past me. I was on foot."

Looking down at the floor, Quist shook his head. "No, no. I'm the one who fucked up."

"You can't change things," Bill said in a quiet voice as he moved into his personal space and put a hand on his shoulder. "No one is expecting you to."

Quist looked up at him, eyes shiny with unshed tears. "I saw how you broke those two vampire's heads open, like they were eggs."

Bill's eyes shifted to mine. "I seem to have gained supernatural strength," he explained.

"Sounds like it," I agreed.

"They're still out there," Quist said, looking dismal.

"Only one or two of them," Bill reminded.

"That one ran back to his nest. By now they all know about you," Quist said to Bill.

"My reputation has grown." Bill smirked. "I'm not worried."

Quist's phone rang and he answered it, spoke briefly with someone and then said, "Thank you." He put his cell phone back in a pocket. "He's at Rosehill Memorial. I'm going there." He was up and moving.

"I'm staying here to speak with Andrew about the demon problem in the towers," I said.

Without another word, but a nod to me, Quist jumped on the elevator, and the one next to it opened, and out stepped Morkel.

"Sabrina? Micheal tells me you were attacked again?" Morkel said, taking us all in. Concern pinching his face, he stepped over to us. "Oh, hello, Mr. Hobart."

"Just Hobart," Hobart said.

"Of course. I see you managed to hook up with Sabrina here." Hobart shook Morkel's hand. He then looked up at the taller man with me.

"Uh, this is Bill Gannon," I introduced. "Bill this is Andrew Morkel."

"How do you... do?" They shook hands. Morkel kept looking up into his face, and could barely let go of his hand. Then, as though realizing he was acting weird, he let his hand go and ran his fingers through the fine blonde hairs on his head.

"So, another attack by a demon?" Morkel came back to the subject, looking back at me.

"Yes," I said. "Well, an attempt."

"Another Ba'al?"

"Yes," I said. "How are these demons getting in, when there's supposedly a ward up?" I asked.

"That's a very good question," Morkel asked.

"Also it seems to keep on happening in the lobby on the north side," I added. "I mean, Ba'al demons don't just pop in unannounced, do they?"

"No, they would have to be called in on a case. Or, they have to arrange to be admitted in order to get through the wards."

"Plus, he made himself look like someone I met at the penthouse party." I squinted. It would seem that someone may have been spying on me. Otherwise how would they know that I had ever met Malcolm? "I'm very sure Malcolm McFeely is not a demon, since he was Letitia's donor." I was second guessing myself again. I shook my head. "No. He was with a friend and they were leaving for the day. Plus I saw his aura."

"You say Malcolm McFeely?" Morkel said. "I can check to see where he is. I'm sure that he is safe enough."

"But my biggest question is how is it that these demons are getting through the ward? We don't have demons staying here in north towers?"

"No. There is a restriction on allowing demons to stay in the towers. They have to register before gaining entry. But we have no demons staying in the towers. I would know. They have certain requirements and have to go through a rigid protocol. Namely go through me."

"So, how is it that gremlins and other bushwhackers find their way in?" Hobart asked.

"Gremlins?" Bill said, looking surprised.

"I breathed fire on them and killed them all," I quipped.

"Oh, no wonder," Bill said and nodded. "I came into the lobby afterwards and they were cleaning up something terrible."

"Yeah. Sort of tough to get demon ashes out of carpet. But they did a marvelous job," I said, toeing the carpet.

"I can't think of how this could happen," Morkel said, looking pensive. "Unless—" he broke off.

"What?" I said. "Tell me. It could mean something to one of us."

"It's highly improbable. I can't imagine why…"

"Just tell me," I said. "As improbable as it might be."

"Possibly a witch. One who practices dark magic," he said.

I knew of someone who practiced dark magic. I would never forget her. But Dante had drained all her powers from her. How would she be able to summon a demon?

"Does it have to be a very powerful witch?" I asked.

"Not necessarily a *powerful* witch. She would only have to know how to conjure a powerful demon. She would have to be in league with a very dark, powerful demon." Morkel's blue eyes watched me and my reaction.

"I think I know who it is," I said, my eyes narrowing. "She was the one who drained me of my powers. But Dante showed up just in time. We—uh—he—" Oh, hell I couldn't tell him what exactly happened. "Let's just say Dante was able to return my powers to me, and then some."

Morkel nodded. "Of course. I remember that. Now I know how you came by all of your powers."

"How powerful of a demon are we talking?" I asked.

"Very," he said. "Upper echelon."

"Like Naamah?" At the name my skin prickled and I had to shiver.

About three tense seconds ticked by before he said, "That's a very powerful demon. And one who doesn't come to our world for no reason. He's possibly the most powerful of them all. Aside from Satan, of course."

"Yeah. Well, I had a visitor the other night. It was the female Ba'al demon who was with Crimmins, that night they came for Lief, but let him go under a technicality."

"I see. She visited you? When?"

"When I was in the hospital, you know, recovering from the gremlin attack."

"What did she want?"

"To tell me Naamah is the one who is behind all this. He wants to kill me for cutting off his tails." I looked up at Bill. "Nearly forgot about that."

"But, surely they grew back, didn't they?" Morkel asked, puzzled.

My hand shot out. "That's what I said. And yes, they did!"

"But he can't send demons in here, unless there's a human link," he insisted. "Tell me, what dark witch would know who you are and be willing to, or dare to contact such a demon?"

"Kiel Saint Thomas." I had something, possibly it was memory of some earlier vision. I had to get to the bottom of things. I had to find out how these demons were coming and trying to kill me. "Could she be found in the hotel's guest list?"

"I could have that checked." He pulled up his cell phone and looked through his list of contacts. "By the way, what happened to this Ba'al demon who came and gave you that message?"

"I let my dagger do the talking." I smiled sinisterly.

Morkel nodded, then smiled. "But of course you did." His phone was dialing and he put it to his ear. "Hello, Rachel, my dear?" he greeted someone on the other end. He chuckled at something she said. "I know. Right?" He chuckled again, followed by more small talk. Obviously he knew this Rachel woman. "Listen, I was wondering if you could do me a huge favor?" He paused for her answer. "Yes. Could you look on your list of guests at the hotel and see if there is anyone by the name of Kiel Saint Thomas. Look through a few days back, just to make sure."

He looked at me. "She's checking. It might take a few moments."

Since I couldn't get a read, I turned to Hobart and Bill. "It would be lucky if she used her actual name, wouldn't it?" I wasn't hopeful.

"She'd almost have to, unless she had an alias as well as a credit card with that alias on it," Hobart said. "They don't take cash in these hotels."

"He's right," Bill agreed.

"Somehow I wouldn't put it past her that she has such things. But you never know. She might have felt comfortable enough to merely use her own name," I said.

"You do?" Morkel said from beside us. He flashed me a smile. "That's the one. Room five-oh-two? Great! Thank you, Rachel. Say hello to Ted for me?" He hung up and looked at me. "Your hunch paid off. She's in five-oh-two."

"How many stories does the atrium go up?" I asked.

"Five floors."

"That explains why the gremlins simply appeared from the ceiling."

The vision hit me like a ton of bricks. Things around me tilted and, then all I saw was the vision.

Chapter 29

The Vision

"She's speaking Arabic," Bill said, holding Sabrina in his arms while kneeling on the floor. "Now, Latin," he said. Sabrina's eyes were closed, babbling while into a full-blown vision. A bit of drool seeped from her lips as she mumbled in those archaic, and dead languages.

Hobart and Morkel exchanged glances.

"You know these languages?" Morkel asked.

"Some Arabic, Latin, yes. Now—now she's speaking Sumerian!" Bill looked up at the two men, and now to the elf nurses who had come up to them with a concerned look. "No one speaks that anymore."

"Who speaks Latin?" Morkel said on a chuckle. "Except priests, professors and students of it, of course."

"She speaks in tongues?" Hobart said itching his beard. "No wonder no one understands it."

"Marking her as the sibyl. She probably won't remember much of the vision," Morkel said.

"It's true," Bill agreed.

Another nurse came up and handed Bill a cold compress.

"Thank you." Bill took the cold compress and placed it over Sabrina's forehead. Sabrina stopped babbling and moved her head side to side. Her eyes blinked open.

"Hi," she said, understanding registering on her face what had happened. "Just call me Chatty Cathy." Everyone chuckled lightly.

Groaning, she moved to sit up, and Bill helped her, taking away the compress. She slid her hands over her face, her dark hair falling down like a curtain. "How long was I out?"

"About five minutes," Hobart said. Bill handed him the compress and he took it and handed it back to one of the nurses.

She looked up at Bill. "You caught me?"

"Yes. I did."

"Thank you." She lowered her head into her hands again.

"Can I make you more comfortable? Maybe on a chair?"

"I can't move. I'm dizzy—"

"I'll pick you up and put you on the couch." Bill didn't hesitate, but picked her up and took her to the only couch in the waiting room. He lay her down on it, carefully holding the back of her head with one hand. Hobart handed him his leather jacket. Bill folded it up and placed it underneath her head for support.

"Thanks," she said.

"Just lay there a while," Bill said, slowly rose and faced the other two men. The nurses all went back to whatever they had been doing. He could tell by the Were's narrowed eyes that he wasn't one hundred percent happy with Bill being there.

"Been a while since I saw her do that," Hobart said, shaking his head.

"I've never seen it, myself," Bill said. "I've only heard stories."

Hobart's thumbs hung from his pockets as he squared off with Bill. "So, you're back—whatever you are—and suddenly in her life again."

"It wasn't my choice. I was fine being dead," Bill retorted, hands spread out to his sides.

"How did you come back?" Morkel asked, his tone held a note of clinical interest.

"I can only conjecture that blood had somehow poured onto my ashes in the cave. It would be the only way I could come back, I would think."

"So, you were a vampire when you came back, but you aren't any longer?" Morkel asked, his arms crossing over his chest. "I don't believe I've ever heard of that."

"I've had… help," he said carefully. Again, his gut told him he couldn't reveal too much to anyone. "I can say no more. But I have a normal heartbeat, and can walk in the sun and eat whatever I like, yet I'm supernaturally strong."

"But what I want to know is what your real reason is for finding Sabrina is this time?" Hobart said. "She told me the reason you hounded her while in your other life."

"I've forgotten. What was your other life?" Morkel asked.

"He was a Nephilim," Hobart said over his shoulder.

"Off-spring," he corrected. "No longer. And she fulfilled my request. It was my dying wish."

"Which was?"

"To donate some of her eggs so that our family wouldn't die out. We've had trouble reproducing. She was chosen by my people to do the task. I was reared to hunt for her, and—well—I was supposed to mate with her. However, because I didn't feel that forcing her into a marriage would be easy, I went with the In Vitro method."

"Nice. And now?" Hobart crossed his arms.

"I'm merely here to keep her from dying," Bill said.

"Now? Tomorrow?" Hobart asked.

"You never know. Perhaps in the next few seconds."

* * *

"Guys, I can hear you bickering and it's giving me a headache," I said from the couch. My head swam, but definitely I was feeling better. I wanted to get up, but knew that would be stupid. I'd be on the floor again and one of my man pals would be picking me back up. Again.

Three pairs of eyes looked over to see me leaning up on an elbow.

"Sorry," Bill said, turning his head to look at me, but turned back to Hobart. "I've told you what I know. I don't know when this will happen, but it will. I've got it on good authority."

"Whose?" Hobart demanded.

"Sorry. Privileged information."

"She's protected by me, and Dante is always with her too," Hobart said. "He's invisible. An Undead." He seemed to feel the need to explain this. Bill nodded.

"I know. We've met. When he was alive," he said, but didn't venture further.

From the couch I said, "I need to go upstairs to get my dagger. Hobart?" I moved slowly to angle my legs off the couch and placed my feet on the floor. *That's it, nice and slow.*

Both Hobart and Bill came to either side of me, helping me become vertical. The wave of dizziness overwhelmed me and I caught both muscular arms that were there. "Thanks," I said.

"You can't move yet," Bill said. I stared into his emerald-green eyes.

"What did I say?" I asked. "While I was out, I mean."

Bill's eyes flicked to Morkel, and then back to me. "Lots of things. Seems the name Naamah kept coming up."

"That's true," Morkel said. Hobart nodded in agreement.

I scrunched up my face. "Anything else?"

"When you went into Sumerian, I couldn't follow. Somethings going to happen," he said. "I think your witch is involved."

"I spoke Sumerian?" I said. "Cool. I flunked Spanish in high school." The men chuckled.

"And don't forget Latin," Morkel said.

"I didn't take Latin—wait—what?"

"And I think you phased into Greek—ancient Greek—for a few words, and then you went into Sumerian," Bill said, smiling. "I'm a bit rusty on those languages."

A mist welled up and darkened two feet away from us. The men followed my gaze and we all watched the vapor coalesce into Dante. With black wings, no less.

"My Lady." Dante went down on a knee and held out my dagger in the sheath with the belt.

"Oh, thank you, Dante!" I took the dagger. He came up to me and touched my cheek, smiling at me. I knew what he was doing. I felt much better from his touch.

"Thanks." I turned to the others. "I need to make an unannounced visit to room 502, Ms. Saint Thomas' room." I looked at the men who stood around me. "Anyone interested in coming with? I'm sure there'll be plenty of entertainment reserved for all of us."

No one left me. That wasn't too surprising. I hesitated at the elevators, thinking about my horrifying vision. Oddly, I did remember it. None of it good, and it didn't end well for me.

"What is it, Sabrina?" Bill asked.

"I have to do this one thing before I go up there." I dug out my cell phone, and struggled with trying to find my contacts.

"What are you trying to do?" Dante asked.

I thrust the phone out to him. "Find my contacts, and Malcolm in there."

He took my cell phone.

I didn't know why I had pussyfooted around about that damned curio and those dogs when I found them.

"Here." Dante handed me the phone. "It's ringing."

"Thanks." Malcolm's answering service came on. I left a message told him what I'd found in my penthouse, and that I would leave word with the staff that these things were his, and that he should take possession of them as soon as he could. If he had any problems, he only had to let them hear my voice on his voice mail. I then asked Morkel to call my pent house, as I didn't know the number. He did that and I spoke with James, telling him Malcolm would be there to pick up his belongings. "And don't make any dinner for me," I added.

"Oh? Are you going to be out for the evening, miss?" James asked.

"Uh," I hesitated, looking at my male friends. "Yes. Until further notice."

I flipped my phone shut and looked at them waiting for me, like they were my soldiers and I was their general. I had no idea what I would walk into up there, but it wasn't going to be good or easy.

"Let's do this!" I said, and felt a small catch in my throat as I turned to hit the button for the fifth floor.

Chapter 30

May the Chips Fall

A few minutes ago, Kiel had stood on the fifth floor balcony looking down on the lobby, watching the whole scene between Sabrina, the demon who had made himself look like Malcolm McFeely, and the men who were with her. *Men were always with her!* Apparently they saw through the demon's disguise, somehow. The one man grabbed him and then they sounded the alarm. It all happened much too quickly, and then it was over.

Frustrated, Kiel stomped back to her room, used her swipe card and slipped back inside her room on the fifth floor.

"Shit!" strands of oily hair hung in her face. With a hand she flopped it back out of her face. "Shit! Shit! Shit!" she said, stomping across the room. Where had once been a bed, now a large, dark circle was burned into the carpet where she had worked her demon magic. The mattresses had burned up a long time ago. Somehow she'd been able to keep the fire alarm from going off. The TV also had a large blackened hole in it, but she didn't remember when that had happened. Demons were not, as a rule, fond of electronics of any kind. Kiel had made certain she did not have her cell phone on her—past experience dictated this.

The witch strode across the room, stopped at the curtained window and strode back, thinking of how she would ever be able to send someone to grab Sabrina while she had so many admirers, and get her to Dark World. The last demon had failed to even get close.

"Fuck!" *Fuck, fuck, fuck!*

Face burning, she spied a glass jar with what was left of the special ointment she was to spread over her body to protect her from certain demons. She surged for it, grabbed it and threw it against the wall. It crashed, the oil splattered and dripped down the wall in gunky globules. The hotel might try and charge her for damages. *I'll be long gone before they even discover it,* she smirked. Naamah had promised her more powers than before. She shivered involuntarily with the thought, and memory of her last encounter with the large demon.

But, if she didn't figure out something quickly, she wasn't going to have squat.

Eyes going to the ceiling, she said, "I have called upon you before…" Her voice raw from chanting endlessly, she called upon her demon helper. "Pharzuph! Come to me! I need your help again. Now!"

Kiel didn't have to wait long—he was so anxious—the demon appeared to her in tight jeans and wore only a black leather vest over his well-muscled chest. Jet black hair was pulled back off his face, wet, as though shower-fresh, but he still smelled like demon. Lustful narrow eyes fell on her. He looked like he had walked off a porno flick set, and wanted to nail her.

The demon gave her a crooked smile, tossing her a nod. "I was wondering when I would get to see you again, witch. You give very good pleasure to me. Naamah was at least right about that."

"Whatever. I need to do this, don't you understand? I need more demons. She's—she's invincible!"

"Who?"

Kiel's hands went toward her head, she grasped her limp, oily hair and pulled it in frustration, and growled, "Sabrina! The one I'm trying to send to Naamah!"

"Oh, yes. That one." Pharzuph leaned against the wall next to the bathroom. He held a paperback novel in one hand and squinted down at it as though what was on the page was more interesting than her problem. "What are you willing to do for me should I conjure more demons?" He turned the page of the book, then flicked his black lash-fringed, glacier-blue eyes on her.

Of course, she would have to pay him with her body again. This time, she had to make sure enough demons were able to take out whoever was with Sabrina, and snatch her to Dark World before she could slip out of their grasp again.

"I will pay you as before. Whatever you want. I don't care. I want as many demons as you can bring me. Every shape, size, color—it doesn't matter. Sabrina must be taken to Naamah tonight!"

"I need an exact amount. A number," he said. His eyes skimming the page of the book, still more interested in the novel than her.

"Okay. A dozen," she said.

"A dozen?" His brow arched at her as though that number was somehow an insult.

"Okay. Make it thirteen, then!"

"You are very reckless, my spirited witch. You must name the demons you want, otherwise..." He cast his eyes to the book, pausing to think. "I might conjure something that might eat or kill you as well as her."

"Fine, fine," Kiel said, one hand on a cocked hip. *Damned demons. What was he reading? Danielle Steel?*

"Which demons?" He asked again, lowering the book. It vanished from his hand in a puff of smoke. Shifting to stand on both feet, he looked ready to do her bidding. "Quickly decide. I want to tie you to the bed again." His crooked grin gave her chills. "I like you helpless while I rape you."

"The mattress was burned the last time," she said, pointing to the burnt remains of the bed's insides.

"Matters not. I will tie you up and thrust my engorged shaft into you and make you scream in sweet release. I love your scream." His eyes dropped to her chest. "I enjoy sucking on your nipples, and holding those delicious globes like ripe watermelons. You have voluptuous curves, my pet."

"Whatever!" She *would* have to pick a demon who read trashy romance novels. "Okay, I'll go with Ba'al demons again." Their blood, if spilled, was lethal. But they were more submissive to her commands than any of the other demons she had called forth. The gremlins, while were a stroke of genius, was actually brought in to make Sabrina pay for Naamah's damaged tails—which were no longer damaged by any means. She could vouch for that. Too bad Sabrina had lived through their attack. Now Naamah wanted her sent to him, and soon. He was growing impatient.

Pharzuph looked a tad disappointed. "Ba'al? Again?"

"Yes. I don't care who they look like. They could look alike, or even look like their real selves, for all it matters."

Pharzuph shrugged. "In any case, you owe me another night of free will of your body."

"Whatever!"

"No. Say it." His arms recrossed, one knee bent, in a relaxed pose waiting.

Kiel's head slumped in defeat. She then looked up at him, meeting his gaze. "I, Kiel Marie Saint Thomas do give you the right to touch my body in any way you chose. I am your servant, Pharzuph, for one night."

"My *slave* for the night," he corrected. "I cannot wait to sink my manhood slowly into your wet depths." The demon clasped his hands together and wrung them as though his anticipation was heightened. "Who do you want them to look like?"

A sharp knock came to her door, making them both stop and stare at it. Neither one said a thing.

"Kiel? Kiel St. Thomas?" the woman's voice said. "Open up. I've got a bone to chew with you."

Sabrina was at her door. "Shit! I need to disappear!"

"That will cost you a second night with me." Pharzuph smiled.

"Fuck!"

"Soon, my pet. Soon." His suggestive smile said it all.

Another knock. This time louder.

"Okay. Give me the demons."

"Who shall they look like?"

"Make them all look like—*me!*"

Pharzuph gave her an up and down look. "Hopefully a more cleaned up version?"

* * *

My shoulders ached, my nerves on edge I thought I might explode. My one hand over the hilt of my dagger, I waited. I didn't like that Kiel wasn't opening the door. I didn't like what my Knowing was telling me, or all my other resources. My vision had been the most shocking of all. *What if I don't make it back this time?*

"She is in there, my Lady," Dante said.

"You'd know," I said to him. He stood behind me. Morkel stood to my right with a pass key-card in his hand. Bill to my left. Hobart stood behind Morkel. We had already discussed our plan of action on our way up here. Since Kiel Saint Thomas was scheming against me, I thought I would have the upper hand in bringing my full entourage complete with an elf, werewolf, Undead and whatever-the-hell Bill was. Dante was very certain her powers were not very strong, but like Morkel had said earlier, she was in league with demons. Strong ones, so we had to be prepared. I'd already unhooked the tabs of my Dagger of Delphi. I'd let it go as soon as the door opened, because I knew a demon was with her—thanks to my telepathic mind. There would be more demons soon, added to the room, this I overheard with my werewolf hearing way before I'd knocked.

No sound, and no one opened the door. Well, what did I expect? I put my fist up to knock again, but Morkel motioned for me not to. Instead, he knocked. His larger knuckles made a louder sound. His other hand held the pass key at the ready. When no one answered again, he slid the card into the slot and slowly slid it out. The green light went on with the buzzer sound. He paused to look at me. "I'm sorry. Where you ready?"

"Not really, but let's do this," I said, stepping forward. Someone grabbed my shoulders from behind, his fingers massaging my tension away. His hands held me until I stopped and looked back. I met Dante's gray eyes.

"In most cases I'd say ladies first, but not this time." Dante squeezed in front of me. He gave a nod to Morkel. Morkel used the pass-key card again. It buzzed and he opened the door.

Chapter 31

Fools Rush In

There was no time to think. The door opened and Kiel was standing there gloating. Actually there were more than one of her. Possibly there were a dozen. All of them dressed the same and had the same look on their faces, and, what the hell? She looked... slimy. My feet were rooted to the carpet in the hallway as though made of lead.

Dante rushed in first, grabbing one Kiel-look-alike Ba'al demon (I could tell—they all had bad hair), twisting its head and it fell. Dagger of Delphi jammed into one demon, and the demon dropped to the floor and expired, then went up in a quick fire and became ashes. Bill grabbed a demon and rammed its head through a wall. Hobart was punching, kicking and snarling his way through the horde. Morkel was the most amazing; he flung his hands out toward a demon who rushed him. A bright jet of light threw the demon back, and it vanished into a black whirl of ectoplasmic vapor. Wow. I had no idea he had these powers himself. I gave him a significant look and he nodded back at me with a crooked smile.

By the time each man had pummeled at least two demons each, and my dagger had jabbed into my second demon, I became unglued and moved one step forward. That's when someone appeared in front of me. He was tall and swarthy looking. Actually he looked like a slimeball. The kind I would not give a second notice anywhere.

"Hello, beautiful." He gave me the usual eye-fuck that any guy does when he's so sure of himself. "I don't think I've ever met a sibyl before. You look like a fragile flower wanting to be plucked and devoured."

"Check out how fragile my flower is, Slimeball." I put my right hand up, and with the power of the mystic ring I threw him across the hall. He landed with a thud against the door across the way. I really hoped no one was in there. That would be unsettling.

Slimeball's greasy hair fell into his face and he swiped it back. He looked startled, but that crooked smile snapped back into place. He got up quicker than I was able to react. His arms were around me like jungle snakes.

"What I wouldn't give to sear your flesh with my lips and sink my tool into your warm depths." His breath stank of brimstone. *Great.*

"Let go!" I said, struggling, anger building up. Where was my dagger?

Then, everything blurred. My body dissolved into a void of roiling nothingness. Everything went black as the demon yanked us through the nearest ley line. I struggled with Slimeball, the demon, who held me from behind. A jolt of fear lit through me as I gathered he was taking me to somewhere unnice and private. I heard screaming—it was probably me. I heard deep laughter—probably Slimeball—and his acrid smell filled my nose.

When things stilled, and sight returned to me, and we were stationary, I stopped screaming and took stock. The demon's breath hot on my neck made me narrow my eyes. His lips trailed along my neck and shoulders, and I realized he was still behind me. His noisome odor made me want to gag. And, to top it off, he was pushing his engorged member against me from behind, like he intended to dry hump me. This had gone far enough! I headbutted him with the back of my head—*Ow! Shit!*—and broke free, shifted my right hand into his face and said, "Get the fuck away from me, Slimeball!"

He vanished in a puff of smoke. Somehow I knew I wasn't safe and sound. Not by a long shot. There was more to come. Lots more. It was red where I'd landed. I knew this wasn't good old Earth anymore.

Alone, I looked up at the cliffs on either side of me, and yes, this looked familiar. I stood at the bottom of a narrow canyon. Tortured rock formations in bands of copper, roan, and terracotta rose up around me and hemmed me in. The air was warm as a desert. Above, red filled the sky along with purple clouds and lots of jagged lightening but no rain. The sky and raw, tortured earth, dry as bones left out in the desert sun, was my clue as to where I'd wound up. Dark World.

"Aw, crap!" I said, as ice prickles rose up my back and I realized where the hell I was.

The sound of pebbles and rocks falling and cascading over the rocky floor told me I was soon to have company.

"Dagger of Delphi, come to me!" I shouted.

The dagger appeared in front of me and I grabbed it. I felt only slightly safer.

"My Lady," Dante's voice startled me. I made an ungraceful pirouette to face him. My dagger in my raised hand, I lowered it upon seeing him.

"We're in—"

"I know," he said, his hands grasping me by the shoulders, gray eyes searching mine.

"We need to leave," I said.

Someone laughed. The sound had an omnipresence to it. I knew that hearty, yet unctuous chuckle and I felt my gut twist with fear. More stones rattled down the incline of the pathway that wound around a turn in the canyon about twenty-five feet away.

"The Powers That Be won't allow it," Dante said low, his voice sounding strained with fear. "I was able to follow you, using your auric path, but I cannot take us back. Something is blocking us."

The ubiquitous laugh echoed once more against the bronze walls. I turned to look toward the corner of stone where someone was coming. One greenish-brown and scaly snake tail came into view and then a second one. I tried to swallow, but I had no spit. My heart sank. *Oh, God, no! Naamah!*

In the next second, Naamah's whole body—which was bigger than any NFL linebacker standing at nine feet tall, weighing in excess of 850 pounds, including twelve foot twin tails (which was how he traversed), emerged around the bend. He was the last demon I wanted to see ever again.

"I am the one blocking you, my Undead friend, because… I can," Naamah said in his characteristically icy voice. His huge membranous bat wings could not be stretched out fully, but it was full enough in our tight twenty-foot space. He walked on his twin snake tails, as he had no legs or feet. His body and arms were that of a human man, otherwise. His head was a smattering of both a bat and a human—more human, since he could speak. His eyes were demon-black in color. His maleness was not at all human-like, and believe me, he was *very* proportional. It was not something I had seen before when I had been here a few months back, and I really, *really* wished I was not privy to seeing it today. I'm not exactly a prude, but looking upon him (it), made me feel faint. My brain told my legs to move, but they couldn't. This was not good. Dagger of Delphi wriggled in my grasp. I wanted to let it go, but held on to it. Something kept me from letting it go. I couldn't be certain, but it seemed Naamah was doing a number on me, despite my ring.

He laughed again. "I was hoping to see you again soon, Sabrina, my dear," he said.

"I've got a feeling 'hope' had nothing to do with it," I said.

Dante stepped in front of me, determined to protect me. How he would do this, I didn't know.

"Oh, and how nice of you to bring your lover. An Undead, now, I see." Naamah clapped his hands twice. "I have something for you, Dante. Your needs are never forgotten here, in my world!"

Appearing in front of the vampire-demon were three women in very sheer robes. They were beautiful. They moved forward, toward us. Correction. Toward Dante. Their curvy bodies moving in a suggestive manner. And they moaned and groaned, their hands rubbing their own bodies, while whispering his name, "*Dante, Dante, Dante...*" over and over and over.

"Ah," Naamah said in that oily voice. "I can see you haven't fed in a while, have you, Dante?"

Dante didn't move. The women came right up to him, their hands were on him. Their moans becoming louder. One woman got on her knees in front of him. One drew her hands around his head and neck and kissed him fully on the mouth. Now a second one fell to her knees, and both drew his pants down, exposing him. They began kissing him there. Shocked by this, I looked away. Naamah was not playing fair. These were succubi.

"Okay, Naamah," I said, my voice thickened with revulsion. "You are king of retch, you know that? I just want to vomit all over the place. You play an unfair game."

"Charming." Naamah's gaze swept over me as he slithered down the path. I stepped several paces back, avoiding his reach, if I could. He slid over the rocky floor of the canyon, blocking out my view of Dante, who was now throwing his head back in the throes of being completely seduced by the three succubi. Then, his body sank and disappeared behind a large rock. The moaning came not only from the women, but his voice joined in.

"You understand, my pet, *you* are what I want; what I've wanted since the moment I saw you. You are a feast for the gods," he said drawing his hands down his chest and to his genitalia, making certain I got the point of this meeting.

I squinted at him. "I'm not yours to have."

"I enjoy your resistance but, really, you cannot dissuade me." He kept moving toward me, and I was really not liking the looks of his manhood—which looked dog-like to me—throbbing all over the place. *Crap-ola!* "You were told to mate with a vampire. You refused. Who do you think made that mandatory? Me. You went against *my* orders. So, since no vampire could do the job, it's up to me to decide who impregnates you." He shrugged. "Looks like I'm the only one man enough to do it." He laughed.

"As if, you narcissistic sociopath!" I tried to snort, but it dried up in my throat. I thrust out my hand that held the Dagger of Delphi. I let it go. It zoomed toward him. I wanted to see him die like all other demons when poisoned by the lethal silver. I wished he would actually explode into ashes, like they do on TV.

Quick as a viper, his hand jutted out and I watched my dagger stop in mid-air and then melt, as though the hottest fire had breathed on it. In less than thirty seconds, the Dagger of Delphi was reduced to a puddle of silver and melted jewels on the floor of the canyon gleaming dully.

I made a sound of absolute astonishment and horror. My dagger! Gone in an instant. That fucker! My eyes pooled with helpless tears. Now what?

One of his long tails whipped toward me. I jumped and reached up. Somehow I grabbed onto a poor little tree that had found a place to send its roots down. I managed to pull myself up, and scramble around the bush, escaping his seeking tail.

"You dare to toy with me, sibyl?" he said, and thrust out his hands to either side. The whole canyon shook like some great hand had grabbed one of those snow globes and shook it, and I was inside it. My feet went out from beneath me along with part of the cliff and the little tree, which still clung its roots deep into the cliff's side. Somehow I managed to hold onto the little tree.

Naamah was a few feet below me, and his tail was snaking its way toward me.

Chapter 32

To Hell and Back

Bill, Hobart and Morkel stood in the now quiet hotel room surveying the damages. Thirteen Ba'al demons all dead, their bodies strewn about the floor. They'd found the real Kiel St. Thomas cowering in the bathroom. In less than it took to sneeze, Morkel had her in silver handcuffs, explaining he would take her downstairs to hold her until the police came—if nothing else the hotel could charge her for all the damages. The witch's oily face and dark hair made her look pathetic. Tears made ugly tracks through the dirt on her cheeks. Her whimpering pleas fell on deaf ears.

"Where's Sabrina?" Hobart asked looking around.

Bill jerked to attention. He rushed out to the hallway, followed closely by Hobart.

"Dante is missing as well," Morkel pointed out, drawing Kiel along by the arm. He pulled her into the hallway.

"That's not like her," Hobart said, worry etched on his face.

"Dante would be wherever she is," Morkel said.

Kiel made a sudden move. Her body so oily, Morkel's grip failed to hold her and she ran down the hall.

"I've got her!" Hobart bolted after her. He caught up with her before she could get to the stairs. How she would open the door to the stairs or press for the elevator Bill didn't know, as her hands were behind her back. Her powers were nearly untraceable, which also was curious.

"I have to find Sabrina," Bill said.

"How?" Morkel regarded him.

"She's gone into the ley lines, I feel it. Another demon with her." Bill squinted as he concentrated. He then looked toward the ceiling. "Nemesis. Help me find her!"

Morkel watched Bill make his own plea with an unseen entity.

"One thing, Bill," Morkel said quickly. "If Naamah has her, he is a god of some sort. Only another god can fight him."

Bill nodded. "I understand." But what Morkel said was unimportant at that second. He needed to find Sabrina and save her from certain doom, or death.

A voice answered Bill's request. "Follow my voice, my son," Nemesis said.

Bill looked back at Morkel before he allowed himself to drop into the ley line opened by Nemesis, awaiting to take him to Sabrina. "I'll bring her home. I promise!" His body dissolved like a snowflake on a warm day. There came a burst of awareness, light-headedness, and a feeling of being pulled along through something that had no weight or depth, it merely existed on a continuum.

Finally, he stumbled onto solid ground, and fell to his hands and knees. Stones cut through his palms and pants at the knees. But he was fine, and ignored the initial pain which vanished instantly. His eyes rose in time to see Sabrina being pulled down off a small scrub tree on a cliff-side by some creature with two tails and bat wings twice the size of his Lexus.

Sabrina screamed when the snake tail grabbed her by the leg and pulled her. She held onto a little tree. The cracking of the limb drew more screams from her. She fell, and her head hit the side of the cliff.

Silenced. Eyes closed. Her body limp in the clutches of that gigantic snake tail, the giant demon looking down on her, his intentions very clear.

"Stop! Let go of her right now!" Bill scrambled to his feet and ran toward the fray. Before he could get within ten feet of Sabrina, a second snake tail grabbed him by the legs. He struggled at first as the tail tightened around him. Then, his attention went to Sabrina who was being hauled toward the large, bald-headed demon.

"Do not interfere, measly human," the demon said. "I will crush you."

"Measly? Human?" Bill said, incensed. Fury built and his wings ripped through the shirt he wore. He spread them wide, believing his were just as magnificent as this ugly demon's were horrific. "I'm not human, you pile of crap!"

The creature's tail doubled its tightness, trying to crush him. Bill hadn't realized the danger to himself, until then. He looked up to find the demon's hands grasping Sabrina by the waist. His tail now used like a wicked tool to rip open her shirt. The material fluttered to the ground. The demon laughed. "Lovely. Such delicate flesh. Oh, and I see you have a crucifix. We hate crucifixes." The sound of something sizzling unnerved Bill. He wasn't sure what exactly had just happened, but there was no question what the demon had in his mind.

He struggled to free himself, but the snake tail was crushing his legs, and now the thing was winding around his hips, moving up his chest.

"Nemesis! Help me! I can't do this alone!"

"*Yes, you can!*" projecting her voice telepathically to him.

"How? He is too strong!"

"*With your touch. Simply think of destroying him, and touch him.*"

"But if I destroy him, won't it destroy her? He's holding her in his filthy hands," Bill said.

"*I will protect her with my essence. Think of destruction. Use your anger, Bill!*"

Bill didn't need to think very hard about destroying the vampire demon as it held Sabrina in the other tail, and his hands were groping her, his mouth on her, all the while Sabrina was out cold, and helpless.

Bill allowed his anger to build up inside. *Yes! I wish to destroy this being who would harm Sabrina. I love her! I do!*

Bill drew his hands across the scaly snake tail and the heat built within his body and he concentrated it through his arms and down to his hands. When the power surged through him, he groaned from the nearly agonizing feel of both his emotions, and the power coursing through him. His hands lay upon the demon's tail, and then melted through the thing's scaly flesh.

A huge roar echoed through the canyon.

Bill's legs were released. He looked up to see the demon being consumed by a red glow that became brighter, grading from brilliant yellow to a blinding white. Sabrina, no longer suspended by the beast's hands, she began to fall.

Bill opened his wings and flew like a shot, catching her in mid-fall.

"*Take her home, where she will be safe, Bill,*" Nemesis said. "*You have done well, my son.*"

Chapter 33

Not Quite Dead

A huge flash jarred me. I opened my eyes, but then closed them against the brightest light—brighter than looking into the sun—which blinded me. I may have screamed, but it was hard to tell since someone else—Naamah?—was screaming as if in mortal pain and anguish.

Then there was almost no sound. The vampire demon no longer held me and I began free-falling.

Someone caught me. I opened my eyes and looked up into a handsome face and a pair of familiar green eyes.

"Sabrina," he said. "Oh, God, Sabrina I have you! You're safe!"

Then, I passed out.

* * *

Bill pulled the afghan from the back of his couch, shook it out and covered her nakedness. Turning, he moved for his closet. Opening it, he pulled down the pillow he stored there for those times when he sat in front of the TV late at night by himself. He gently lifted Sabrina's head and settled it underneath it. Her eyes were still shut. Still unconscious. Was that bad or good?

Heart hammering, he tore up the stairs, two steps at a time, and ran to his room, flicked on a light and stepped toward his drawers. His shadow and reflection caught his eyes—something seemed odd. *Too large.* He looked up into the mirror above the bureau. His bare chest exposed it caught him by surprise. *When did my shirt come off?* He took a double take. More surprising were the wings that had unsheathed moments ago while in the Underworld. A tingling sensation of jubilation rushed through him at the sight. They were not the ugly bat-like wings he had at first been given upon awakening to this world after being dead. They were made of soft feathers and the most startling purest white he'd ever seen, whiter than his original wings. His body slumped with the surprise as the elation overwhelmed him. He covered tear-filled eyes with a hand, whispered a soft, "Thank you, Nemesis," but could only afford a few seconds to take it all in. Sabrina lie unconscious on his couch.

Recovering after a moment or two, and knowing exactly what drawer the sweatshirt was in, he pulled out the old gray Oxford sweatshirt. He exited his room, flipped off the light, and darted back down the hall. He took two steps at a time again down the stairs—in fact he wasn't even sure he hit any of them, but merely *flew*.

He stood over Sabrina's still form, taking her all in for the first time. A line of blood that had leaked from her mouth had dried. *Had she bit her tongue?* Or was there more damage inside than he'd thought?

"Okay," he said, more to himself than to her, because she was definitely out. "I'm just going to put this on you so that you won't wake up wondering why you don't have a top on." He swallowed. He'd never touched a woman to the extent of either putting clothes on her, or taking them off his entire life. *I can't believe I'm in this situation.*

He settled himself on an ottoman and shook out the sweatshirt. He made sure the lettering was facing him. *It's like dressing a child,* he told himself. *That's all.* Pausing he thought if he did it quickly enough he wouldn't see much. Not that he wouldn't mind, but this was definitely not the time nor place to be looking at a woman who'd been so abused, nearly raped by a demon, and now was unconscious. *I wonder how doctors can separate their male libido in order to examine a woman?*

Licking his lips, he leaned forward, grasped the afghan and pulled it down, exposing her upper body. When his eyes wandered to her chest, he pulled in a gasp of horror. A terrible red welt, oozing mucus in the center of her chest in the shape of a crucifix held his eyes. *How did I not see this?* It were as though someone had branded her. Then he noticed the lines drawing up toward her neck and around it. Obviously the crucifix she had been wearing had been burned off of her by that monster.

"No!" Horrified, he drew his hand over the area, hovering about an inch above it. Bill's hand drew the heat into himself. A mild, not too unpleasant, energy coursed through his hand, and then a coolness, and he pushed that energy into her exposed flesh. When he lifted his hand, the burns were gone. She was unharmed in that region, except for minor redness in the shape of the cross.

He gasped again, but his sharp intake was one of pleasant surprise. He had somehow healed her.

She was a magnificent specimen of womanhood. And while he wasn't the only male who could appreciate a woman's body, he had had very few chances in his 110 years of life.

Averting his eyes, Bill wrangled the sweatshirt—which was so huge, it looked like a gunnysack—over her head and managed to shove her arms through the armholes. The arms of the sweatshirt were so long he had to fold the sleeves halfway up. As he picked her up with one hand, pulling the sweatshirt down over her stomach, he saw the blood stain on the pillow case. About the size of an egg. He remembered she'd hit her head badly, on the cliff-side, when that monster pulled her down. There was a bump, about the size of an egg, on her forehead. But this wasn't bleeding. Gently, he felt the back of her head, his fingers finding the tacky blood in her hair, and a large lump here too.

He let her down gently, running his hand across his bearded jaw, hearing it scrape his palm. Could he heal her? *What if I do something wrong? Something irreversible.*

"Well, you're dressed properly, at least," he muttered to Sabrina. Another man would have said that he was foolish for being so gallant as to not want to linger his eyes over her nakedness. *It's not proper. I barely know her—and not in that way.* It was exactly how his superiors had expected him to seduce and mate with her. He had made sure he would not have to force her. *Thank goodness for the egg and sperm donor program.*

Hand to his brow, he rose trying to figure out what to do. She needed a physician. But who? He had nearly reached for his phone twice to dial 911. But after dealing with the 911 operator for Emma, he didn't want to go through that again. He needed someone he knew. Someone who was on his team, so to speak. There was one such person nearby. He'd gone to him once—asking about the sperm donation program. Dr. Don Phillips MD, was a member of Nephilistic League of Young Men, just as Bill was. Dr. Phillips was two hundred and fifteen years old, but looked around fifty-five and had a thriving medical business nearby.

In a way the doctor knew about Sabrina, because Bills life-long mission was to find the sibyl and mate with her, as it was general knowledge among their members.

The matter was now in the past—the breeding in or out of the womb, it didn't matter. His lifelong mission was accomplished, in his former life.

He reached for his cell phone. The doctor was low on his contacts but he was there. It was late, but he would leave a message on his personal number and hope that the doctor would check it, and get back to him. The phone rang twice and there was a voice.

"Hello?"

Startled to get the doctor awake at this hour, Bill stuttered, "Oh, uh, hi. This is Bill Gannon? I don't know if you remember me."

"Oh, of course, Bill. How is the, um, project?"

"Completed. But now there is a huge problem with the woman. She's been injured. Head injury. She's unconscious. Has a large bump on the back of her head and it's bleeding."

"That sound serious. Why didn't you call the paramedics?"

"It might look rather bad—for me, I mean. And I can't afford problems, if you get my drift."

"Of course. Can she be moved?"

"I'm not sure. I'm afraid to move her. Actually, it might be that I've moved her too much already. I've got her at my home. Is it possible you can come here? I'll definitely pay you."

The doctor breathed into the phone as though he considered it. "Where are you?"

Bill gave him the address.

"You're not that far from me. I'll be there in a half an hour."

"Thank you. I'll be waiting." He hung up.

The moaning sound brought his attention back to Sabrina on the couch. She rocked her head slightly. He knelt next to her and took her hand.

"Sabrina? Sabrina, can you hear me?"

Her brow furrowed as she moved her head back and forth a few times, making little fretting sounds.

"Sabrina? Please. Open your eyes." He lightly touched her brow above the eyes, but away from the other bump. *Maybe I should have gotten a cold cloth for her head?*

She opened her eyes and met his gaze.

"Hi, there. I thought I'd lost you for sure," he said soothingly.

She looked around, then her eyes returned to his face.

"Where am I?" She grimaced and touched her head. "My head hurts."

"Don't worry. I have a doctor coming and we're going to get you into a hospital. You're in my house. For now."

"Who are you?" she said, her brow crinkled deeper.

"I'm Bill. Bill Gannon. Don't you remember?"

Looking fretful, she gripped her bottom lip with her teeth. She shook her head slowly side to side. "No." Then she asked, "Who am I?"

* * *

Dear reader,

We hope you enjoyed reading *Requiem*. Please take a moment to leave a review, even if it's a short one. Your opinion is important to us.

Discover more books by Lorelei Bell at
https://www.nextchapter.pub/authors/lorelei-bell.

Want to know when one of our books is free or discounted for Kindle? Join the newsletter at http://eepurl.com/bqqB3H.

Best regards,
Lorelei Bell and the Next Chapter Team

The story continues in:
Interlude by Lorelei Bell

To read the first chapter for free, head to:
https://www.nextchapter.pub/books/interlude-urban-fantasy

About the Author

Lorelei's interest in vampires came in her teens watching the original Dark Shadows on TV, and old horror movie classics of "Dracula" on TV late at night. As a result, she was considered odd because of her interests in the macabre, horror/vampire movies—way before it was 'cool'.

When not at her day job, Lorelei works on her novels, inventing new characters and places/parallel worlds where her main character, Sabrina Strong, has a few adventures, lovers, solves a mystery or two, and comes within a hair's breadth of being killed—all in a day's work by a sibyl like Sabrina. Her writing has been compared to Anne Rice's more gritty novels, but with a humorous twist in the tradition of Charlaine Harris.

Sabrina Strong Series:

Book 1 - Ascension

Book 2 - Trill

Book 3 - Nocturne

Book 4 - Caprice

Book 5 - Crescendo

Other books

Spell of the Black Unicorn

"I wanted to create a heroine who has to learn who and what she was from the beginning and throughout the series, rather than plopping my readers in the middle of things and doing a lot of back story.

My vampires all have their own personalities; you will not find a cardboard baddie among them. They each have their own needs, wants, and desires, and do fall in love—in other words are capable of human emotions.

I hope you enjoyed this book!

Thank you!"

Lorelei Bell
Lorelei can be found on Facebook and at her blog:
http://loreleismuse-lorelei.blogspot.com/